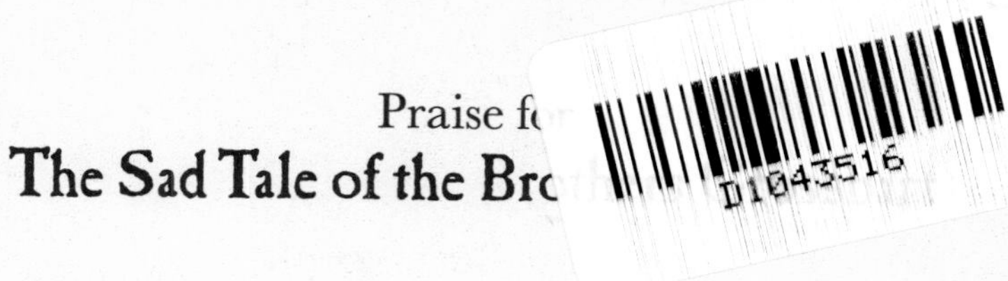

Praise f
The Sad Tale of the Br

"This debut novel is kind of like the unexpurgated versions of Grimm's fairy tales, as imagined by Chuck Palahniuk on some seriously bad drugs. Bullington clearly has a great appreciation for the rich history of folklore, and his viscerally evocative writing is excellent."
—*Library Journal*

"Striking and often funny."
—*Publishers Weekly*

"Discomfiting, disgusting and at times as grotesquely pleasurable as picking at a scab."
—*Kirkus*

"As the antithesis of conventional fantasy, this is a tour de force."
—Telegraph.co.uk

"A novel of great humor, deep theology and gratuitous murder and quite unlike anything I've read before. I absolutely loved it...one of the books of the year for sure!"
—Sfrevu.com

"The wicked sense of amorality and humor will appeal to many who like their humor dark. Like its amazing cover, it is a satisfyingly clever, well-plotted book that never takes itself too seriously and a very promising debut."
—SFFWorld.com

"Bullington paints a world appropriately dark and sinister with a confidence that makes you wonder if he knew someone who lived there."
—Graemesfantasybookreview.com

"Darkly funny, profane, erudite, bawdy, and wickedly original... the debut of an amazing new talent."
—Jeff VanderMeer

By Jesse Bullington

The Sad Tale of the Brothers Grossbart
The Enterprise of Death

The Enterprise of Death

JESSE BULLINGTON

www.orbitbooks.net

Orbit
Hachette Book Group
237 Park Avenue, New York, NY 10017
www.HachetteBookGroup.com

First Edition: March 2011

Orbit is an imprint of Hachette Book Group, Inc. The Orbit name and logo are trademarks of Little, Brown Book Group Limited.

Library of Congress Cataloging-in-Publication Data
Bullington, Jesse.
The enterprise of death / Jesse Bullington. — 1st ed.
p. cm.
ISBN 978-0-316-08734-6
1. Renaissance—Fiction. 2. Magic—Fiction. 3. Alchemists—Fiction. I. Title.
PS3602.U42E58 2011
813'.6—dc22

2010026564

10 9 8 7 6 5 4 3 2 1

Printed in the United States of America

For

All Those Who Go Before Us

Prologue

The Worst Beginning Imaginable

Pity Boabdil. King of Granada, last Moor lord of the Iberian Peninsula, reduced to a suppliant outside his own city by a Spaniard sovereign, an exile from a home hard won. The truce signed by kings and Pope, all that remained was for Boabdil to bow before his victorious adversary and kiss the man's ring. The victor was supposed to refuse the offer, thus preserving some shred of Boabdil's already tattered honor, but this stipulation must have slipped the Christian's mind as he extended his pudgy fingers to the Moor. There was nothing for it. King Ferdinand's seal tasted salty as the strait Boabdil would soon cross, and the man's onion-pale queen leered at the Moor as he rose.

That dreadful Genoan sailor who hung around Isabella like a fly around a chamber pot stood a short distance off, and when they made eye contact Boabdil supposed the weather-beaten bastard was imagining his head on a pike. At the signing King Ferdinand had mentioned something about the explorer sailing for India the wrong way round and Boabdil had paid it no real mind until now, with the scheming seaman appraising the former ruler of Granada's venerable pate. Boabdil hoped he drowned.

The handover continued, a grand display of pageantry and pomp, with the humbled Boabdil bowing in all the proper places as the procession carrying aloft a weighty silver cross all but stuck out their tongues at the defeated Moors leaving the city. Of course the treaty had many articles detailing how the Moors who chose to stay in Granada or thereabouts would retain all their rights and be under no pressure to convert and be protected as they had before, and of course each and every article would be cast down and shattered before Boabdil's mustaches gained even a few ashen strands. The Christians had given him a token patch of broken Spanish earth upon which to reestablish his noble person, but Boabdil held no illusions, and so south they departed to sail to a continent Boabdil had never known.

When they came to a prominence upon the road where Boabdil could view the Alhambra of Granada one final time, history recalls the heavy sigh that escaped his lips, a sigh as weighty as if the whole country issued it. Indeed it might have—with the passing of Boabdil the tolerance and culture that the Moors had slowly cultivated over hundreds of years of conquest was likewise expelled, and within Boabdil's lifetime the Jews and Moors who lived at peace with the Spanish Christians would be banished, murdered, or forcibly converted, the lanterns of illumination that mutual respect fosters traded for brands used to burn Qur'an and witch alike. Small wonder Boabdil might sigh, and smaller wonder still that this most famous of sighs was actually a ragged, choking sob.

"Must you cry like a woman over that what you could not hold as a man?" his mother asked him, which, predictably, only made him weep the harder. She could be unfair, could Boabdil's mother.

Boabdil did not simply cry for his lost kingdom, he cried for his lost daughter. The son the Spaniards had kept ransom during the siege of Granada had been returned, but in his place Ferdinand, ever the son of a bitch, had claimed Boabdil's daughter Aixa, and there was not a single thing the broken old ruler could do about it. A king should love his sons most, of course, but Boabdil was no longer king and so allowed his sorrow to run down his face in snotty dribbles.

The viscous, golden grief dangling from Boabdil's nose and lips as his belly shook with emotion made him look for all the world like a walrus chased off a honeycomb by a greedier bear, for Ferdinand's piggy little eyes and boxy jaw lent him something of an ursine face. None present had ever seen a walrus, however, and the only man who had encountered a bear was Boabdil's second cousin, who had been severely mauled by the beast on a hunting expedition. The poor fellow had to be carried around in a lidded basket to keep those weak of stomach from fainting at the sight of the gnawed-up stumps where his legs used to be and the terrible scars crisscrossing his face. The result was that no one commented on the walrus-and-bear imagery, and Boabdil's second cousin spent the rest of his life haunted by nightmares of the furry monster that had put him in his box. Pity Boabdil's second cousin.

Ferdinand, king of This, That, the Other, and now Granada, was very fond of sexual relations so long as they were not with his wife. It was Isabella's eyes, eyes so widely spaced she looked more sardine than woman, and seafood gave him gout. That the portly Boabdil had sired such a gorgeous girl as Aixa pleased Ferdinand greatly, and almost quicker than he felt the pinch in his hose the lecherous ruler had her baptized, renamed after his wife—a coup to Ferdinand, but a choice that unsettled everyone else he told about it—and established as a mistress. Behaving in a beastly fashion to Moors was something of a hobby for Ferdinand, and so as Boabdil kissed his ring that fateful January day in 1492 the conquering king murmured in his fallen adversary's ear that were Boabdil to send him a beauty who outshone Aixa then the Moor should have his daughter back, thereby ensuring Boabdil knew just what carnal fate awaited his beloved child.

The time for pitying poor Boabdil has now passed. Upon

emigrating to North Africa and settling in Fez, the still obscenely wealthy Moor did little but acquire pretty young girls in hopes of offering one to his old enemy. He thought his daughter peerless in beauty, however, and as the years passed and—whether or not he would admit it even to himself—his memory faded, he remembered his daughter as being yet prettier and prettier still, until a manifest goddess would have been hard-pressed to get an approving nod from the gloomy old walrus, and so none of the bought women ever made it further than his personal harem.

At long last the would-be royal pimp came into possession of the Egyptian jewel of a local merchant's harem, a girl who caused even Boabdil's rheumy eyes to sparkle and widen. She was little older than the son Isabella-née-Aixa had by this time borne Ferdinand, but the former king of Granada saw the potential her beauty hinted at and so he wheedled and maneuvered and finally managed to get her sent straight toward Gibraltar, accompanied by a dozen slaves to tend to her and two dozen eunuchs to guard her and three dozen servants to carry the crates of incense and wine and dates and other presents he included to help persuade Ferdinand to release Aixa.

Do not pity Boabdil, who committed vile sins in the name of fatherly love. When he heard that the ship carrying his nubile gift was sunk by Barbary pirates, he did not believe the herald and had him flayed, and the second one to bring him the same news he had burned alive, and the third he had quartered, and the fourth he had buried alive, but the fifth he believed, and was saddened. Having now lost two peerless beauties—which should not be possible in the first place, but pity the pedant who told Boabdil that—the former sultan finally gave up on freeing Aixa, and his sorrow was so pronounced that in his dotage he scarcely enjoyed his prodigious harem, or his sumptuous table, or his magnificent hunts, or his impressive stable, or his pleasure cruises.

As for Omorose, the young Egyptian girl Boabdil had sent to exchange for Aixa, she did indeed fall victim to piracy and shipwreck on the crossing from Ceuta to Spain. Rather than surrendering to the notoriously ruthless corsairs, the ship's captain had sunk his own vessel, Boabdil's incense perfuming the waves as the less suicidal crewmen dumped out the chests to use as rafts. The pirates were able to fish out most of the servants and slaves and eunuchs and sailors to sell into bondage, but a few drowned along with the captain, who had tied himself to the mast to ensure a proud end. Only Omorose and her least favorite slave, Awa, escaped both pirates and sea by dint of a courageous eunuch named Halim, and after a terrifying night at sea with Omorose sitting in a myrrh-stinking box as the other two clung to the sides, all three washed up on the coast of Spain.

Omorose was the oldest of the castaways and barely a woman herself, and her sheltered life had made her as skilled at taking charge of calamitous situations as it had at flying through the air. The two younger adolescents had weathered much harsher lives, thankfully, and Omorose deigned to heed their counsel when both Halim and Awa advised moving inland in search of fresh water. Instead of a stream or spring they found a gang of bandits, who wasted no time in tying their hands and feet. Omorose allowed her hands to be tied with a haughty dignity and poorly concealed relief at being discovered by someone, even if it was only a pack of mangy thieves. Halim took more umbrage at his mistress being thus detained and so had his nose broken before finding his own limbs bound, but Awa, who had fled bondage several times on her native continent only to find herself with a new master whenever she sought shelter, knew well when she was caught and obediently offered her wrists.

Off they went toward Granada, where the chief of the bandits had a brother who spoke the heathen tongue of the Moors and could appraise the worth of the incomprehensible foreign prisoners accordingly. Away from the coast and over plain and mountain they went, into that highest Spanish range to avoid the known roads where servants of King Ferdinand might cheat an honest businessman and his partners of their fairly found booty. Up and up they went, along paths unfit for goats, until they were forced to take shelter from a thunderstorm in a narrow cave. None of the three Africans had ever known such chill as the wind whistling down into their damp shelter, their weather-ruined garments small protection, and there, in that cold, miserable cave, their nightmare began in earnest.

I
Death and the Artist

The corpse gaped up at its killer, who squatted over it with a panel of pine steadied on the ruffled velvet covering his thigh, intently sketching the dead man's startled, stupid expression with a nub of charcoal tied to a thin stick. It had taken no small effort to locate this particular body, the first man the artist could be sure he personally had killed in the battle. The youth had not died in a manner any would call brave or noble, instead fumbling with his intestines like a clumsy juggler as they fell out of his split belly, and he looked even worse with the grime and blood and filth and the reek of shit and sunbaked offal, but soon he would become a saint. Which saint exactly, the artist had yet to determine, but a saint to be sure; it was the least he could do.

"You're a sick bit of whore-crust, Manuel," said a fellow mercenary as he cut the thumbs off the corpse nearest the one Manuel drew.

"Say what you will, Werner," said Manuel, scowling down at his handiwork and finding the representation no more pleasing than its model. "At least I don't fuck them, you godless piece of shit."

"Somefinn's in his arse," a third man said with a laugh as he strode up behind them, and, giving Werner a wink, he trotted the last few feet and kicked Manuel in that very spot.

Slipping forward from the blow, Manuel held his sketch aloft as though he had stepped into a creek that proved deeper than it looked. His exposed left knee fell directly onto his subject and he cursed as the fashionable slit he had cut in the fabric welcomed the warm push of rank meat, gutlining now lining his hose. He scrambled up and pursued his guffawing assailant Bernardo, and after settling matters with that jackass Manuel had to go so far as to draw his hand-and-a-half before Werner would surrender the thumbs he had nicked from the artist's kill.

By then the light was ruined, a crimson sunset outlining the Lombardy hillside Manuel trudged toward. The bald stone prominence rearing up into the bloody sky reminded him of a skull, with eye sockets and a nose formed from the command pavilions and the grove of mercenary tents at the base of the mount creating a jagged maw. But then he was an artist and so everything looked like a symbol for something else, and because he was also a soldier most of the symbols he saw made him think of death.

"Manny, my little cowherd!" Albrecht von Stein did not stand to greet Manuel, reminding the artist at once why he despised the captain who sat across the obscenely heavy ebony table he insisted be brought from camp to camp with him. Von Stein was a large and hairy man whose blunt face would not have seemed amiss in some turnip field instead of wheedling at foreign courts, and his ogreish manners were little better than his looks. Were the bulk of Manuel's fellow mercenaries not also Swiss who would testify to his military prowess upon returning to Bern, thereby aiding in his local ambitions, the artist would have sought out a less odious captain to serve under.

Von Stein had followed the scent of bloody metal south just as surely as Manuel had, however, and the mercenaries of Bern had gravitated to von Stein's service rather than working directly with the French or the various local—and therefore unstable—

dukes and mayors. The Lombardy city-states were constantly pouring coin into the trough-coffers of the French and Imperial commanders providing the muscle for their squabbles when the foreigners were not fighting each other directly, and the old crown-eater did have a knack for tactics. Noticing the disheveled state of Manuel, von Stein pouted in the same fashion he had at a dinner several years before upon realizing the young artist he had just met was not actually gentry.

"But you've spoiled your pretty little dress!"

"I think a splash of color lends it something distinctive," said Manuel as the flap of the tent fell behind him. "Papal paint and all that."

"Oh, that's good, good." Von Stein nodded. "Can't have too many cute names for the wet red, and it's distinctive to be sure. But do you know what the Emperor said about your little hose and silk and all? Your baubles and laces?"

Manuel knew what the Emperor Maximilian, former employer and current adversary, had said because von Stein had already told him thrice on the campaign road—another hazard of knowing the commander personally before enlisting in the mercenary company. "No, what did he say?"

"He said *let them.*" Von Stein beamed, thrilled as ever to recite the magisterial ruling as Manuel sweated in his brightly colored confection of puffed sleeves and tight hose, swatches of padding and finer cloth stitched jauntily onto the garb by the artist's nimble-fingered niece. "About wearing that foppery and all, instead of proper attire. *Let them,* he said, *let them have something nice in their wretched, miserable lives!* As if we were hurting for sport or coin down here where all good men are trampled, as if we were wretched to play at wars other than his!"

"How generous of him," said Manuel. "I don't know how men could manage to serve were they lacking in ostrich feathers for their hats."

"For all that piss, the plume of your toque is brighter than most." Von Stein frowned. "Or do an old soldier's eyes mistake your halo for mere millinery accoutrement?"

"I find a handsome presentation best for ingratiating oneself with the enemy. When they turn to fetch me wine and cheese I run them through. It's quite less than Christian, really."

"You give me the impression you don't enjoy the work I pay you for," said the captain, his frown deepening. "A pity when the butcher has no stomach for slaughter, and that's all these little squabbles have been. How's your wife?"

"Well, last I heard. And yours?"

"Well." Von Stein narrowed his eyes.

"Well." Manuel cleared his throat. "A very deep subject. But while it's true I don't relish the slaughter, as you say, I do appreciate the coin. One dead Milanese or Venetian or whoever will buy a lot of paint, the useful sort, and when we return to Bern I would beg the privilege of having your wife model for me—the powers that be mentioned a possible commission for the cathedral's choir."

"Oh!" Von Stein perked up. "What sort of painting do you have in mind? Nothing provocative, mind you—my wife is a lady."

"I haven't decided on the motif yet," said Manuel. He had—she would be Salome, and John the Baptist's head would be as closely modeled on her husband's as Manuel dared.

"She will be delighted, simply delighted," said von Stein. "She's been pressing me to ask, but, I don't know, I thought it might, well, it might seem..."

Manuel was taken aback that von Swine, as he was rather unimaginatively dubbed by his men, had actually demonstrated something resembling decorum. "Tell her it is my dearest wish, and that I hesitated to ask only out of respect for her esteemed husband."

"Oh, wonderful! Good, good." Von Stein nodded enthusiastically, and Manuel felt a twinge of self-loathing to put his verbal fingers even the slightest bit under the codpiece of the man's raging ego. "So we need to get you home safe to paint, and you don't like this business anyway, so..."

"I wouldn't have come if I didn't need the money," said Manuel. "And if I had enough to go home I... I don't have enough to go home yet. Sir."

"Now you do." Von Stein plunked a bag down on the table, a purse closer in size to a saddlebag than a pouch. The captain leaned forward, clearly delighted with his presentation. Manuel waited to see if the man's enjoyment would shrivel if he let it alone long enough, but when the smile did not fade Manuel sighed and took the bait, reflecting that unless one is quite blond or white of hair having teeth that match your beard is a most unfortunate circumstance. The captain's beard was a pepper-flecked auburn.

"A raid at midnight into a fortified city? A one-man assault on a gunner embankment? An assassination?" Manuel hefted the bag, poorly concealing the strain it took to lift it.

"An errand. You deliver something to the Andalusian border, then you go home. None of that Papal dye or what have you, unless complications arise. Brigands on the road, that sort of thing."

"Spain?" Manuel cocked his head at von Stein. "What do I deliver? And how many men do I pick to go with me?"

"Five men, and I've already picked them. Werner—"

Manuel cursed.

"Bernardo—"

Manuel cursed louder, glowering at the stained knee of his hose.

"And the Kristobel cousins. The three that are left—"

"Two."

"Eh?"

"We're down to two Kristobels as of this afternoon, which is still two too many. Why do I get the dregs?"

"Are you really asking? We march tomorrow, Manny, you would prefer I give you my best and boldest?"

"Let me take Mo, and you keep the rest. The two of us—"

"You *would* prefer I give you my best and boldest! No no, my powder maid stays, and you take the five. Er, the four."

"You said five. So let me choose someone else, anyone else, to mind my back. Werner and Bernardo aren't too choosy about where their thumbs come from."

"They're cowards, Niklaus," said von Stein, the sour expression on Manuel's face at the use of his first name a welcome sight to the captain. "They'll listen to you because you're not. Now, along with the package I've got a letter for you to deliver, and if I don't receive a letter back confirming that everything went smoothly you will find yourself in a bit of trouble."

"Right." Manuel still held the satchel aloft. His arm was hurting, and he liked it. "Spain. What's the delivery?"

"Her." Von Stein nodded behind him at a lump on the floor of the tent that Manuel had hereto failed to notice amidst the tent's clutter, a faint smile on the older man's lips, lips that looked oily as poached eels in the light of the candle on the desk between them. The lump was shaped like a human sitting with her legs crossed, a thick sack over her body with two bands of chain encircling it, one at the throat and the other at the waist. Manuel dropped the satchel on the table.

"Get fucked." Manuel turned toward the tent flap, his face gone as pale as his most recent model.

"She's a witch," said von Stein, and Manuel did not need to look at him to know he was still smiling.

"Of course she is," said Manuel, willing his feet to carry him outside and down to the mercenary tents, to wine and food and murder in the morning, good honest murder with a crown bonus for each thumb. "Spain. Of course. I've heard about what they're doing."

"Have you?"

"Yes. Have you?" Manuel turned back to look von Stein in the eye.

"No. I can imagine, though. Spaniards are evil cunts, as we both know from—"

"What's special about her? Those godless bastards don't have enough heretics or madwomen to burn, they've got to import ours now? Fuck that, and fuck you." Manuel's wife Katharina would like that when he told her, he knew, and that helped propel him out of the tent.

"They'll rape her," von Stein called after him, and he saw Manuel's boots pause underneath the flap. "I knew you wouldn't do the poor bitch, being as high and mighty as you are, so I wanted you to head it up, but if my work's not to your liking I'll put Werner in charge and hope—"

"Fuck that, and fuck you." Manuel came back in, his lips drawn back like the cadaver of a hanged man. "I'll take her."

"And I suppose you're too saintly to accept payment for safeguarding the maiden?" Von Stein reached for the satchel.

"Why?" Manuel grabbed the man's wrist, surprising both of them. "What's she done? There's no such thing as witches! And why in Christ are you talking with her in the room, you cruel bastard?"

"As I said, I don't know what she's done or accused of." Von Stein wrenched his arm away. "And I don't care. I know a churchman, well, he's an Inquisitor now, but you follow. He wants her, and he's paid handsomely for her, and so he'll have her, and in as good condition as you can manage to deliver. It took my best dog-snout to catch her. You know Wim?"

Manuel nodded, having seen the former huntsman go into the

ground that very morning. Before the battle. At the time Manuel had not thought much of it, scouts being even more exposed to the elements than most and thus more susceptible to all sorts of maladies. "They buried him around Matins."

"Caught something on the way back," von Stein sniffed. "Fever must have worked his mind before he went, boy was raving all sorts of horrors. *He* certainly believed she was a witch, and worse. A black devil, he said."

"Did he?" Manuel peered over the commander's thinning pate at the hooded prisoner and lowered his voice. "Don't you worry about her listening? She might, I don't know..."

"Cast a spell?" Von Stein smiled. "Eavesdrop? We both know that where she's going they won't listen to a word she says, and even if they did, what of it? We're men of war speaking of just that, albeit a spiritual combat."

"You don't mean you approve of what the Spaniards are doing, or those bastards in Como?!"

"It's not just Spain or Lombardy, they're going after them in the Empire, France, and even our precious little Confederacy. As I say, I am not as well-read as you regarding just what they're up to," said von Stein, and Manuel saw he wore the same unhappy, fearful expression as when his employers, be they French, Imperial, or whoever he was working for at the time, came to inspect his troops. "Rome certainly hasn't condemned it, and I'm nothing if not obedient, something else you could learn from me, obedience, but yes, I'm obedient to Rome, so who are we to say if what they're doing is the Lord's work or not?"

"And if the pay is good—"

"The money they're paying if we deliver isn't the issue, it's what we lose if we don't. Our souls, Manuel, our souls!"

Manuel crossed his arms, trying not to look at the bound witch.

"Tell a single man and I'll have you hanged, I swear it." Von

Stein nibbled his lip. "What was promised me, what was promised all of us when I donated that stallion to the Church, is in jeopardy! Forgiveness, Manuel, for everything we've done! They'll take it all away! If I don't deliver the witch there will be no indulgence, Manny!"

Manuel's eyes widened and his hands shook. "Are you fucking serious?"

"Yes, yes! They mean it, too, and of course the Spanish cardinals are—"

"You actually believe God will forgive your sins if you give the Spaniards a woman to burn?" Manuel looked like he was going to be sick as he forced a dry, barking laugh. "And that story about you trading your horse for blanket indulgences is true? You really believe the word of pardoners, you sad-eyed old cock? I thought only merchants with more coin than sense bought that claptrap!"

"What I believe is no concern of yours." The fear von Stein had poorly concealed ignited into rage, and his fists tightened as he stared at Manuel. "What should concern you is getting that witch to Spain, because if you don't hand me a letter with a certain seal on it you'll be burned yourself, you little tick! Yes yes, I see you, Niklaus Manuel *Deutsch*, tacking a little Imperial flourish on your name, clawing your way up, here and at home, ever anxious to have a word with your betters, ever eager to pretend your father wasn't a fucking peddler. You say you want to get involved in politics, my boy? Loose those lacey breeches, bend over, and take your first proper lesson, you mouthy fucking peasant!"

The men glared at each other, Manuel's left eye twitching until the older man finally exhaled, deflating like a sack of wine around a table of good friends.

"Take her and get out," von Stein ordered. "We'll be in Milan, playing nanny until the Emperor arrives to throw his hired landsknechte against we fine Swiss confederates, our French employers, and whatever thick-headed Milanese are still about. You meet us there and give me the letter, I give you the crowns, and then you go home to that nice little house on Gerechtigkeitsgasse or whatever fashionably unpronounceable street you've set up on, yes yes?"

"I don't have a choice, do I?" said Manuel, knowing full well that one always has a choice.

"No. You're the only one I can trust to deliver her, Manuel, and you can tell your confessor it was my fault. And even if she isn't a real witch and you aren't doing God's work, what's another mortal soul on your tally? I wager you've lost track of how many you've killed, yes?"

"No," said Manuel, finished with lying to von Stein for the night. Not only did he know the exact figure but he knew all their faces, most sketched from memory but a few on the field, and if he returned to his workshop in Bern he would have another seven saints to add to his pile of planks. He wondered if he could bring himself to sketch the witch—to date there was a dearth of female martyrs in his collection.

"Go on, then," said von Stein, waving toward the witch. "Better you set out tonight and camp some leagues away, lest the rest of the boys get a whiff of her. Hard on them since Paula and the rest of her whores skipped off back to Burgundy. The Inquisitor's name is Ashton Kahlert, and he's got men waiting to receive her at the church in Perpignan, off the Barcelona road."

"Kahlert isn't a Spanish name," said Manuel, but he was looking at the witch.

"They're all Spaniards to me," said von Stein.

"I'm going to lift you up now," Manuel loudly informed the lumpy, bagged woman. "We're going to march for a while."

"She's got a leash round her neck," said von Stein helpfully, and with a sigh Manuel untied the tether and fixed it to the chain around her waist instead.

Von Stein rolled his eyes, put the money satchel back into a small chest under his table, and retrieved a sealed letter. He waited until Manuel had taken the letter and awkwardly led the witch to the tent flap before setting his pistol, a glorified hand cannon, on the table next to the sputtering candle. Just as the flap fell behind Manuel, his kidskin boots visible under the edge, the captain called out a final warning.

"And if you find yourself imagining it's your wife or little niece under that witch-sack, and if you then find yourself imagining that maybe I won't be quite so cross if tragedy strikes and the delivery does not transpire for any number of reasonable excuses, then, dear Manny, then I want you to remember, and you will not need to imagine because we both know that it is true, then I want you to remember that I know just where your wife and niece sleep this night, and every other." Von Stein smiled and raised his pistol toward the tent flap as it was ripped aside, the touchhole at the base of the weapon hovering beside the candle. Manuel took three steps before he noticed the gun, and then the long blade of his sword slowly slunk back into its scabbard as the artist backed out of the tent. Von Stein smiled in the empty, bright pavilion, while outside in the damp night Manuel futilely tried to stop picturing his wife or his niece under the sackcloth and iron as he led the witch into the darkness.

II

The Coming of His Acolytes

Something other than the wind howled in the darkness of the Sierra Nevadas, the Andalusian currents blowing rain straight into the mouth of the grotto as if the world had turned on its side and the African captives were in a pit instead of a cave. Despite the cold and wet the beautiful harem girl Omorose slept, and could scarce have awoken had she been of a mind to. Days spent in idle abandon had ill prepared her for forced marches over the cruelest terrain her bare feet had ever blessed with their presence, and bundled in the soggy clothing her servants had stripped off, she groaned and tossed on the stone floor of the cave.

Halim crouched naked behind his mistress, staring at a point in the blackness at the rear of the cave. When lightning flared the bandit chief was illuminated, his eyes likewise fixed ahead so that when the weather permitted he could return the eunuch's glare. The man stationed at the entrance was the only one more exposed to the storm than the three Africans, and he entertained no false hope of sleep in such conditions and so amused himself by waiting for the lightning to give him more glimpses of the two naked Moors.

The slave clung to Omorose's back, confident her mistress slept too heavily to awaken and discover her impertinence. Awa had never before touched Omorose, or any master, without permission, and the sensation of Omorose's heart beating against her chest brought new and strange thoughts to the girl. On the hard march Omorose had tried to hide her pain and fear but her hazel eyes had bubbled over like the fountain in the harem's courtyard when Awa offered her lady her own share of water. Omorose had smiled as she took the drink, an honest if sad smile. Such kindness in spite of hardship confirmed for Awa that she had come into the company of an extraordinary creature indeed, a girl not unlike herself but one previously gifted with a far grander existence.

Awa recognized that her own chaotic life was again mutating, and that life had taught her that when armed men force you to accompany them on treks through the wild the end result is never for the better. She would have run, and escaped, too, for these men were clearly not slavers by trade, but she had resolved not to abandon Omorose even before the calamities of the recent days. Her mistress was only a few years her senior and mayhap that made her seem more agreeable, and unlike the rest of her former masters, Omorose never shouted or beat her. That she would come to prize and consider rare such simple courtesy never occurred to the happy daughter of the Fon headman Awa had once been, but experience is just that.

Crouching beside the young women, Halim had decided that the flashes of lightning were infrequent enough that he could throttle Omorose and her slave to death before being discovered. Whether he would, or should, Halim was not so certain, even with Boabdil's orders that Omorose be granted a quick and royal death rather than fall into the hands of lowly men should piratry or banditry occur. When the lightning lit them up the bandit chief saw that the eunuch had broken his blind stare and looked instead at the sleeping women beside him. Then the cave went dark again, only the rioting storm giving indication of where the cavern's exit was located in the blackness. He would not, Halim decided, not admitting that upon seeing Omorose's beatific sleeping face he could not.

Omorose awoke to feel someone holding her down but was too terrified to scream. The wet cloth against her cheek and the quaking of the naked slave pressed against her back cheated the noble girl of any hopes that she had been suffering a nightmare. She realized the girl was not pinning her down but hugging her gently, and while a few days before the indignity of having the slave touching her might have sent Omorose into hysterics, there in the freezing darkness the warmth Awa provided was palpable and calming. Confident neither the wretched creature on her back nor the men could see, Omorose let her tears join the growing pools on the cavern floor.

Awa drew away as her mistress shook with a barely contained sob, then gingerly returned her fingers to Omorose's shoulder. The wind ran down the gap between the girls, a growing chill spreading from Omorose's back toward her feet and neck. Disgust again trumped by need, Omorose snaked her own bound hands up through her layers of wet cloth and took Awa's shuddering fingers, wiggling herself backwards to again press against her slave. Awa found herself smiling in the dark as she squeezed Omorose's fingers and her mistress squeezed back, and after enjoying the clammy feel of the girl's silk-soft palms, she pushed her fingers down and set to working at the leather straps tying Omorose's wrists together. She would rescue her lady, just as Halim had rescued them from the sinking boat.

"We'll get loose, and then we'll run," Awa whispered in the seashell that was Omorose's ear. "The rain will hide our footprints if we get out of the cave."

"What?" The thought of escape had not crossed Omorose's mind after Halim was beaten into submission upon initially resisting the bandits.

"They have a guard, but only one, I think. The rest are behind us, out of the rain." The clumsy knots at Omorose's wrists confirmed for Awa the bandits' inexperience in the ways of transporting slaves.

"But if there's a guard—"

"Shhh," said Awa. "I untie you, you untie me, I untie Halim—"

"Who?"

"The eunuch. Who saved us?"

"Oh."

"I untie him, and then we three run." Awa lowered her voice even more. "He's biggest so they'll likely grab him before you or me, and he'll fight for you if you're the one they catch."

"Are you sure?"

"I've done this before," said Awa, trying to keep her nervous fear in its own cave as she got the last knot loose. "Once we're free we'll have to avoid being caught again, but let's worry about that rain when next we're dry, alright?"

"Alright."

"Now we must be very quiet so they think we're sleeping," said Awa. "Don't pull on my knots, find the root of the twist and work it backward."

Her skin free of the biting leather, Omorose enjoyed the sensation for a time before choosing to acknowledge the slave's still-bound hands pressing urgently into her shoulder. Omorose remembered what her old handmaid had said about Awa's scars meaning she had run and been captured several times, and remembered how they had laughed at the idea of the plump wretch running anywhere on her short legs. She set to freeing Awa's wrists, pausing as her slave had done when she heard the faint scraping and squelching of their captors moving about in the dark, and although it took her much longer she eventually got them loose.

The storm died down only to periodically flare up like the

white coals of a long-burning fire. Dozing in his cramped squat, Halim felt a creature crawl across his foot and almost stomped it when fingers tightened around his ankle and tapped just above where the strap dug into his skin, the length between his feet having been shortened to a hand's width after they had stopped moving for the day. Halim let her work at his ankles, praying that the lightning kept at bay a little longer. It did, and he lowered his wrists, which she made short work of. Flexing his fingers, he winced as the joints cracked loudly in the dark.

Feeling around, Halim soon found a jagged piece of stone and tightened his fist, intent on giving his life if it meant the escape of Omorose. Then the cave lit up as the lightning returned, and three sets of eyes widened. The back of the cave was empty.

As the thunder pealed across the peaks, Awa slowly rose to a crouch and helped her mistress up, the slave's numb, slick skin starting to remind its owner of its presence as pain and cold began jumping all over her body. Another flash, much closer, and again they saw only the black and empty cavern, the dozen bandits vanished without a trace. The thunder came again and Awa wondered if the mountain had eaten the men who hid in his mouth, and now laughed along with his ally in the sky who had driven the prey to seek such shelter. They had to leave before he swallowed again.

"Now we run," Awa said, finding Omorose's hand in the dark. "You must follow me, mistress, no matter what. When we run we cannot stop."

"Where are they?" Omorose tried to stand but her overworked legs fought against her, cramps forcing her to lean against the wall of the cave. "What if it's a trap?"

"Then it's not a good trap since we were already caught. Please, mistress, before we find out what happened to them."

"But." Omorose bit her lip in the dark. "I'm too . . . I can't run, I can't, I—"

"You can." Awa squeezed her mistress's quivering hand. "You can, Omorose."

The cheek of Awa using her name momentarily made Omorose forget her fear of the dark, empty cave. "Don't you—"

"Quiet. Now." Halim had seen something more than an empty cave and he scuttled away from the whispering girls. Patting around in the dark, he asked for light from above and was granted his request as three bolts crashed down just outside the cave, the wind screaming and the rain biting as he scooped up two discarded swords, the hilt of one sticky and wet. Then he noticed that the puddle in which he stood felt comfortably warm on his bare, blistered feet, and over the thunder rattling his senses he heard Omorose scream.

The attacker smashed into Halim and he felt both swords fly away as fists pummeled his sides. He slid down the wall of the cave, the assailant's bony fingers cutting into the eunuch's ribs with each blow. Omorose's scream broke off and Halim lost his breath as a cudgel bruised his stomach, and then the man pinned his arms behind his back and hoisted him up, the eunuch's back scraping on the man's rough armor as he was carried out into the storm. Lightning blasted the earth just above the cave and Halim saw their new captors, and his own scream drowned out both Omorose and the crackling thunder.

Awa had smelled them even before the first flash of lightning had made Omorose scream, and now that the sky-fire showed her their faces she understood why her mother had never answered her questions about how she would know if the spirits visiting her were those of the dead and not some more common, natural thing, like the water spirits that misted her face by the waterfall or the storm spirits that filled her nose with their hot odor before the rains. Now she knew, for these spirits rode their old bones, and some still wore their carrion flesh in the same loose fashion her mistress wore the dangling wet rags of her servants.

The bonemen hoisted them up before they could move. As they were held aloft by the strongest arms Awa had ever felt, lightning illuminated the skull appraising her and she screamed for the first time since she had been taken from her village by the slavers, when she had vowed that no matter what fear she felt she would not give any spirit or man that power over her. Yet as the sky revealed the undead things carrying her and the first person she had cared about since childhood up the mountain into death she screamed and screamed, the spirits passing their three victims among them as though the youths weighed no more than satchels of limes.

Halim lost himself in his terror, gibbering along with the clicking jawbones of the monstrosities carrying them high into the mountains, but Omorose had recovered enough to realize what had happened and why the bandits had disappeared from the cave. Their captors had murdered the three of them in the cavern and now she was on her way to Hell, the lightning flashes Allah seeking in vain for her soul amidst the vast nightscape of the damned. She cursed Him then, cursed Him as weak and unfair to those who had praised Him even if they could not understand Him in the way He was explained to mortals such as she, and as she was juggled from skeletal fingers to rotting, soft arms she vomited into the swirling rain, the stink of her sick and fear mingling with the fell stench of the demons.

A tiny light appeared high above them in the darkness, the lightning left far below as they climbed higher and higher, the skeletal members of the host casting themselves against cliff faces, their bones scattering up the sheer surfaces to become animate ladders for their riper compatriots to scale with their prisoners held high. Several times they came to vast chasms and the skeletons climbed atop one another and formed bridges over the gulfs, the farthest-flung amongst them snatching the ankle of the one before him and in this fashion retracting themselves to the opposite side once their sharp spines had been crossed by the fleet-footed, capering dead. Racing up a gully, they emerged onto a plateau and here they were blinded by the light shining from an open door in the darkness, a glowing passage to another world, and before any of the three youths could recover from their journey they were shoved wailing through the doorway.

III
The Crucible of Madness

C

The animated corpses stayed outside. Omorose, Halim, and Awa collapsed in a pile on the floor of the hut. A small oil lamp sealed their eyes into leaking slits with its brilliance, and as a shadow passed over the huddled youths Halim squealed and Omorose groaned. Then the door was closed behind them, and with the devils shut outside all three wept with relief and gratitude.

None of them ever fully recovered from that night, their minds hammered into strange new shapes by white-hot fear, but after no small time of babbling and begging and praying and moaning the three Africans returned to their senses. Being so close to Heaven, dawn came early on the mountaintop, and as the only window slowly ate up the shadows in the hut, first Awa, then Omorose, and finally Halim sat up and took notice of their surroundings and their savior, who had sat watching them the entire time.

The room was cluttered but clean, the stone floor rubbed smooth and the adobe walls free of cracks. A granite table dominated the chamber, a crude wooden chair pulled back on the other side of it, and set in the rear wall above this was the window, through which one of the animate skeletons watched them. Noticing this brought on another fit in Halim, but Omorose and

Awa were already paralyzed by the sight of a monster hulking on its hind legs beside the window, a furry behemoth that Boabdil's second cousin would have recognized all too well. Eventually they realized it must be dead or a statue, although Awa suspected that given the walking corpses outside the bear's seemingly inanimate nature in no way rendered it harmless. Every wall was striped with shelves that bowed under the weight of clay jars and bowls and less identifiable objects, and a cauldron hung inside a small fireplace to their right.

Their host was less mundane. He was human enough, but his cold jade eyes were set deep in the tight skin of his face and he appeared far too aged to even sit up in a bed and chew solid food, yet he now darted around the room with an easy alacrity, his withered limbs piling the table with bowls and a jug. Then he opened the door and Halim buried his head between his legs, Omorose grabbing Awa's hand as three of the skeletons marched into the room and squatted down beside the table. With a muttered word from their host the skeletons fell apart on the floor, only to have their loose bones crawl over one another and snap together in new formations, and in less time than it takes to cleanse oneself before prayer three stools were waiting at the table. This bothered the young women quite a bit, Awa convinced that he was a sorcerer and Omorose that he was a devil.

"Please, sit and eat," the man said, his Arabic crisp despite his pale skin. "Now."

Even Halim acquiesced, none of them eager to see what might happen should they disobey. They all balked at the stools, but the rib seats scooped their bottoms comfortably and were not as sharp as they appeared. Halim and Omorose stared doubtfully at the gray chunks floating in the stew that he ladled out, but Awa's mouth flooded as the familiar goat spirits rushed into her nose and rubbed their musky backs on her tongue, and she forgot her fear.

Seeing Awa slurp up the food, Omorose set her dignity aside to sate her hunger, but Halim only drank water from the jug out of his smaller bowl. His knotted, burning stomach advised against attempting anything solid, and only with great effort was he able to keep himself from checking the window to see if the skeleton still watched him. He wondered if it all were punishment for not following his master's order to throttle Omorose rather than risk her defilement, and he cursed his own cowardice.

"Now then," the man said, reclining in the chair across the table from them. "Welcome, welcome. My apologies for any discomfort experienced but I assure you the mercies of those men who had you bound would have proven no gentler. As a matter of fact, I don't think it would be any exaggeration at all to say that you children owe me your lives."

Omorose did not say anything. Awa did not say anything. Halim swallowed, and picked up his bowl of stew.

"I am, as you see, a simple hermit." The man leaned forward and leered at them, exposing a set of uneven yellow teeth. "A lonely goatherd, I lack enough stock to feed every beggar who crosses my border, and so you will have to earn your keep by doing as I say. I live a sparse life, as you see, and have little room under my roof. I therefore suggest you work together to build a shelter before the next storm. Winter comes quickly up here, and you don't want to be caught without something substantial when the snow falls."

Unaware if her companions' silence meant lack of manners or a surfeit of terror, Omorose shakily stood and managed a quavering "Thank you."

"It's nothing, nothing." The man waved his hand dismissively. "I always need more hands, more backs."

"No." Omorose closed her eyes, swallowed, then opened them again. "Thank you, but no. We...we have to go. Now. We have—"

"Pressing business?" The man widened his grin. "Loving parents? No no, I don't think so. You're mine now, just like my other little helpers. You will help me, won't you? You'll do what I ask, without my having to order?"

"I—" Omorose could not stop shaking, even when Awa's fingers found her hand. "I—"

"Run!" Halim hurled his stew in the man's face and leaped on top of the table, his heart pounding harder than his feet as he took one, two, three steps across the granite and fell upon the hermit. Awa and Omorose were both knocked to the ground by their stools as the skeletons shook themselves back into their old shapes and followed Halim over the table.

The eunuch landed atop the old man and brought them both to the floor. Halim punched in the hermit's long nose, blood splashing hot against his cheeks, but to the eunuch's horror the ancient man howled with laughter instead of pain, putting his hands to his hollow cheeks and hooting as the boy's fist fell again. Halim's second punch made a wet slapping noise and he felt the man's jaw shift in his face, but then bone fingers were tightening around both of the youth's wrists and his neck and his legs and Halim was yanked off of the old man by the three skeletons, who held him aloft as the hermit shakily got to his feet, his face a giggling red smear.

Awa threw open the door and was confronted by another walking corpse, this one carrying a bundle over its shoulder. She darted past it into the night but stumbled as she heard Omorose scream behind her. The girl had frozen in the doorway, and before Awa decided whether to run or go back another boneman came around the side of the hut and seized her by the shoulders.

"Hold them still and make them watch," the hermit commanded, and as Awa was dragged back inside she saw that Omorose had her arms pinned behind her back by the new arrival, a shriveled husk of a corpse that had deposited its bundle on the table. The bundle moved, and as her skeletal captor hoisted her up Awa saw it was the bandit chief who had originally captured them, jagged splinters of bone jutting out of his broken arms and legs. Only Halim tried to avert his gaze, but the skeletons holding him got their fingers under his eyelids and made sure he saw through his tears, the sensation of gritty bone pressing against exposed eyeballs arresting his struggles. The eunuch knew he would never escape if they blinded him.

"Have a look, children," the hermit said, blood bubbling in the center of his swollen, mashed face as he drew a dagger from under his cloak. "Look close, now!"

The blade cut into the bandit chief's face and he began to scream. Omorose and Halim joined him, but Awa managed to keep her jaw set even when the man's nose came off, the hermit popping the glistening lump into his mouth and chewing it with a serene expression on his desiccated face. The screams grew louder as the old man swallowed and wiped his bloody face on the front of his cloak. Looking back up at them, the hermit's caved-in nose was again straight and jutting out of his face like an accusatory finger.

Then the old man began screaming along with the broken bandit and Halim and Omorose, dancing around the hut and shrieking in their faces, rubbing imaginary tears from his cheeks and skipping about like the happiest of spoiled children. When he noticed Awa was not screaming along with the rest he paused for only a moment, giving her a saucy wink as he snatched up a clump of dried stalks studded with silver-trimmed green leaves from a basket by the hearth and ignited them on the fire. Puffing his cheeks and blowing out the flaming wormwood, the hermit inhaled the thick smoke billowing off of the plants and howled even louder, prancing back toward them and shaking the smoking clump in their terror-taut faces.

Omorose began to squirm and kick as her tormentor returned

but it was too late, and as the licorice-sweet fumes filled her nose she calmed and then quieted, her legs dangling and her eyes crossing. Halim had nearly screamed himself unconscious before the smoke even reached him and so went almost at once, but Awa held her breath even when her eyes burned and her lungs boiled, and then she finally coughed and hacked and faded on the cloying smoke, the last thing she remembered the old man putting his hand on the dying bandit chief's shoulder and whispering,

"Pity Boabdil."

IV
The Three Apprentices of the Necromancer

He was, of course, a necromancer, although it was some time before his pupils learned that word, and of course he meant them ill. They were trapped atop the mountain, and even had they outrun their undead handlers there was still the matter of the chasms that boxed in that high and desolate spit of rock and ice, and the sheer cliff that fell away on one side of the prominence. The atoll of stone where they were imprisoned cast its shadow over another, lower island of rock and hard earth, and there the necromancer's semi-wild goats, sheep, and ibex pastured in the summer when color returned to the lichens and grasses of the mountain.

They were his apprentices whether they liked it or not, and of course they did not. The chestnuts they had found so delicious the first few days soon became disgusting as they ate little else, be they roasted plain, ground into flour, or cooked with the little meat he granted them. During the days he had them beat at one another and the skeletons with sticks under the tutelage of the reanimated bandit chief, who had escaped the cave and for a time held his own against the deathless that fateful night before losing first his nose and then his life, and so was deemed a suitable fencing instructor.

They erected a crude lean-to against a boulder as far as was possible from the necromancer's hut without sleeping on the actual cliffside like swallows. The old man oversaw their construction and laughed at them for choosing the shrieking wind that raged along the precipice over his quieter company, and often he did not even allow them to stay in their meager shelter. On the nights he forced them into his hut he taught them to read in the only book he had, and in that book he only ever let them see the first page, yet he could make the letters bend and warp and dance into new shapes and languages and thus one page was enough.

"The power is in the symbol," he told them one night after they had eaten of the bandit flesh kept cool year-round in the snow of the glacier behind the hut. Before they had discovered the actual source of their meat Omorose had told Halim that prohibitions against pork meant nothing to the damned, and even after they realized that he had made them cannibals they soon found that hunger goads worse than any god and so they continued to eat the stringy lumps in their stew. "What are we but symbols? Our flesh is merely an imperfect shadow cast by our spirit, what your imams call the soul. Our bodies are powerful because of the soul they symbolize, and with that power we can alter them, and we can alter other symbols."

Halim had given up trying to unravel what the witch meant with his words and simply followed Omorose's and Awa's leads as to when to nod or shake his head. The old man never singled him out with questions the way he did the young women, and Halim attributed this to the prayers he still sent east as often as he dared.

Awa found the sorcerer's ruminations cumbersome and often wrong, the spirits clearer than ever there atop the world. Trafficking with the powers was something else entirely from the spirit-infused charms coveted by her people, however, and as she learned how to address the fire spirits that hid in rocks as well as the spirits of the stone themselves she slowly plotted their escape.

Omorose struggled with the concepts but appreciated the results—her tutelage on the mountain was more formal than anything she had learned as a child, and far more useful than hours of squeezing as if she were holding in her water to one day please a prick. The necromancer's exercises made her capable of altering little things to suit her purpose, made her able to bend what she thought was real to the breaking point and then ease it back down once the world had given her what she wanted. Little things only, but she was beginning to appreciate that little things stacked up, and things that ought to be mundane became something more if she focused enough. The tongues of the bandits he had made them eat while concentrating on what the muscle-paddles symbolized had taught them Spanish in as much time as it took to chew and swallow the tough meat, and she was confident that were she to eat the tongue of Halim or Awa she would learn their savage native languages in the same short order.

"Omorose," said the necromancer, switching back and forth from Arabic to Spanish to get them used to the subtleties of their fresh linguistic knowledge. "What sort of symbols am I talking about?"

"Everything is a symbol," Omorose said quickly, her eyes darting to Awa for support. Her former slave gave the slightest of nods, and Omorose continued. "This world is nothing but symbols, which is why I thought we were in Hell when we came here. I thought we had gone from one world to another but only... only the symbols had changed. The world seemed changed because things I knew"—seeing his sour expression Omorose amended herself—"because things I thought I knew, like death being the end, had changed."

"How? Why?" he demanded.

"You changed them," said Omorose. "Because nothing in this

world is true, and everything is a symbol. You can take what is true, what the symbol stands for, and you can change the symbol. You took the bones of men who had come here before us and changed what they stood for, life instead of death. You took the truth behind the symbols of the men, their souls, and you put them back into their bones and changed their symbols and, and—"

"Bah! Awa, tell me plainly, girl, what do I mean by symbols?"

"You mean different things at different times with the same word. But now you're talking of spirits." Awa licked her lips, uncomfortable under his gaze even after all the long months on the mountain.

"And what is it we do when we change symbols, as your little friend calls it?" Omorose bristled to hear her flawless recitation of the words he had driven into her skull used in such a chiding manner. He was never satisfied with anything they did unless it made the others look bad, her especially. She looked to Awa, who stared past the necromancer and out the dark window.

"You can't change spirits," Awa decided, looking back at her tutor. "You use words to make spirits and symbols sound the same but they're not. When you say you're changing symbols you mean you are controlling spirits and making them do what you want, which is not what they want. The spirits of the dead want to leave their old bones but you draw them back and bind them and make them do what is not natural. So when you say you're changing symbols you are making the spirits do unnatural things for you."

"Closer. How do we do this?"

Awa shrugged. "I ask them."

"You do, don't you?" The necromancer shook his head. "Fascinating, the shapes it takes. Make the fire hotter, Omorose."

Omorose blinked and looked at the smoldering coals, focusing on the flames crawling up the back of the stone hearth. Her temples began to pound and sweat ran down her neck as she strained herself. She wanted the fire to grow so badly it hurt her throat and back, and she felt the pinching in her bladder and bowels as she concentrated. Finally a white jet of flame came hissing out of the center of the blaze, the plume of heat warming the room in an instant even as it died, and Omorose relaxed, her breath coming hard and her body trembling.

"Now you, Awa." Omorose saw him smiling at her old slave and she bit her pretty lip, fury mingling with the nausea that focusing so intently always brought on. Awa paused for a moment, then stood and went outside. She returned a moment later with a log from the woodpile and tossed it on the low fire. It flared up instantly, yellow flames dancing all over the dry timber.

The necromancer brayed at this, clutching his sides as he laughed and laughed, and Omorose felt her eyes boil with embarrassment. The slave was always cheating and he always laughed, as though the ape had done something clever. She had told Awa about making her look foolish but the little black beast seemed not to care at all.

"It's not just the wood," Awa told Omorose, recognizing the pained expression on her friend's face. "You didn't hear because it was my spirit talking and not my mouth, but I asked all the logs if any were ready to join the wind, and he was, and then I asked the fire if she would burn especially hot if I gave her a log ready for her touch, and she said she would, and so it was very hot, hotter than just wood and fire."

"Don't listen to her," said the necromancer, mercurial in his praise as ever. He took a hawthorn box from a shelf and opened it to show them the half-dozen round stones inside. "Bartering's for higher powers, everything else will do as you say if you follow Omorose's example and make them. Take these salamander eggs. They only hatch in fire, but as their mothers can't be expected to find a hearth out in the wilds they are born with the innate knowledge of what fire truly is, and when the mother whispers the true word that all our human words for fire symbolize the eggs flare up, igniting the nest she has built, and so the fire born of their own true selves warps the symbol of the wooden nest and..."

Halim dozed in the warmth of the hut, waiting as patiently as a scorpion on a frog's back for his opportunity. As time had stretched over them and he had come to terms with the new road his life meandered down he recognized that the necromancer had been hurt that first night even if he had healed himself, and what could be hurt could be killed. Learning the letters was hard, and the witchery impossible even had it been wanted, but he was outpacing Omorose and Awa in the martial training, and he had found where the skeletons kept the rusty swords they took down to the low passes for their raids. Soon he would be good enough to kill the necromancer in one blow and escape with Omorose, and if the necromancer did not die then Halim was confident he would at least be fast enough to spare his mistress any more pain and witchcraft.

Their first winter on the mountain the three Africans almost died a dozen times over, the necromancer begrudgingly allowing them to sleep on the floor of his hut after the third time he had to nurse Halim's frostbitten feet back to health. The only method of restoring the blackened toes that the necromancer trimmed off and cast into the fire as the gang of skeletons held the wailing boy was to have Halim eat the corresponding digits from the supply of bandit corpses, which was dwindling. That winter waned slowly beside the glacier, and slower still when the necromancer chose the windiest, coldest, stormiest nights to amuse himself with his dead playthings.

He would make the preserved bear corpse in the back of the room drop from its fearsome rearing posture onto all fours, and as his disciples tried to sleep he would cavort amorously atop its back with the rankest of his undead, the emaciated one that had brought in the bandit chief that first night a personal favorite. Omorose's observation that this gnarled thing was female was slow in coming, and Halim would have used these frequent occasions of the necromancer's distraction to attempt his murder had he been able to bring himself to look at the loathsome conjugal bed. For Awa, the only thing more disturbing than the moans of the undead concubine were the nights when she lay motionless and silent, a simple corpse mounted by the sweaty necromancer.

Menarche finally arrived in all its cramping glory for Awa that spring, slow in coming as good news, and she received a sharp rebuke from Omorose when she asked for some of the little linen they had left amongst them to bind herself. Understandably reluctant to request precious cloth from her tutor, Awa finally broke down when a scrap of rough wool proved every bit as unbearable as she had known it would be the first time she ran her hands over it. Rather than putting her through his usual undue unpleasantness, though, he simply sniffed the air as she entered the hut and went to the rag basket, fishing out several scraps and tossing them to her.

"That's a different symbol, of course," he said as she picked up the cloth and winced, knowing it had gone too easily. "Useful in all sorts of ways. Were I you I'd postpone bearing a child for some time, better to parlay down the years. Babes fetch a high price to the right bidder, and none more than a firstborn."

Awa fled the hut shame-blind as the necromancer cackled along with his concubine, whom he had granted a tongue for the purpose of conversation, as well as less polite uses—Awa had once made the mistake of looking up when the necromancer gave an especially zesty grunt to find the husk of a man posed on all fours like the more robust bear upon which he rutted, the dead woman's face buried in a place Awa thought unfit for romance. Hiding in the lean-to, Awa wadded the cloth uncomfortably in place under the leggings that the necromancer had taught them to knit from the wool he put through his rickety spindle.

As soon as she finished the bandit chief found her and led her to the dusty plateau for her daily training. Instead of sticks she saw that Omorose and Halim already held rust-reddened swords, and she silently took one for herself when their skeletal instructor offered it. The necromancer had repaired the bandit chief's broken bones and cleaned his flesh to help fill their larders, and like all the rest his retreat from the sparring circle was accompanied by a cacophony of grinding and clicking.

The transition from chestnut staves that bruised skin and occasionally cracked bones to sharp metal that could kill in an instant altered the style of their training not a bit. Halim came on fierce as ever, Omorose beguiling in her feints and jabs, and Awa defensive to a fault. The bandit chief danced about them to add the element of constant distraction, and to parry with the speed of the dead any blows that slipped past their defenses. Even with his aid they often ended their training early to carry someone to the necromancer's hut after a stab went too deep or a gash would not stop bleeding. By the time winter again loomed on the mountain Omorose and Halim each had stripes to match the old scars of Awa. Unlike her companions, Awa never screamed when the jagged metal tore through her flesh and dragged across her frame, leaving crimson wakes flecked with shavings of bone and rust.

"When should we try again?" Awa asked Omorose one frigid autumn night as the three huddled in their lean-to after the necromancer evaluated the light snowfall and told them they would not be allowed to sleep inside for another fortnight.

"I didn't know we'd already tried," said Omorose. "Or is *escape* what you call it when we get one foot down the cliff only to have the bonemen pull us back by our hair?"

"I'm sorry for that," said Awa, cheeks darkening. "But I've

thought of something better. If I distract the bonemen by trying to go over the glacier and down the far cliff they'll follow, and if they leave a few behind you've gotten good enough to stop them."

During a recent sword session Halim had smashed in the skull of one of the skeletons, and to his immense pleasure it did not rise again. Awa had further determined the nature of the creatures' mortality—if their existence could be described in such terms—by focusing on decapitating her undead sparring partners. When she had finally succeeded that very morning it had simply picked its bony head off of the dirt and reattached it, proving that the destruction of the skull itself was required to fell the monsters.

"So we get to try and fight our way out?" said Omorose. "That's an even better plan."

"I'll fight," said Halim, perking up.

"You two go ahead," said Omorose, bundling her blankets around her, "but I'm through being punished by him. We don't seem to be in any more danger now than we were the first night."

"But don't you worry about what he's planning?" asked Awa. "No good can come of staying here."

"He's going to eat us," said Halim, a far longer chain of words than he was normally wont to link.

"Fattening us doesn't make sense," said Awa. "We've already eaten more than we'll ever put on, no matter how much we grow."

"He seems to like his bed companions seasoned," Omorose said. "He probably wants a little more age on you and I before adding us to his collection."

Omorose smiled at the horrified expression on Awa's face. Being young, pretty, and vivacious had formerly been assets instead of detriments in currying a keeper's favor, and though Omorose was in no way disappointed to be excluded from that particular arena of the necromancer's attentions, she found herself struggling with alternative methods of pleasing him. If you were not the favorite you were a glorified servant to the favorite, and she would sooner hop onto the bear and try her hand at changing his perceptions of living partners than be forced to dote on her own slaves. Or so she told herself when she was cross.

"Perhaps he's simply bored, and this is how he amuses himself," said Awa, making her mistress flinch. Omorose had recognized the familiar markings of ennui on the necromancer's gnarled face from the outset—the way his snotty eyes lit up when he provoked a reaction from his wards, the way he chortled to see them cry. That her rival now suspected the same could complicate Omorose's task of proving herself the most interesting pupil. The methods of allaying the necromancer's boredom might differ from the customary variety, at least for they the living, but she had done little but combat her own boredom in the harem, and knew many a diversion and trick yet to be employed.

"Bored?" Omorose sniffed at Awa. "Oh yes, I'm sure that's why he teaches us his sorceries and everything else, and why he sends us out every day to spar with the bonemen. Bored. Really, girl, what a stupid thing to say."

"Oh," said Awa, wondering how she had scared her friend. Omorose only became nasty when she was frightened or upset, otherwise having thawed toward Awa on the chill mountainside. Her former mistress might still eschew using her name instead of "girl," but the tone of that word had warmed to Awa's ear, and she felt a rare heat on the coldest nights when Omorose would murmur, "Hold me, girl," and their prickly skin would touch and—

"Just stupid," said Omorose. "Don't you think, boy?"

Halim grunted his assent, amazed as ever at how they pretended everything was alright, how they played the little games Omorose knew instead of casting themselves over the cliffside the first chance they got. Still, he would not abandon his duty even in the hell he now inhabited, although, truth be told, the times he had slunk off to the cliff while the young women slept he had felt a fear even worse than what the necromancer inspired in him to see the moonlight glinting on the rocks far below, and even without the bonemen watching him from the darkness he would have balked. This was a test, he told himself, a test to be overcome through strength of will as well as arm.

The glowering eunuch's disapproval meant nothing to Awa, who pitied him no more than she pitied herself and far less than she pitied Omorose. At least Omorose tried, which was more than could be said for Halim. If Awa were to be honest with herself, she would have admitted that she was relieved he remained so unapproachable lest Omorose turn to his thicker, warmer body when the wind pushed through the chinks in the stacked stones of their shelter. Quick in all her lessons, Awa had learned that if you are not the favorite you sleep alone all of the time, instead of most of it.

V
The Final Test

"There's not enough meat to last out the winter," the necromancer told them, the storm clouds hovering above them like a displeased father over a noisy cradle that had suddenly gone quiet. The three apprentices stood in front of the door to the hut he blocked with his withered body, their meager blankets bundled in their arms in anticipation of being allowed to set up before the hearth as they had the previous winter. The necromancer nodded at the bandit chief, who marched in front of the youths with three sword blades clutched in one bony hand. He planted the blades in a line where the hard-packed earth met the stone shelf that comprised the floor of the shack.

Omorose, Awa, and Halim looked at the sword hilts gently swaying at waist level like an iron harvest, the only crop this high, barren field would bear. Then one of them moved the slightest bit and it all happened very quickly. Omorose and Halim went forward and Awa jumped back, and as a peal of thunder came from the south they made their moves.

She had to go back for her, Awa thought as her tough, bare feet slid down the side of the gulley leading away from the hut. She had to turn around. She had to stop running or Omorose would die. Her feet did not listen, and the twilight fell around her as her eyes filled. Awa was afraid and so she was abandoning her friend, like a disloyal beast that knows only fear, that—

A pursuer came down the opposite side of the gulley but Awa was ready and ducked past him, snatching his femur to arrest her own dangerous momentum and sending the skeleton crashing into the ground where its left elbow blasted apart on a rock. She caught herself from falling, and seeing that no others were yet upon her, she grabbed a large stone. The skeleton scrambled up just as the rock caved in its skull, and down it went. She blasted its knee off, and with the long bone of its femur in one hand and the rock in the other she resumed her flight.

Omorose was scared, Awa knew this, scared just as Awa was, and hurt inside, just as Awa was. Awa tried to stop herself from remembering her former mistress's smiles, her sad eyes, the nights when she went to her old slave and wrapped her arms and legs around her and sobbed quietly, Awa not daring to move lest Omorose pull away. She would come back—Awa lied to herself and knew it, but could not do otherwise for fear that she might slow for an instant and be caught by the new pair of skeletons that now chased her pell-mell down the steep crag; after she escaped she would come back and rescue Omorose.

Three steps separated Halim from the necromancer as the eunuch darted forward, and with the first step he drew a sword from the earth. The miserable old monster was quick but none were quicker than Halim, who had so carefully hidden his true strength and speed. Seeing the necromancer gape as he took his second step Halim grinned, for the bandit chief was only now moving forward on his left, and none were quicker than Halim as he brought the sword up underhanded, its point level with the necromancer's stomach. The old man was not moving so fast now, his hands coming up far too slowly to intercept the sword, the first syllable of some incantation only now forming on his surprised mouth, and none were quicker than Halim—

Save Omorose. The sword she had drawn came around to the right of Halim, the rusty point nicking the necromancer's shoulder as it passed him and found its target. The eunuch's knees buckled and his arm jerked, his sword twisting in his suddenly clumsy fingers, and he smacked the necromancer's chest with the flat of the blade instead of running him through. The force of Omorose's blow flipped Halim backwards, the cold sky above and then the upside-down image of the bandit chief running toward him and then the earth he was crashing down onto, fat red raindrops spattering the dust and snow, and then he landed, having come fully around to see one of the necromancer's corpses swaying in front of the laughing old man, a small, headless thing with more meat on it than most of the undead.

"Oh." Halim's lips made the shape as he realized she had decapitated him, and then the world grew dimmer and dimmer as he saw Omorose approach him, the last thing he felt her fingers hoisting him up by the hair.

"Very nice, very," the necromancer managed, and Omorose suddenly felt dreadfully weak and began to cry, her dripping tears washing some of the grime from Halim's severed head as she carried it to her master. He had never before praised her so openly, and as if she were purring instead of sobbing he stroked her again with his words. "Excellent work, truly. You're as unpredictable as the weather."

Snow began drifting down and more thunder came from beneath them, where the true storm lurked over the lower peaks. The necromancer dusted himself off and looked from Omorose to the skeletal bandit chief. With a sigh he patted Omorose's shoulder and said, "Cut Halim's tongue out and give it to yon sword master. He'll catch her for us, but perhaps words will work better than other weapons on little Awa. Bring her to us, bandit."

Omorose's wild, dangerous smile found its twin on the

necromancer's face as she clumsily used the sword to free Halim's tongue. Tossing it to the bandit, she saw it fly between his jaws and then vanish as if Halim and his tongue had never existed and she were simply a young woman having a most peculiar nightmare in her harem. Then she saw the tongue had somehow adhered itself to the interior of the skull's hollow mouth and now licked the horror's teeth, and Omorose knew she would never wake up.

Awa came to the end of the unbroken prominence and looked across the wide chasm—she had spent countless hours jumping around the mountaintop in preparation, but standing on the edge she realized, as she always did when she surveyed even the narrowest part of the crevasse, just how impossible a leap it would be to the far side. If she did make it, though, she could run all the way down the steep mountain instead of trying to descend the cliffs. Or so she hoped.

Then Awa turned away from her treacherous escape route to face her pursuers, a stone in one hand and a femur in the other. There were still only two, and she hurled the fist-sized rock with a skill she had steadily honed over the previous year. She turned to meet the charge of the second skeleton without looking to see if her missile connected with the first. It did, the spirit in the stone honoring the deal it had silently brokered with Awa and flying true. The targeted skeleton's skull exploded and its body tumbled in a heap at her feet, but its fellow launched itself off a boulder with its sword coming down to split Awa's shoulder.

Awa had watched them meticulously, and occasionally the necromancer even allowed her to inspect an unanimated example so that she might learn how each piece fit together and worked in harmony, and so she knew exactly how the bones could and could not move, and she sidestepped the leaping skeleton at the last moment. Its twisting shoulder blade cut her underarm as she brought the loose bone in her right hand down into the gap where its extended sword arm met its body. There was a grating sound as it landed and tried to raise its weapon, and she pulled down on her bone like a lever. Its arm popped neatly off as she planted her foot on its spine and shoved it off the cliff. Its other hand swung around to grab her face but she kept her hair shorn close to the scalp and it found no purchase as it tumbled away over the precipice. Before it even broke apart on the rocks below she had tucked its sword into the worn belt that her leggings fastened to and began trotting along the edge of the chasm.

"There's nowhere to run," she heard Halim say, and her left foot twisted underneath her as a loose piece of stone slid out from under it and clattered down the side of the crevasse. A year before, the skeleton who appeared beside her would have been indistinguishable from its fellows, but Awa had taught herself to look closely at the bones, and the faint fissures where his broken arms and legs had been fused back together identified him at once. The bandit chief held a sword loosely in his arm, and behind him she saw a pack of skeletons fast approaching.

"Awa," the bandit chief said. "Listen to me—"

Awa did not, limping toward the prominence she had long before chosen as her leaping-off point, resolutely refusing to consider how a sprained ankle might impact her jump. He quickly circled in front of her, his sword raised. Her hand tightened on the hilt of her own weapon and she grimaced to put weight on her left leg.

"Don't," the bandit said. "I have every advantage and—"

Instead of her usual cautiousness, Awa came at him hard as Halim would have, and he fell back as their swords met and she tried to drive him over the edge. He spun around her on the plateau side, their backs bumping, and she lost her balance. His hand snatched her tunic and pulled her back from the precipice, and then their swords connected again as she used the momentum he had granted her to attack.

Without being able to speak he had lacked the ability to instruct the children as well as he might have, and his bones had tallied many more years than she of swinging iron and steel, but still she drove him back, her teeth gritted, her sword a russet blur. He tried talking to her but the ringing of metal on metal sang louder than he could speak. At last she overextended a jab and he kicked her in the stomach, bringing her to her knees as she gagged on the pain in her gut. Instead of running her through or pinning her down he dropped to a squat and hissed at her.

"Awa, listen to me"—he glanced over his shoulder—"you can't get away, not now. I've tried finding ways to help but there are still too many of the mindless ones under his sway. The dead travel fast, girl. Now quickly, before she comes, Omorose means to kill you. She killed Halim and—"

"You killed Halim," Awa said, still on her knees with her head bowed but slowly curling her toes under her feet to spring up. "You brought us here, didn't you? And if Omorose is, is confused, who can blame her? Who can blame any of us?"

"I"—the skeleton turned its skull away from her—"I didn't—"

Awa's sword blasted his wrist into powder that joined the snow now falling around them, and as both his sword and the hand that gripped it fell she pivoted on her good ankle and hobbled along the chasm. The other skeletons had reached them now and came pouring down the mountainside toward her, a flash flood of clattering bones. She was panting and her left leg stabbed her from toes to groin with every footfall but she pushed herself faster, shards of muddy ice coming loose from the precipice beside her. Then three skeletons dropped down in front of her, and she limped even faster toward them, her eyes focused on the spit of rock jutting out between her and the skeletons. A small tree grew from a crack near the top of the cliff on the opposite side of the chasm.

"Death won't save you from him!" the bandit chief cried from just behind her, but then she turned, the toes of her good foot pressing down on the edge of the rock. Awa leaped over the gulf, the far side rearing up through the thickening snow, and she hit the trunk of the tree chest-first. The cracking of her ribs was louder than the cracking of the wood under her impact, her legs slamming into the sharp stone of the cliff. Her arms flopped around the base of the tree from the collision but her strength had been driven out along with her breath, and after a single triumphant instant she limply fell away from the tree and the cliff-side, into the abyss, her last thought of Omorose's crooked smile.

"I was hoping it would be you," the necromancer told his apprentice as they stood waiting before his hut in the snow, and Omorose returned his grin.

VI
The Soldier and Death

The mercenaries were three days out from the camp when the men did what Manuel knew they would, which was a day more than he had expected. The first night was free, what with Werner and the rest elated at the promise of wages away from the front line and the fat sacks of rations given to each of them. Manuel had actually gotten an honest night's sleep once they had stopped a few leagues off, with the witch's tether wrapped around his wrist and the hope that she would scream if she were disturbed in the night.

The front of the witch's hood had a tightly laced slit, which Manuel opened to give her food and drink. The glimpses he caught of her features when he did were vague, especially with the blindfold she wore under the sack, but von Stein's parting words ensured that to Manuel's gray eyes she bore more than a passing resemblance to both his wife and his niece. Her arms were kept pinned down by the second chain and so he had to hold the waterskins and hard loaves to her dark lips after removing her gag, but she made it easy for him by being neither resistant nor overly eager to be fed and watered. He did not replace the gag after pulling it down around her neck the first night.

The first day proper it rained from dawn to dusk and Manuel let them keep the road, with the men taking shifts to scout ahead lest they encounter a contingent of any variety—the roads were only safe so long as one had strength of numbers. The day after that one of the men had probably noticed something, perhaps when he was hoisting the bottom of her heavy, musty sackcloth to help her relieve herself. They had enjoyed quite the laugh when Manuel had noticed her trying to squat and gone to assist, and they must have noticed how small her feet were or something, and then his already dubious claim of political hostage turned into what spattered his boots. After that they spoke more to themselves, eyeing the bundled prisoner with renewed curiosity, and Manuel did not sleep that night.

Obviously he could not stay awake the entire trip west, and so some part of him was relieved when they made their move in the morning. Get it out of the way now, and quickly. The Kristobel cousins were key, and if he could break them then the odds were back on his side.

"Manuel," Werner greeted him, and from the man's honest grin Manuel knew what he was about. "Think I'll help'er with the business this morn so she don't mess your boots gain. Sir."

"You can't have her." Manuel addressed the bunched-up trio of Kristof Kristobel, Kuhlhoff Kristobel, and Bernardo as much as Werner. "Von Swine's kept the pay until we get back with a letter, which we won't get if anything's done to her, right? So a fat purse later or a poke with a witch now and maybe a hanged neck for the trouble, which is no choice to my mind. Put yours from it."

"Witch?" said Werner, and Manuel hoped he had not erred in disclosing this. He had. "Well then, I figure it ain't my fault what I'm bout, is it? She done bewitched me. She bewitched you lot?"

"I ain't fuckin no witch," said Kristof, crossing his arms. That settled it for Manuel—if he took out Werner quickly that would leave Bernardo, and with the Kristobels—

"I will," said Kuhlhoff. "Why not? See if she's cold inside like they say, eh?"

This left Manuel with a serious problem. One Kristobel simply was not enough, and he doubted—

"Settled, then," Werner said, and Manuel noticed the dagger in the man's left hand. When had he drawn that?

"Ya said we could toss fa first," said Bernardo, pushing between the Kristobels. Manuel let his eyes flit over their camp but did not back down as the second man advanced up the small rise. Terrain was far from everything in a battle but he had the high ground for a moment, the rest having set their fire lower on the side of the hill facing away from the road, but the lack of vegetation save for hazel trees would not help her hide even if she were able to get away, and Werner was too close, far too close.

"Right," said Manuel, recognizing that they had left him little choice if he wanted to safely return to his vulnerable family. Werner and the rest would take turns with the witch on the hillside, leaving the wet sackcloth and chains in place, her silence of the march possibly broken by muffled screams. Manuel would want to go off a distance, maybe vomiting from the sight and sounds, but he must force himself to watch lest they get carried away. If she were to survive the rest of the trip to Spain he would have to make sure none of them were too fierce, and that meant observing every time, especially with Werner. She was a witch, and so of course no questions would be asked when she was delivered, and then back to von Stein and payment, and back to his family. Katharina—

Bernardo hoisted the sack-covered woman to her feet, Werner still watching Manuel closely, and in that instant the artist resolved never to see his wife again. Better not to see Katharina at all than not be able to look her in the eye, better to sleep forever than never be able to sleep well again. Fuck that, and fuck them.

"Sacrifice," said Manuel. "God is sacrifice. I heard that, somewhere, but it stuck. The very idea that money, money earned through evil acts, that money could be more important to Him than to act in His image, to sacrifice oneself... it's preposterous, isn't it? Preposterous!"

"What?" Werner tightened his hold on his dagger. "What in fuck are you on bout?"

"What in fuck." Manuel nodded sagely. "Indeed. I'm talking about sacrificing the little lamb there. Oi, Bernardo, I get first go and there'll be no fuckin tosses for it, other than who goes second."

Bernardo looked at Werner, who squinted at Manuel. Behind them the Kristobels relaxed their shoulders, and Manuel wondered if they would have backed him after all. Too late now, and he winked at Werner as he pushed past him. Would the rapist plant the dagger in his back or in his neck? Manuel held his breath as their shoulders brushed, but then Werner clapped him on the back.

"You're alright then, Manuel!" Werner laughed. "I like goin last myself, anyhow. Give *Master Artiste* first go, Bernie."

"You said—" Bernardo began but Manuel cut him off.

"I've got some butter in my bag that's a little sour. Fetch it for me and I'll give you next." Manuel's grimace must have looked enough like desire for Bernardo not to question him further, and he trotted to the artist's pack. Werner was saying something loud to the Kristobels and Manuel roughly grabbed the witch's shoulders, wondering if he addressed the back of her head or her face as he chanced a whisper.

"When I said, you are run," Manuel said in perfectly lousy Spanish. He almost gagged on his words, his voice sounding impossibly loud. "Fuck, I hoping your comprehend."

"I understand, Niklaus Manuel Deutsch of Bern." The witch's voice ghosted through her hood in far smoother Spanish than his, and Manuel froze. Her use of his name unsettled him greatly, and for just a moment he wondered if she really was a witch. Then he asked himself if it would change his actions if she were, and he had to admit it would not. She had not given any previous indication she understood him at all, and certainly none that she could speak—

"Take the chains off," the witch whispered. "But first the mask. I'll be blind until my eyes adjust, so stall them once it's off. Don't be rash."

"Did she fuckin say somefinn?!" said Bernardo.

"She's begging me to not let you fuck her," Manuel replied, unlacing the slit in her hood and widening it enough to get his hand inside. He felt her hot cheek as he clumsily fumbled with the blindfold, the stink of neglect and waste wafting out of the hole in her covering making his own eyes water. He got the blindfold up, and as he removed his hand he saw her brown eyes blink and begin bubbling over even in the shadowed interior of her hood. She was a Moor, he saw, and he laughed nervously at his folly—he had thought her face and bare feet were simply stained and dirty.

"Are you takin that off'er?" Werner asked, and Manuel heard his boots squeaking in the wet leaves as he approached.

"If I didn't care what my hole looked like I'd have stuck a sack over one of you bastards soon's Paula and her stargazers jumped boat," said Manuel, spinning the Moor around to get at the clasps on the chain at her back.

"She's a witch," said Kristof, panic in his voice. "If you let'er go she'll do something!"

"Aye," said Werner from beside Manuel, and it did not relax the artist to see the man had traded his dagger for a sword. "She'll do somethin, alright, four somethins. Five, if you stop bein a cunt, Kristobel!"

Manuel removed the pin locking the waist chain in place and

the heavy iron fell on his boots, the edges of the sack bulging and popping as she flexed her arms. Werner gave Manuel a smile, the sort of smile fishermen exchange when one of them has landed something big, Bernardo beside him with the olive-tinted butter pooling in his sweaty little hand. Manuel almost threw up, far more nervous than he ever felt before a battle. Werner's sword was right there—

"I hope you're a fighter, bitch!" Werner barked beside Manuel's ear. Manuel's fingers were shaking as he slid out the pin from the neck chain. The iron had been tight as a dog collar against her throat, and as he tossed it aside he heard her take a deep breath but he could not warn her, he could not say anything, Werner was too close—

"I'll give you space to work, Manuel." Werner nodded knowingly, walking around the witch so that he stood above them on the hill, Bernardo still holding the butter out to Manuel to his left, and the Kristobels somewhere behind them. Manuel held his breath and, bunching the sackcloth in his fists, pulled the heavy, damp bag up and over her head, finally releasing the woman.

She was a girl, a naked girl, and there was nowhere for her to go. They were surrounded, and now she was standing nude and shivering in the pale dawn on the hill, and Manuel realized what he had done. They would both die on the hill, and she would be raped, and if he had not intervened he could have kept her alive, he could have kept her from seeing what they were doing to her, he could have—

—One always has a choice, Manuel knew, and he had made his. Werner's sword was still out but he had backed away enough that Manuel stood an honest chance of drawing his own in time, assuming nobody stabbed him in the back.

"Well aren't you gonna kiss'er?" Bernardo's fetid breath drifted over the artist's shaking shoulder, and Manuel tried to pull himself together.

"You actually kiss them, you fucking ponce?" Manuel grinned at Bernardo and snatched the lump of melting, rancid butter out of the mercenary's extended palm. He took it with his left hand, his off hand, which Werner might have noticed if he were not laughing at Bernardo's expense, and Werner laughed harder as Manuel shoved the butter in Bernardo's mouth and shoved him backwards. Then Werner stopped laughing as he saw how hard Manuel had pushed, Bernardo falling backwards with his arms flailing, and Manuel saw the Kristobels were even closer than he had thought, and for some reason the assholes had their weapons drawn as well. For fuck's sake.

Werner was hoisting his sword back and bounding forward even as Manuel's right hand closed on the hilt of his own weapon, and before Bernardo had crashed onto the moist earth behind them everything went to shit. The witch ran exactly the wrong way, bumping into Manuel as she spun away from Werner and went behind the artist, directly toward the Kristobels and Bernardo. Manuel's sword was still only half drawn as Werner brought his weapon around, but the prospective rapist had swung it side-armed and so Manuel was able to intercept the blow with the non-sheathed half of the blade, his wrist twisting painfully and his belt loops popping off as his scabbard was torn loose from the impact.

Manuel's right fist was shaking and could not hold on to the heavy sword, his wrist sprained from the awkward parry. The sheath fell off the end of Manuel's hand-and-a-half as he clumsily traded the weapon into his butter-slickened left hand, and then Werner was bringing his sword down again. Manuel hopped back out of the way, slipping down the hillside, but Werner did not hesitate, pressing the advantage. Manuel knew he had a moment or two before Bernardo was up and swinging behind him, to say nothing of the Kristobels, and he had to put Werner down at once or all was lost. More precisely, he thought *fuck fuck fuck*, but surely the veteran was aware of the rest.

Both of their swords were long and heavy, and once committed to a maneuver difficult to alter in their deadly course. Manuel waited for Werner to swing again, and when the blow fell he again jumped out of range, only this time he swung his own sword sideways as he dodged, his swing perfectly timed to cut into Werner's overextended sword arm. Unfortunately, the rancid butter coating Manuel's palm collaborated with his momentum to send the sword leaping out of his hand, flying past Werner and embedding in the dirt.

"Fuck!" Manuel screamed as his botched attack sent him stumbling into Werner, but rather than trying to get his sword up in time Werner threw his elbow into Manuel's ribs. Manuel fell past Werner but one of his kicking feet caught the mercenary behind the knee and Werner lurched forward down the hill. Manuel's sword was right there, and he planted one hand on the ground beside it and snatched the weapon with the other, propelling himself to his feet. That was the idea, at least, but his sprained wrist buckled as he tried to push himself up and he fell back down, his buttery left hand slipping off the hilt of his weapon.

Werner was charging back up the hill toward him and, still on his knees, Manuel could gain his feet or his sword but not both. He chose the sword, and as Werner's steel blade arced down at him Manuel twisted around. Seeing the flashing metal above him, the artist pitched himself forward to avoid it, belly-flopping onto the cold ground only to feel something stop his sword.

It was Werner, the tip of Manuel's sword flush with the man's spine. The hand-and-a-half had bounced off the top of Werner's codpiece and passed through his linen and silk shirts and into his stomach. The momentum of Werner's own missed swing carried him over to the side, skin and cloth tearing as he was disemboweled on Manuel's sword. Werner was still screaming as he fell, his uncoiling intestine tangling on Manuel's handguard and arresting the man's fall for a long and terrible pause until his gut tore and he hit the earth. Werner screamed and screamed as Manuel rolled onto his back, knowing Bernardo or one of the Kristobels was right behind him, knowing he was about to die but laughing in spite of it because at the very goddamn least he had field-dressed Werner like a deer.

There was no one there. Scrambling up and peeling Werner's innards off the guard of his sword, Manuel saw two bodies at the base of the hill, and then a scream came from deeper in the wood just as Werner's finally trailed off. Trotting cautiously down, he saw that the Kristobels lay side by side, their shirtfronts soaked with blood as though they were conjoined brothers fallen victim to an unsuccessful separation, clean swords still held in lily-white hands. Hearing the high scream again, he set off after Bernardo and the witch, delaying further investigation of the corpses.

Beyond the base of the hill was the undergrowth Manuel had longed for on the hillside, and when the scream did not come again he slowed to a walk, every juniper patch and hornbeam thicket carefully examined. Then he found a blood splatter on the ground, and, following the trail toward another hillock rearing up among the budding hazels, he heard a moan. Pushing through a clump of junipers, he found them at the mouth of a small cave in the side of the hill.

The witch wore Bernardo's clothes, and the naked man lay at her feet making small wet noises and holding both hands to his bloody mouth. As if she had been waiting for his audience, the witch nodded at Manuel and squatted over Bernardo, slitting his throat with a dagger. With his dagger, Manuel realized, and even though he could see the weapon his hand went to the empty sheath at his waist. She must have taken it when she bumped into him on the hill, and she must have used it on the Kristobels and now, obviously, on Bernardo.

In the better light she looked older than he had originally

thought, but not by much. She was short but surprisingly well-built, her close-cropped hair the dull, grayish brown of the bistre Manuel used for his ink, her skin darker than the dead leaves at her feet. And in the time it had taken him to kill one man on equal footing she had killed three, and all with his dagger.

"You're a witch," said Manuel, a bitter metallic taste in his mouth. He realized he had bitten his tongue when he had fallen during the fight, and he spit red. "Is that it?"

"Yes," the witch said in Alemannic German to match his, and he saw her mouth was smeared with blood.

"And you used your witchcraft on them?" Manuel smiled to hear such words leave his mouth.

"No, I used your knife on them," said the witch.

"I saw that." Manuel nodded, pushing the rest of the way through the prickly bars of the juniper and looking down at the witch and Bernardo's leaking body. "That's your witchcraft, isn't it? Being so good with a blade? The way so-called learned men attribute—"

Then Manuel stopped. Bernardo was getting up, planting his bloody hands in the thick crimson pool his neck had created, and he jerked up to his feet, the flow at his neck quickening from the exertion. He stood swaying beside the witch, who smiled faintly at Manuel. The artist was also a soldier and knew a dead man when he saw one, and Bernardo was most assuredly dead, the wound in his neck as wide as Manuel's thumb and deep enough that as the risen corpse turned its head Manuel saw the hint of bone that must be his spine. Manuel was going to be sick, he was—

Manuel started awake in a shadowy cave long after the rain started, thunder murmuring its displeasure to be left outside. His wrist hurt and he had no idea where he was, confusion and pain adding a sinister edge to the gloom. Between the artist and the mouth of the cave was a small campfire, and Manuel lay very still, trying to straighten out what had actually happened from what his exhausted mind had made him dream before collapsing. Yet the whole morning seemed implausible, and he was cold and damp and sore and could smell the char of cooking pork, and so he got up and went to the fire where the witch sat in front of a joint of roasting meat and a simmering stewpot.

"I wonder at you, Niklaus Manuel Deutsch of Bern," said the witch, and when she did not offer him her waterskin he rooted through the piled bags at his feet until he found one. He dug deeper until he found another skin full of wine and an apple, and then he sat down.

"Do you?" He sounded scared to himself, and realized that he was. He did not know where his sword was, nor his dagger. Fuck.

"I do. I wonder if those men hadn't meant to rape me if you would have set me free. I wonder. When you found me, when your master was ordering you to deliver me, you said the Spanish men would burn me, yes?"

"At best." Manuel took a slug of wine.

"So that is alright. You were not happy about it but you would have done it, but when they decided to rape me you told me to be ready to run. That was foolish. We both would have been caught, and I still would be raped, and you would probably be killed. Are you foolish enough to think you could have fought them all when one of them almost finished you?"

"No, I didn't..." Manuel took another pull. "I didn't think they would be so close. I thought you might be able to get away, or that the Kristobels would come around if I put Werner down quick. Still foolish, as you say."

"If they hadn't tried what they did, would you have tried to let me go, or would you have given me to this Inquisition?" The witch was watching him closely, and something he could not place nagged at him.

"I don't know," Manuel said, reserving his lies for those who paid him. "I'd thought about it, of course, thought of little else. I'd like to think so, but we'll never know, will we?"

"No." The witch sighed, and then Manuel realized what was bothering him. The first thing he had remembered upon waking was Bernardo's corpse getting to its feet, but he had dismissed that at once as fancy. But the other shapes in the light of the meager, smoky fire were not boulders nor the walls of the low-roofed cave nor bits of fancy. They were four men, four men whom he could now smell over the cooking meat and the woodsmoke and the loamy scent of the cave. They smelled like old blood and early rot, like sweat and piss and shit, like all the notes subtle and strong that combine to create the perfume of battlefields and slaughterhouses; the unmistakable smell of death. And they were watching him with unblinking eyes, Werner, Bernardo, and the Kristobels, they were watching him from where they sat blocking the only exit to the cave.

The thunder came again, and Manuel slowly backed away from the fire, into the dark recess of the cave. He kept his eyes on the dead men she had brought back to life but soon his sore hands assured him the back of the cavern ended in cold, wet stone and earth, a dead end. She was a fucking witch, not some poor midwife or Jew or madwoman, but a real fucking witch. And he had loosed her.

VII
The Last Apprentice

Awa fell, and then the bandit chief crashed into her back, bones encircling her limp body. Both of her shoulders were dislocated as their plummet was arrested by the interlocking spines of the necromancer's pack of skeletons that tethered the chief to the near side of the chasm. They swung into the cliff face, breaking Awa's previously uninjured right ankle, and then they were slowly reeled back up, Awa drooling red from her internal wounds. The loose skeletal arms jammed into cracks in the rock and hauling up the line of their spines quickly rejoined the rest of their bones when Awa and the bandit chief were finally hoisted back to safety.

The snow felt warm on Awa's cheeks as the bandit chief carried her. He was talking to her with Halim's voice but her rattled mind could not pick out individual words until she saw the necromancer and Omorose waiting in front of the hut, and then her fear cut through the pain coursing through her, pain as rich and widespread as the blood in her veins.

"Now *that* I saw coming," the necromancer said with a smile at Omorose. "The runner runs, just as the fighter fights. How are you feeling, little Awa?"

Awa tried to tell Omorose to do everything she could to live, to tell her mistress how much she loved her, but only more stringy blood leaked between her teeth.

"She destroyed three," the bandit chief said as he laid Awa down in the snow at the necromancer's feet. "Got to the far ravine, cut off my hand, then made a jump for the other side when she couldn't run anymore."

"A runner and a fighter, eh?" The necromancer looked at Omorose. "I think the fight's left her, don't you?"

Omorose looked down at Awa and her twisted mouth began twitching at the corner as she remembered the way her former slave had held her on the worst nights when Omorose could not pretend anymore, the countless times Awa had labored to make Omorose's shortcomings appear to be her fault instead. The younger girl looked up at her, a strange and frightening smile creasing Awa's bloody mouth as their eyes met, and Omorose knelt to put her out of her misery. The slave must have seen the knife in her mistress's hand then, Awa's eyes widening, and she managed a gurgling cry.

"No!" Awa tried to warn her but then his hand touched the back of Omorose's neck, the necromancer's glittering eyes locked with Awa's. Omorose fell dead in the snow, and Awa began to sob, trying to crawl to her friend despite the agony it brought.

"None of that, now," said the necromancer, and with a murmur Omorose sat back up. "Bring Awa in and lay her by the fire, then bring me Halim. She'll need his shoulders and ankles by the look of it, and probably more beside. You'll be at the mortar and pestle all night; much as I hate to waste good bones she'll be useless without them. We'll do a soup with the powder, I think."

The snow settled on Awa's cheeks, on the salty brooks both clear and red that trickled down them, and then Omorose's corpse picked her up and carried her in. When she tried to refuse the food in the coming days the necromancer merely had to threaten Omorose's mortal remains and Awa would do as she was told. Eventually she was able to speak without crying.

"I'll do anything you want, and not run, nor disobey," said

Awa, unable to keep her eyes off the corpse of Omorose standing behind the necromancer as they sat at the table, the bone broth steaming between them. "But you let her go."

"Where to?" His bemused smile sickened her.

"To wherever the dead go when sorcerers don't enslave them," said Awa, her voice unwavering. "You let me bury her, and you never touch her again, or let your servants touch her, or eat her, or anything else. You let her sleep, and if you do then I will be as good an apprentice as you could hope for."

"Alright," said the necromancer, and with a wave of his hand Omorose's corpse collapsed in a pile on the floor. "Now eat your supper, it's getting cold."

Refusing the help of the bonemen, Awa found the mountainside less than accommodating to an amateur gravedigger. She eventually settled on the far side of the glacier where the rock shelf reemerged from under the ice just before the cliff fell away. On the narrow outcrop of stone she built a cairn over her mistress, and the spirits of the glacier promised to keep Omorose cool lest the summer sun ripen her into something delectable to scavengers. Awa stacked the rocks high, her fresh wounds nothing more than fresher scars and minor aches after only a few days of taking the necromancer's cure.

That first winter alone with the necromancer was the worst, with him jumping the bones of his beloved restless dead on an almost nightly basis. Between his romps she discovered where he actually slept, and how. In the mornings when he sent her out to spar with the bandit chief he animated the bear corpse, which would rear up on its hind legs while the necromancer unlatched a catch in its fur, making its whole chest swing open on a hinge. Then he would step inside, careful not to snag himself on its ribs, and pull the furry door shut behind him. The undead bear watched Awa intently whenever she came in to bind a wound or start cooking their dinner but only growled if she approached it. Knowing she would have to learn all his secrets to avenge her mistress, Awa became the model pupil and asked him about his sleeping habits one midwinter day when they were snowed in.

"If you mean to ask why I sleep inside a giant, monstrous beast instructed to rend apart anyone who might disturb my rest I would ask what happened to your previously acceptable wits." The necromancer's concubine tittered from atop the bear's back—it was still on all fours after the previous night's activities.

"I think there's more to it," said Awa. "You don't always sleep, and when you do it's always during the day, when I'm out."

"Any old sod can see when the sun is up, but by keeping a nocturnal regimen I train my eyes to see better than an owl in the dark." With his long nose and fat, round eyes he did look something like an emaciated owl, although Awa, never having seen such a bird, did not realize it.

"There's more," said Awa.

"More?"

"More." Awa nodded. "You don't want me to see you sleep, and not just because we're all vulnerable when we sleep. You've your bear, after all, and I couldn't hurt you if I tried. So why do you hide?"

"She's calling you afraid!" said the concubine.

"Not afraid," said the necromancer, but his left eye twitched as he spoke, and he snapped his fingers to dismiss his paramour. Her desiccated corpse went limp atop the bear and he steepled his fingers, watching Awa closely. "And no, you couldn't hurt me if you tried. Iron, as I've told you, is one of the only symbols that represents what it truly is, here and on the so-called Platonic level of reality, and thus it can hurt even one such as myself. Because it is a true material and not just a symbol of something else, iron restricts our ability to alter the world, be it talking with spirits or commanding symbols or however you put it. But the usual methods will heal an iron-caused wound, and if I feared it in general I wouldn't give you a sword of the stuff, would I?"

"No," said Awa, suddenly quite nervous. She had suspected that iron might be the key to undoing him, for she dimly recalled that in her homeland the metal was supposedly important to sorcerers. Accordingly, she had stashed one of the swords under the ice of the glacier near the hut to always have cold iron close at hand were he to give her the opportunity to use it. If he were sleeping unguarded, for example. She swallowed, his large eyes ever on his sole pupil. "So why do you sleep inside the bear?"

The necromancer forced a sigh and pushed his chair back. "Come on then, let's teach you how to die."

"What? I don't—"

"Just a little death, dear Awa, although that means something quite different to the Normans. Beware Norman lovers, their hearts are made of iron even if they're softer elsewhere." Awa knew better than to run. His bluish fingers brushed the nape of her neck and she felt her whole body fall away. She remained seated on the bone stool but her heart had stopped and she could not even make herself blink. She began to panic. She was dead, but she was still trapped in her body, and the terror that death was an eternity trapped in one place and nothing more settled onto her cooling heart.

"You're dead," the necromancer breathed in her ear. "But you're not. It's how we can prolong our lives—instead of sleeping I let myself die for a little while, so that the days granted my mortal flesh are extended. Yes, days. Picture your life as a day, Awa, with dawn your birth and sunset your death, and everything in between a single, impossibly long day. The sun keeps its pace regardless of whether we are waking or sleeping, and eventually twilight comes for even the most long-lived creature. You already know several means for healing yourself, for slowing the sun, as it were, but now I'll teach you something better—how to freeze the sun in the sky of your life, to bring it to a standstill. The only way to cheat death is to die first, to give yourself willingly, and with the methods for revival."

Then his fingers scalded her neck with their warmth and her heart lurched forward and she gagged on the air as her lungs pushed and her body jolted. Her temples pounded and she felt sick, icy sweat coating her instantly. He resumed his seat.

"We are living, of course, and if we were to truly die then no necromancy could revive us to this marvelous mortal coil that all undead envy. Any seeming advantages to be gained from lacking a heartbeat are suspect at best, and pathetic. The undead are wretched, jealous animals, Awa, all of them!" His sudden fury would have frightened her far more had he not recently killed her, or close to it.

"How then?" Awa managed, sure the secret to his vulnerability lay at hand. "How did you, how do you..."

"It's not true death, of course." The necromancer shook his head to dispel whatever spirits darkened his mood. "Your organs would putrefy in no time at all. They do freeze up, however, and returning can take some getting used to. The *truth* of Awa, of course, is everything—you were aware even though your heart had stopped and your brain, supposed home of all your ability and knowledge, was dead. You *were* dead, were you not?"

"I was." Awa shuddered at the memory.

"The body, the symbol, had died, but unlike real death the spirit, the spark, the *truth*, remained, and with that you could bring your body back, you could unlock your flesh and live again. But only assuming no damage was done in the meantime, yes? Pity the witch cast on the pyre while in the torpor of a little death!"

"So when we die normally, the spirit does not linger?" Awa was intensely relieved.

"Of course not," the necromancer snorted. "Not all of it

anyway, and where the bulk of the spirit goes is anyone's guess. The dead cannot tell lies, not a one of them, but when they are brought back to this world they cannot remember where they were, only what they knew in life and what has befallen their bones. What happens after a true death is beyond our ken, but a piece of the spirit lingers ever after, enough to weld bones together even in the absence of tissue, enough to power the dead to do our will. Can you guess where that little piece lingers, the sliver of spirit that does not get to toddle off to ever after?"

"The skull," said Awa.

"Correct. So long as the skull is intact the remains can be raised, and even if the skull is ruined you can salvage the other pieces and attach them to working servants. My own tutor was obsessed with building new creatures instead of being content with the shapes men and beasts take. He was a peculiar man, and quite dreadful. He had me flogged by a six-armed rotten ape whenever I displeased him, which was often enough, and two of the ape's hands were seal flippers so you can imagine how it stung."

Awa could not.

"So this is the day you become a necromancer." The old man looked a little moist around the eyes, but it could have been from the steam of the wormwood tea he had just topped off. "First you learn to die, and then you learn to cheat death. Understanding how to revive our own bodies is easier once we've mastered the simpler method of raising the mindless ones, your so-called bonemen. Show me what you can do." He waved his hand and Awa's skeleton stool collapsed, the bones cutting her legs as she bruised herself on the floor.

Dusting herself off and ignoring the necromancer's guffaws, Awa peered down at the bones. She remembered well what he had taught her but hated the notion of ordering any spirit to do her will, even, were the necromancer to be believed, a piece of a spirit. She would do as she always did and ask instead of order, much as it might displease him, and with a bit of concentration she saw the shard of the skeleton's spirit crouching like a little gray mouse in the skull's eye socket. Yet when she asked it to pull itself together in exchange for a proper burial once she disposed of the necromancer she received no answer, nor any sign it understood.

"What have I told you?" the necromancer sneered, cottoning on to the delay. "This parleying with spirits you do is pure sheep-shit, it's just what you tell yourself you're doing to justify to little Awa what she's about. Now stop talking to walls and raise the fucking thing already!"

The bones came off the floor in a cloud, passing over the table like a swarm of bees and re-forming atop the necromancer. He yelped and spilled his tea, falling back as the skeleton dug its fingers into his throat. Then the necromancer jabbed his finger and it passed through the skeleton's skull as though it were soft clay, the heap of bones rolling off of him onto the floor. He clapped a shaking hand to his bloody neck, Awa staring open-mouthed at her injured tutor. She had only thought it for an instant but—

The door burst open behind her and the bonemen snatched her up and threw her on the table. The necromancer reared and struck like a riled serpent, something sharp and metal in his hand, but Awa did not scream even as the knife bit into her stomach, the blade breaking its point on the granite table as it passed through flesh and skin, shards of metal splintering off inside her, and then the night took her.

The necromancer was feeding her when she awoke, and to her intense dismay Awa realized she was lying on the bear, bundled in his stinking, crusty blankets. She was still too weak to move other than to lap up the stew, which was rich and salty and free of the chestnuts the bonemen gathered from the foothills for a change, precious chunks of meat bobbing in the bowl as plentiful as the various aches Awa felt. She sucked on a piece of fat, trying not to focus on her frowning nursemaid. His neck bore new scars but they were frustratingly shallow.

"That was good," said the necromancer. "Very, very good. I'm sorry I lost my temper with you, but I think we both understand each other better now, don't we?"

Awa nodded, slurping up the stew. Already the icicles of hurt embedded in her stomach and chest were melting, and her numb left foot began to itch. She had been rash, but he had been frightened, or else he would not have—

"To make sure we understand each other, I have taken certain measures," the necromancer said, ladling another spoonful up to Awa's mouth. She did not take it, looking anxiously at him. "With all the import you put on spirits this and spirits that, I thought it might behoove me to take a little of yours, just so you know that I can."

Awa felt queasy but knew only the stew could take it away, and reluctantly took the offered spoon. After swallowing, she steeled herself and said, "You can't. Not unless I give it to you, or I'm dead."

"No?" The necromancer leaned in. "For one of my skill gobbling up spirits isn't just easy, it's profitable. I take their knowledge, I take their strength, I take everything. I could gnaw the spirit off your bones like a fox on a chicken leg, were I so inclined, and then you'd be nothing but a lot of meat on a little skeleton. Believe you me, Awa, that's far worse than any sort of death you've heard of, having your spirit consumed. There's no coming back from that."

Awa flinched and whispered, "Do it, then."

"So brave!" The necromancer stuck out his lower lip. "Or are you just sour, my little Awa? If I ate your soul who would I have to cook my supper, to darn my leggings? Who would I have to learn my many lessons? No no, you stay with me. A little bite to tide me over, though, to convince you I'm serious. Your name would be one thing, not that little evening moniker you've given me, *Awa*—"

She froze. He couldn't know—

"You don't know it yourself anymore, do you? Were you so young when you were taken that you never learned it, or did you make yourself forget, maybe to keep your captors from having more power over you? You always were the bright one, *Awa*, weren't you? Nothing's more powerful than a name, a birth-name, and with that you can do all manner of mischief—very clever to blot it out!"

One of her first owners had called her Awa, but she had not forgotten her true name for the reasons he said—she had forgotten because it was easier to pretend she was dead, the same as she had forgotten the faces of her parents, the name of her mother. She made herself forget as much as she could, to make the fragments that would never dissipate somewhat less heartrending. The slavers with axes, the last time she had screamed before encountering the mindless dead—

"Over here, Awa." The necromancer was snapping his fingers in front of her face. "Don't look so scared—it's not your name I'm taking today, it's something much smaller—I know what you refuse to give me, and so, on principle, I will take it. I will take everything from you if the mood strikes me, Awa."

Awa could no longer focus on him, instead looking down at the cooling stew. He meant it, she knew he did, and the thought made her long for oblivion, for an end to everything. Was that what he was doing, making her so miserable that the only succor she might find would be through losing herself entirely? She would not fall for it, she decided, she would be strong.

"But to prove I'm a sport why don't we play by your rules?" The necromancer offered her another spoonful, and she took it. The stew no longer tasted delicious, it tasted like mud and tears.

"I know what you're afraid of, little Awa, I knew the night you arrived what you wouldn't give me. I let you keep it because you pleased me but I see now I've been too lenient, too soft, too much the friend and not enough the parent. So now you give me a little scream, and with it a little piece of your soul. Or so you believe, yes?"

He offered another spoonful, his exaggerated pout offset by the firelight that made his wide eyes all the more mischievous. She knew he was capable of anything but she would not give him that, would not give anyone that, not for anything. She had failed herself that first night in the cave, but he was not there then, he was waiting atop the mountain, and all those who had heard Awa then were now dead. The necromancer was right—if she were to let herself that would mean giving him a part of her soul, and she had given him all that she could bear. She—

She saw the small bones rising out of the spoon like a windfall branch in a puddle after the rains, a pair of little white pieces still connected by pale tissue. A toe. Nothing special in that; cannibalism had been the least of Awa's troubles for quite some time. What made her pause was that her own left foot still itched terribly, and as she flexed to wake it up the bones in the spoon bent of their own accord, sending a ripple across their tiny pool. She dropped the spoon back in the bowl.

Later, after it was done, Awa wondered how such a simple trick could have broken her after all she had seen and experienced on the mountaintop, but break her it did. Following her gaze down toward her swathed legs, the necromancer stood up, his lips making a surprised O, and, handing her the bowl of soup, he yanked the blankets off. She clung to the bowl as if it were the myrrh crate all those years before when she had almost drowned with Omorose and Halim, and again she was almost drowning, only now the sea was inside her.

Her left foot was missing, her ankle bound in bloody linens.

She felt it, it was still there only invisible, and she flexed it as hard as she could. She saw the toe bones bend again in her bowl, and something larger sloshed in the cauldron over the fire, stew splashing down to hiss on the coals, and for the first time since she had seen the dead walk Awa screamed.

The bowl clattered on the floor. Then the door burst open and the bonemen pranced inside, led by the necromancer's concubine. Some of them carried swords and rocks to bang against each other and the rest scooped up the unused cooking implements by the fire, beating pots and pans together as they jumped and spun around the room. Awa scarcely noticed, staring at her stump and screaming and screaming, the necromancer jabbing his face in front of hers and screaming right back at the top of his lungs, matching her shriek for shriek, tears of happiness splashing down his cheeks as Awa wailed and the dead danced.

VIII
Awkward Adolescence

ち

Awa grew a goat foot. The necromancer told her it was prideful and stupid and that ensured her decision; after she strained herself out of the stewpot and picked the pieces out of the pools of vomit surrounding the bear she buried what remained of her left foot with Omorose. She ground the hoof into a powder after promising the creature's spirit that she would eat soft summer grass a few times a year, and as she suspected the new foot grew in quickly, although it did take some getting used to.

As soon as the weather began to turn she broke down the old shelter she had made with Halim and her mistress and moved it farther down the glacier, using Omorose's cairn as one wall of the new hut. By the time the next winter arrived she had filled in all the chinks and even had a crude fireplace, but not a week into the snows she admitted defeat and trudged miserably back to winter in the necromancer's hut—a fireplace was worse than worthless without wood, and her tutor was not sharing. He welcomed her with a grin and a hot cup of wormwood; ever since the scream he had been nothing but cordial to his pupil.

Years passed atop the world, and as Awa grew she passed through many hells. Self-loathing and self-pity jostled each other for dominion but she fought them both, and in the absence of other company she found herself talking quite a bit with the bandit chief. The necromancer would not allow idle chatter, and so their conversations took place as they sparred. Awa had long since stopped blaming the man for her situation, except when she was angry with him.

"I'm jealous of you," Awa told him as her sword whipped toward his skull.

"Oh?" The echo of metal tolled across the high places as he parried her.

"Foraging down the mountain." Awa ducked, his sword grazing her sweaty scalp. "With the bonemen."

"Well, it—" Before he could finish she was on him again, and it was not until she had cracked his shoulder blade and then mixed up the powdered-bone-and-water mortar to fix it that he went on. "Well, it is a change of—"

"What's this, what's this?" The necromancer had crept up behind her, his concubine on one arm. "Lollygagging, by the look of it. I trust you to manage yourself and yet here you sit, gossiping away."

"I hurt his arm." Awa tried to relax her tight jaw but the rest of her body was not as adept a liar as her tongue. "We were only talking about parrying while I repaired it, not—"

"Hurt him, did you? I suppose that means you've learned all you can from the old boy, eh?" The concubine whispered in his ear and the necromancer smiled. Awa knew what was coming next, she knew him well enough to see that, and the best thing would be to deny him the satisfaction of a response. She knew that, but it was so unfair, it was so petty and cruel, it was so—

The shoulder blade she was daubing stayed gripped between her fingers but the rest of the bandit chief fell apart on the stone, his skull bouncing in the dirt to settle in front of the necromancer. Awa ground her teeth and felt her fury slowly begin to cool. She had expected that, but then her tutor put his bare foot on top of the skull and began lifting his other leg, clearly intent on balancing atop the skull while his rotten little girlfriend egged him on.

"Stop it!" Awa shouted. "Please!"

"Oh." The necromancer hopped off the skull, then hooked his foot under the jaw and adroitly kicked it up into the air, catching it in one hand. Halim's tongue remained on the ground, coated in dust. "What's the matter, he can't feel anything now."

"You could break him." Awa felt her fingernails, gnawed to the quick though they were, digging into her palms. "You pull those tricks and his skull lands on a rock, and then what? He's gone forever."

"And what a tragedy that would be." The necromancer rolled his eyes.

"I want to play with him," said the concubine, the little cords of brown musculature remaining on her face pulling up into a smile. "Don't you? We could teach her how to get some friction off the bones."

"Tut-tut," said the necromancer, leaning down to pick up the dirty tongue. "We'll need this, then, though I imagine Awa won't—"

Awa did not. She was already halfway across the glacier, all her recent scabs peeling back as her feet kicked up the ice. She did not cry, and had not in some time, though on occasions like this she dearly wanted to. That night she heard them carrying on for hours, personal sounds made public on the wind, but even after they quieted she could not sleep, tossing in the warm summer night on her pallet of dried boughs and old hide. Few things make one more desperate than insomnia, and when she could bear it no longer Awa began removing the stones from the far wall of her hut.

The draft of cool air that wafted out was reward enough, and she lay down, her back to the small cavern she had opened. She had raised and put down dozens and dozens of the bonemen at her tutor's instruction but never had she done so unbidden. The thought had lived with her since the day her mistress had died, of course, but Awa feared becoming like the necromancer even more than she feared the man himself. She had almost done it, she had almost done what she had promised herself she would never do, but then they started up again at the necromancer's hut, the she-cat yowls of the concubine digging into Awa's once-soft eyes and finally drawing forth the tears.

"Hold me, girl," said Awa, and Omorose crawled out of her grave, wrapping her frigid limbs around her former slave.

Awa awoke later than usual and immediately sent Omorose back into her cairn, walling up the grave after her too quickly to do it properly. Awa felt sick, and when she peered through the last gap in the wall and commanded Omorose to die again the guilt brought more tears and snotty vomit. Awa paced the edge of the cliff all day, ranting at herself, and only when the sun set did she realize the necromancer had not come for her, nor had his bone-men. She also remembered she had not eaten since the previous lunch, and it relieved her somewhat to know the sickness she felt inside her might in some part be the result of her famished stomach. Had she eaten a proper dinner she never would have done that.

But of course she would have, and of course she did it again before a week was out. The necromancer kept the bandit chief's skull balanced in the bear's mouth, baiting her to ask for him back, but she simply ate in silence, answered his questions with a flat directness, and returned to her hut with that peculiar excitement, that bizarre, alien illness working on her mind and stomach. Awa had forgotten what it felt like to be happy, and the return of the sensation confused and worried her.

The glacier had done what it could, and so Omorose retained a good deal of her beauty. Her eyes were deep and still as the blackest wells, and Awa's thirst to drink from them grew and grew throughout the sultry days. Best of all was the realization that Awa had prevented the necromancer from plucking a single hair from Omorose, let alone her tongue, and so after only a few nights Awa worked up the nerve to actually talk to her mistress instead of leaving her mute.

"You can speak?" Awa asked her as Omorose settled in behind her, those marble-smooth and cold arms a marvelous weight on Awa's side and shoulder.

"Yash," Omorose said, her voice muffled. Awa led her mistress outside to inspect her properly, something she had not dared do before lest the necromancer see her. The ice crystals in Omorose's long hair rendered her ropey, snarled locks into an extension of the stars set in the black firmament blazing down on them, and Awa had Omorose open her mouth. There was the problem, a thick mold clogging the poor girl's mouth. After thoroughly cleaning her mistress's palate with her shaking fingers, Awa quickly took her back inside.

"Hold me, Omorose," Awa whispered, and Omorose did. After a deliciously long pause, Awa asked, "Did you miss me?"

"Of course," said Omorose, and with ever-softening fingers she stroked the tears from Awa's cheeks. "I've been waiting for you. Why did you make me wait so long?"

"I was scared," said Awa.

Omorose laid her hands on Awa's back and sighed. "So was I. I was worried you wouldn't come, after how I'd treated you. I was worried you would think I meant those mean things I said, I worried..."

"No!" Awa rolled over to face Omorose in the darkness, her nostrils far too deadened to appreciate the strength of her mistress's aroma. "I knew, I mean, I thought... I hoped..."

"I was confused," Omorose said, her hands finding Awa's in the darkness. "I was confused and scared, and I didn't know what I was doing. I'm sorry, Awa, I'm so, so sorry!"

These words that Awa had longed for, had needed so badly, melted her like fat on a fire into a spluttering, sobbing mess as she clung to her mistress. Some wicked part of Awa had always maintained that Omorose did not care about her, did not care about anyone but herself, and this secret self had whispered its lies to Awa even after Omorose's death, had told her to forget the witty, sarcastic mistress with hair dark as the heart of a storm and eyes bright as lightning. Awa's love was vindicated, and then she realized Omorose had said her name for the first time. Rather than bringing on more sobs, this gave Awa a terrible case of the giggles, and soon Omorose was laughing along with her, and for one night everything that had befallen Awa seemed a fair price for what she had gained.

"Rare night," the necromancer said a week later, after they finished supper.

"Oh?" Awa was sure he suspected something and so tarried before returning to their hut.

"Yes indeed." The necromancer glanced at the cauldron and Awa quickly fetched him his tea, the sweet anise smell reminding her of Omorose. "The heavens will spill fire down on our lowly world, or so the peasants will fear. Those bastard charlatans will be at their devices, of course, plotting their charts and making up their reasons. Claptrap!"

"Oh?"

"But pretty claptrap," the necromancer said, and Awa thought he cast her a strange glance. "Fancy a little stargazing with your old master? I can point out the few alignments that matter to us."

"Of course," Awa said too quickly, wondering how much her face showed. "That would be, ah, yes please."

The necromancer eyed her carefully. "Or maybe I'll sketch them here, and have you look alone, and then tomorrow we can go together and see if you've done your work."

"Yes!" Awa realized she had almost shouted, and blushed. "If that's alright, I like trying first. The spirits are hard to read up there, so it's a challenge. Fun."

"Fun," the necromancer repeated, and retrieved his book. Using the long quill taken from some strange bird with an eye hidden in the feathers, he began sketching several constellations on that first blank page. He used no ink but as the quill touched the book sparkling red stars appeared, and after Awa had nodded at each one he closed the tome. She knew that same page would be blank the next time he opened it, just as it always was.

Setting down his book he raised his palm into the air. The bear towering over him opened its mouth and the bandit chief's skull rolled free and landed in her tutor's hand. He placed it on the table and sent it spinning across the table to Awa, who caught it easily. "Suppose you can have that old layabout back."

"Thank you," said Awa, a little guilty for not feeling more excited about it. "Can I go now?"

"Aren't you going to call him up?" asked the necromancer, blowing on his drink and taking a sip. "I'm rather curious to see if you're able."

"Oh?" Awa blinked. She had already raised dozens of skeletons at his behest, and grew ever more paranoid at his odd behavior. "His bones are where you left them, so why don't I tomorrow?"

"Alright," said the necromancer, "he's your friend. Give him back to me, then."

Walking around the table, she saw him eyeing her spirit and wondered as she always did what he saw there. For Awa the spirits were but scraps of shadow, big ones for the necromancer and the bandit chief, little ones for most of the bonemen, but who knew what he could read in a spirit. She would have to see how big Omorose's spirit was; she had never really looked. Then Awa caught herself, horrified to be thinking of her mistress with his gaze upon her, and forced herself to wonder about fire from the sky, which made her think of lightning, which made her think of the night they arrived, which made her think of—

"Well?" He was looking up at her, and Awa realized he had already taken the skull from her hands.

"Oh." Awa swallowed, half expecting him to seize her arm and ruin her life again. "I'm feeling odd, may I go?"

"Off with you." The necromancer waved her away but she knew he watched her back as she left.

Awa knew she had to pull herself together if she wanted things to last, and, preoccupied with upbraiding herself, she stumbled over the bandit chief's spine in the dark. That guilt rubbed at her again, but guilt is no match for hunger and Awa trotted across the glacier, her other friend forgotten as Omorose greeted her at the mouth of the hut. Awa had stopped putting Omorose down when she was absent, knowing that if she let Omorose return to her natural death the process of decomposition would resume at its usual pace, whereas in an undead state the corruption was greatly slowed. Omorose remained fair as ever to Awa, the least objective of beholders.

They sat against a rock with their feet jutting over the abyss, Awa's pallet dragged out to cushion them as they watched the stars. The celestial fire the necromancer had mentioned was not lightning but falling stars, and although she had seen them before, never had Awa beheld so many, slicing down like knives cutting through the sun's veil only to have the ebon cloth seal instantly behind them. Together they found a few of the constellations, and as the stars slowly turned they spied another, and then another.

"He's onto us," Awa finally said, having put it off as long as she could bear to keep a secret from Omorose. "He suspects, and he'll take you away if we're not careful. I'll have to put you back down for a little while."

"I know," Omorose sighed, and Awa let out her own pent-up breath. She had worried her mistress would not understand, and the thought of disappointing her was excruciating. "But not until dawn? Please?"

"Of course! Tonight is, is beautiful, isn't it?"

"Beautiful," said Omorose, but she was not looking at the sky. Awa felt herself tense up and drew her feet back from the edge lest the world turn any farther and pitch her over the side. "Will you give me something before you put me away again?"

Awa nodded, unable to speak, and Omorose scooted closer to her on the pallet. It happened as slow as the twisting of the constellations above them, their hair finally tickling each other's foreheads, and then their lips tickled each other's, and stars fell around them as they kissed on the edge of the world.

Awa broke away, too anxious to properly speak, scrambling to her feet and wringing her hands, and she would have stumbled over the cliffside if Omorose had not caught her arm, pulling her back. Too many horrifying nights were welling up in Awa's mind, the bones of the bear creaking, her eyes running along with her nose, but then Omorose gripped her tightly by the nape of the neck and drew her back in. Omorose tasted bittersweet, like liver and wormwood and certain nightmares, and Awa felt her mistress's hand pushing up the bottom of her tunic. She caught Omorose's wrist, felt soft skin and knotted muscle sliding over bone, and then they sank together onto the pallet.

Omorose doted on Awa by the light of the heavens, kissing her hoof as tenderly as she kissed other regions, and before dawn discovered them sprawled with every limb intertwined Awa had achieved things she did not even realize existed. They started awake and hurried inside lest they be discovered, and cried together before Omorose went back inside her tomb. As the wall was half filled in she knocked it back down and pinned Awa again, her well-trained hands reaching above her occupied head to massage or restrain her lover, as befitted the situation. When it was over Omorose gently kissed Awa on the cheek and climbed inside her barrow, building up the wall from the inside. Awa wanted to help but could do nothing more than whimper, eventually dragging herself to the necromancer's hut lest he come looking.

Awa paid for their excess with each step, resolving to be more moderate to prevent such stinging rawness in the future. That night she identified each constellation to the necromancer's satisfaction, and only remembered that she had failed to raise the bandit chief when the necromancer mentioned it several days later. That old guilt returned, but faded soon enough as her tutor informed her that he had called up the skeleton himself and sent it off to fetch firewood and chestnuts in the low valleys. When he returned Awa apologized profusely but he waved it off, commenting on her improved mood.

"I guess I've just gotten used to living here." Awa shrugged, and if that answer did not ring true to the bandit chief he did not say.

Omorose and Awa had resolved to wait until autumn to throw the necromancer off their trail. They lasted a few weeks, and before very long at all they were together again every night. Awa could not remember having been so happy.

IX
Medicines Bitter as Wormwood

One morning Awa felt a dull burning in the region one least wishes to feel discomfort, and to her consternation and eventual misery the sensation grew worse instead of better over the next week. It became so vicious that she could not sleep, Omorose holding her as she wept and shuddered. The next day she heeded her lover's counsel and staggered to the necromancer's shack.

"Feminine problems are not my province," the necromancer sniffed after she had finally stammered out her symptoms. "I've told you, gnaw a little huteri, the root, not the flowers, and some yarrow can't hurt while you're at it. Did you know the Spaniards call yarrow 'bad man's plaything'? How's *that* for—"

"It's not that," said Awa, her pain overriding her embarrassment. "I know myself well enough. Something's wrong."

"Hop onto the table and let's have a look," said the necromancer with a sigh, closing his book. The tome floated off to the high shelf on the wall behind the bear, and had Awa not been so distracted she would have noticed the bound air spirit sit down heavily beside the book upon delivering it. Instead she stared at the necromancer, not moving. Every time she thought he could not be worse he revealed a new method of shaming her. "Hop to, Awa. Or would you rather Gisela here examine you?"

Awa looked to the concubine and back to the necromancer.

Knowing the thing had a name did little to warm Awa to her. Anyone was better than the necromancer, though, so she nodded quickly and eased herself onto the table. She remembered the dying bandit chief laid out on the same table the first night, remembered countless unpleasant meals eaten here. She tried not to cry as the rancid concubine left her master's side and came around the table to stand at Awa's feet.

"Spread your legs," Gisela said, her voice gruff and masculine from the anonymous bandit's tongue the necromancer had given her. The concubine's clammy hand felt like an old leather glove on Awa's knee, her thin leggings soaking up the corpse's chill. Awa whimpered as the concubine lifted up her tunic, spreading her legs farther in a bid to bring on more pain to distract her from the scene. She told herself that as bad as it was, once it was over she would have survived the worst experience imaginable, as people often do in the midst of deep and abidingly awful situations, but that gave her little succor. Bony fingers prodded Awa; it felt like they were digging in a wound.

"A scream from little Awa used to be a rare thing, indeed," the necromancer said when she yelped. "But I suppose after you've let one out what's the harm in howling down the moon most nights, eh?"

"You callt it," said the concubine, the sharp removal of her digits somehow worse than their intrusion. "Bad, too. Surprised she can walk."

"Like papa, like daughter, I suppose," said the necromancer, reminding Awa that she could no longer remember her real father. "You want to make it go away?"

Awa nodded, her eyes still bolted shut rather than showing him what they both knew surged behind them.

"Right then, if you're old enough to play with them you're old enough to learn the remedy," and his words cracked her dams, the tears hot on her face, the sob catching in her chest as he snatched her wrist and yanked her up from her reclined position. She tried to twist her hand away but he held her tight. "If you do it yourself you won't have to come here next time, and believe you me, there will be a next time. But where's the sport in love if it's always safe, eh?"

Awa went limp and allowed his hand to guide hers down between her legs.

"Cover it with your hand," he said, and she flattened her palm and fingers against her mound, only her dirty tunic between sore skin and rough hand. "Now find the intruder. It's pulsing in there, cooking you up, propagating itself in the little hearth you've built it with grave filth for mortar. A foreign spirit, as you'd have it."

Awa gasped, the sensation suddenly clear and unmistakable as a kite's cry over the silent peaks. Some spirit had invaded her and was roiling in her most sensitive instrument, feeding off her heat and moisture and swelling ever larger. He was still talking but she no longer paid him heed, her face set as she focused on the spirit.

The necromancer had taught her early on how to use her spirit to close like a mouth around another spirit, to bite that spirit and sever its tie to its body. It was how he had killed Omorose with a brush of his hand, how they could kill anyone or anything not guarded against such an attack. All that she need do was touch her victim, and this vile stowaway was already touching her quite thoroughly. Awa did not even remember her promise to herself never to use that wicked technique, and even if she had the circumstance would surely have allowed for an exception. Her spirit tightened around the interloper and the heat began hissing out like a coal tossed into a snow bank, her pain diminishing along with the invading spirit, and before her tears had dried on her cheeks the spirit was gone, and her discomfort with it save for the mild sting from the concubine's fingers.

"Well?" he whispered, releasing her wrist as she let out a sigh. "My arts aren't all so impractical, are they now?"

"What was it?" Awa shook her head and hopped off the table, a new vigor coursing through her. "The spirit that was haunting me, how did it—"

"*Haunting* you?" the necromancer hooted. "You didn't have a haunted snatch, Awa, you picked up a case of the rot, and I can imagine where!"

He knew, she realized, all his asides finally sinking in. Awa was halfway to the door when she caught herself, curiosity momentarily trumping her hatred for the man and his laughing concubine. "It *was* a spirit, I felt it, but a different kind of spirit from others I've met. Tiny, invisible if I weren't looking, and without any body."

"Maybe not a body we could see," said the necromancer as he settled down in his chair. "Aren't you always going on about spirits, and how everything has one? Well there's your proof. When a wound turns sour and starts leaking pus that's not because the flesh has died; on the contrary, it's because new life has settled in the injury. The maladies men ascribe to humoural imbalances are simply creatures men cannot see, beings of spirit but not of flesh. The Great Mortality a century and a half in its own tomb was not divine wrath, it was a proliferation of creatures beyond the ken of men, creatures as mindless as they are dangerous. Some say they were built by demons, some say they *are* demons, and some say stranger things still. Personally, I think those cocky bastards in the Schwarzwald have something to do with it, a nice little present for we men who so offend them with our very presence."

"Spirits without bodies..." said Awa, wondering at another reference to men in the Schwarzwald. Usually when the necromancer got himself worked up he would allude to that place, the local lack of Germanic tongues preventing Awa from knowing quite what he was on about but inferring from his references that it was some sort of school populated by thieves and frauds.

"Of course, there's plenty that do more good than harm, so one has to be careful and only remove the more troublesome spirits. A fellow apprentice of mine became obsessed with removing all the parasitical creatures sharing his body—took out some useful spirits from his guts and next thing you know he stopped being able to digest food properly. Went mad and finally hanged himself when he couldn't get rid of all the little spirits swarming inside him. We may think we hold dominion over our flesh but we're actually crawling with uncounted poxes and other riffraff, and it's best to let them carry on unless they start acting up like the little fellow you caught in your lointrap. Mindless spirits can be more dangerous than sentient ones, mark me—they can't be reasoned with, for one."

"I see." Awa nodded, eager to get back to Omorose since he did not seem to have any more to say on the matter of her paramour. She had been out of commission for far too long and like any addict needed to fall back into the perfection she had found. "Thank you, sir."

"You need to know these things," the necromancer said sagaciously, taking the mug of tea his concubine had prepared. Gisela began to speak but he raised his eyebrows and she pitched onto the floor, her taut skin slapping the stone. "Now, since you've found me up and about let's move on to the next stage of your training. I've been trying to teach you how to raise the souls of the dead for ages now but you always seem to be too busy for your old tutor."

"I already know how," said Awa, unable to hide her smirk. "How many times must I tell you that when you treat spirits with respect they make things much easier? I don't need to order them about to get results."

"Oh really?" The necromancer put down his tea. "Young Awa has surpassed her tutor, has she, just like she surpassed her fencing instructor? So tell me, why didn't you return his soul to his bones, hmmm? Too busy? Not in the mood?"

"I—" Awa blushed, unhappy to be reminded of her selfishness in forgetting her friend.

"Or is it just possible you're not half as clever as you think? Is it just possible you can't back up that shit you're so keen on talking once your old tutor's taken away the ouch-ouch, eh?"

"Alright," said Awa, striding around the table. The old bastard had a surprise coming, just like the first time she had animated a skeleton. She remembered the panicked expression on his face when the skeleton had gone for his throat and she smiled, her hoof clicking on the floor. She reached out to the spirit of the concubine that hovered over her splayed corpse, called her back to her bones as she had with Omorose. The corpse sat up and clambered to her feet, but weirdly enough the bulk of her spirit hung around Gisela's exterior like a cloak knit of shadow and mist.

"Any chump can bring back the flesh," said the necromancer. "I thought you said you could return her soul to her bones."

"I..." Awa's heart began to trot. "Didn't I, Gisela?"

"No," the concubine said. Somehow her voice sounded even deader than usual.

"You're making her do this, to mock me," said Awa, raising her voice. "I told her she could go back to her body so that means she must not want to, she must be resisting because you told her to. You're trying to make a point about the difference between asking and ordering the spirits, aren't you?"

"Did I ask you any such thing?" The necromancer looked at Gisela.

"No," said the concubine.

"So why is your spirit still absent?" The necromancer smiled at Awa as he asked.

"She did not do what must be done," said Gisela. "My soul needs her help to return."

"She's lying!" Awa said, refusing to acknowledge that the concubine had lost her rough masculine accent and was speaking with a flat cadence, like the mindless bonemen the necromancer had given tongues to report on what they saw in the chestnut forests on their forays down the mountain. "You're making her lie to upset me!"

"The dead can't lie," the necromancer said patiently. "How many times have I—"

"You lied about that!"

"No, I didn't. Even those cheats in the Schwarzwald can't let even a little one slip out, it's impossible for them. Believe me, Awa, you just can't do it because I haven't taught you yet. Not everything is as easy as making a log burn on a fire, you know."

Awa felt sick but knew he was wrong, at least about some of it. Maybe if a spirit wanted to return badly enough it could even without whatever means he employed. Still, she heard herself say, "Show me, then."

"Right ho," he said. "Put her back down."

"Alright," said Awa, and she released the little bit of spirit holding Gisela up. The concubine fell back on the floor.

"Only the first time's tricky, and after that the soul will listen to you and hop up or down at a word or a poke. Here's what you do—roll her over, and kneel by her head."

Awa did.

"It's not so difficult but hardly the sort of thing your average gravedigger might think of. She'll be easier than most because her spirit's already right there, yes? Now, if you focus you'll notice it stems from her head. Normally there would be no real spirit to see, only a sort of tether leading from that little piece of spirit that stays in the skull into nothing, and that's what you have to pull on, normally, you reel them back in from wherever they've gone. So you focus on that, on drawing them back to their body."

"Yes?" Awa said impatiently, looking down at the chipped teeth jutting out between the gaps in Gisela's shredded lips.

"Focus on drawing the spirit back, and breathe into their mouth, willing your life into their chest. And that's it, though caution is never more justified—you can put them down just as easily as the rest but they're no longer mindless, so they're not bound to follow your ord—"

"Get offa me!" The concubine shoved Awa away, the young necromancer falling down hard as Gisela scrambled up. "Why couldn't you make'er practice on that bandit?"

"You were handy." The old man shrugged. "Where are you going?"

"Home," Awa said numbly, getting up and pushing open the door.

"As the devil told the sinner," the necromancer called after her, "you *are* home."

X

Cruel Youth

Omorose was not waiting at the door when Awa came home. She sat in the back of the hut, staring straight ahead, and Awa bit her lip. She wanted Omorose to tell her it was different, to tell her it was a lie, but the corpse only sat there until Awa told it to get up.

"You're not Omorose," Awa said, her voice cracking.

"I am her body," said the corpse.

"You're not supposed to lie. He said you couldn't lie."

"I never lied," said the corpse.

"You did!" Awa shouted, her stomach heaving. "You did! You told me those things, you told me, you told me you loved... oh no no no, not that, no, not that."

"Yes," said the corpse, its eyes still staring ahead. "I've been talking to myself using her, her body, I've put the words I want to hear in her mouth, and I made her touch—"

Awa was sick, hunched over and crying and unable to think. When she finished she staggered away down the cliff face and sat on the edge wondering how much she had imagined, how much she had dreamed. She had known her tutor was mad, obviously mad, but was madness contagious?

It took the better part of the day for Awa to pull herself together, but when she did she knew what she had to do. She marched straight back to the hut, more frightened than she ever had been before but resolute. She owed her, and after Awa had put Omorose's corpse back down she squatted by her face, that stricken, long-dead face, and looked. There it was, the little shard of spirit she had been using to raise Omorose lurking in her mistress's mouth, and if that were the anchor then the line ought to be...

Awa saw it then, growing off of the spirit fragment and vanishing, and she reached down along it with her mind, searching for Omorose. Then she exhaled into Omorose's gaping mouth, and as she did the coldness hit her like a wave of frigid water, the rest of her breath sucked out of her lungs by the corpse. Omorose's eyes fluttered and her lips rasped together, and then she opened her eyes and she opened her mouth and she sat up, not some simulacrum or hollow vessel but Omorose herself.

"You..." Omorose focused on Awa, who stared aghast at her lady. "You black bitch!"

The first few blows Awa accepted passively, letting Omorose tackle her and pummel her face. She deserved that, surely, but through her teary, swelling eyes she saw Omorose hoist a rock and she drew the line.

"Stop!" Awa managed, but Omorose did not listen and so Awa pushed the woman's spirit back out of her body, her corpse slumping forward on top of Awa and the rock clattering down beside them. Awa lay there as the sun set outside her door, Omorose's weight heavy upon her, and marveled at her own folly. Several times she caught herself talking to Omorose or herself, and finally she heaved the sticky body off of her and sat up, twilight settling over the mountain.

"Bitch!" Omorose came at her again, and again Awa dropped her back down, wincing to see her beloved's jaw crack open on a rock as her empty corpse hit the side of the hut. The third time Omorose used an obscure Egyptian curse word but the stone she snatched up informed Awa of her unchanged purpose and so back down she went.

A different thought occurred to Awa, the harshness of Omorose's reaction justifying sterner measures. She tried and found that raising just the body as she had before still came easily, the amorphous blur of Omorose's spirit shrouding the corpse but unable to possess it of its own volition. Awa thought to kiss her one last time but the body no longer appealed to her, the long years since Omorose's death no longer so slight a concern, the hard work of the glacier no longer quite so successful.

"Get back in your grave, and cover yourself with stones," said Awa, the corpse silently obeying her but Omorose's shade letting off a high whining sound. Once Omorose's corpse had blanketed itself with rocks and lay facing the gap in the wall, Awa addressed her old mistress: "Omorose, I'm going to let you back into your body now but I can't let you attack me. So don't move or I'll just push you out again, alright?"

Awa focused and Omorose jumped into her old skin. "*Let* me back into my body? You dirty, sneaking *animal*! It's mine!"

"You're dead." Awa swallowed.

"Damn right! And you think that gives you the right to rape me? To make me lick you, you horrible fat ape?"

"No, I didn't know, no, I love—"

"Why don't you lick me, girl, why don't you lick my rotten slit if you're so keen on me?"

"Alright," said Awa, her composure falling away like the bones of a skeleton with a cracked skull. She dropped forward on her knees and began pulling the stones away from the barrow to get at Omorose. "Alright, I'm sorry, I've been selfish, I didn't think, and when I offered before you told me not to and—"

"I didn't tell you anything!" Omorose screeched, the stones covering her rattling like Awa's teeth as she shifted in her grave.

"And stay the hell away from me, you nasty beast! Don't you dare touch me again, don't you dare!"

"I thought it was you," Awa pleaded. "I did, I thought it was you, I thought I'd brought you back and—"

"I loved you? I wanted to fuck you?" Omorose's blackened lips pulled back to reveal mealy green gums. "I'd sooner have our tutor touch me than have a mud-black little monkey clinging—"

"What's wrong with you?!" Awa screamed at her. "Why are you always so mean?! You weren't even in your body so why do you care? Why do you care if I'm happy for one night in a thousand?!"

"My body," said Omorose, her shift to calm, rational discourse even more frustrating to Awa than her shouting accusations. "Mine. I might not have been in it but I certainly knew what you'd been up to as soon as I got back. My flesh remembers, that little bit I left behind remembers, I remember. My body, not yours. Ape."

"You weren't." Awa gulped, timing her words to fit between the sobs. "I didn't know, and you weren't using—"

"So if you're asleep and the old man wants to give you a poke that's alright so long as you don't wake up? They kill rapists where I come from, ape, they chop them up and burn them."

"No," said Awa. "No, I'm not—"

"This is why he killed me," Omorose said sadly. "You got me killed because you're so nasty."

"What? No—"

"Yes you did. You're just like him, that's why. He knew you were just like him, a pathetic fat bitch who can't have what she wants unless she steals it, who has to open graves to find a girl who will suffer her kiss. You're just like him, you—"

"No!" Awa shrieked, wrenching Omorose out of her corpse and snatching up stones, walling in the cadaver. "No no no!"

When the tomb was resealed Awa wiped her tears away with gritty fingers and gathered her blankets. Turning in the doorway, she yelled at the crypt, "You stay in there until you behave!"

The necromancer did not protest when she dumped her belongings in front of his hearth and informed him she would be staying. The concubine began saying something vile but Awa ran out before she could finish, her tutor chuckling in his chair. Awa paced the perimeter of the mountaintop, her hoof kicking pebbles over the edge, her ragged sniffling unheard by all but the dead.

"Awa." She heard him behind her in the darkness, and she paused as the bandit chief approached. "Is everything alright?"

She turned and looked miserably at the bones of the man who had brought her there, who had brought all of them there, and then she threw her arms around him, his ribs jabbing her chest, and she cried and cried. He comforted her as he had when he delivered her back to the necromancer following her escape attempt, his fingers catching in her short, matted hair. She had no water left in her eyes and her chest hurt, and though she had never heard the expression she knew her heart was broken.

"I've got a surprise for you," he whispered when she had pulled back, past embarrassment but tired of feeling the dead press against her.

"Oh?" she said, almost able to stop thinking about Omorose for a moment.

"Do you like wine?"

"What?" Awa blinked. "Wine?"

"Wine." His skull bobbed in the darkness. "We had some, my friends and I, and it was left in the cave when we all were taken. I retrieved the cask on the way back from fetching wood on one of my first trips below, and have kept it hidden. I was waiting for a special occasion to give it to you."

This brought on the longest jag yet, and being a dry run it

hurt more than ever as Awa sobbed. He helped her along to the little pit in the stone where the keg was stowed, and, fishing it out, they sat side by side on the edge of the cliff and she drank. The bandit chief had her pour a little from her cupped hand onto his extended tongue so he could taste it, which caused him to make spitting noises.

"Don't drink it," he said. "It's gone sour, I'm afraid."

"I don't care," said Awa, slurping out of her hand. "At least it doesn't taste like chestnuts or wormwood."

"It will make you sick."

"Don't care," said Awa. "And if it does I can take the sickness away. I'm a necromancer, I can do that."

"Oh," said the chief, and after a pause, "Do you want to talk about her?"

"No," Awa lied, wondering just how everyone on the mountain knew—were the goats laughing at her as well as the skeletons and the necromancer and the concubine and Omorose herself and... She stopped herself, knowing such paths were unhealthy, and anyway, who were goats to judge? The bandit chief let her drink in silence, and the unique illness it brought upon her was no more bitter and cramping than her grief. Finally a thought landed on her like a biting fly, and she turned on the bandit.

"You've got your spirit. So you don't have to do what he says."

"No."

"Then why didn't you let me get away that time? Why did you bring me back instead of helping me run?" Awa was not angry, simply very tired.

"It wasn't the right time," he whispered, looking around the desolate, dark plateau. "He can still banish me from my bones with a glance, and his mindless ones are dangerous in numbers. We'll find a way to get you out of here, Awa."

"And what then?" Awa smiled wryly. "You Spaniards aren't very accommodating to young Moors, in my experience."

"Men are not accommodating to strangers anywhere," said the chief. "Most of them, anyway. I have learned from my wayward life, and I repent. I—"

"I was only fooling," said Awa, slurping up more wine. It was growing on her, the sting it brought to her starved palate a better balm than any she had yet found. "We've all made mistakes, and I forgave you a long...a long..."

Where did the grief hide, Awa wondered as it came on her again, ambushing her every time she felt safe, where did it lurk and why could she not vanquish it with the knowledge that she was, if not righteous, innocent in her intentions? She never would have done it, done any of it, if she had not been taken from her village outside Dahomey, if her family had not been murdered before her eyes, if the voice of her mother was not lost to her. She had struggled to forget that voice, had struggled to forget the faces of both her parents, because to remember their faces was to remember the axes cleaving them, to remember their voices was to remember them screaming. Now that she had succeeded in banishing them from her memories she realized her folly but could not call them back, she who could call back the flesh of her beloved somehow incapable of raising a simple thing like the memory of an old face she had kissed countless times, a loving voice she had heard sing countless songs. Awa felt the pain in her chest as palpably as a broken rib, a cracked wrist, a stolen foot, and, biting her lip, she tried to push the hurt away as she had the memory of her parents, the deepest, darkest part of herself relieved to be thinking of anything but Omorose for even a moment.

While she rubbed her face on her tunic the bandit chief began telling her about his family who lived in Alpujarra, where Moors still lived in peace with Spaniards, about Granada and far Aragon and the forging of one Spain from the pieces once held by Boabdil and Queen Isabella's family, about the world beyond that even he had not seen. He told her about real wine and honest laughter and the way starshine transformed the plains outside Lorca from shattered desert to seamless dreamscape, the way the sea brought tears to his father's eyes, the way his brother danced when the zither played just for him. He almost managed to convince her that life could be enjoyable again.

"When we get away," Awa said long into the cask and the night, "when we're free and we've burned down his hut and we can go anywhere we want, where do you want to go first? What do you want to do?"

"I want to go into the ground," said the bandit chief. "I want to die once more, though I cannot remember what it was like to be properly dead. I have lived enough, and I desire nothing more than to rest."

He did not want to make her weep again, but the dead cannot lie.

XI
The Soldier and the Witch

Down the years, and the mountain, Awa stared at the soldier who had freed her as he wept and gibbered and pawed at the damp walls of the cave. Their interaction had been going well until he had noticed the resurrected corpses of his former companions, at which point things went rather downhill. Awa decided there was nothing for it but to be direct.

"I'm not a witch," she told Manuel as he cowered in the back of the cave, and he realized he had been whispering that word over and over again, his eyes still fixed on the risen dead and the curtain of rain behind them at the mouth of the grotto. "Or maybe I am. He preferred the term 'necromancer,' though I gather there's no real difference so 'witch' if you like. Bruja, warlock, wizard, sorcerer, witch, necromancer, diabolist, all the same—I can raise the dead, Niklaus Manuel Deutsch of Bern, and I can command them to do my will. I can parley with spirits, with demons, and I can kill any man that lives with only my touch."

"Fuck," Manuel squeaked, knowing she spoke the truth.

Awa took the cooking flesh from her fire and blew on the slick, oozing meat she had cut from her would-be rapist's thigh. The pot bubbling over the fire contained the mashed-up hand and forearm of one of the corpses that she had prepared before the soldier had awoken, some naïve part of her thinking that it would be as simple as giving him a bone soup to heal his injured wrist, thus repaying his rescue, and then they would go their separate ways. She had not told Niklaus Manuel Deutsch of Bern that, of course, nor anything else—not about her past or Omorose or her current predicament. Nor would she, much as she suddenly wanted to.

In the three and a half years since she had left the mountain he was the first living person to freely help her, to show her compassion, and now he crouched like a beaten dog, his eyes wide, his nostrils flaring, his trousers wet with piss. Why had she made such a show of raising them? Why had she raised them at all? She might have talked with Niklaus Manuel Deutsch of Bern. They might have passed a day together in conversation, drunk wine and laughed, become fast friends. Instead she had ruined everything. Again.

The witch set down her meat and all four of the dead men tipped over, Werner teetering for a moment before he pitched onto the fire. The witch cursed and kicked him out of the coals, and Manuel thought he saw the pommel of a sword shining on the belt of one of the fallen Kristobel cousins. He scooted forward the slightest bit and her head snapped around, her eyes dark and her head haloed by the firelight behind her. She looked less like a saint and more like a wrathful angel to the terrified artist.

"Please," Manuel said, "I won't tell anyone. Please."

Awa wished he had not said that. Of course he would tell someone, and even if he did not she would have to worry about it for the rest of her days if she let him go, which was far more trouble than it was worth. He had mentioned God to the other men just before releasing her, she had heard him through the sack they had covered her with. That made it a little better, as he presumably would be less frightened of death than the animals she trapped and killed for her dinners.

Manuel recognized the resignation in her shoulders as she clambered up to a crouch, the weary sigh as keen an indicator as her shouting in his face, *I'm going to kill you, Niklaus! I'm going to kill you even if I won't really enjoy it!* His own shoulders had bowed under that same weight many a morning, after all, and did his breath not fall out of him with equal dismay when his prayers were said before battle instead of bed? She was going to kill him because, well, who really knew why witches killed people? Maybe because he knew she was a witch and might tell—

The witch was reaching out toward him and Manuel kicked her hand away, hardly the dignified march to his Maker he had seen for himself but there it was, and he kicked again as she came closer. He had painted himself a few times, which always made him feel a little bit like an asshole, but now he was suddenly wishing he had written plays or poems instead, about himself, about all this, so he could write some choice final words for himself, something concise and graceful and—

"Fuck fuck fuck," Manuel wailed as her fingers stung his ankle like the nettles that had grown beside his great-aunt's hut, a burning chill racing up his bones and striking his heart, quick and sure as water running down the sluice of the little red millwheel he always passed on his way home to Bern, to his family, and then Niklaus Manuel Deutsch died. His chin hit his chest and he floundered backwards, his legs twitching on the ground as his breath froze on his lips. The artist was just another bland and anonymous corpse, the destiny of many a soldier not blessed with extraordinary luck or skill, and the fate of quite a few with plenty of both.

Looking down at the body, Awa wondered why she had not killed the man completely. If she did not restore him in a day or two his organs would no longer work properly, but the little death was, for the time being, hardly different than putting him to sleep. Supposedly—she had never applied it to herself and never would if she could help it, her experience with the trick at her tutor's hand enough to put her off it forever. She returned to her fire and cooling meat, and as she ate she considered whether or not to give back what she had taken.

Strange, how she had been resigned to die only a few days ago, to abandon the impossible quest that had wasted almost four precious years, yet as soon as men tried to help shuffle her toward her end she fought like a desperate beast, like a woman with everything to lose. She had actually been scared of being raped, of being killed, even though she sometimes thought she deserved both. Had she not given up, resolved to lose something far more precious than her life?

"Stop," Awa said as she realized she was muttering to herself again, and after she had eaten she sifted through the bags of her captors. The satchels were carefully emptied one at a time by the fire, sorted through, and then put back precisely as she had found them. She tried to guess which bag went with which dead man, but the first two bags contained identical blankets, bowls, and food, although in the bottom of the second she came across a moldering human thumb. The third bag seemed just as bland, but then her fingers felt a small, smooth oval plank of wood. Carefully removing it, she gasped and then grinned, holding the picture before her. On the flat circle of wood was a mildly smudged black sketch of a nude woman—her breasts pert, her short hair and sharp nose and sly smile all distinct despite the wear the image had received. Awa stared at it for a long time, tilting it this way and that in the firelight, and then she put the treasure aside and returned to the last two bags.

Awa could tell one of them was different at a glance and so she put it aside, first picking through the other bag with less attention than she had the others, her eyes flitting back to the lumpier satchel as she hurried through her search. Then she wiped her greasy hands on a dead man's back and carefully uncinched the last bag.

Awa allowed herself a long, sighing "Oooooh" as she carefully removed one plank after another of smooth pine, some covered in hide to protect the image, others blank, virginal, and she separated the laths into two piles. Continuing her investigation, she found three large, rough cylinders of charcoal wrapped in more of the hide, several small wooden dowels and twine, a handsome little case containing a stylus and a pouch of black powder, and several more personal effects—a tiny doll made of sticks and bright green cloth, and a gold crucifix on a leather thong. There was also a wineskin containing much finer drink than she had thus far found, and after building up the fire she settled in with the wine and the sketches.

They were unlike anything she had ever seen, or at least remembered—Omorose's harem must have contained art of some variety, but that was a lifetime ago, and there in the cave Awa doubted the images were equaled anywhere in the world. They were of dead men, mostly, though eyes less versed in the markers of the grave might not have noticed these subtle details in many of the portraits. There was also a larger nude of a woman with curly hair, which Awa did not let herself focus on until last. A few were clearly done using charcoal, and these were much more smudged than the ones he had evidently gone over with some kind of ink.

Finally she held the image up to the light, the shadows making the woman come alive, and Awa felt her chest tighten at the beauty of the creature, and she bit her lip, keen to allow herself a tiny bit of sport with such a fine inspiration to help her along. Then the image of Omorose shoved herself in the way of Awa's arousal, and she had a compulsion to cast the plank into the fire. Instantly horrified by the impulse, she quickly covered the sketches back up and stowed them in the pack, save for the small nude she had taken from the other bag—this she wrapped carefully in dry cloth and put with the large satchel she had claimed for herself.

The sketches decided things for Awa, who now realized why Manuel's thumbs and forefingers were stained black. She ordered the corpses of Werner, Bernardo, and the Kristobel cousins to their feet, and then had them go out into the rain and dig their own graves, their swords biting into the gray mud. Once the graves were sufficiently deep she had them crawl inside and, after shedding her clothes and leaving them in the dry cave, she buried them. The rain felt good on her skin, and the fire felt even better when she was finished, and then she brought Manuel back from his little death.

"Get up," she ordered, releasing his spirit back into his body. Rather than promptly rising like the undead he rolled on the ground, gasping and clutching his face. Before he could fully recover, Awa launched into her spiel. "You've been sick ever since you rescued me, Niklaus Manuel Deutsch of Bern. You've had a fever and told me you saw dead men and that I was really a witch, but I'm not. You seemed to see a lot of things that did not really happen. This happens to men with fevers. Do you still have a fever, Niklaus Manuel Deutsch of Bern?"

"Blart," said Manuel, vomiting all over himself.

"You're still sick," Awa observed.

"You killed me," Manuel groaned, his headache distracting him from any potential, and indeed advisable, duplicity in the matter. "My heart stopped, I heard it. Felt it. You looked through the gear, and took them outside. The dead—"

Manuel dry-heaved and Awa licked her lips, watching him. She had forgotten that when her tutor had applied the little death to her she had been perfectly conscious the entire time. That was a problem. She approached him again.

"Saved you," Manuel panted, strings of bile dangling from his chin like an old man's last few beard hairs. "I fucking saved you! Please!"

Awa reached toward him again, and he drew back with a

whine. She stopped, her fingers still stretching out toward him, and then closed her hand into a fist. They could talk whether he was alive or dead, and it occurred to her that if she killed him again she could raise his corpse and interrogate it as to Manuel's character, especially in regard to his opinion of witches. But she did not know if by doing so she would actually kill him instead of giving him the little death—could those whose spirits were not fully removed from their bodies be raised as mindless ones? The question certainly bore looking into.

The witch was considering him, her fist between them. She did not look so young anymore, nor so slight. She was thick and made of nothing but hard angles, her dark skin making her appear more statue than woman to the artist.

"You can kill me anytime," Manuel said before her hand could unclench. "Please, let's, let's talk for a while. Please?"

"Talk?" This broke the witch's reverie, and she stared at him as though toads were hopping out of his mouth instead of words. "What would we talk about?"

"You," Manuel said, and as her face sharpened into a scowl he added, "And me? I'm an artist. You saw those sketches? Mine. And the nude I sold to Bernardo, the one you saw first, that's mine, too."

"That's mine now," Awa said. "I like your...pictures. Tiny little shards of their spirits live in them."

"Ah," said Manuel, his sudden flush of pride instantly cooled by the creepiness of her appraisal. Perhaps his old master Tiziano had been right—he should have stuck to still life. "I can sketch one of you, if—"

"No!" Awa backed away from him. "If you try it you go back to death, Niklaus Manuel Deutsch of Bern, and I won't wake you. Understand?"

"Of course." Manuel nodded. "Absolutely. Whatever you—"

"Think I'll fall for your tricks?" Awa demanded, although she wondered if the hazy remnants she felt in the planks would be strong enough to have any influence at all over a complete spirit like hers. "I know others can do as I do, or like I do. Are you a witch, Niklaus Manuel Deutsch of Bern?"

"No," Manuel said, relieved that she had given him a little room. "I'm an artist, and I'm a soldier, and very often I'm a fool, if my wife or captain are to be believed, but I'm no witch. I'm a man of God."

"Man of God?" Awa said. "The same god that walked as a man and then returned from the dead, that god?"

"God." Manuel nodded, not sure what she was driving at. "The only God."

"Where I was born men thought the spirits were gods," said Awa, remembering her early conversations with her tutor more than the actual faith of her mother and father. "And here men believe in a man who was a god. How do you know he was not a trickster, a necromancer? How do you know he was not my tutor, or his tutor, or some other like them? How do you know you don't worship a monster that has deceived you, a man capable of stealing bodies, raising the dead, and living forever through sorcery?"

"Ah," said Manuel, not having anticipated anything so complicated as a theological debate with a witch when he had set out to earn some paint as a mercenary. At least she was sounding more like the witches he had heard about, being completely fucking heretical and all. "Well, faith, you know? Faith."

"Faith." Awa crinkled her brows. "You mean belief?"

"Well, yes," said Manuel. "I believe God is who He is, and that He will redeem me, if I please Him."

"How do you please him?" Awa eyed him. "Killing his enemies? Killing the worshippers of his enemies?"

"No," said Manuel, deciding that he had no more to lose than his life were his honest answers to displease her, and he had already lost that once tonight without any continued ill effect. "Some think that way, but I don't believe it. I believe we please Him by living good lives, by following His example."

"What is good to the fox is not good to the hare," said Awa. "He was a soldier, then? Your god? He wore a blade and delivered witches unto their death, but only so long as his friends did not seek to rape them? This is his example?"

"No," said Manuel, the incongruity of his current occupation with his belief something he had gone over enough times on his own that he did not hesitate before answering. "I am not living up to His example. I was trying to, but then I went to war, and the only recent time I have done as He would was when I helped you escape and—"

"You *helped* me escape?" said Awa, taking a pull of his wine. She could not remember being so happy, the fire warm and the questions bubbling out of her lips like tea-water over the side of the cauldron. Not for the first time, she wished she had wormwood close at hand. "Before you said you saved me, yet now you acknowledge that you only helped, and that, had I not fended for myself, all might have been for naught. How long, I wonder, until you admit that without my blade you would have died, that I saved you?"

"My blade," Manuel snapped, unwilling to let her take all the credit for his near martyrdom. "Your hand, yes, but my blade that you took from my sheath. I'd say that means we saved each other, or helped each other if you prefer."

"Yes." Awa nodded. "That's true, Niklaus Manuel Deutsch of—"

"Manuel," said he, "is what I'm called. There's no need to say it all like that."

"Oh," said Awa, a little embarrassed.

"But we were talking about God," said Manuel, and as the words left his lips he started to giggle. She looked at him curiously but he could not stop himself, and soon he was howling with laughter. Witches were real, the dead could walk, and here he was explaining his most private thoughts on faith to a strange woman, a Moor, who had performed a miracle comparable to the Lord's resurrection, and upon his own flesh. For fuck's sake.

"What's so funny?" Awa asked, worried that she had broken the man's mind. She hoped not, for already she liked him more than any living person she could remember. That perhaps was not so remarkable in her case as it would have been in another's, but there it was. If she had driven him mad with her tricks she would be very annoyed with herself.

"Nothing, nothing," Manuel managed, the realization that the witch was watching him a sobering one. He had to keep her entertained or she would kill him, or worse. Perhaps if he kept her talking until dawn she would— It was the middle of the day, he realized, the slackening rain revealing not night-shrouded darkness beyond the cave but a dreary afternoon. Fuck.

"Are you mad?" Awa asked.

"No." Manuel shook his head. "I don't think so, anyway."

"Are you hungry? Or thirsty?"

"Yes," said Manuel, realizing how famished and parched he was. "Very much so."

"Eat," said Awa, motioning to Werner's stewpot that simmered over the fire. She was pleased the restorative soup would not go to waste. "And this is your wine, I believe."

"Thank you," said Manuel, taking his lightened skin and draining it in one long, sloshing guzzle. Quite tipsy herself, Awa switched to water and watched him scoot around to get at the stew.

Every time Manuel glanced up she was smiling at him, which did little to assuage his worry. Maybe he *was* mad, he thought, or consumed with fever, or simply dreaming. Then he wondered where she had gotten pork for the stew, and concluded that one of the other mercenaries must have been holding out on him. He shook his head. He, Niklaus Manuel Deutsch, gobbling up the tastiest meal he had eaten in months directly from a witch's cauldron!

"You said that before you went to war you were trying to live like your god," prompted Awa when he had finished. "Were you a priest, then? A monk or some other holy man?"

"No," said Manuel, the wine soothing his panic. "Between the two of us, I very much doubt many monks or priests are living as He would like. Through a friend of a friend I was able to read a treatise by this Italian fellow, Niccolò Muck... Niccolò Mack... Niccolò. This Niccolò, he wonders if any ruler can practice what they preach to their subjects and remain in power, and though he was talking about lay leaders the point could, and maybe should, be applied to the Church as well. Maybe the clergy couldn't stay in power if they expressly followed His tenets, but the whole point is living just lives, not maintaining the power you've inherited, which seems at odds with pardoners and all the rest."

Very good, thought Manuel, *since you're dining with a witch why don't you go and voice some blasphemies while you're at it? Maybe later the two of you could eat a baby or something.* Did witches eat babies? Manuel had not given any heed to stories about witches once he had grown up, and so found himself unsure of what she might be capable of.

"You don't think all of your holy men are just?" Awa could not believe her luck in finding an actual breathing person critical of the world around him, another person who thought instead of blindly believing. Such had prevented her from making many—or any, she corrected herself—friends among the living. She could account for faith, though she did not share it, but not the unquestioning obedience that brought about the horrors of the Inquisition that she had almost experienced firsthand.

"No," said Manuel, resigned to let his wine-whetted tongue

run its course. It was rather liberating, for she seemed quite interested in what he had to say. *Of course she does,* he thought ruefully, *she's a witch, and you're speaking her language now, alright.* "Men lose their way, just like sheep, no matter how careful the shepherd. It's not the shepherd's fault, for even the best shepherd will, when his flock becomes large, rely on his dog, and if his dog is not dependable then sheep will be lost. Our Shepherd has a flock that requires a great many dogs to tend it, but dogs are hungry animals, and when there are tasty morsels everywhere to distract them the dogs—"

"What are you talking about, Manuel?" Awa interrupted. "Dogs or priests?"

"Priests," said Manuel, "but the metaphor—"

"Your priests are hungry? You seem clever enough to speak in clearer terms than dogs and shepherds. There are many followers of your god, and so your god has many priests, yes? After that I could no longer follow you."

"Yes," said Manuel. "The priests, well, the priests have become distracted by the world, I think, by material rewards instead of spiritual ones. Follow?"

"No," said Awa.

"Look," said Manuel, "I'm no Erasmus but I'll see if I can't explain. Priests are supposed to be concerned with God, and with helping we mortals follow God. Yet in the time between the foundation of the Church and today, right now, much of the clergy has stopped doing so selflessly, instead demanding payment for their service to God. Men no longer need to live just lives, but instead can be as corrupt as they wish so long as they pay the Church to forgive them. Sins, wicked acts that displease God, are forgiven by the Church in exchange for wealth, instead of the acts of contrition and penance that God had stated was the only way to be restored to His graces."

"How do you know all this?" asked Awa.

"From what I've seen, and what I've heard and read." Manuel shrugged. "And not all priests are like that, of course, but enough to give one pause."

"You still haven't told me how you were living like your god before you became a soldier."

"No. And I said I was *trying* to live like God, not that I was succeeding. You asked me if God was a soldier, and I said no. He kills, yes, and we servants of He are soldiers when we have to be, yes, but He is not a soldier Himself, for soldiers follow orders and He—"

"So you had to be a soldier?"

"No," said Manuel with more guilt than he was accustomed to feeling about the matter. "I became a soldier to feed myself and my wife and niece and maybe one day my children, and to better serve Him in my own humble fashion—through my art, through the pictures you liked. I do not think God is a soldier, but I do think He is an artist."

"You have not struck me as humble," said Awa. "But I don't know if you should be. Your god is an artist?"

"Yes," said Manuel. "He made this world, did He not? It is a beautiful place, and no living man may match His skill in creating. Look around you at this realm, and the creatures that populate it. Yet I struggle to emulate Him, to create beauty, to venerate Him through my art."

"And you seek to do this outside of your god's church, which you consider corrupt?"

"Well," Manuel sighed, looking at his charcoal-stained digits. "Most of my paying jobs are done for churches and abbeys."

"You're a hypocrite, then," said Awa, quite pleased. She was a hypocrite, too.

"No," said Manuel. "Well, maybe a little. I take their money, it's true, but it's all to serve Him, and I turn a little coin glass-blowing on the side. You see—"

And on they went, until the sun set, and they ate cold meat

and drank warm wine, and talked on until Awa began to yawn and blink and Manuel had almost forgotten that he was keeping company with a sorceress. He remembered sure enough when she went outside to relieve herself and killed him on her way out, those fingers stopping his heart as abruptly as a bandit's breaking-pole stopping the spokes of a wagon. He lay on the floor of the cave, unable to move or speak or breathe, terror and panic driving his mind to the threshold of sanity, and then she returned and addressed him.

"Niklaus Manuel Deutsch of Bern, I know you can hear me despite being a dead man. I like you more alive than dead, but I also prefer being alive myself and know that I cannot trust you, for your fear of me is as obvious as it is justified. However, I also know you will never trust me so long as I keep killing you every time I take a piss or a nap, so we must agree that a better solution is needed. Get up."

Manuel did not vomit this time but his head still pounded and he glared up at her. "What the fuck do you want from me?"

A fair question, and one Awa had not considered. The answer came of its own volition. "You saved me, this is true. Yet it is also true that you took me away from where I was. Therefore I want you to escort me back to where I was before we met, and then we may part ways."

"Back to the camp?" said Manuel. "But—"

"What? No, to where I was before that, a day and a half north-west of there, I believe, beside a stream. My belongings are still there, I hope."

"What, ah, happened there?" Manuel asked, sitting up. "The man who captured you, Wim, died the morning of the battle, before von Swine gave you to me."

"I was stupid," said Awa harshly. "Careless. Feeling sorry for myself. I—" She looked up sharply but seeing that Manuel was not smiling at her expense she cleared her throat. "He threw the chain around me. This Inquisition must have told your master how to bind me, and he told the man. Before he tightened the iron I touched him, but the chain must have already dampened me enough that instead of dying at once he persisted long—"

The witch broke off, her eyes widening, and Manuel nervously glanced over his shoulder to make sure some worse horror was not approaching. Awa could not believe how stupid she was, detailing to Manuel her principal weakness. Most men were not versed in witchcraft, especially not the minutiae of debilitating a necromancer, yet here she had gone telling him the last thing he needed to know. Her fingers twitched and she almost killed him again before appreciating just how confused he looked.

"So we journey back toward the camp, which isn't even there anymore, and then you go your way and I go mine?" said Manuel carefully, his eyes on her quivering left hand.

"Yes," said Awa, adding quickly, "Unless you'd like my help with your master."

"Who, von Stein?"

"He's threatened your family," said Awa, her brown eyes stabbing into his. "I know about serving masters we despise, and I think you will need to kill him for your family to be safe."

"Yes," Manuel said numbly, although already he was imagining how he could get her back into her sack and safely to the Inquisition. She *was* a real goddamn witch, after all, so it wasn't like she was some innocent he would be turning over. What had she said about iron binding her?

"I am going to sleep now, Niklaus Manuel Deutsch of Bern, and we both know the only way I can ensure you do not try to kill or capture me is for you to die."

"Wait, no—" Manuel put his hands up.

"Shut up," she said, her face suddenly looking very young and sad. "You listen to me, and then you speak. You did not think I was a witch, and that is why you freed me. You thought I was a madwoman, you told your master, and you pitied me as such. Your god and his servants do not pity witches—I know this, and your master threatening your family certainly does not compel you to help one whom you consider wicked by nature. But I'm not wicked, even if your church thinks that I am. I have done things I regret, it is true, but who has not?"

"I wouldn't..." Manuel began but she looked at him and he knew she had more to say, and so he let her.

"I had a master, and he would have me kill to save myself. I will not do this, because it is what he wants and because I do not believe innocents should suffer so that I may live. Instead I sought to free myself, but in the years I've searched for a way to thwart him I've found no escape, no alternative but to do as he bids, to slaughter children to lift the curse he put upon me."

The flat tone of voice and the despondent expression on her young face magnified the horror of her words, and Manuel felt lightheaded. She was speaking of the devil, of course, and could he doubt her after all he had seen and experienced that day? He leaned closer as she continued.

"Yet I will not. When I was captured I had just put the last of the dead I had raised into the ground, and I intended to desert my quest. I decided to try and live as a simple woman instead of a necromancer, to find some place in this world where I could exist for a few quiet years. I was content to wait for my death, my oblivion, and so I will be hard-pressed to begrudge you if I wake up and find myself wrapped in chains, a sack over my head, a gag in my mouth. Think of your family, Niklaus Manuel Deutsch of Bern."

And with that Awa went to the fire, lay down, and went to sleep, the wrapped-up portrait she had taken clutched to her chest. Manuel waited until her breathing evened out and then fled the cave, stumbling through the darkness back to the scene of the morning's altercation. By the light of the moon he eventually found the discarded chain and the stinking sack they had bound her with, and he took them back to the cave, approaching the dark mouth much more slowly and cautiously than he had left it. She still slept beside the dying fire, and Manuel stood over her, the iron chain gripped in both hands.

XII
Something Sweeter Than Unspoiled Wine

"One more task," said the necromancer one autumn afternoon, "one more ritual, little Awa, and then you will be free to go, a necromancer in your own right. It's enough to make me get out a handkerchief."

"What?" Awa felt her breath dash away and hoped it came home soon; she had much more to ask on the matter.

"You don't think I meant to keep you here forever, did you?" said the necromancer, and Awa realized she had thought exactly that. Considering any alternative might have given her hope, something she tried to weed out of her emotional garden lest it choke her seasonal apathy and perennial pragmatism.

"You're going to let me go?" Awa marveled at the words even as she knew they had to be another of his games. "You would not let me go without a reason. I am too useful to you."

"True enough!" He laughed, in better spirits than she had ever seen him. "The fact is, you can't go where I'm bound, so there's nothing for it. Getting there will require your aid, but once I'm gone you can do what you wish—stay up here for all I care, or see the world and all its wonders. I only ask that you stay alive so that we may converse again some sunny day, and I will be most displeased if I have to call you back from where the dead go. And don't think a split skull will stop me, either—even if your body's dashed I can summon your shade, put it in a bottle or something. So live, Awa, live!"

"Ah," said Awa. "That's it. You're not really letting me go, you're just going away for some reason, and someday you'll come back and put me back under your thumb."

"Must you always think the worst of me?" The necromancer scowled, clearly put out. "Here, I've got some presents for you."

"Presents?" Awa took a step back. "I really don't want—"

"Are you sure?" asked the necromancer, and Awa was no longer.

"What I meant," she said carefully, "is that I don't need—"

"Need's a funny, fleeting thing," he clucked, opening his bear and rooting around until he found a small chest. Setting it on the table, he gave her a strange smile and opened it up. Awa looked around to see where his concubine had slithered off to, suspecting a trick, but then he beckoned her around the table. "Put that hoof of yours on my chair."

Awa obliged, and he took a thin, shimmering black rope from the box. He wrapped it twice around her ankle where goat fur met skin and tied it in a bow. Nothing happened. She looked up at him, and he grinned and nodded, pointing back down. Returning her gaze to her hoof, she stumbled backwards, nearly tipping his chair. Her hoof was gone and her old foot was in its place, the black twine bowed around her ankle.

"I don't want this," Awa said. "I liked it!"

"It's still there," the necromancer said huffily, hurt, or something like. "I just hid it so you won't be burned at the stake by the first peasant you run across. The rest of the world isn't so understanding of our talents."

"Oh," said Awa, and tapping her heel on the floor she felt her hoof clatter instead of a too-soft sole.

"You still see the string?"

"Yes," said Awa. "Shouldn't I?"

"It's only visible to you, so you can take it off if you like, and even with it on you're liable as not to leave cloven hoofprints, so be mindful of mud when you're walking about muddy villages." He rooted through the chest for something else as Awa held her foot up and tried to wiggle her illusory toes.

"What is it made of?" she asked.

"A braid from my tutor's beard," said the necromancer, making Awa lose some of her excitement over the gift. "And here's his skull."

Awa looked up and saw him holding out a small, hexagonal piece of bone with a circle punched through its center. She took it and peered closely at the burnished band. "His skull?"

"The hardest part of it, expertly carved and crafted." He tapped his head. "That beard string of his will work fine for a foot or a hand but isn't good for much else, though I once tied it around an adder's throat to make it look like a grass snake."

"But this piece of skull?"

"A ring," said the necromancer, and, taking it back from her, he slipped it onto one of his fingers. Nothing happened. "Well, look away!"

Awa glanced to the bear and back to her tutor. Omorose stood before her, alive and radiant and smiling from ear to ear. Awa looked away again. "Take it off. Not funny."

"No?" He dropped the ring onto the table and reached back into the box. "You can look any way you like when it's on, and more than that, it disguises the sound of your voice and even your smell—useful if dogs are after you. For you I'd recommend the visage of a burly Spaniard fellow, lessen your chance of trouble on the roads. Not much respect for women or Moors these days. Ah, here they are!"

He placed a familiar hawthorn box on the table. "Best way to start a fire in even the wettest weather, though you'll need to get them out of the kindling quick once it's lit—if they stay with the fuel they might hatch. Hardly a salamander left in all the world, so if you lose these don't count on finding another. You recall how to ignite them?"

"I tell them the word for fire, like their mother would." Awa opened the box and removed one of the half-dozen petrified eggs.

"You have to focus on one at a time, though, which is nice—keeps you from setting your bag on fire when you've got one in the tinder and the rest in their box and you speak those sacred syllables." He took a dagger out of the chest, its handle an ibex horn and its sheath black leather. Glancing at Awa, he quickly put the weapon back in the chest and shut it. "You can have that after I've left. The bear will open right up for you once I'm gone."

The necromancer turned to put the chest back in his ursine hidey hole and Awa surreptitiously made her way over to the cooking area. A quick perusal confirmed that all the iron tools were gone, including his cauldron.

"What are you doing?" He was right behind her.

"I was going to make some tea," she said, careful not to look him in the eye. "Where are—"

"Stowed, in preparation of my departure," said the necromancer. "Now piss off until tonight, I've got to prepare a few things."

"Alright," said Awa, gathering her new possessions. "Thank you, sir."

"No," he said, "thank *you*, little Awa."

More convinced than ever that he meant her imminent mischief, Awa forced herself to wait quite a while before strolling down the glacier to where she had secreted one of the swords. It was gone. Worrying her lip, she tracked down the bandit chief and asked if he would spar with her.

"I would, but he had the mindless ones gather all the swords last night and cast them from the high cliff. Might we use the old sticks?"

"No." Awa worried her lip more. "Have you seen Gisela? His whore?"

"Not today," said the bandit chief. "And the mindless ones are off somewhere as well. Something must be brewing. I would be very careful, Awa."

She nodded. "Getting rid of the iron might mean he's vulnerable, or is going to be. He said he needed me for one last ritual tonight and then he would set me free."

"That sounds suspicious."

"I know it."

"Be careful not to play into his hands. He is very clever."

"I don't have much choice." Awa sighed. "We've all lived in his palm for a very long time, and I can't refuse to help."

"No."

"What if he is, though?" It came out quickly, Awa giddy at the thought. "What if he really is leaving? What if he's not so wicked but just mad? Mad and lonely? I know I—"

"He is not *just* mad, nor is he lonely. He is dangerous and cruel, a monster. You know this, and you know I cannot lie so you should feel assured by my assessment."

"Yes, but if we believe the things we say they are not lies even if they are untrue, yes? He gave me things," said Awa. "Look at my foot, he made it—"

"Do you not remember what he did to that foot, Awa?" he said, and at the memory her sprouting hope withered. "Be wary of him, today more than you ever have before. Did you not tell me he was in a kind mood as he fed you your own flesh?"

"I'll be careful," said Awa, doubting she could be careful enough if he intended her harm.

She spent the rest of the afternoon playing with the birds she had brought back to life, the littlest of them a skeletal swallow that sported mouse bones she had gathered from raptor pellets instead of feathers. It jumped from rock to rock and landed on her finger, its delicate skull cocked at her as she walked it to the end of the cliff. One by one she had the vultures and other bird carcasses hop over the edge so they could have one last flight. Awa sadly watched them plummet down, wings vainly flapping, until they smashed apart far below. She thought she saw the cauldron shining at the base of the cliff but it might have simply been a bright piece of rock reflecting the setting sun. Finally she had her littlest bird leap over the side, but the mouse bones actually worked and it glided out, buoying itself in the stern winds, and to Awa's delight it returned and landed on her shoulder.

Pleased by the good omen, she walked back toward his hut cooing to the little bird. When she reached the door she looked at her tiny friend and saw what she was looking for, and with a quick peck on its skull she restored the creature's soul to its bones. It jabbed her palm twice with its beak, leaving little rubies in the furrows of her hand, and then it flew up into the darkening night. A good omen.

Awa felt queasy as she shut the door behind her, the air thick with wormwood smoke. Through the haze she saw that he had drawn all over the black tabletop, diagrams she had never seen before etched into the stone and filled with oil rendered from the fat of men, judging by the rich smell she made out through the licorice-tinged miasma. He talked quickly, anxiously, having her grate mandrake root onto a circle he had carved at the foot of the table while he poured sheep's milk into a bowl full of ground bone and rusty iron shavings.

"You said iron couldn't be used in—" Awa began as she watched him work but he cut her off.

"I said iron dampens our ability to work our arts," said the necromancer, stirring the bowl with a finger. "Try raising a skeleton the next time you're holding a sword. Now, if it's on your belt that's something else... provided your belt's not iron, of course. It's all about binding, Awa, about trapping reality in a certain shape, which is the last thing we want sometimes and the first thing we need at others. We usually need reality to be malleable, mutable, open, not closed and set. Now drink this."

"What?" Awa frowned at the bowl. Since moving back in with the necromancer she had been plagued with vivid, traumatizing nightmares, and if they did not involve Omorose they invariably featured her tutor torturing her. Several dreams had featured poison. "Why?"

"Because I am, for one final night, your master. Shall I make you?"

"No," Awa said, and drank the mixture. She tasted other elements in the draught but there was nothing for it, and despite the rarity of luxurious, thick milk she gagged on her fear and the flakes of metal. He was going to murder her, she knew it, but why had he told her to live and—

"You'll pass the iron soon enough, and then your abilities will return," said the necromancer as he drew his fingers back inside his tunic and began pulling it over his head. "We all have a little in us, in our blood. It's part of what makes blood such an essential element—it contains the mystical properties of incomprehensible life, yet it also carries cold, hard reality. Drink a little sometime and tell me I'm lying; you can tell by the taste. That's why so few are disposed to working our wiles—too much iron, dampens them to the point that practicing witchcraft is impossible. That's why you have to start young, to train yourself to fight against your very blood, to— What's the matter?"

Awa had backed away as he stripped nude, the haze in the room making her dizzy, the milk curdling in her belly. She glanced into the fire to see if the pot hook was still there but he had removed that, too. He was moving toward her, his spindly nakedness disturbing in a way that no cadaver could match—they were supposed to look dead, after all.

"Don't touch me," she whispered. "Don't you even—"

"Touch?" He blinked once and then laughed. "No, little Awa, no no. You won't even have to touch me! My skin just needs to touch the stone, nothing more. I'm sorry to blather on, but I'm appreciating how much I never told you, how much you have to learn. Too late now, too late, too late. Now come over here and listen."

He turned and clambered onto the table, and she saw that a wide flap of skin was missing from his mid-back down to his left buttock, the beet-red, rectangular wound only now scabbing over. Wincing as the granite met his exposed meat, he settled his puckered body down onto the oil-brimming channels like a starved hog in a nearly dried-out wallow. The smoke grew thicker and Awa realized he had blocked the chimney, her eyes stinging and her lungs burning. He gave a pleased sigh as he stretched out, his head turning to Awa.

"The iron's taken effect by now." His voice quavered the slightest bit, like an accomplished but nervous liar trying to fool his mother, and like an astute parent Awa picked up on the tremor though all other ears would have missed it. "You can't do anything, so don't try to be smart or it will end worse for you than it did for Omorose. Just do as I tell you and you'll have your freedom."

"Don't you speak her name, you horrible thing," Awa did not say, though she might have were his green eyes not so focused, so sharp. Instead she nodded her head softly. Had he let it go things might have turned out very differently.

"I'm serious, little Awa. Don't think I can't smell what you're thinking. You can't hurt me, you can only hurt yourself, and if you try I'll make you suffer in ways you can't imagine. You think it was bad that I let you rape your little friend's bones before cluing you in to the way things work? You have no idea. I'll play with her myself, and have your bandit friend do the same, and you'll have to watch, you'll have to watch your Omor—"

"Don't speak her name! You horrible thing!" She was crying and her fists were balled. "I hate you!"

"So long as we understand each other, anything's better than ambivalence," said the necromancer. "Now do as I say, yes?"

Awa stared down at her seemingly matching feet for a long time, then wiped her stinging eyes and nodded.

"Right. All you do is take that sheet hanging over the bear's arm and pull it up over me, all the way to my head, and then you let it lie atop me, and then you slowly pull it back down again. I can do what I need to do whether you oblige me or not, but my chances of a complete success are far stronger if the sheet covers me during the process. Understand so far?"

Awa numbly walked around the table to the bear and took the sheet draped over its forepaw. The linen was covered in lines and scribbles, much like the table. Drawn in blood, of course, but also fouler substances, gauging by the smell. Then she noticed the bear was dead, stone dead without even a fraction of its spirit, and she froze, her heart beating so hard she nearly threw up. If—

"The smoke can't be helped but get on with it," snapped the necromancer. "No excuses for dawdling, not now. Bring the sheet to my feet and wait until I start the invocations. Don't cover my head until I've gone quiet, and then count my heartbeats. After exactly one hundred heartbeats slowly remove the sheet, and I'll tell you what to do next."

"Why?" said Awa, trying to make herself sound out of sorts and drugged from the smoke. That was easy enough. "What are you doing?"

"These aren't exactly traveling clothes," said the necromancer, pinching a wattle of loose skin under his chin and shaking it. "Have to trade in this old hide for something fresh, something new. The sheet and the smoke help obscure the transformation—recall how with the ring and the rope the process did not take effect until you had looked away and then back? If you don't do as you're told I won't be able to become as young as I'd prefer, and I'll be very cross. That's the worst you can do, but I would still not advise it. You have not seen me cross yet, Awa."

Awa did not know if she believed him, but she focused on his words rather than letting her mind settle on what had flitted through it, like the little bonebird arcing over the abyss for an instant before sailing back to safety.

"Do not fail me, Awa," the necromancer said quietly. "Please. I have been harsh, I know, but I think in time you might understand even if you cannot forgive. I love you, Awa, I love you and I only seek to keep you safe from a world that would bind you in chains, that would make you a slave to selfish children who spurn your kindness, who resent your mercy. I love you, and that is why I have been cruel. But no more—after tonight you will be a favored daughter instead of an abused pupil, a queen instead of a slave. Understand?"

How could she? No words he had spoken, no blows he had delivered, no dreams he had crushed stabbed her as viciously, broke her as thoroughly. She felt disemboweled, she felt on fire, she felt icy water fill her lungs. What could she say, what could she do? Her tears cut through the smoke, and she heard him begin the invocations. No gods or goddesses were mentioned, no prayers given, only commands, and Awa realized she had already drawn the sheet up to his neck.

Looking down at his face, weathered and leathery, Awa wondered what it would feel like to have those grubby, murmuring lips kiss her on the cheek or forehead, to have those emaciated arms hug her like her father must have, like her mother must have. Again she tried to remember her mother's name, her father's name, but they were gone forever. Names were powerful things, and her tutor had never given her his. Would he when the ritual was completed?

The necromancer's mouth froze on the last word, his eyes staring blankly at the ceiling, and Awa pulled the sheet over his head. She heard it, his heart, beating with brooding slowness, and she began to count along with it. She knew she had to pull herself together or she would lose count and he would be cross, and she did not want him to be cross. She wondered if she would recognize him as a younger man. She had never tried and—

The little bird clattered its bones against the window, and though she could not see it through the boards covering the portal she knew the sound at once, the mouse bones she had given it whirring against one another as it flapped just under the eaves.

Fifty.

Fifty-one.

Fifty-two.

Fifty-three.

Awa scanned through the haze, peering at the boarded-up window, and that was when she noticed it, hiding on the ceiling. The necromancer's spirit had somehow exited his living body and floated above it, the wormwood vapors running over but not through it, the wavering bond tying the spirit to his head curling up like smoke from a snuffed candle.

Sixty.

Sixty-one.

Sixty-two.

The bird flew back over the cliffside in her mind, but now it dived down and Awa dived after it, moving too fast, too clumsily, letting herself focus fully on the deadly thought she had kept at bay all through his explanation of the ritual. She knew she had to calm down, knew there was time aplenty if she were methodical and practical. She banged her hip on the table and fell, the smoke finally starting to choke her, and she cried out as she scrambled up, pawing the front of the bear. Somehow she could still hear his heart but had lost it just long enough to terrify herself even more.

Was that seventy or seventy-five?

The door in the bear would not open but she got her fingers into the seam and wrenched it, peeling back a fingernail but springing the catch. She felt about in the dark cavity and it was gone, of course he had removed it, of course he had secreted it somewhere else, of course.

Seventy-five or eighty?

The shelf, the high shelf where he always placed his book—she had seen the chest there when she came in, had seen it but not had time to acknowledge it, and with a sob she pushed past the bear and jumped high, her now-bleeding fingers catching the ledge and bringing the whole rickety shelf crashing down on top of her. She felt the smoke part around her, felt the spirit of the necromancer run itself over her neck in warning of what lay ahead, but there could be no turning back; instead the contact confirmed that for a dozen more heartbeats, at least, he could not return to his flesh to thwart her.

There was too much smoke, the billowing clouds pouring out of the small blaze in the hearth blinding her further even as the firelight was gobbled up, converted into the obfuscating fumes. Then she felt the curl of an ibex horn under her palm and cried out, on her feet and blundering around to find the table, her fingers shaking so hard she could barely loose the clasp keeping the blade in its sheath. His heart was beating faster, a blatant cheat, and then she felt his leg under the cloth and followed it up to the head of the table. A high whining was coming from his spirit, the same noise Omorose's ghost had made when Awa forced her mistress's corpse to bury itself, and she made out the shape of his head through the smoke.

One hundred.

Clear as lightning and loud as thunder, she knew it, she felt it, and the spirit did, too, building itself up like a storm cloud, and then they raced for the necromancer's skull, blade and spirit evenly paced. The cloth over his mouth sucked inward just as the tip of the dagger reached him, the wide blade cracking his left eye socket as it passed through all the way to the hilt. Awa shrieked and wrenched the knife sideways, and the ibex-horn hilt told her fingers who told her hands who told her arms who told her mind that his skull had split open like a log under an ax.

This did not stop her from making sure, and when she could not pry the blade out of the slick, shrouded head she jerked him onto the floor and used the hilt to lift him up and smash him back down until his skull caved in enough for her to free the knife. She knew exactly where his heart hid and there the blade went and out he bled, and, finally, Awa let herself stop. He lay dead, swaddled in what had become his winding sheet, his skull fractured, his heart run through with cold iron, and Awa closed her eyes. She was alone.

XIII
The Counsel of Corpses

Awa was not alone. The smoke shifted, billowing waves breaking over her face, and she heard the familiar sound of his laughter. The cackling came from just behind her and, slowly opening her eyes, she turned to see what she had done.

His spirit floated free and unfettered, a smear of bright, oily blackness in the dark smoke, serpentine and long and coiling above her, faint yellow light shining from two holes in its blurry head. She could not breathe as she looked up at it, her head aching from the strain and the fumes, and it looked back at her. *He* looked back at her.

"I knew you were the one," he said. "Predictable. Easily manipulated. Clever, but so very stupid. Stay safe, little Awa, stay very safe or your spirit will suffer, and those of your friends as well. Safe."

They stared at each other, Awa unable to speak, and then he slid across the ceiling, a dozen branching, many-handed arms bursting from his sides and propelling him along, and then he slipped through the crack over the door and was gone. Awa looked down at his corpse, the bloody shroud stuck to her legs, and she began to laugh. It hurt like the time he had stabbed her, each sound that left her lips summoning another ghost of the blade jabbing into her lungs and stomach, and as she laughed she slipped from her knees onto her bottom and kicked at his corpse with her hidden hoof. Of course he wanted this, of course he planned this. Of course.

When she realized the fire in the clogged hearth had spread instead of dying she moved to salvage what she could, but as soon as she stood upright in the burning hut she fainted, the smoke too thick, the night too long. If the bandit chief had not pulled her out of the blaze she would have died, and that prospect had not held much allure in some time. He also rescued the dagger, a leather satchel, the spinning wheel, and the box of wool, but everything else fluttered away on ashen wings as the hut burned to the ground, and Awa returned to the world of the living in the skeletal arms of her only friend.

"Bury me here, and take care to dash my skull before you stack the cairn," said the bandit chief several days later, after he had nursed her with the little lung meat remaining on the last glacier-preserved corpse in their larder.

"Get out, then," said Awa, and before he could say another word she pushed his spirit from its body. She scowled at the dim gray shade hovering over his remains as she raised him up as a mindless boneman. The skeleton stood before her, Halim's unnaturally moist tongue still in place. "You can't tell me what to do, not after taking me here, after taking us here. You don't get to rest while he plays some new game with me. No, you're going to do what I say, aren't you?"

"Yes," said the skeleton.

"I bet your spirit's not too happy about that, is he?" Awa raised her voice, looking past the boneman at his hovering spirit. "Are you!?"

"I do not know," said the skeleton.

"I bet you don't," she said, and whirled away. "You're with me for as long as I choose. Let's fetch Omorose."

Walking over the glacier, Awa's pace began to flag. She knew exactly what she was doing, and it was terrible, but she could not stop herself. Of course he wanted to be dead; so did she, after all, but if she could not, then neither... then neither...

Awa stopped, the snow cutting into her ankles and burning her buried foot a pleasant sensation, a real sensation. She would not do this, because she was alive and being alive meant making decisions, meant choosing instead of simply being. She turned back to the ruins of the hut, her boneman following her. The rest of the skeletons had leaped over the cliff while she was helping the necromancer with his last ritual and so he was the last, just as she was the last apprentice. Except he would go into the ground and not return, and she would persist, alone.

She did not make him dig his own grave but had him lie on the soot-covered granite tabletop in the wreckage of the hut, piling the rocks onto his body in the place where he had died so long ago. She felt his spirit worrying at her arms as she worked, trying to convince her to let him help, or maybe just to let him back into his bones to say goodbye, to thank her. She could not or she might not let him go, and this self-awareness gave her strength even as it sickened her.

When the entire body was buried under the high mound of rocks save for his skull, she addressed his spirit: "I never asked your name because he taught us that names give power, and I never wanted to have power over you. I was a child and so I did not appreciate that this was impossible, that the living and the dead can never be equal, that I always had power over you. I beg that you forgive me for what I considered doing to you, for even thinking of treating you like, like a slave. You are the only friend I have, and I will miss you every day that I live, and if I one day find myself in the same resurrected position that you have suffered, every day after I die. I love you."

His spirit was pushing even harder then, trying to get back inside its skull, and Awa wondered if she had moved him to change his mind, to desire her companionship more than he desired rest, and so she brought a stone down on his pate as hard as she could before her weakness overpowered her compassion a second time. The skull shattered, ricocheting teeth stinging her arms, and she heard a faint hissing noise as his spirit faded into the air and the rock, but as it went a name impressed itself into her mind: Alvarez.

"Sleep well, Alvarez," Awa said as she covered his broken skull with rocks, and when the cairn was built she turned to her small collection of possessions and began lugging them to the abandoned shack she had shared with Omorose. She would restore Omorose to her body and see if her mistress's ire had cooled during her banishment from her flesh, but first she would knit her a gift, a fine pair of new leggings. She had plenty of black wool, and some lighter wool she would dye with ibex blood. Nothing was stopping her from going down to the pastures now, the beasts already penned in their winter enclosures, and she would make a stew that very night, and maybe dine on a little grass in honor of the goat that had given her its hoof.

Then Awa saw her little bonebird flitting over a patch of snow to her left and paused, the spinning wheel hoisted over one shoulder. She reached out to its spirit and called it to her but the bird lit down onto the snow and tapped its beak, as though it were searching for ethereal worms amidst that spectral field of snow. Knowing she had time aplenty, Awa delivered the wheel and wool to her hut and then relocated her bird, which was still hopping in place on the glacier. As she neared it she noticed that she was approaching the thin region of the glacier, the dangerous section shot through with thin ice and deep chasms. She moved slower, not as confident as she once was that the spirit of the glacier could be trusted to tell her when she was going too far.

Awa's bird had cleared the snow away from Gisela's face with its wings and Awa grinned, knowing at once what had transpired.

The concubine lay in a hole in the ice, the snow packed in tight around her. The powder above her would melt during the days and freeze during the nights to restore the unbroken surface of the glacier, and very soon she would be hidden as skillfully as a single blond hair in a field of wheat.

The concubine's spirit had nicked off to wherever they went, not having foreseen so early a rise, and Awa's smile widened. He wanted to dig her up at some point, the old sneak, and he knew his pupil might interfere with that goal if she were to remain in plain sight. The potential for mischief was mind-boggling, and Awa reached out and reeled in Gisela's spirit.

"Get up," Awa said once she had relocated the spirit.

"You found me?" Shriveled eyelids blinked over the frozen yellow pools that her eyes had deteriorated to, rotten grapes set in a moldy gourd. "Told'em you couldn't be trusted."

"Get up and do as I tell you or I'll push you out and make you watch what I do to your bones," said Awa, confident her tutor had disciplined his favorite paramour to the point that she would know better than to disobey those with the power to banish her spirit with a nod or a word.

"Couldn't do worse'n what he's done," Gisela said but crawled out of the grave all the same, frozen bones shrieking inside saggy skin as she moved.

"You can't lie," said Awa, "and I'll push you out and ask your corpse if you give me trouble."

"Course you will," said Gisela. "You're the same's he."

"No." Awa forced herself to keep her voice level. "I'm not like him. But I know how to hurt you, so behave. He hid you here to keep you safe from me, and so you'd stay fresh for when he came back to get you, yes?"

"Yeah," said Gisela, squatting in her grave and rubbing her knuckles.

"When will he come back for you?" said Awa.

"In his time," said the concubine, her bandit's voice husky as ever. "When he's done with you."

"Done with me?" The queasy feeling this brought on told Awa she was on the right track. "Do you know what he is planning as far as I'm concerned?"

"Yeah," said the concubine, looking rather pleased with herself for a dirty old corpse crouched in a snowy grave.

"*What*," Awa said sharply. "What is he planning as far as I'm concerned?"

"He's plannin on takin your pretty body and makin it his. Can't live forever, not even he, but he can get somethin new, somethin fresher. Spirit'll last for all days, tis the blood and bone what sours."

"What?" She cannot lie, Awa told herself, she must be telling the truth. "What do you—"

"Did you have a vision of bein out your skin?" the shriveled concubine asked, and Awa's heart froze at the memory. She had felt the cold air on her exposed musculature as she lay dripping on the floor, the necromancer hunched over the large bloody membrane he held stretched flat on the table like new vellum, his quill racing over what she had known must be the inside of her skin. She had awoken with a scream, her whole body racked with fever, but until that moment she had been able to force herself to believe it had been nothing more than an especially vivid nightmare, that even for her tutor there were limits to what reality would allow. The concubine clapped her hands together gleefully. "You remember, don't you, lil Awa?!"

"Yes," said Awa, her taxed mind as numb as her ice-crusted ankles. "He wants my body. His spirit wants my body, and he did something to me, when I was asleep."

"Marked you! Marked you for his touch!" said Gisela. "And once he's in you wager on those hands of yours touchin me a bit! Wager on that tongue of yours—"

"I don't think so," said Awa, pushing the concubine's spirit out of her body, the shade moaning as it was unmoored. The dead do not lie, however, and so that wager— "Get up."

The corpse sat back up from where it had fallen, the loose soul of Gisela expectantly settling around her body's neck like a stole. Awa smiled at that, knowing the bones remembered as well as the spirit, and chided herself for allowing the hideous concubine to enjoy even a drop of pleasure, an iota of sensation. *You stay and you watch*, she thought, and smiled at the cadaver.

"Your fun's over, Gisela," said Awa, pleased to see the spirit writhe over her bones. "But first you watch your body tell me what I want to know, and then you get to watch what I do to it. I warned you, and you gave me that shitty attitude you always do, having a laugh at my expense, except he isn't here to protect you, is he? He isn't here to watch your back, and if he means to steal my body I don't really care too much for staying in his good graces. So bite off all your fingers and swallow them, and *feel* it, you nasty thing."

The shriveled cadaver jammed her blackened digits into her mouth and began to chew, faint whines slipping between the sharp teeth and frozen meat and crackling bones as she ate her own fingers. Saffron tears flooded the long-dry riverbeds crossing Gisela's face, and Awa laughed. Soon her guffaw turned to a dry heave and she waved at her to stop, the necromancer gagging at the sight of what she was making the corpse do. Torturing the defenseless was what he would do, not her. Not her, never her. She was different. Gisela's spirit might have been giggling or crying, the droning noise obscure and alien.

"Now you speak what you know, and in detail," Awa said at last. "He marked me, and he intends to steal my body. Why me?"

"The ritual required his intended to slay his flesh, but in such a fashion to free his soul instead of banishing it to where the dead go, to make it something else," said Gisela's corpse evenly. "An esoteric and difficult ceremony. He could not leave this place in his own body, and only vessels prepared from youth can master his arts, even with a new spirit. Few children were brought to this place, and of them you were both open to the art and easy to control."

"I'm not," said Awa. "I'm not!"

"You were," said the corpse. "He needed you to murder his prepared body with a certain tool, and if you had not done that then the ritual would have destroyed him utterly. He tricked you into murdering him."

"So what now?" Awa said after a long pause, only her bone-bird returning to her shoulder dispelling the hopeless torpor that strangled her tongue. "Where is he, and when will, when will he return?"

"I do not know where he is," said the corpse. "He will return in ten years, upon the night that is called the Autumn Solstice. It is then that the curse he put upon you will fade, and then he will return."

"What curse?" said Awa, genuinely surprised that matters could actually worsen at this juncture.

"The curse that marks you as his intended. No dead may harm you so long as it bides, no dead in all the world. But upon the Solstice it will pass, and he will take your body."

"And my spirit? What will happen to my spirit?"

"When the curse dissipates your spirit will be naked and vulnerable, and no wards will keep him from it. He will devour it, and any scraps he leaves will be but an extension of his will."

"Oh." Awa sat down on the glacier. "Oh."

So after all she had weathered he would return in a decade, steal her body, and obliterate her soul. She often lusted after an end of consciousness, an absence of memory and pain, but he had convinced her it was not possible, that even were she to have her own skull split he would still find a way to draw back her spirit. That there was a way to achieve that precious oblivion did not bring her comfort, however, only more misery. Things we want often seem sweeter until they become attainable.

"I don't want him to be happy," Awa said to herself as much as to Gisela's corpse. "I want him to be disappointed. If I kill myself, if I have my head crushed, will he be able to find a new body? Will he be able to call back my spirit?"

"I do not know," said the corpse. "He told me only what he told me. I do know that when he wore his skin he could call back the spirits of the dead that had no bones at all."

"Oh," said Awa, and sat some more, her legs and bottom becoming as stiff and cold as her feet. As she ruminated on her unhappy circumstances, she had Gisela's corpse climb down to the low meadows and retrieve an ibex from its pen, the fingerless horror snapping the animal's neck and returning with it wrapped around her shoulders. Awa continued to brood, and eventually looked up at the spirit-shrouded corpse. "Is there a way to stop him?"

"He told me there was," said the corpse. "He instructed me to tell you, if you found me and asked that question. He said that if you take one hundred children, and you kill those one hundred children using the knife he gave you, then your curse will be lifted and he will never trouble you again."

Awa nodded glumly. "He knew I would find you."

"He told me you were clever but stupid," said the concubine.

"Is there any other way to break the curse? Any at all?"

"If there is, I do not know it."

"Oh." But Awa did not think long before a different, welcome thought occurred to her, one that shone its light through her darkened spirit and brought blooms of hope to her neglected inner plot. "His book wasn't on the mantel, it wasn't there! His book might have a way to take it off!"

"It might," agreed Gisela's corpse.

"Did he take it with him? Do you know if he took it with him? I didn't see it, I didn't see him take it!"

"He could not take anything with him. He is a creature of aether now, and cannot take such things as are made of more than spirit."

"He's hidden it, then, like he hid you!"

"Yes."

"Where?!" Awa leaned closer and took Gisela's slippery, fingerless hands in her own cold-cramped palms. "Where has he hidden it?"

"I do not know—"

"Shit!"

"—where it is hidden, but I do know he sent it away with his familiar spirits, demons made of the high mountain winds."

"Oh," said Awa, then seized on a discrepancy. "But you said beings of spirit could not take physical items with them!"

"No," corrected the corpse, "I said that he is a creature of aether now, and so he is and so he cannot move his book, nor otherwise manifest himself beyond the absence of life he has become—he might smother a small bird by settling upon it, but little else is possible until he again dons flesh. His familiars are made of wind, real wind, and as such they can blow the breeze about your hair or swirl the snow around my grave or even, if several muster their strength, take a book from one place and put it somewhere else. I do not know if he intended me to see or not, but these eyes saw his familiars take the book and fly away with it. But I do not know where they have taken it."

"How will I find it then?!" Awa cried. "It's gone forever!"

"It has your blood inside it," said the corpse, arresting the fit Awa was on the verge of suffering. She had not intended it as a question but was not very well going to tell the corpse that. "He took a page of flesh from his back, and prepared it, and when he inscribed the inside of your skin he also added a new page to his book, and wrote upon it using your blood. This is how his art is crafted: your blood on his skin to add a new page to his book, his blood on your skin to bestow his curse. Yet your blood is just that, and if you draw near enough your stolen blood will cry out to you, if you listen. This will help you find the book."

"Oh!" This news cheered Awa far more than it had any right to. "And if I find the book I can remove the curse!"

"I do not know."

"But it might!"

"Yes," said the concubine. "It might."

"Thank you!" Awa threw her arms around the ice-coated corpse, making Gisela's spirit squeal faintly. "Thank you thank you!"

Let there be hope, then. It scared her almost more than there being no hope at all, to have such an impossibly small chance, such a mean and tiny scrap of hope, but hope she did. She would find the book, and she would break the curse, and even if he killed her, even if he found another way, even if all were for naught, she would have this delicious warmth, this knowledge that she could choose. She had no options before, she knew that now, that she had been as weak and open to suggestion as the mindless bone-men, but at this moment she had the choice of whether she would wait hopelessly for his return or whether she would work to thwart him. To those spoiled on countless options and fattened on limitless choices such a selection might appear to be no choice at all, but there on the mountaintop Awa wept at the luxury.

"Thank you," said Awa, wiping her face on her tunic. "Oh, thank you so much."

The spirit of Gisela buzzed around her vacant, lolling head, the animated body waiting for another question. None came.

"Gisela." Awa addressed the spirit as much as the body, and it quieted its droning. "Lie back down in your grave."

The corpse obeyed her, and as soon as it lay flat in its grave of ice Awa shoved Gisela's spirit back into her desiccated head. Her putrid eyelids fluttered, and the last thing the restored spirit saw was a dagger plummeting into her eye. The sensation of the skull splintering inward as the blade sunk in delighted Awa, but then she doubled over and gagged, wondering what had happened to her and how she might stop herself from ever again acting so wicked, from ever again taking pleasure in such evil sport.

The concubine had it coming, Awa thought as she wound her way across the glacier back to her hut, the evening sky ablaze around her, and she almost convinced herself she was the only victim atop the mountain. Then she reached her hovel and saw the left wall of her hut, Omorose's tomb, and burst into tears. That night she soaked the lighter wool in ibex blood but did not eat the creature's flesh, instead smoking it for later consumption and eating the pile of brown grass she had collected until she threw up again. When the last of the chestnut wood had burned away and the half-smoked meat lay piled outside her door she slept with her back to Omorose's crypt and hoped for their future together.

The next day the dyed wool dried and she knit by starlight, adopting the necromancer's nocturnal schedule in preparation of her journey to the world below. Safer to travel at night, he had told her many times, and here at least she believed him. Days later she had several sets of black and rust-red striped leggings, and a coarse black cloak, and a new goatskin tunic, and then it was time to see if Omorose would behave herself.

She would not, although at first she did seem calmer. Then the reason for her lack of aggression became apparent: "Girl, I'm trying very hard to pick up a rock to brain you, but my body won't listen. What have you done to me?"

Awa had awoken early and brought her mistress outside just before sunset, and as the sun sank between the peaks like the lidless, bloody eye of a dying beast, Awa shook her head, disappointed but, she found, hardly surprised. "He's cursed me, Omorose, so that the dead cannot harm me."

"Isn't that a tragedy," said Omorose, and she knelt and picked up a rock. Awa watched her closely, and saw the exposed musculature tighten around the stone, Omorose's entire arm going rigid. She turned and tossed the stone over the cliff. "Poor little ape, protected yet again by her beloved daddy."

"Don't," said Awa, her tongue feeling as fat and stupid as Omorose insisted the rest of her was. "Please, Omorose, don't. I know what I did to you and—"

"You're sorry?" Omorose said sarcastically. "Apology accepted, beast, just as soon as you fling yourself off that cliff."

"I won't," Awa said quietly, relieved she had not been asked to do so the first time she had returned Omorose's soul to its body. She would have, then. Probably.

"Oh well," said Omorose. "Then why don't you get on with raping me or whatever you're going to do?"

"I'm not." Awa felt the tightness wrap around her throat, as though her mistress were choking her. "I'll never touch you again. I, I found a way to make it so you'll be alright, so you can be normal. So we can be even."

The words sounded so foolish that Awa could not blame Omorose for the incredulous look on her raw, frostburned face. Taking out the ring the necromancer had given her, she offered it to Omorose. The undead horror blinked at it and said, "Am I supposed to be touched that my violator made me a present?"

"I didn't." Awa swallowed, resisting the urge to throw it over the cliff and send Omorose hurtling after it. "It's, it was his. It will make you . . . normal."

"Normal?" Omorose plucked the ring from Awa's palm and slid it on. "You mean *not so much rotten meat* when you say normal, beast?"

"Yes," Awa whispered, looking away. "Focus on how you

would like to appear. Now. But if you call me beast again I'll ruin you, understand? I'll take you apart and—"

"Oh!" said Omorose, and looking back at her, Awa echoed the sentiment. The young Egyptian woman looked even more delicate and lovely than she had in life, and her tattered, stained shroud was replaced with a lovely blue-and-green silken abaya embroidered with tiny trees and flowers. She took Awa's heart yet again as she admired herself, and for a moment she seemed to forget her antipathy as she gazed at her own flawless hand. "Am I... is the rest of me so fair?"

Awa nodded and, finding her limbs slightly more obedient than her mouth, retrieved the clothes she had made Omorose and offered them next. Glancing at them, Omorose sneered. "What use have I for that trash? My garments are made of far finer stuff, are they not?"

Awa nodded again, and striking a low bow, managed, "I would use the ring to make myself inconspicuous on the road, but I have done you a great wrong and don't know a better means of making amends. Please forgive me, my lady. Please. All I have is yours, and I would give you my life if I did not need it to better serve you."

Omorose made a low sob, and Awa kept her head low so her mistress could not see her smile. She had finally forgiven Awa, or if not that, then at least realized that her servant was contrite. Awa would be washed clean in the tears of Omorose, and no longer need blame herself.

Except Omorose was not crying. As her mistress laughed and laughed, Awa supplied the tears she felt the occasion deserved, and only when the dry chuckles faded with the light did Awa daub her eyes with the rejected tunic she held clutched in both hands. Then Omorose demanded she explain what had transpired to allow her to leave the mountain, and with a wondrous ring to boot. Awa told her, in as clipped and dead a tone as the mindless ones giving their answers to any who asked.

"Well, beast," Omorose said when Awa had concluded, the night fully around them. "I have no use for lizard eggs, and as I cannot bury it in your wretched breast I do not want your dagger, either. I do want his book, though, and I will find it, and I will break your curse."

The last words obliterated the first, and that small patch of hope in Awa's breast grew larger and wilder, her palms damp, her mouth dry. "Together we'll find it, and once the curse is gone I'll find a way to make you all better. All better, I swear!"

"Once the curse is off I'll carve out your eyes and tongue and cunt and every other thing that gives you joy," Omorose snarled, and before Awa could draw back in hurt or lash out in anger her mistress had spun away and was dashing across the glacier. Then Awa's indignation trumped her naïve surprise, and she pushed Omorose's soul out of her fleeing body.

Except Omorose was already too far away, and moving farther with every instant. Appreciating just what she had done, and finally dispensing once and for all with her unrealistically charitable opinion of her beloved, she scrambled up in pursuit lest Omorose get away and make good on her threat. Awa could outrun anything on the mountain, and—her right leg was asleep and she tripped, falling in the snow.

Crying out in frustration, she got up and hobbled after Omorose, but by the time she had shaken the limb awake her reanimated mistress was gone, swallowed by the night mountains as neatly as Awa's tutor would swallow her spirit if she did not find his book, and find it before Omorose. Chastising herself, Awa returned to her hut and changed into the clothes she had made for Omorose. They fit perfectly, given that she had knit them based on her own proportions, and putting the dagger, the box of salamander eggs, the smoked meat, her blanket, and extra clothes into her leather bag, Awa turned her back on the only home she now remembered.

XIV
The Long Walk to Golgatha

Two individuals of the opposite sex will, if forced to go on a journey together, fall in love. Often begrudgingly, and with a great deal of reluctance by at least one of the parties, to be sure, but love will fall as surely as night after day. In the unlikely event that one of the two is homosexual, asexual, already in a loving relationship, or otherwise disinclined from romancing their traveling companion, love will fall all the harder, like cannon fire upon a charging cavalry; indeed, the less likely the two are to fall in love naturally, the more certain it is that the sojourn will bring them together.

Somehow, preposterous though it may sound, Awa and Manuel did not fall in love on their journey together, in spite of the wife at home who adored Manuel, in spite of Awa's lack of sexual interest in men, in spite of their mismatched personalities, and in spite of their growing and mutual fondness for one another. The best they could muster was a lessening of fear on Manuel's part and the honest—if painfully disinterested—observation on Awa's that Manuel was not so bad-looking, and that was only observed as the result of some self-deprecating jibe the artist had made about his own downward-angling nose. Pathetic.

The more time Manuel spent with Awa, though, the more he wanted to draw her—to sketch and then paint her likeness, and not upon wooden boards but canvases and abbey walls. Her full lips contrasted her hard cheeks in a splendid fashion, and the bulging muscles in her arms and legs endowed her with a body reminiscent of Minerva, tempting to an artist who had spent so long paying tribute to Venus-like figures. She was, in fact, just as strong as he, yet lacking the androgynous looks that characterized the few other women he had met who carried a sword instead of a spindle, and in her unorthodox and scarred fashion she represented the ideal model.

She would have none of it, at first, but eventually he wore her down with the same disarming charm he hoped would convince von Stein not to have him killed once he returned to the front and reported his mission a failure. He had stood over Awa for a long time the night before they set out on their journey together, the weight of the iron burdening hand and heart alike as he debated with himself whether or not to bind the witch. Part of what it had come down to was, unflattering a light though it may shine on Manuel's soul, her obvious fondness for his work—had she been a critic that would have made things much easier.

There were other factors, of course. The way she clung to the little piece of smut Bernardo had commissioned as she slept, for one, so much like the way Manuel's niece had held on to the doll he had made her when she was young, the doll she insisted he take with him for luck, the doll he had seen the witch remove from his bag, hold as reverently as a relic, and then carefully return to his bag as he lay dead on the floor of the cave, watching.

Manuel had wondered if she would struggle as he put the chains on her, if she would resist the bag and the blindfold, both of which would be necessary. He couldn't very well look at her after that, nor have her look at him. He didn't think she would fight him.

Fuck that, and fuck him for even thinking it.

Manuel the martyr, he had thought as he envisioned himself beheaded like John the Baptist or pierced with arrows like Sebastian or dunked in tar like... like... Manuel's memory for the gory ends of God's servants failed him there due to the stress of the moment, but his imagination helpfully supplied a picture of all three grisly ends happening to him at once, von Stein cackling, his family shrieking, but then he remembered Awa's expression when she had asked him if he was living as God would want, or however she had put it, and that was that. Manuel the martyr and the nameless witch, fast friends and road partners. Ludicrous.

Awa could not believe she had a living friend, and sometimes found herself victim to giggling fits to match the one Manuel had suffered in the cave. He was conceited, incredibly conceited, and thought he knew everything, and he came off as condescending even when he was obviously trying not to, but still. A friend, a breathing friend who knew she was a necromancer yet still shared a wineskin with her. Ludicrous.

"You seem like a decent girl," Manuel said once she had, to some extent, stopped frightening the ever-loving shit out of him. "So why traffic with the devil?"

"I'm a *woman*," Awa snorted. "And I've never dealt with your anti-god, if he even exists."

"But the raising of the dead is an evil act, rife with—"

"So I'm to understand the taking of lives is less evil, as you say, than the returning of them?" said Awa.

"Now, putting it like that is dodging the issue," Manuel argued.

"No it isn't," said Awa. "You kill other men for money, never knowing, as you yourself admitted, if they're desperately protecting their homes or simply after the lucre like you."

"I said that?" It did sound a bit like something he might say.

"You did. So you kill other men, possibly innocent men, for

money. You told me that first night it was to feed your family, but you seem like a smart enough man to earn wages doing something else. I, by contrast, restore life to those who have lost it, and not for money but to help those cut down before their time."

"Now, I don't know if Werner and—"

"An exception, and a rare one. These last few years I have scoured this world on a desperate errand, and as I often stopped in churchyards on my travels I found cause to raise the occasional corpse, it's true, but always, with only a few exceptions, at the behest of the spirits of the dead, souls returned from wherever the dead go."

"Ah!" said Manuel, careful as ever not to ask about her history. "But you admit there's a Heaven and a Hell! You said where the dead go! You did! And how can there be a Heaven without God?"

"I didn't say anything of the sort," said Awa, exasperated. "Do the sort of people you usually debate with tolerate these, these shenanigans?"

"The people I usually debate with aren't versed in arcane mysteries." The artist laughed.

"That's it, mysteries," said Awa. "You're learning. What I do is simply mysterious, not impossible or, as you would have it, evil. As a child I was taught that we are born even, balanced, and maintaining that balance is how we live a just life."

"You mean a balance of good and evil? That would justify evil actions, wouldn't it?"

"Using those words, yes, I do mean a balance of good and evil. I think that's what she meant, anyway, my mother. It's as sure as daybreak in the east that we will act in our own self-interest at the expense of others, but so long as we maintain a balance we are living... good lives."

"Leaving aside that not all evil is simple self-interest gone awry, would you admit then that something so unnatural as raising the dead is evil, and you have much to atone for?" Manuel asked cautiously.

"I have much to atone for, but I don't think necromancy is intrinsically good, evil, or unnatural. Much of what is natural seems more than to the ignorant."

"The first time I saw a gun fired I nearly shat myself," admitted Manuel, "but that's simple alchemy!"

"Simple." Awa nodded. "Doing what I do is quite simple, I assure you."

The artist was relieved to discover that his wrist was not nearly so injured as he had initially thought, and after a few days of drinking her special broth he could barely remember which arm he had hurt. Other aspects of her witchiness were taking more getting used to. Manuel's legs had locked up and his jaw had hung open like a busted trap when he noticed that one of her bare feet left cloven hoofprints in the muddy road, and when she lightly informed him that this had always been the case and he had just failed to notice on the march out from von Stein's camp he gave a little squeal of disbelief. Then she had bent over and made a bit of loose string appear between her fingers, her left foot instantly replaced with that of a goat. Manuel had nearly fainted, but when he recovered he wished to paint her more than ever, he *needed* to paint her. Out of the question, said Awa, secretly delighted.

"So there I am," Manuel said conspiratorially, though theirs was the only fire for many leagues on that cool spring night. "Falling-down drunk, with the abbot walking around my studio. If I'd been sober I'd have told him I was ill and he should come back the next day, but if I'd been sober I wouldn't've needed him to come back, would I? Normally Katharina, my wife, would've run'em off, but if she'd been there she wouldn't've let me get so drunk, either, would she? So in he's come, middle of the day, wanting to see my work fore the commission gets under way."

"So when your wife's not around you just get drunk all the time?" Awa asked, more than a little in the staggering way herself. They had reached their last four skins and opted to have a proper occasion with them instead of sipping the vinegary swill for the rest of their journey. "Very responsible."

"It's not like that!" Manuel protested. "I was celebrating the commission, wasn't I? And the brandy was stiffer than I'd thought, and I'd been too excited to break the fast fore meeting the abbot that morn, and afterwards I'd needed a drink, and there he was, no more'n an hour or two after I'd left his abbey, sneeeeakin in like some white mouser fattened on a night's rattin."

"Mouser? Rattin?"

"Mouser's a cat, isn't she?" said Manuel. "Called such because they go ratting... eating rats. Mice? Mouse? Mouser?"

"You're doing it again!" Awa guffawed, her honest laughter still grating and harsh from neglect. "You and your animals!"

"Can I finish?!" Manuel shouted in mock indignation. "Can I finish?!"

"Finish, finish." Awa waved him on. "Tell me about how the abbot had a friend who was a snake, or maybe a fish, and the Pope who's an owl, or the dog-priests or whatever."

"Thank you, m'lady." Manuel bowed so low he nearly singed the feather in his cap on their roaring bonfire. "So the abbot."

"The cat abbot. Cabbot?"

"The same. So in he comes, and I'm too slanted to protest or send'em off, and I start showin'em around. So—if you had an abbot in your studio what's brimming with pictures of saints being martyred and angels and biblical scenes and even antique scenes of mythology and all, what do you think'd be the first thing I show'em?"

"What's the commission supposed to be?" Awa asked after giving the question far more thought than it deserved.

"Conversion of Constantine. He's an old emperor. Was pagan, went straight."

"Oh. Something from his book, then? You said you had biblical pictures, right?"

"Sure." Manuel nodded. "Lots of it. But you agree then, dear friend, that maybe showin the abbot of my fucking local job my personal collection of *nude women* might not've been the keenest idea I've struck on?"

"Manuel," said Awa, setting her skin down and blearily trying to meet his erratic gaze. "The two ladies I've seen of yours are the finest, best things I've ever seen. I think you should show anyone who will look, I think you should show the world, I think... yes, yes, show him the naked women. Why not?"

"He's the abbot," Manuel protested. "He might catch a peek around the baths, sure, but vows of chastity! He's sworn off it, hasn't he? And I'm not talking tasteful religious pieces with a little tit, either, I'm talking raw stuff, vivid."

"What's the matter with vivid?" said Awa defensively. "You say your god's an artist, and if I were to agree with your beliefs I'd say the finest of all his pieces is women. Some of them, anyway."

"And you'll hear no disagreements from me on that," said Manuel, trying to maneuver back to his story. "The one I made for Bernardo, though, is tame compared to some of my private pieces. I'm talking top-to-bottom, *vivid* detail. Things an abbot shouldn't be interested in."

"Why not? If you say—"

"Can I finish? Thank you." Manuel sighed, too drunk to acknowledge or care that his story was more or less ruined. "So I show'em the nudes, lasses spreading their legs, pushing their chests up, bottoms out, you name it. And he's makin these noises in his throat like—"

"Like a sheepdog! Like a sparrow! Like a—"

"Like a angry abbot, damn it! Like a really furious abbot, alright!?"

Her laughter was punctuated with a sound that might have been "alright."

"And then...bam! I'm sober as a churchm—I'm sober as he is, dead sober, well, not really *sober* sober, but a helluva lot more sober than I've been, and I realize what I've done but there's *nothing* for it and he's turning bright red and he's shakin and then I stop worryin bout losing the commission because he's about to keel over dead of shock, and then I'll have a dead abbot on my hands and..."

"And?" Awa said when Manuel did not continue. "And what?"

"And"—Manuel grinned—"and he turns to me, and says, *My boy, I'll buy the lot*!"

"Oh, Manuel," said Awa, suddenly feeling more sober than she actually was. "Your art won him over! That's, that's so...it's so wonderful!"

"Well." Manuel deflated a bit. "*I* thought it was funny. Cause...cause I thought he was horrified? But he was really just excited? Abbots aren't supposed to be interested in women."

"I still don't see why not," said Awa, and, picking up on his disappointment, she added, "And it's funny, too, really it is, it's just kind of beautiful, too, isn't it? Not even him who's supposed to go without to please his god can resist your ladies!"

"Yeah?" Manuel blinked at her.

"Yes! You didn't sell them all, did you? I'd love to see your vivid ones, Manuel, I'd love it so much!" Awa had gotten to her feet.

"Well, I sold those," said Manuel, "but I've got loads more, and yeah, once I go home you should visit Bern, I'll show you all my ladies."

"Yes!" Awa spun around on her invisible hoof. "Pretty, pretty! I love your ladies, Manuel!"

"I've got one in my pack of Katharina, I think you saw her when I, when I..."

"Was dead? I did indeed, Niklaus Manuel Deutsch of Bern, and I tell you now, on my word, I did not know one could fall in love with a picture before seeing her, and the smaller one I kept. I wanted to press the plank to my lips and..." Awa stopped spinning. She knew from her tutor's nigh-endless ridicule what men thought of women who liked other women, and for all his open-minded qualities Manuel might—

"You like, *like* girls? Like I do?" Manuel blinked. "Ohhhhhhhh. I see. I do."

"You do?" Awa gnawed the inside of her cheek.

"I do," said Manuel. "My friend Monique's, er, lady-minded, too. Likes girls, I mean. So that's, you know, not a big deal. To me. Most women, right, and men, they don't get it, but yeah. Women *are* beautiful, aren't they?"

"Yes," Awa said, amazed yet again by her fabulous friend. She might cry, and of course as soon as she thought that her eyes started in with their old dampening.

"And I'll pass on the compliment to my wife." Manuel frowned at his empty skin, and seeing Awa's confused expression said, "The model. For the bigger one? Curly hair. Katharina. Don't use her for the commissions, she asked me not to, the one I did for Bernardo's a pretty little whore was with us just fore we hit Lombardy. Can't recollect her name but she was decent enough a subject. *She'd* make a good Salome, yes indeed..."

Awa had stopped paying attention, too guilt-ridden over her amorous thoughts regarding Manuel's wife. She had nearly taken matters in hand while looking at the portrait, and with the artist—and husband—lying behind her watching, a little dead and powerless to speak. Awa imagined herself sliding her hand down the trousers she had stolen from the dead Bernardo and shuddered—could they have ever been friends if she had done that, if he had seen what a nasty little beast she was? Could she—

"What?" Awa's mouth said, capturing the attention of her mind. He had said something.

"I said," Manuel repeated, "I'll introduce you to Monique. My friend? She likes whores but I always imagined that's cause they're more inclined to keep secrets and play different. Never know, you two might hit it off—"

"No thanks," Awa said quickly.

"Already got someone?"

"No!"

"Oh," said Manuel, finally appreciating that he had hit a nerve. "Well, you know, if you change your mind..."

They stood together by the fire for some time, utterly missing the many opportunities to look into one another's eyes and cast aside their old loves, the myriad chances to at least see if they enjoyed the taste of one another's wine-stained lips, and eventually they made their beds and lay down beside one another. Manuel fell asleep first, snoring loudly, which meant the first watch fell to Awa. For all her earlier anxiety she had no compunction against fishing out the small sketch of the whore she had taken from Bernardo's satchel and creeping just far enough into the underbrush to be out of sight while still being able to clearly see the image. She enjoyed herself a bit there, and with some effort was able to keep the memory of Omorose from souring things until she was done.

The von Stein problem came to occupy more and more of Manuel's thoughts as they neared the end of their short journey together. Assassinating the man was, while delectably appealing, out of the question—his guards even followed him to the privy. He would also expect Manuel to try something, and would have taken measures. The man was, in a word, a shit, but he had not made his reputation and fortune by being negligent or deficient in his tactics, be they the stratagem of the actual battlefield or the political arena.

Manuel the martyr pressed on down the road, and when they hit the river where they were to part ways he generously offered to escort Awa back to the very spot where she had been abducted. Awa was more than happy to accept, and so upriver they went as Manuel's brow grew ever moister. Every bole in every tree looked like a tortured saint, every ray of sunshine cutting through the gnarled canopy overhead reminding him of the judgment awaiting him. He really ought to put himself on a plank before meeting von Stein, and then entrust Awa with returning it to his wife. Yes, that was quite good, actually, and—

"This is it," said Awa, breaking away from the river and cutting between two willows that hunched low on the bank like overladen gleaners. "Back in here. Yes, there's my old tunic."

Manuel saw what must be her old clothes trampled down in the sandy soil and followed her to the place where she had decided to give up on ever finding the necromancer's book. Two obvious graves were on the edge of the clearing but he did not inquire, instead turning his attention to the pile of dead limbs and logs stacked in the center of the clearing. Awa knelt beside it and then crawled into the heap of twisted, dry wood until only her feet jutted out. Then she backed out, a clutch of round stones in her fist, and after rooting around on the other side of the woodpile she picked up a nice-looking wooden box and into this she deposited her rocks. Witch business did not bear prying into, by Manuel's thinking, but then she looked up at him and smiled sheepishly.

"I was going to let them go. I still will, before he takes me, but the hassle we had getting your flint working these last nights convinced me I might have use for them yet. Ah!" Awa noticed her old satchel hanging from the goat willow where she had left it, and loosening the straps she saw that the leather pack had kept her extra clothes dry. She quickly stripped off her stolen trousers and shirt and changed back into her worn leggings and tunic, Manuel blushing but not looking away. He had his obligations as an artist, after all.

"So this is it, eh?" Manuel said after they had eaten the rest of her meat for lunch. "You go your way and I go mine."

"Yes," said Awa, hopefully adding, "If you're sure you don't need my help in dealing with your master."

"I've got that worked out," Manuel lied.

"Good," said Awa, and glancing at the ibex-horn dagger she had retrieved from her old pack and fixed to her belt, she took the stiletto she had taken from Manuel during her escape and handed it back to its owner. "It was my pleasure to use your blade, Niklaus Manuel Deutsch of Bern."

"Keep it," Manuel said, standing up and brushing the sand off his legs. "We call them Swiss Swords, and excluding the commissions I put one on every painting, so I've got plenty."

"What?"

"My signature," said Manuel. "I draw a little dagger. A little cheesy, maybe, but it's my flourish."

"No, I mean . . . I can really keep it?" Awa was crying suddenly and silently, the tears running down her cheeks making Manuel take a step back.

"Yes, of course. Please. And if all goes well with von Stein I should be back in Bern before winter, so do call. My house is white with green trim, on Gerechtigkeitsgasse. If—"

"My name is Awa," said she, and Manuel nodded, recognizing from her previous stark refusal to tell him that she put a high commodity on keeping it secret. "Awa."

"Thank you, Awa," said Manuel awkwardly. He should be frightened that she would kill him or curse him, he knew, but somehow he could not raise a single hackle. "Well then."

"Do you think I could find work in Bern?" Awa said, wiping her eyes.

"I don't really know..." Manuel suddenly imagined her showing up on his stoop, all Moorish and witchy, and that got his heart going. "I don't know if it would be safe, I mean, people are scared of Moors, and what, what do you do? Other than, you know, knife things? Witch things?"

Awa shrugged, not really needing the reminder that she was a pariah but accepting it just the same. "I can make traps and catch small animals with them, and I can clean and cook them, and I can sew and I can knit and I can turn wool into yarn, and I can heal wounds, and I can read, and I can—"

"Enough, enough." Manuel smiled. "You're overqualified to be landvogt, er, bailiff, let alone a washerwoman or servant. I—"

"You..." Awa watched him, the smile on Manuel's face widening and contorting into a very strange look indeed. "You what?"

"I know a leech who was haunting the camp when I left, a Swiss leech calling himself Para-something. Everyone thought he was a magus, a sorcerer, and he certainly didn't do much to counter the rumor. I drank with him a few nights before I met you, before the battle, and one thing that struck me about him was his openness to witchery. That's right...he was almost obsessed with the occult, was saying we ought to be learning from witches instead of burning them."

"Really?" said Awa. "Why didn't you tell me about him earlier?"

"Everything's been so crazy I didn't think...Now, I'm not saying you ought to tell him you're a witch or anything, that could be really bad, but if you pass yourself off as some sort of heathen healer—"

"I could pass myself off as a convert," Awa interjected. "I know enough about your faith to pass."

"Whatever," Manuel said excitedly. "But we could enlist his

help, maybe. I know he absolutely despises von Stein, and the reverse, which is good news for us, and had some harsh words regarding the Inquisition as well. That way you could be close at hand whenever my mercenary days are done, and then I could help you get established in Bern."

It was the worst plan imaginable, and Manuel knew it. The Swiss doctor was definitely a drunkard and probably a madman, and such a scheme would involve bringing Awa back within von Stein's easy snatching if he should find out about her. *Manny, your little cowherd? Why, he walked in with a Moorish woman yesterday, I think she's staying with that doctor you hate. Shall I fetch them, sir?*

Just as Manuel opened his mouth to tell Awa to never mind, it could never work, forget it, he saw the overjoyed expression on her face, and that decided it. They gathered their wares and left the camp by the river, two daggers and Bernardo's sword at her belt, a hand-and-a-half at Manuel's, and together they marched back toward Manuel's judgment. For fuck's sake.

XV
The Judgment of Milan

As Manuel entered the lavish room where von Stein waited, he realized why both sides of the doorway were smashed open when the palatial residence itself had been spared from the artillery their French employer had clobbered the besieged city with the year before—that great big fucking desk the bastard moved everywhere with him would not have fit through the frame, and so his men had widened the opening to fit their commander's prized piece of furniture. Anything smaller would only call attention to the man's girth, Manuel knew, but did he really need a desk built of solid ebony? The men who had carried the thing up all three flights of stairs had wondered the same thing, and at much greater length.

"Manny, my cocksucking little Judas!" von Stein crowed, standing to meet Manuel. This did not relax the soldier in the least, especially when he saw that the commander had traded his old hand cannon for an expensive-looking matchlock pistol, the cord already cocked back and smoldering.

"Good afternoon, sir." Manuel bowed, wondering if the gun would actually penetrate his skull or if the shot would merely mangle his face into a pulpy mess of bone and tissue. His sword had been confiscated at the door, which was a shame as he had resolved to murder the prick rather than grovel or hop around his own execution. Such harsh resolutions had always been abandoned in the past, but it was nice to have the option that a handy weapon afforded. "How's your wife?"

"Very well, very well," said von Stein, his cheeks beaming, his nose valiantly resisting the sneeze that the feather of smoke wafting from his matchcord was trying to coax out. "And yours?"

"I don't know," said Manuel, lightheaded with nervousness. "How is she?"

Were Manuel a bachelor he would not have given a wet fart for the dance he now maneuvered through, he would have come back with blade flashing or not at all, but he had a wife, and he had a niece to look after, and he had put them both in mortal danger for the sake of a confirmed heretic and witch. While von Stein was not so mad as to needlessly harm innocent women and children he was certainly ruthless enough to slaughter a thousand families if he found some advantage in it. Manuel knew this because he had entered towns as they fell, had personally heard his captain give free rein to his men to do what they wished to those naughty, naughty besieged citizens who had callously locked the invaders outside their walls.

"How should I know?" asked von Stein. "I've been out defending cities and waging wars, not taking holidays with my chummy-chums. Where are your chummy-chums, Manny?"

"Dead," said Manuel, meeting the man's gaze, which meant looking over the muzzle of the pistol. "All of them."

"Oh my!" Von Stein gasped and staggered about in an exaggerated swoon. "How tragic! How dreadful! How perfectly predictable."

"I told you to let me pick my own men," said Manuel, and forced his legs to march toward the gun, toward his martyrdom. With every step he took, von Stein took a step back, until the larger man had almost reached the rear wall and the artist had reached the front of his desk. Then Manuel pulled out one of the uncomfortable chairs and sat down, still eyeing von Stein. "Aren't you going to ask me how Spain was?"

"How was Spain?"

"I didn't go."

"Ah." Von Stein advanced on the table as Manuel took the open bottle of wine next to the commander's glass, gave it a sniff, and then tipped it back. He wondered if it would be the last thing he ever tasted. "And why didn't you go to Spain?"

Manuel wiped his mouth. "The witch got away before we got there."

"Ah. I thought you said there was no such thing as witches. I thought you said she was a madwoman." Von Stein rounded his table, which meant squeezing between the desk and the wall. He kept his pistol on Manuel.

"I was wrong," Manuel chortled. "Very wrong. She's a witch."

"And how did she escape, Manny?" Von Stein had lowered his voice and was moving behind Manuel now but the soldier did not turn to follow his captain, instead taking another pull from the bottle and looking straight ahead. This was much closer to how he had always imagined his death, a dignified discussion followed by a quick and brutal act of violence. No cowering in a cave, whimpering at witches, just pure, self-righteous pontificating concluding with his martyrdom. Better, then, but still bad enough to sour the wine in his stomach.

"They tried to rape her, and once the chains were off she stole my dagger and killed both Kristobels and Bernardo." Being entirely honest with von Stein was actually quite a bit of fun, but while he dearly wished to see the look on the man's face, Manuel did not want to spoil his presentation by turning toward him.

"I see," von Stein murmured, just behind Manuel now. "And what were you doing at the time?"

"Killing Werner," said Manuel, and almost giggled.

"I see," said von Stein, and Manuel felt the metal cylinder push through his hair and rest gently against the back of his head. At least his face would be spared, and it seemed his family would as well. Manuel was almost disappointed, with death so close, that von Stein lacked the imagination for a more fitting martyring. "You know what that means, don't you?"

"I don't get the pay you offered to deliver her?" Manuel smirked, closing his eyes and imagining his wife and niece in the garden, von Stein's sharp intake of breath the wind stirring the ivy on the side of the house. He heard the pistol's mechanism clicking, metal ratcheting on metal, and marveled at how impossibly slow time had become. Had the gun gone off already?

"You could at least act contrite, you little cow-fucker," said von Stein, removing the pistol from Manuel's scalp and cuffing him hard on the back of the head as he went back around the desk. Manuel opened one eye and then the other as von Stein settled into his chair, muttering to himself as he removed the smoldering matchcord from his gun and dropped it into his wineglass, the dregs bubbling as the cord hissed out. Tossing the priceless pistol onto the table between them, von Stein crossed his hands on his stomach, pursed his lips, and frowned long and hard at Manuel.

"I'm sorry?" Manuel eventually said to break the silence.

Still wordlessly eyeing Manuel, von Stein opened his desk and took out a letter. Letting his dour gaze fall away from the soldier to the parchment in his hand, he opened the letter and pretended to read it with the same ham-fisted mock surprise he had employed when talking with Manuel before.

"Do you know what this is?" von Stein finally whispered, shaking the letter at Manuel. "Do you?"

"It's a letter saying I never delivered the witch?" Manuel hazarded, but von Stein shook his head slowly, sadly, as if he were a doctor bearing exceptionally bad news.

"It's a fucking pardon, is what it is," said von Stein.

"Oh?" Manuel leaned forward and reached for the letter. "From whom?"

"From God, you ungrateful bastard," said von Stein, putting the letter back in his desk before Manuel could take it. "And me."

"That's awfully generous of the two of you," said Manuel, hoping his voice was not shaking as badly as his boots.

"You—" Von Stein pursed his lips again, shaking his head even more vigorously. "You are a lucky, lucky boy, Niklaus. Kahlert's been excommunicated."

"Who?" Manuel was terrible with names, but that one sounded familiar.

"The Inquisitor! The one you were supposed to take her to?!" Von Stein finally lost it, which pleased Manuel immensely. "You... you need to get your shit together, Niklaus, and quick!"

"So the Inquisitor's been sacked, is that it?"

"I thought his demanding we find a particular witch in our vicinity or lose our indulgences sounded harsh, unreasonable." Von Stein sighed. "*In our vicinity.* Apparently that same letter went out to every commander, captain, and mayor within five hundred leagues of Barcelona, and while the cardinals were discovering the letters, firing the bastard that sent them, and sending us retractions and apologies we were busy actually capturing the bloody witch and sending you lot to deliver her. So as I don't care for being threatened by distant Church functionaries"—*didn't hear you saying that the last time we spoke,* thought Manuel—"I'm actually rather pleased she got away instead of being handed over to this Kahlert cunt."

"Happy day," said Manuel, having swallowed quite a bit more wine than he had intended during the captain's posturing.

"Indeed it is. You missed out on most of the fun outside, I'm afraid. We stumbled over another Imperial contingent a day out, and much sport was had. Mind, they had some tasty guns." Von Stein nodded at the matchlock on the table between them, the pistol inlaid with silver filigree. "But rougher though they may look, our guns were just as loud, and my maid kept her men cool and fire was met with fire, though I gather she's caught a different sort of fire herself. A shame, that, she'll be difficult to replace. We've already hung all the Imperials we caught, and the bulk of them have run home, tails tucked, without even knocking on the door of this fair city. They're saying the Emperor might be out of the fight with this one."

"Good show, sir," said Manuel, taking another pull from the bottle. "So you've led my countrymen to victory over your countrymen and your former masters, and all for the fucking Milanese."

"All for my fucking self," said von Stein, opening his desk again. "And the Kakerlake King, of course—the Milanese stay fucked and French, which is perhaps redundant. If you're really interested in politics you ought to pay more attention to whom you're working for, Manny. As for countrymen, well, your countrymen are my countrymen, and the word is Maximilian had even more Swiss marching this way than us, so be thankful they changed their minds and went home before brother had a chance to slay brother, eh? Or might you have relished the chance to stick it in some Basel-backer, or whoever you Bernese are squabbling with this week?"

"All members of the Confederacy are Swiss," Manuel said numbly, suddenly wondering how many of the saints he had martyred along the road to Milan were cowherds or merchants' sons from the next canton over and not, as he had previously assumed, Imperial. Both sides were paying, so why should he think all the Swiss would gravitate to one foreign banner instead of whoever approached them first? And why the fuck should it matter if the boys—the *men*, he corrected himself—if the men he had killed were confederates or not? They were saints just the same...

"—Manny, and we both know who's in charge here." Manuel might have sighed at von Stein's redundant tapping of his own chest if the man's other hand had not taken another saltpeter-soaked cord out of his desk and lit it on one of his gauche purple candles. Manuel might have snatched the gun away but he was a little drunk and by the time he fully registered what was happening von Stein had picked up his pistol and cinched the sputtering cord into place after cocking the hammer. Then he stood and moved around the desk as Manuel finished the bottle, the artist's hand around its neck to bash von Stein if he got crazy. Manuel had listened to far too much of the man's shit today to allow himself to go quietly and—

"The campaign's over," von Stein said. "For me, at least. I'm going home, and suggest you do the same. The Emperor's fled and Milan's saved, which means we're finished."

"But I haven't got enough money yet!" Manuel protested.

"Then find a new master," von Stein sniffed. "Or go back to painting. Everyone else will be nipping off, and those who actually helped defend the city earned more than enough to be happy for quite a few years to come, so you might be lonely if you stay."

"Defend from what!? You said the fucking Imperials never showed up!"

Seeing von Stein's expression, Manuel shifted his approach.

"I would've helped!" He stood to face von Stein, the bottle still gripped in his left hand. "You sent me away or I would've been here, you know it!"

"I do." Von Stein nodded. "But you weren't, and you disobeyed my orders. I'm a gentleman, Manny, not a cheap, cheating little peasant, and if you had done as I told you I would have paid you for it, even though it would have pained me, knowing as we do now what a fraud that Kahlert turned out to be. So if you had followed orders you would be just as rich as if you helped guard the city, if not more so, but instead you played the martyr, strolling in here with your head held high like you'd just fucked the Duchess of Ferrara *and* her daughter instead of losing a little girl and getting all your men killed. You Bernese can't take a punch to the nose or a hard shit without slapping yourselves on the back."

"What am I going to do?" said Manuel, as much to himself as to his gloating captain. He was smarter than von Stein, much smarter, and nobler, for being of a lower birth, and a hell of a lot more handsome and talented, so how the fuck did he always end up with the short end?

"Paint," said von Stein, waving his gun in the air with a flourish. "I'll commission a piece for my wife, and another for my mistress. Just don't go getting them mixed up!"

"Paint." Manuel sighed, knowing too well just how poorly that paid.

"Don't worry, Manny," said von Stein, putting his free hand on Manuel's shoulder and leading him back toward the door. "I'm flush as a virgin's cheek on her first poke, so expect a fair price for your work. Which hand do you paint with?"

"My right," said Manuel, still distracted from the wine and his pardon and his diminished prospects, and so he failed to notice von Stein stepping behind him until the gun went off. He shot the fucking bottle, Manuel thought as the glass exploded and smoke enveloped them both, and then he realized his left hand had caught fire. Stumbling forward, he held his arm in front of him and saw a ragged hole punched through most of his palm, his middle two fingers attached to the rest of his hand by nothing more than raw, scorched skin. Then the blood came and he reeled, collapsing on the carpet as von Stein delivered a few lazy kicks to his backside.

"—orders, you self-righteous little shit," said von Stein, and through the massive gaps on either side of the door Manuel saw the guards storming the room. The last thing he heard as two men scooped him up was von Stein saying, "And don't take him to the good leech, give him to that batty fraud. The boy's fond of witches."

XVI
Syphilis and the Magus

"Theophrastus Philippus Aureolus Bombastus von Hohenheim," said the ugly little man as he bowed. "But you may call me Doctor Paracelsus."

For a moment Awa could not speak, amazed by the length of his name and trying to commit it to memory.

"Right," said Manuel, cracking his knuckles and trying desperately to forget that if his reunion with his captain did not go exceptionally well he might be dead within the hour. "And remember, Doctor, von Swine *hates* Moors, so not a word."

"The lady's presence in my clinic will be a secret known only to the inner sanctum of we three now present, for I shall adorn her as a bandaged nun upon your departure," said Paracelsus. "In truth, I doubt your commander's prejudice to those of the darkest land can compare with my aversion to his good graces, and so upon calling in the future request Sister Gloria instead of whatever unpronounceable, to our honest tongues, and esoteric name the Moor has gone by in the past."

"The Moor?" Awa blinked. "Me?"

"Know thyself, Sister Gloria, and be free!" said Paracelsus. "What herbs do you use in your practice?"

"Ah, wormwood," said Awa, looking fearfully at Manuel. This

so-called doctor was barely older than she and very clearly blind drunk. "Lots and lots of wormwood."

"A fine plant, useful in so many applications! Those with trouble of stomach would do well to sample its leaves, and the root, when mashed and mixed with—"

"Right, take care, Sister Gloria," said Manuel, backing out of the small room Paracelsus had ushered them into. "I'll be by to visit from time to time."

"Be careful," Awa called after him, but then Paracelsus had seized her arm, looked her up and down for the umpteenth time, muttered something in a language even she did not recognize, and then set to swaddling her with a roll of thin white linen bandages. After this layer he provided her with a musty, oversized habit that had a small cut and a large dark stain on the right shoulder, and finally gave her white gloves. Only her eyes, nose, and shards of her temples were not obscured by the bandages, and he then smeared a pale ointment on these visible patches of skin.

"Fortunate for you I had this Spirit of Saturn, Sister Gloria," Paracelsus said as he rinsed the lead paste off his fingers. "I wish you to know that in this mortal flesh you have found an ageless hunger for knowledge, a timeless receptivity to the arcane and the so-called unnatural. We both know that all things come from nature, do we not, that God is a gardener, yes?"

"Ah," said Awa, simultaneously terrified and curious. "I think—"

"You do, you do." Paracelsus bobbed his head. "How many would listen, though? How many would admit that a Moor and a woman are both capable of thought, and the skull of even the *Moorish woman* must be tapped for milk like a coconut from her savage shores, the milk of knowledge, the elixir of information!"

"What?" Awa took a step back, resolving to put the man down like a crazed animal if he tried to bore into her skull to get whatever milk he thought might be there, friend of Manuel's or not. Their journey to Milan had been uneventful, although they had needed to hide from the retreating Imperial mercenaries as they approached the contested city, and upon gaining the walls Awa discovered it was unlike any place she had ever been, an overwhelming jumble of impressive buildings and once-impressive buildings reduced to rubble and ruin. Now, in the broken heart of Milan and the doctor's clinic, Awa felt far less optimistic about her current prospects—the man was deranged, and the entire low building echoed with screams and wails.

The actual hospital lay deeper in the city and was much larger and cleaner, but Paracelsus's clinic was not intended for war wounds and mundane illnesses. Rather, the warehouse he had cordoned off with clothesline and sheets into something resembling an infirmary was devoted to treating the Great Pox, and with the siege finally ended the doctor was overjoyed to eject the combatants he had been forced to tend and return to his never-ending supply of syphilitics. After he finished adorning Awa in her disguise he led her out of the crowded storeroom and down the makeshift hallway, pointing from one curtained-off chamber to another and rattling off the required care.

"But what is it?" Awa finally managed to sneak in a question as Paracelsus took a pull from his flask of schnapps. "I know what a pox is, but what is this particular pox? How is it caused and how is it spread and—"

"The French Disease?" said Paracelsus, and, noting her continued confusion, he clapped a pudgy hand to his forehead. "The Italian Disease? Dutch Disease? Wherever-the-soldiers-or-sailors-or-whores-come-from Disease? I suppose they don't teach such things in the convents, of course. I suspect it's caused through contact with the infected, especially by coitus, intercourse, *sex*. The inflicted dribble their noxious fluids into one another, not that those high asses at the university would admit it. So long as you live up to your habit you won't have much to fear, but tell that to all my deserters. It's you and I for now, sister, everyone else has abandoned us for the *real* hospital." The scorn in his voice was palpable to even a novice in the ways of nuance such as Awa.

"But what does it do?" asked Awa, all of the patients obscured by the hanging sheets.

"Why, it ravages the body and destroys the mind!" said Paracelsus with obvious relish, and suddenly snatching her arm, he dragged her between two curtains. A patient lay in a bed, staring at the ceiling. "Behold the wages of fornication, the cost of rutting like a beast!"

Awa took a step toward the man. At first she took him to be an animated corpse, meaning Paracelsus knew more than he let on, and meaning she was in a great deal of danger. She turned to the doctor, convinced he was performing some strange experiments on the dead and masquerading it as a pox epidemic. Then she heard the patient's wheezing breath and turned back in horror, disgusted and fascinated that life was capable of persisting in so decayed a vessel.

The man's face—no, his entire body—was rotting, the stench wafting from him something she had not experienced in quite some time. Paracelsus watched curiously as his new nurse approached the man instead of recoiling in horror. She did not even hold the clove oil–soaked sleeve of her habit to her nose, instead leaning in to get a closer look at the poor, damned mercenary.

The spirit of the malady thrived in the man like maggots in a dead boar's belly, Awa could see, the invader pulsing and wriggling through its victim, gobbling up spirit, flesh, and mind alike. She had never encountered so virulent and terrible a creature, and leaned ever closer, staring with wide eyes as it worked. She wondered if the little stowaway spirit she had picked up from Omorose their first night together would have grown into something so powerful if she had not caught and destroyed it early on. No, she decided, this was much worse.

"Of course, there's not much to do for them at this point but hope they die quickly, the doomed wretches," said Paracelsus. The patient's eyes grew wide at this and he tried to speak, a gurgling rasp escaping his blistered lips. Paracelsus frowned. "You *are* Swiss, aren't you? Do you happen to speak any other languages, sister?"

"A few," said Awa in Spanish, and, lapsing back into German, whispered to the patient, "Would you like to die?"

The man jerked away, shaking his head, and Awa withdrew her hand from his moist shoulder. Paracelsus was watching her curiously as she turned back around, and, also in Spanish, he said, "This isn't that sort of clinic."

"Oh? And what sort of clinic is this?" Awa followed him out into the hall.

"More than just hospice, if that's what you're driving at," said Paracelsus. "Your task is to see the patients remain hydrated, fed, and as comfortable as their loathsome condition allows. The administering of any cures is the sole province of myself."

"So there's a cure?" said Awa.

"There's a plant in New Spain that's said to be effective, but I haven't been able to lay hands on it. This leaves us with the traditional remedy, though I've yet to hit on a wholly effective method of administering the hydrargyrum."

"What's hydrargyrum? A plant?"

"Quicksilver," said Paracelsus. "Tell me, Sister Gloria, would you spend a night in the arms of Venus if you knew it led to a life of mercury?"

"What?"

"Nor I, though I've pioneered some new delivery methods for the treatment, certainly more credible means than the fumigation those charlatans taught."

"The charlatans of the Schwarzwald?" Awa asked, his use of the term nearly identical in context to that of her old tutor's.

"Who?" Paracelsus blinked. "No, Ferrara, though the piss-gazers weren't much better at Vienna. So-called universities, both as riddled with ignorance and superstition as these lost souls are riddled with pox, and with the same result—infection, proliferation, death."

"Oh," said Awa. "Can I see this quicksilver?"

"Certainly," said Paracelsus. "I needed to refill my flask anyway."

Back in the storeroom, Paracelsus lit a lamp and set it on his cluttered table. Then he took a small metal pail with a wooden lid from a low shelf and heaved it onto the desk with a sloshing sound. Then he took two flasks from his pocket, one clay and one steel, and a small metal funnel. First he removed the stopper from the clay flask and knocked it back to make sure it was empty, then inserted the funnel and poured an amber liquid from a bottle on the table into the container, his lips counting off several seconds and then stopping the pour at the brink of overfilling his flask. Capping and pocketing it, he took a sip from the open bottle and passed it to Awa before placing the funnel in the steel container.

Awa coughed on the liquor, prompting Paracelsus to snatch it back. "Careful, little sister, this is the real stuff. Now hold the beaker straight, over the bucket."

She obliged, savoring the heat the liquor had brought to her gasping breath. Then she saw a stranger marvel still as Paracelsus removed the lid from the pail and turned to retrieve a ladle. The iron bucket, which appeared to be lined with some sort of stone or wood, was full of molten metal, its surface rippling, yet it emitted no heat. Spooning up the liquid, he beamed at Awa and motioned for her to hold the flask and funnel over the surface. She did so and he slowly filled it to the brim with the quicksilver.

It was beautiful and alive with spirit, utterly unlike iron or other dead metals, and the doctor must have noticed her fascination for he took the bottle from her, pocketed it and the funnel, and bid her hold out her cupped hand. She did, and he ladled a little of the mercury into her palm.

"Oh!" Awa let the cold fluid roll around, and bending her pinky inward was able to brush the surface of the tiny pool. Unlike blood or grease it did not leave a residue on her fingertip, and she was about to taste it when Paracelsus raised his eyebrows and pointed back to the bucket. She reluctantly let it run down the side of her hand into its pail, and he put the lid back on and returned it to the shelf.

"I've been known to get my flasks mixed up," Paracelsus said with a wink. "Not that the debauchees complain to have a taste of schnapps, mind you."

"That's truly wondrous," said Awa. "But is it really a good cure if it's poisonous in its own right?"

"What makes you think it's poisonous?" said Paracelsus, not angry or accusatory, but with some other, stranger emotion in his eager, bulging eyes. "You were unacquainted with it, I believe?"

"Oh." Awa swallowed, knowing she could not very well tell him she had asked the spirits of the mercury as she held them in her palm. "I—"

Awa was saved for a second time by Manuel as he was assisted into the clinic by two of von Stein's guards, his clumsily bandaged hand spattering blood on the hay-covered floor as he was half dragged up the hallway. His low moans would have been lost amidst the usual syphilitic symphony of the clinic had they not come in through the door beside the storeroom, and so Awa went straight out, followed by Paracelsus. Any protests the doctor had about bringing a non–venereally afflicted patient into his clinic instead of the regular hospital were silenced by Awa and the guards, all of whom turned angrily on Paracelsus when he started in.

"Oh, it's Manuel, isn't it?" Paracelsus finally observed as the guards trotted out of the stinking clinic. "Let's get him a bed, then."

They made Manuel as comfortable as they could in a cot beside the storeroom, no real distance from the stench and cries of the infected. Paracelsus examined the hand, lamenting that Manuel had not taken von Stein's weapon. "I possess an elixir that goes on the blade instead of the cut, and had we the tool of your injury we might undo its mischief!"

"Sounds like a witch to me," Manuel said through gritted teeth when the doctor went to his storeroom, leaving him alone with Awa. "How're you getting on?"

"Quiet," said Awa. "He did this to you, your master?"

"Yeah," said Manuel. "But I gather that's the worst of it. That Inquisitor that wanted you's been kicked out of the Church, so his order to catch you's void."

"Did you find out how this Inquisitor knew of me, or why he wants me?"

"I was a little fucking busy being shot to ask, actually," said Manuel. "If you'd care to ask von Swine yourself—"

"I intend to," said Awa, getting out of the chair she had brought beside the pallet. "And I'll also ask him where he gets off threatening the family and injuring the flesh of a man of more character and worth than the god he claims to worship."

"Hold on, hold on," said Manuel, catching her wrist with his good hand. "Damage is done, isn't? And you're off his mind as well, which was a boon I didn't expect but am happy for. So sit down, calm down, and tell me how the doctor's treating you."

"I'll tend to you." Awa lowered her voice. "His remedies are... suspect. He uses wet metals that don't seem to do much but make him a little crazy."

"Oh." Manuel nodded. "And what will you use?"

"Is there a graveyard near this place?"

"Never mind." Manuel shook his head decisively. "Bring on the wet metals. And the drink. He's got spirits here?"

"Spirits?" Awa whispered, her eyes widening. "I wondered if he might. He seems to know more—"

"I've just the thing, Manuel!" Paracelsus returned from his office carrying a large board laden with terrible-looking tools, and setting this across his patient's thighs, he shooed Awa out of her chair and began inspecting the wound. "Sister Gloria, if you would be so kind as to take a pitcher around to water the weeds."

"What?"

"The patients?" Paracelsus arched an eyebrow.

"Oh, yes, of course," Awa said after catching Manuel's smile. "Call if you need me."

There were several rain barrels set just outside the main door, and Awa filled her jug with the brownish water many times throughout the day as she tended to the patients. Most were not as bad as the first man she had seen, and there were also a few women down on the left side, closest to the building's only fireplace. Once she had watered them all she brought them gruel from the large cauldron that had been warming since breakfast, then collected the bowls and washed them in a rain barrel. After this she emptied their chamber pots, and then cleaned the beds and bodies of those too wasted away to reach the pot at all. Manuel was dozing in bed, Paracelsus dozed in his chair, and on Awa worked into the night.

Taking a break from her already intuitive routine, Awa slid past Paracelsus and examined Manuel's hand. The tincture Paracelsus had smeared on the wound stunk like old mushrooms, and Awa could tell at a glance it would fester before a week was out. With a sigh she wrapped it back up and returned to the first patient she had met, the desperate, decaying man. He did not wake as she entered, and drawing the sheet along its string behind her to cordon them off, she killed him with her touch.

"Doctor," Awa said, and when he did not rise, "Paracelsus!"

"Yes!" The physician started awake. "What?"

"One of them died. The man you showed me?"

"The Swiss? Well, I'm Swiss, Manuel's Swiss, but *the* Swiss? The one I showed you?"

"Yes."

"Well, drag him outside, then." Paracelsus stood and stumbled toward his storeroom.

"And what then?"

"Eh?"

"After I take his body outside, what then?" said Awa.

"Leave him in the street," Paracelsus said slowly, gesturing with his arms as though she were deaf, "and come back inside. Someone takes them to the potter's for us; we can't well be expected to do everything."

"Oh. Thank you."

"Of course, of course," said Paracelsus, retiring into his storeroom.

Awa returned to the man she had murdered, and, cutting his left hand off at the wrist with her ibex dagger, she dragged him out onto the damp street. After she had cleaned up the smear his stump had left on the floor she set to cleaning the hand and digging out the needed portion, going back and forth between the dead flesh she was working with and Manuel's injury to make sure she did not miss anything. She went wide in case there were internal injuries she could not see, and then dipped into the storeroom for cooking gear rather than tossing it all into the gruel cauldron.

Paracelsus slept on the floor with his arms and left leg wrapped around a sword almost as tall as he was, and stepping over him, she retrieved a small pot as well as a mortar and pestle. After rinsing out the powdery residue in the latter and scraping out the black crust in the former, Awa ground up the pieces of hand she had taken, bones and all. Making a pudding from them, she set the pot over the low fire in the rear of the clinic. She was almost done when a shadow fell over her, a shadow much taller than Paracelsus or Manuel, and Awa went still, wondering if the disposal of the dead in Milan was not as casual as the doctor had implied.

"Imma have some of that puddin," a gruff voice said in clumsy Italian, and turning to answer her guest Awa saw the largest woman she had ever seen hulking over her like some animate larch or ash.

"This is for another patient, madam," said Awa. "But if you return to your cot I'll make you some as well."

"Harrumph." The woman squatted down, her clothes less soiled but just as pungent as most of the patients'. She had yet to acquire the stink of impending death, however, and only the fragrances of old sweat, blood, and halitosis wafted from her. Even hunched over she was a giantess, with hair the color of dead grass pulled back in a ponytail as thick as its namesake. She only had a few of the lesions on her face but Awa could see the spirit of the malady had already rooted itself deeply in the woman. "Wait 'ere with the good stink, if it's all the same."

"*My* name is Sister Gloria," said Awa, happy to be talking to another living woman for the first time in far too long. "*I'm* a nun who tends to the sick."

The woman peered at the bandaged Awa and shook her head skeptically. "Ya don't look so good yourself, Gloria. If I'd knowed that's whatcha got up ta in the abbeys I'd 'ave married the Christ myself!"

Then she made a terrible chortling sound like a consumptive man gasping for air and she slapped Awa so hard on the shoulder that the mock nun toppled to the side. The woman immediately helped her up, apologizing profusely. "Don't take no offense ta my strongarm nor my fat tongue, this pox 'as me spoutin at the mouth like a piked pig."

"It's alright," said Awa, "but I've got to feed my other patient now."

"Manuel, is it?" said the woman. "Recognize that snivelin anywhere. He's mad, mind, he'll wade in with the best an' the beast, but for such a fuckin martyr he bellyaches enough ta rile Mary an' all the saints."

"Is your name Monique?" Awa asked, having transferred the contents of the pot into a large wooden bowl.

"How ya know that?" The woman stood quickly, blocking the hall.

"I'm a..." and Awa smiled beneath her bandages, because she knew it was true. "I'm a friend of his, and he mentioned you."

"Why'd he do that, then?" Monique was not moving.

"Well," said Awa, "well."

"Wells run dry," said Monique. "What reason that wide-mouth 'ave to bring me up?"

"He said we had things in common, you and I."

"Ya look strong enough but what else? You a daughter of Barbara?"

"No, my mother—"

"Talkin bout *Saint* Barbara. She minds after us what carry cannons, so if ya pack powder you'd best learn'er name quick."

"Pack powder?" The more the woman talked the less sense she made to Awa.

"If it ain't guns, it ain't cunt, is it?"

"Well." Awa was relieved her disguise covered her blushing cheeks as she looked down.

"You mean I was right bout whatcha get up ta in the convents?" Monique seemed genuinely impressed. "Fuck me. Not now, obviously, but still. Quack says it's the cunny an' cock what spreads it, so ifin the nuns've got the pox what hope do the 'ores 'ave, eh, sister?"

“I don’t...” Awa sighed. “I have to feed Manuel before this cools.”

“Right, right.” Monique stepped aside. “Don’t tell’em I’m here, right?”

“Alright.”

“And you promised me a taste of your puddin, don’t forget.” Monique leered as Awa passed her.

“As soon as I’m done I’ll—” Awa paused and stiffened, looking up at the giantess. “That’s... really not something to say to a stranger.”

“I was jus talkin bout the puddin you offered,” said Monique, raising her lesion-covered palms. “An’ us what wears the same ’abit ain’t ever all-strange to one another, is we, sister?”

“I’ll cook you something soon,” Awa decided. “But the coals are a little low for more pudding tonight.”

“I got tinder plenty.” Monique winked as she went back toward her cot. “You jus say the word you need them coals stoked.”

Terrifying though the pox-stricken woman surely was to most who encountered her broken-toothed visage, Awa had never been flirted with before, and the experience filled her with the same heat as Paracelsus’s schnapps. Rousing Manuel, she almost asked him about Monique when she remembered the woman’s request, and so stayed quiet on the matter as she fed her drugged friend. Through his haze of pain and alcohol, Manuel struggled to keep the food down, wondering why the hell Awa was humming happily to herself, and where she kept getting pork from.

XVII
The Hangman's Sword

33

"Why would a hangman have a sword?" asked Manuel. "Wouldn't he have rope? Maybe a knife to cut the rope, but why—"

"Sister Gloria carries a sword, and she's a nun," said Paracelsus. "Everyone carries swords."

"I—" Awa began but Paracelsus was already on his way.

"—heard there was to be an execution, so in the name of education I endeavored to attend. My fellows were too squeamish by half, refusing to admit that we as men of medicine could learn anything from watching a man die. I'll be the first to acknowledge that studying dead bodies is impractical, just as studying an empty stewpot is impractical if you wish to know what was had for dinner—without life a body is just so much sulfur, salt, and mercury, but that's no reason to think watching someone actually die is *worthless* and *morbid*. The presumption of those fools, the conceit! I rode alone, my horse old but quick, and came to the hamlet just as the sun set, a boon, for this was one of those backwaters where the gates are locked at night and they won't open until dawn for king or countryman. I found an inn and—"

Paracelsus's schnapps was better than his storytelling, but he could not speak and drink at the same time, so the three listeners were content to let him prattle on as they passed around his bottle.

Paracelsus recounted his tale from a stool, the door to the storeroom closed to block out the hoarse screaming of the patients, and Manuel, Awa, and Monique sat on various uncomfortable cushions. It was late in the evening of the day after Manuel had been brought in, and even with the benefit of her pudding and the accompanying pleading with the spiritual residue of the dead man's hand, Manuel's palm still leaked blood and lymph. The good doctor could not believe the miraculous recovery, and only Monique's arrival at the bedside had distracted Paracelsus as Manuel scrambled from the bed and threw his arms around the giantess, devastated to see the telltale lesions bulging from her face like acorns under a handkerchief.

Awa had smiled at his grief, for she alone knew the woman would not die of the Great Pox. Severing the spirit of the malady and consuming it entirely had taken far more energy than Awa had expected, and she thought that Monique had almost awoken as the necromancer doubled over beside the bed gagging. Before, ingesting the spirit of infection had given her strength and warmth, but this spirit had sickened her, and she lay awake all night racked with fever. Awa was well by morning, however, and at a glance she could see that the pox was entirely removed from Monique. The more time Awa spent in the clinic the more resolute she became in the decision she had recently made—she would stay in the clinic and help alleviate the suffering, instead of accompanying Manuel to Bern when he recovered.

"—the execution was to be held the next morning, so I was just in time, but there in the hills such a thing as an execution attracts quite an audience, and so there was no room at the inn."

"Stay in the manger, then?" said Manuel.

"I stayed," said Paracelsus, ignoring Monique's guffaws and letting the sentence dangle long enough to quaff from the nearly empty bottle, "with the hangman!"

"The hangman with the sword, or some other—" Manuel began.

"The same!" Paracelsus thundered, which made Awa, who otherwise would have been able to keep it in, explode with laughter. It took the doctor's retrieving a fresh bottle to quiet them down. When order was restored he went on: "This hangman, it seemed, had a problem that was truly *diabolical*, and as the priest could not relieve him I thought to pit my own mental prowess against this mystery."

"I'm very sorry," said Awa, "I must not have heard you, but what was the mystery again?"

"I hadn't told you yet," said Paracelsus, to more laughter. "But I will! Directly! The problem was this—the town had the custom that when a man was hanged, the hangman was charged with severing his head just after his neck had snapped from the noose, and this hangman, being a consummate professional, always chopped the heads free in one swipe before the body could bounce twice."

"Why?" said Monique. "What purpose such a thing 'ave, stead of leavin'em ta swing?"

"Local customs are profoundly weird," burped Paracelsus. "Better to come to terms with this and move on than to examine the peccadilloes of peasants. Probably why they got such a good crowd. But I digress! The hangman was haunted."

"Haunted?" This finally interested Awa. "By who?"

"By *the heads*," said Paracelsus, turning and blowing out a few candles for better ambiance. "They would roll up the side of his house and down his chimney, and so his home was always cold, for on the nights he lit a fire they came just the same, dropping down into the hearth, and the stink of charring skin and burning hair would force him from the place. Every night they came, and so, he told me as I stood at his door after finding the inn full, he could not possibly put me up for the night, for he would suffer none to suffer as he suffered from those infernal guests.

"But I, a doctor then in deed if not yet in title, swore to see him through the night, and break the curse beside. And so I did, and in payment he gave me his sword, which I keep ever at my side." Paracelsus leaned back on his stool, quite pleased with himself.

"Bullshit," said Monique. "Lies."

"The Lord God knows I am no liar," said Paracelsus.

"But wait!" said Awa. "What about the rest of the story?"

"What do you mean? I broke the curse, I got the sword. End of story." Paracelsus shrugged.

"How? How did you break the curse?" said Awa.

"Such things as how a magus lifts a curse are hardly the sort of topic for casual discussion," said Paracelsus.

"He 'asn't made that part up yet," said Monique.

"Alright, then," said Paracelsus, miffed. "Here's what I did. First I asked when the trouble started, and he told me it came about the night after he had hanged and beheaded a warlock—*the same warlock whose sword he now used.* The condemned sorcerer had bequeathed it to him at the gallows, and upon retrieving the weapon from whatever farmer-with-a-barn who served as jailer in that awful place he found it to be of fine make, and all down those years it never lost its edge. So I examined the sword, found a secret compartment in the pommel, and inside the compartment was a piece of bone tied to a lodestone, with which the sorcerer had bound an imp to the sword, and by sprinkling this charm with salt and invoking the Lord's name I forced the imp to tell me how to break the curse, which I then did, after sending the familiar, the imp, that is, back to Hell."

Paracelsus's audience had grown very silent, which was how he liked it. He went on:

"The task was simple—I had to smash each of the heads with

the sword as they appeared in the hearth, which I did, and when the last desiccated skull was dashed the curse was broken. The hangman was so relieved that he gave me his sword as a gift, and that was that. The hanging I watched the following morning was, needless to say, not so interesting."

The silence continued for a spell longer, then Manuel said, "That makes *absolutely* no sense at all."

"Fuckin lyin quack!" Monique offered.

"No, it does, it does," said Awa thoughtfully. "Breaking the skulls would sever the spirits, and if the charm in the sword had some other spirit, a familiar or imp or what you will, then it might summon..."

Awa realized she was talking aloud, and quickly snatched the bottle from a very interested Paracelsus. Manuel began laughing, a dreadful, strained cackle, and Monique joined in, slapping Awa on the back and nearly chipping her teeth on the lip of the bottle. This obnoxious riot continued until Manuel came up with something, which most assuredly was not much:

"She's... always imitating the way other people sound for a laugh, is our Sister Gloria," Manuel said. "Pretty good, eh?"

"Sounded just like the doctor," agreed Monique. "Think ya'd picked up an echo, Doctor P?"

"My dear, tell me—" Paracelsus started but Monique cut him off.

"Now assumin for the moment ya ain't a lyin fuckin quack, what say ya explain why ya believe in imps an' other such devilry? Doctors not supposed ta be superstitious."

"Superstition is equal parts imagination and reality we don't yet understand," the doctor said stuffily. "The Philosopher's Stone, for example—"

Paracelsus rambled on for some time on matters alchemical and obscure until he had talked himself hoarse. Then Monique, who had not listened to a word he said, endeavored to explain the nuances of some of her more colorful colloquialisms to Awa, who could not make sense of most of them. Paracelsus dozed off on his stool; the man's attention was prone to flagging when he was not at the root of the scene. Manuel had staggered off for a shit.

"What'd I miss, then?" said Manuel as he came back in.

"Jus a lot of prayin, nuthin ta beg your confession on."

"That's a shame," said Manuel. "I do love a little sin."

XVIII
A Discharge, with Some Weeping

"Ya got me pure of this pox," said Monique as she finished packing her bag. "The how've it don't concern me. Ya keep denyin all you want but I *felt* it comin outta me, woke me up from a dead sleep an' fever an' seen ya cuttin out away from my bed, coughin an' all. Lyin don't become no nun."

"I'm not a nun," said Awa lamely.

"Oh really?" Monique smirked. "Yeah, that weren't obvious a'tall. Ya got the pox under them rags?"

"I'm a Moor," said Awa, and at this Monique first drew back, then leaned close, her Delft blue eyes narrowing as she peered into Awa's copper brown ones.

"Like, a fuckin *blackamoor*?" Monique whispered, glancing around at the stained curtains boxing them in.

"Yes," Awa whispered, her guts twisting up into a noose to throttle her hopes of finding any kind of friendship from the woman.

"Fuck me," Monique exhaled.

There it was. Awa thought about telling Monique that judging a woman by where she was born made no more sense than judging her for liking other women, or for having brown hair instead of blond. Telling never did any good, of course, but—

"In that case I can't very well make ya a full fuckin partner even if ya do 'ave the scratch," said Monique thoughtfully. "But we kin work somethin out, ta be sure. How much ya got?"

"Excuse me?" Awa blinked, the tears she had not even noticed smearing the lead makeup around her eyes.

"I'm out, right?" Monique set her bag down. "An' you're the one what got me out, an' I don't mean to forget that, blackamoor or no. Ya kin do for others whatcha did for me?"

"Now, what I did—"

"Rub a little paste or somethin, yeah?"

"Well, actually—"

"*Rub a little paste or somethin, yeah?*" Monique flashed Awa a ludicrously exaggerated wink. "What goes in that paste is the doctor's business, not mine, an' not the 'ores', neither. Important thing is the nasty goes away, aye?"

"I'm not a doctor," Awa protested. "Did you say whores?"

"See, that's why I need ya, sister, cause of them wits of yours. Course we can't call you a doctor, anyone with more'n half an eye kin see your great tits an' call the shit on that claim at once, an' then we're in it for claimin ya's a doctor when ya's jus, I dunno, an apothecary or midwife or some such. Midwife sounds good an' all, aye?"

"Monique," said Awa firmly. "What are you talking about?"

"Talkin bout gettin ya your own practice, an' some cunny besides, if you're interested."

Awa took a step back. "Now, I'm... I'm flattered, but—"

"Not me, you chit!" Monique laughed. "I'm talkin bout the 'ores! Sure, most of'em don't have the willin or want ta go lappin tween our legs, an' of those that will a fair sight less will go down ta blackest Afrik, sure, but the 'ores I got in mind are the dirtiest of the dirty, an' we'll find us a choice chicken or two for ya ta pluck if you'll say yes, sister. Say yes, sister!"

"You want to go get whores," Awa said carefully, sure she had missed something and trying not to take the woman's offensiveness personally. "And you want me to go along to, to tend to these whores, so that you don't get another malady?"

"Sister Gloria," said Monique, "an' we *will* have ta getcha a new title an' clothes, cause keepin some 'abits at hand for clergy or whoever ta wear or put on they girls is one thing, an' havin a fuckin blackamoor nun sittin bout a brothel all day is somethin else. But I got waylaid—point is—I fuckin love 'ores. I love fuckin'em, I love drinkin with'em, I love eatin with'em, I love jus sittin bout talkin with'em. Love 'ores, I do, an' ya kin ask Manuel if that ain't the Lord's truth. So down all these days stead a puttin way funds for some of them fillygreed matchlocks I've been keepin on with my old guns instead, an' squirrelin away every coin I get, excludin the occasional bottle or piece of mink from one of said obligin girlies. Kin ya guess why?"

Awa could not.

"To open my own brothel," Monique whispered conspiratorially. "An' with this last bonus a von Wine's I'm set. Got me a beard named Dario, a game little dandy who'll sign the papers an' lease an' all, an' o'er my travels I planted enough seeds in the heads of enough 'ores that ifin we stop in a few towns along the way ta the new digs we'll 'ave us a regular caravan of cunt rollin into Cathar Country, an' then we're set. I pony up the cost so I run the show, Dario's the frontman an' gets a small take an' a room for his part, 'ores get a bigger cut than they's accustomed ta keep'em 'appy, an' you, Sister Gloria—"

"Me?" Awa was not sure if this was the worst idea she had ever heard, or the greatest. "Me?"

"You, Sister Gloria," said Monique, "are resident cunt-cleaner. See, I got it all worked out—ifin my 'ores is clean all the time, an' I mean, *really* clean, word'll spread, and that'll give us the edge to justify payin the 'ores better, an' any other costs we might incur by dent a bein a real classy fuckin venture."

"But Paracelsus says that most people don't know the pox

comes from, from that, they thinks it's the water or the gods or—"

"Word'll spread on all counts, mark me there, an' then my 'ores legs'll be spreadin like brains on bread." Monique licked her lips at the thought. "Sides, havin a house wholly free of the pox'll be good for morale an' establishin a certain, whataya... ambiance. A certain fuckin poxless ambiance. Ifin ya got capital ta help start us off I'll give ya a cut of the cunny-money, an' even if ya don't you'll have *private* fuckin chambers, three meals a day, four bottles of wine or two of stronger stuff a week, an' the free ass of any 'ore willin to give it. An' mind what I said—I'll assure ya got a choice of no less than three different obligin fannies, kind of girlies what'd teach the devil's own stable how ta properly service everythin from blackamoors to blacksnakes."

"I... don't... I." Awa had never considered anything remotely like what Monique was suggesting, and told herself that any interest she might possess had everything to do with gainful employment far removed from Paracelsus—who grew creepier by the day—and not the promise of carnal relations with women who drew little distinction between her and a serpent. Awa *had* wanted to find a way to distract herself for the next few years, to enjoy life instead of surrounding herself with death, and to restore any tipped internal balance in the event the nigh-forgotten beliefs of her mother came to be true. While she had decided tending to the afflicted pox victims would be a more fitting and fulfilling occupation than washing Manuel's laundry in Bern, it sounded like in purpose working for Monique would be essentially the same as working for Paracelsus, only with a rotating choice of women and drink. This seemed more and more appealing as the young necromancer considered it. A wet shriek came from just beyond the curtain to her left, the sound deteriorating into a gurgle as the patient gagged and vomited on the stench of his own putrefying body, and that settled it.

"Alright," said Awa, though she had learned enough of the ways of men and women to avoid putting up her own substantial fortune of grave-gained treasures she had acquired over the years since leaving the mountain. "I don't have money to spare but I'll be your, your... I'll tend to your girls, and I thank you for your offer."

"Least I kin do, right?" said Monique. "But you'll be tellin me your real name fore we go any further, less your Infidel fuckin parents thought Gloria sounded proper in their Turk fuckin tongue."

Awa frowned, not having considered this condition, but of all the people she had ever met Monique seemed the least likely to exploit something as subtle as the power a name gives a person. "Awa," said she.

"Right enough, Awa," said Monique, clapping her on the shoulder. "Let's getcher gear an' get shy of this shithole."

They went to the storeroom and gathered Awa's satchel, which she had never unpacked. She had slept on the floor beside Paracelsus and with the lack of privacy had not wanted him examining her dagger or salamander eggs by leaving the unusual items lying around. As she shouldered the bag Paracelsus burst into the room behind them, his arms wrapped around a small cask.

"And just where do you think you're off to, my dear?" The physician panted as he set the keg down. "And look at you, madam, fully recovered in so short a span!"

"We're leavin," said Monique. "An' where we go ain't concern of man, beast, nor nuthin betwixt'em."

"And when will you be back, Sister Gloria?" asked Paracelsus, straightening up and looking at Awa.

"I..." Awa glanced at Monique, who raised her palms and took a step back. "I don't intend to return. I thank you very much for your time, of course, and your generosity, and—"

"My understanding, of course," said Paracelsus, narrowing

his puffy eyes. "Most people in this wide world of ours would not be so understanding, I don't think."

"Of course, your—" Awa began, but he cut her off.

"Most people would not tolerate *a witch* to sleep under their roof, let alone a Moor." Paracelsus raised his eyebrows, glancing at Monique. "No, most people might balk at the idea of a woman composed of more sulfur than salt being allowed to live, let alone—"

Which is when Monique closed the short distance between them and punched him dead in the jaw. Paracelsus seemed to hop nimbly backwards onto his table, but then all his limbs flailed about and glasses were breaking and his canisters went rolling onto the floor. Monique might have hit him again but Awa grabbed the taller woman's arm.

"Call'er a fuckin witch again an' see what happens!" Monique bellowed before Paracelsus's eyes had even come back into focus. "Say it again, ya quack, an' I'll drown ya in your fuckin pox-metal!"

"I *am* a witch," said Awa. "He just didn't want you to think I wasn't when—"

"The fuck he had anythin but blackmail in mind," Monique fumed. "I know when a fuckin cock's workin a threat into 'is words, an' that's what he was doin. Threatenin."

"Monique, I am a witch. Did you hear me?" Awa squeezed her friend's arm, unsure whether she wanted her to punch the physician again or not. He had seemed a most understanding man, albeit a peculiar one, and until this he had given her no definitive reason to think his concern for her was less than altruistic.

"Maybe if you'd put a pox on me stead a takin one off I'd give a shit," said Monique. "As is, I'm more'n happy ta pay ya for your wiles with more'n a spot beside me on the floor and fuckin gruel to eat like this lump's been doin. Ya wanna fuckin tell me she's a witch again, lump?!"

"No." Paracelsus dribbled a little blood as he spoke, glaring at Monique. Awa saw his eyes dart over to his sword propped against the wall, and she quickly stepped between him and it. At this his shoulders sagged, and the sullen young doctor said, "Go on then, Sister Gloria, I can see when my friendship is no longer required. I would not have exploited you, though; I would have had you for a tutor. I only hope that in time you will not allow false impressions to color the facts, that I was a man open to you in ways that those who could never understand you could, could never understand."

"An' jus what the fuck is that supposed ta mean?" demanded Monique, bowing up further.

"That in only a short time I have learned much from our mutual friend," Paracelsus spat, a small rose blooming on Monique's tunic where his bloody spittle fell. Tears were running down his cheeks as he continued, but Awa did not know if these were the result of emotion at her impending departure or being struck in the face. "That much of what we, in our ignorance, think of as medicine is actually poison, but that very poison, in the proper dosage, can be a medicine. That there is more at work than we know, and that if we but listen to the swarthy witch, the seemingly mad diabolist, we may discover more than all the wisdom of antiquity. Go if you must, Sister Gloria, but know that by doing so you shut me out, and by shutting me out you shut out all of modern medicine. You will not find another so willing to believe, to hear you out. Spirits in the mercury? Of the mercury? The world teeming with all sorts of spirits, and not divine nor diabolical but simply spirits who—"

"I never said that!" Awa cried. "I never told you, how did you—"

"But you did!" Paracelsus nodded. "As you slept you would mumble to yourself, and often when you were awake as well. I have transcribed some of it, and much of it is in line with what—"

"You want me to break 'is head in?" Monique looked very seriously at Awa.

"It's my fault," said Awa. "I shouldn't have, I mean, I know I talk to myself sometimes but... Theophrastus Philippus Aureolus Bombastus von Hohenheim."

"Yes?" Paracelsus blinked, pleasantly surprised that someone, anyone, had remembered his full name.

"Theophrastus Philippus Aureolus Bombastus von Hohenheim, what is done is done, but I cannot have you telling people about me. Use what I have given you but trouble me no more." Awa stepped between Monique and the physician, who tilted his head back at the sudden intensity of his nurse.

"Trouble you? Why, I—" Awa touched his knee and he died. A little, anyway, and it was the most marvelous, exciting experience of the doctor's life.

"Christ!" said Monique, backing away. She knew a dead man when she saw one, and even if he had not noisily voided his bowels she would have known he was murdered.

"Theophrastus Philippus Aureolus Bombastus von Hohenheim," Awa said his name a third time, and leaning in, whispered in Latin, "You are dead, but I shall spare you this end so that you may help the living, so that you may use the little wisdom I have given you to change the minds of men, both about witches and about the world we all inhabit. It would be far safer for me to leave you as a corpse, but instead I give you life. Do not make me regret my decision, Theophrastus Philippus Aureolus Bombastus von Hohenheim."

And up he sat as she returned his life to him, only to double over again in agony as a migraine ricocheted behind his temples. By the time he had recovered enough to realize he had soiled himself, Awa and Monique were gone, as was his schnapps cask. He did not even clean himself before scribbling down the monumental experience of dying, the stench and itchiness not nearly distracting enough to delay him a moment more.

Manuel was waiting for them by the north gate with two horses Monique had acquired for their journey, a large bay and a dappled mare hardly bigger than a pony. The rapidity and thoroughness of his palm's recovery, as well as Monique's drying lesions, pleased Manuel greatly, and he waved his scarred hand at them as they approached. While Monique quibbled with Manuel over the strapping of the saddles, Awa tried to calm her unhappy heart enough to recite her farewell speech to her first and best friend among the living, Niklaus Manuel Deutsch of Bern.

"What's this?" Manuel interrupted her before she really got the tangle of her words sorted out. "But I'm, that is, we're sharing a horse, aren't we?"

"What?" Awa could scarcely believe it. "But we're not going to Bern."

"Well, yes, but I thought I might—"

"Earn some coin," said Monique. "I hired us some muscle for the road, lean though it fuckin is. Bern's got 'ores, bein a civilized spot, an' so we'll pop in there long the way."

"Really?" Awa could hardly believe it. "I can see your ladies!"

"Ah," said Manuel, picturing himself riding up his walk with Awa and Monique, picturing his wife and niece and servants and maybe his already disapproving father-in-law coming out to meet them. "Ahhhh. Maybe we could, I suppose. I wouldn't want to, you know, slow you down."

"Don't worry, Awa," said Monique, swinging onto the larger horse. "There'll be ladies aplenty soon enough, an' ones what'll put up with his queerness!"

Manuel turned a very deep shade of crimson, arousing Awa's

curiosity, but when she asked him about it later he muttered something about being an artist and having responsibilities to his craft. In the meantime, he simply blushed and got onto the smaller horse. Awa had never been so close to one of the beasts, let alone ridden one, and was more than a little reluctant. Her insistence that she walk along beside them was met with derisive laughter from Monique, who wasted no time in hoisting Awa onto the saddle before her.

"You're a fuckin big girl, right enough," Monique breathed in Awa's ear. "Fit enough ta wrestle me down, maybe, and sure enough wrestle down a Manuel or two. You like wrestlin, Awa?"

"I'm not..." Awa began, but then Monique nudged the horse into a canter and whatever words Awa had on the matter escaped along with her breath. They were moving far too fast for the necromancer's liking, but Monique's burly arms anchored her reasonably well, meaty hands holding the reins in Awa's lap. They were on the road and making good time, Manuel trying to keep up on the little horse, and once she triumphed over her motion sickness and vertigo Awa leaned back into Monique's solid chest and tried to enjoy the ride.

XIX
The Smith's Guns

♀

Awa and Monique fucked twice before arriving in Bern. The first time Manuel had insisted on sleeping in a tavern's common room because he claimed his back would never sit right again if he did not have one honest night's sleep on a pallet, please, and as Monique was more frugal with her money she camped in the foothills outside the hamlet's walls with Awa. Dusk drifted down through the grove of red willows as Monique and Awa washed the road dust, grime, and sweat from themselves in the frigid stream running beside their camp, both women growing less and less subtle in the glances they took of each other's shivering bodies.

"Your nips're pink enough, for a blackamoor," observed Monique as she squatted in the stream, gasping as the current struck the warmest part of her body.

"Thank... thank you?" Awa scrambled over the rocks to quit the stream when Monique grabbed her arm, tight but not unwelcomely so.

"Why doncha rinse like I done?" The seriousness in Monique's eyes made Awa turn away.

"It's cold, and—"

"Ya wanna fuck, Awa?"

"What?" Awa blinked at the dripping, scarred mercenary, Monique's freckled face and beech hair glistening in the twilight.

"Not sayin I wanna make ya my sweetin, Awa, I'm jus askin if ya wanna 'ave a nice little fuck while Manuel's off cryin ta himself in the tavern. Ya don't like what I'm doin call it off, an' if ya do ya throw me some face, aye?"

"Just...just fuck each other?" Awa swallowed.

"Never fucked a—yeah, jus fuck each other. Do. You. Wanna. Fuck?"

Awa did, unreservedly, though the Dutch giantess was a far cry from what she had previously considered beautiful. Monique was, however, a tremendous amount of fun in bed, or would have been if they had a bed to employ. They built up the fire then went deeper into the grove lest a traveler come upon them, and Monique proceeded to give Awa something she had been lacking for years. The woman's hands and lips were no softer than the rest of her but the strength in them felt wonderful to Awa, the feeling of breath on her neck and ears and breasts and stomach and everywhere else a novel sensation, and a welcome one. The warmth of Monique seemed to burn Awa as her partner reached her destination and began running her scalding tongue up the sides of Awa's labia, and when that slick, blazing tongue gently spread Awa open and took its time reaching her clit the younger woman began to buck uncontrollably. Fingers and tongue rhythmically pressing toward one another with only Awa's most sensitive region between them, Monique finished her partner with aplomb.

"That storm a yours' been brewin awhile, yeah?" Monique grinned as she crawled up beside Awa, who stared at her wide-eyed and awed. Then Awa burst into tears and threw her arms around Monique, who awkwardly tried to soothe her so she might find some recompense sooner rather than later. When she finally got her settled into place between her thighs Monique found Awa every bit as enthusiastic as she was clumsy and inexperienced, but eventually Awa brought her friend to an occasion, the woman nearly tearing out a patch of Awa's scalp as she gripped her hair and ground against her face and fingers.

The fire had burned low but they built it back up, drinking and talking and smiling at one another, Monique occasionally pinching or throwing her arm around Awa. Late in the evening Monique withdrew one of her matchlock pistols at Awa's request and passed her the weapon. "Aye, I 'ad the same look in my eye, Lord'll vouch, first time I got close enough ta see what they was an' what they was bout. See, ta tell it right it went like this..."

The girl grew up amidst the estuaries of what had been the Groote Waard before the Flood of Saint Elizabeth transformed fertile countryside and village alike into an inland sea of sweet, brown water. On the newly formed banks willows grew, and on the islands that had once been hillocks many leagues from any stream or pond more willows grew, and the girl grew up on these banks, on these islands. They cut the willows, the girl and her mother and father and brothers and sisters, and they sold the willow bark, which was good for doctors, who ground it up with their mortars and pestles for their medicines, and they sold the willow wood, which was good for everyone else, as it smelled sweet and burned slow and hot, and they sold the baskets they wove from the willow boughs, which were good for doctor and farmer alike, being light but strong and sturdy.

The girl was named Monique, and her parents sold the willow, and when times grew lean they sold Monique. She was stronger than all her brothers and sisters, and so the man who needed bellows worked thought himself fortunate, for in addition to being an ox Monique was also a woman, and so there would be no risk of her pursuing more recompense than her master gave her. This man was a smith of small arms, and he knew the family because he found the willow ash to be the best for making powder, and like any good smith he tested everything before selling it, and testing guns meant using powder, and that meant either buying it or making it, and there was nothing the smith would buy if he could make it himself—that both his wife and would-be heir died in childbirth was the only reason he sought outside help in working his works.

Monique worked very, very hard for the smith in his shop in Rotterdam, and guarded his forge when he went off to broker deals or simply get out for a little while, and being far from stupid she paid much mind to what the smith did to build his guns. When he was out she examined the castings, the tools, and the pictures in the manuals she could not read, and as years passed and the smith grew older she unobtrusively began helping more and more with finer and finer details of the smithing process, until quite without his knowing it she was as good an apprentice as any craftsman could seek.

When the smith decided to sell his shop, having made enough coin from the French sojourns into Lombardy politics and the accompanying need for lots and lots of guns and powder, he tearfully dismissed Monique with a few coins and the clothes on her back. When her request for a letter certifying her skill at smithing was laughingly rebuked, she asked what exactly she was meant to do with her life, and he suggested whoring. The guns she took with her would have afforded her a comfortable purse had she sold them, but Monique had no intention of parting with them, especially as they might prove useful if the smith recovered from the drubbing she had given him and sent men after her.

She knew the guns she had helped make had always gone south, and so did she, hoping to find one willing to overlook her gender and employ her in a smithy. None did, not in Burgundy and not in France and certainly not in northern Spain and not in the Empire and not in the Swiss Confederacy, but there at last she found some work that enabled her to earn coin while working with guns. During the years of traveling and seeking out wealth she had found herself in many, many dangerous circumstances, and had been in countless fights, and one evening in a tavern, after she beat three disrespectful Swiss mercenaries to a pulp, their captain, a brute named von Stein, hired her on the spot.

Monique was so overjoyed to find someone willing to take her on despite her being a woman that she did not even realize what she was hired for until the next day, when she was sober and enlisted. If anyone asked she was supposed to tell them she was an unfortunately feminine-looking man, but usually the willow-cutter's daughter simply responded by pistol-whipping the offending party in the mouth, and that seemed to get the job done well enough. She recognized better than most the limited capabilities of her preferred weapon and, courtesy of von Stein, received dispensation to occasionally act in a more traditional mercenary capacity while still carrying her guns, instead of always being left behind with the rest of the often ineffectual gunners.

"In the fuckin shitstorm's where the blood gets hottest," she concluded, "which is 'ow me and Manuel got so fuckin close—boy kin stick'em like a born butcher."

"You're amazing!" said Awa at last. "You overcame your cruel master and lived to tell the tale!"

"He weren't such the motherfucker," said Monique. "I felt a bit bad, for a time, seein's he was nigh sixty when I laid'em out, an' lay'em out I fuckin did. Some men 'alf 'is age don't recover from a beatin like that, teeth everywhere, an' he did teach me what I know, or knew. Don't wager I could cast a turd out my ass after these years without a smithy."

"I'm sure you could!"

"Well, maybe I could cast that," admitted Monique. "But what's your yarn, little sister? How'd a nun come ta drink with the damned, eh?"

"That's a story for a colder night," Awa said nervously. "I just, I don't—"

"No worries, no hurries," said Monique. "I'll hear it when ya tell it, an' not a day fore then."

"Thank you," said Awa, her severity giving Monique pause.

"Well, we waited down the stars, so ta bed then?"

The next morning Awa found herself more than a little infatuated with Monique, but the woman was far cooler than she had previously been with Awa, and positively glacial compared to the previous night. Still, the hurt of Monique's standoffishness was slight compared to the pain Omorose had caused her, and Awa attributed her friend's demeanor to not wanting Manuel to pick up on the shift in their relationship. Awa focused instead on the sharp green pines and sharper gray stones girding the road, the pale blue sky and paler wisps of cloud wreathing the peaks as they rode into the Alps—being once again enclosed by mountains was a comfort to the necromancer.

The second time they fucked all three had been drinking by the fire, and they snuck off when Manuel became viciously sick, throwing up and moaning like a gluttonous hound that had eaten too much of a stolen roast. This encounter was just as disappointing as the first time had been fulfilling, with Monique bringing along one of her pistols and insisting Awa rub the barrel against herself while the mercenary watched, masturbating, and only when the heavy, cold bronze became too abrasive and Awa stopped did Monique consent to giving her partner the laziest of attentions with her tongue. Awa's orgasm was little more pleasurable than those she gave herself, which were also less embarrassing than rubbing a weapon over her most delicate parts as her paramour drunkenly gave her instructions and pleasured herself rather than having Awa assist.

The next morning Manuel noticed the change in Awa and Monique's interactions even through his pounding headache, although it was another day, and a miserable day it was, before he guessed at what had happened. When he did, he remained as silent as the two women had become, neither giving him much opportunity to talk to one or the other alone, and so they came down from the wildflower-speckled meadows of the high country where marmots whistled among the overgrown boulder fields and snowmelt waterfalls crashed down through cataracts, the trio drawing closer and closer to Bern. At least his hand was fully healed.

They encountered no excitement along the valley roads, and so Manuel had no opportunities to earn a bonus for being an active as opposed to merely present bodyguard. Passing the little red millwheel outside Bern gave Manuel the same heady rush of relief it always did—he was coming home, and the wheel turned the same as it always did, like life, like war, like everything he could think of. His delight was only tempered by the realization that he would be arriving without nearly as much of a fortune as he had hoped for, and with two very strange women. His wife knew and tolerated Monique, but how she would react to a Moor dressed as a nun, and what their servants might think—now that his journey with her was almost concluded, the alien witchiness of Awa reasserted itself in his mind, and even as he looked over the bramble thicket of her short hair he wondered just how the hell he had ever thought of her and their friendship as anything remotely normal. Then he glanced at his scarred but intact left hand holding the reins, and sighed. Befriending a necromancer had proven somewhat advantageous, he had to admit.

Manuel felt his face break into a stupid, uncontrollable grin as they turned onto Gerechtigkeitsgasse, but then Monique slowed her horse and said, "I'm ta look up some mink was here last pass, those pig-assed Swiss 'ores you introduced me ta last time I was up."

"Oh," said Manuel. "Well, come by when you're done. Katharina will be disappointed if you don't at least dine with us, and of course you're welcome to stay as long as you like. We've got pallets I can put down in the studio."

"You wanna come meet some pig-assed 'ores, Awa?" Monique said, trying to catch her friend's eyes. Awa found the ears of the horse she shared with Manuel rather intriguing. "Get rid of some of that tension if—"

"No thank you," said Awa, finally meeting Monique's gaze. The larger woman seemed taken aback by the ferocity of Awa's expression. "I would much rather see Manuel's ladies than your pig whores."

"Suit'cherself," said Monique, wheeling her horse around. "Though his ladies don't eat ass on no account, and certainly for no handful of pennies. I'll be by for dinner after I've sealed the deal."

"Take care, Mo," said Manuel, turning his horse back down the street. Awa was rigid as a halberd on the horse before him, and Manuel tugged his hair, wondering how to balance this new wrinkle with his imminent reunion with his family. Then Awa let out a long sigh and relaxed, and Manuel chanced it. "So," he said, "you and Mo, then, did you, ah…"

Awa turned her neck almost all the way around like an owl, staring at Manuel. Shit.

"Look, she, well." Manuel shrugged. "She's never stuck with anyone for longer than a night or two so long as I've known her, though she's had plenty of girls who'd have stopped charging her from what I've seen."

"From what you've seen?" Awa narrowed her eyes at Manuel. "And you introduced her to whores here in Bern? *Pig-assed* whores? What are you doing in brothels, Niklaus Manuel Deutsch of Bern?"

"Not fucking," sighed Manuel. "Just looking, and painting."

"Just looking and painting? Nothing more?"

"Look," Manuel said, eager to conclude the matter before reaching his house. "Katharina knows about anything I do—

we've got arrangements, my wife and I, but for your own puerile curiosity, no, I don't fuck them. Satisfied?"

Of course this only increased Awa's curiosity, but in the moment she was still bitter over Monique's attitude. "Satisfied. Your friend Monique has a shitty way of dealing with people—people who care about her. And this is coming from me!"

"Well," said Manuel, "I'd guess she's had a hard life—"

"*She's* had a hard life?! Growing up in a warm workshop, not getting beat or tortured, to hear her tell it? Hard?"

"Workshop? She's never told me anything about where she came from or what she did before she joined up with von Swine, so that must mean something, right?"

"Means she tricked me into thinking she was more than just a dumb bitch," said Awa, though she knew guile and Monique no more went together than Paracelsus and brevity.

"Look," said Manuel, spying an open white shutter at the end of the block, the green trim on it bright as the last time he had touched it up. "Did she make any kind of promises or claims? I've never known her to go back on her word, she's honest to a fault. Now, if she made some kind of pledge or whatever you do then I'd say to hell with her, sure, but I'm wagering she—"

"She didn't say anything like that," said Awa, chiding herself for not taking her friend at her word. Awa wondered why it always stung worse when people told her the truth. She had hoped to leave that cruel honesty behind with the undead. "I'm just...I really thought she liked me! But I...I know what I am. I'm not pig-assed, though I am a beast."

"Hey, now, you're a fit woman, and you'd be a perfect model, as I've oft told you," Manuel said, slowing the horse even more, hating her for staying silent for a week only to blurt it all out now, and quickly hating himself for being so selfish. "You're hardly a beast, just...unique. And your body is, well, I've no idea what Mo means by pig-assed, but you've got more muscle than most men I've met, and the little padding you've got is..."

"Niklaus!" At this Awa straightened up and Manuel quickly dismounted, and as Awa wiped her eyes on her browning bandages she saw two women in the doorway of the house before them. One was barely old enough to be called such, and the other clearly Katharina; despite being older and fuller of middle, Awa recognized Manuel's wife from the nude portrait he kept of her, and blushed.

"What is this thing on my doorstep?" said Katharina, throwing her arms around her husband. Awa smiled down at them, for some strange reason suddenly missing the mother she did not remember. Katharina then hopped back from her husband, looked him up and down with a sly smile, and turned to Awa. "Excuse me, sister, but my husband has been away sometime. My name is Katharina, and I would be honored if you would enter our home for something to refresh you."

"I'm sorry, love," said Manuel, "I seem to have left my manners in Milan. This is Awww, Sister Gl—"

"Awa," she interrupted him. "Please, just Awa."

"Awa?" Katharina laughed. "What an interesting name! But please come in, sister, please! And you! Come and meet your daughter, Niklaus!"

XX
Manuel's Ladies

Manuel was a father. Katharina was certain when he had left for war but he had not let himself believe—he never would have gone if he was sure that she was pregnant. He wanted to go to the crib he had built several years before, when he had briefly flirted with the idea of becoming a woodworker, but his wife shooed him off to pour them drinks for a toast in the kitchen. When she returned, a swaddled shape held in her arms, he put his unsampled glass on the table. The witch standing to his left was forgotten, as was his dear niece on his right, and as Katharina brought his daughter to him Manuel teared up, extending his arms to take his child.

Katharina cradled the babe in one arm, and with the other she gave it a vigorous rub. It seemed terribly rough to the artist but he did not know the first thing about babies; maybe that was something that needed doing. He would leave it to his wife if so, he could never be that firm with his daughter.

The kitchen was silent as a lull in mass as he took his daughter, and then the happiest day of his life became a nightmare. As soon as he took the bundle of soft linen the babe thrashed and twisted out of his hands, as if his bloodstained fingers burned the innocent child, and he barely caught her before she fell. Then the cloth covering her face fell away and Manuel shrieked, his child a monster. Her orange eyes matched the fur coating her flat face, her needle teeth and too-pink mouth shining as she bit at him, only the blanket she was wrapped in protecting him from her kicking legs and arms.

Lydie, Manuel's niece, began shrieking as well, as did Katharina, and Awa backed away from the table in horror. The realization that the two women were howling with laughter instead of fear only amplified Awa's concern. Then Manuel was laughing as well, the cat leaping from the blankets and dashing out of the kitchen.

"Evil baby," he managed through his laughter, leaning against his laughing wife. "Evil fucking baby. I fucking forgot. Evil baby. His face. Is. Too terrible."

"I'm sorry." Katharina remembered Awa, looking up at the anxious nun and panting another apology. "So sorry, Sister Awa. It's a game we'd play with the kitten, wrapping him up like that."

"Evil baby." Manuel shook his head, still trembling all over. He looked to his niece, who had slid down to the floor and was the only one still giggling. "I suppose you had a hand in this cruel plot?"

The teenager nodded, glancing up at Awa and bursting into another fit of raucous laughter. Katharina tugged on her husband's arm, sobering a bit at his serious expression. "Come on then, Niklaus, let's introduce you to little Margaretha."

"You mean—" Manuel looked at his wife, then his niece, and finally at Awa, who had finally relaxed. "Just what I need, another woman."

"Come on, then." Katharina slapped him lightly on the chest, then led him to the bedroom where his infant daughter slept.

Awa could not remember having been so nervous as the day wore on in the Manuel house, her friend cooing over the baby that cried more often than not at being held by her still road-fragrant father. Lydie poorly concealed her fascination with the bandaged nun, and, exchanging clumsy conversation with Manuel's pretty young niece, Awa reflected that the girl was probably the same age as she had been when she had first brought Omorose back from the dead. Awa doubted Lydie had even seen a corpse, let alone—well. The girl was as soft and pink as the marrow in a freshly cracked bone, and did not appear to have the slightest idea of what happened out there, beyond the sphere of her adoptive aunt and uncle. Awa hoped the girl never knew a fraction of what she did about the world. The idea of a rival tribe bursting into this magnificent house, hacking the adults with axes and abducting the children, seemed ridiculous, but then she remembered what the armies Manuel had served with had apparently done—according to her friend, the only difference was that the children inside the besieged cities might be cut down, burned alive, or raped instead of merely taken as slaves.

Awa's dark thoughts were interrupted by Manuel, who ushered her out of the kitchen where they had sat holding the baby and listening to his stories about the front line, with brave pikemen and gunners fighting the good fight against the hordes of the enemy. His studio was much smaller than she had imagined—smaller than he deserved, she thought—but even more spectacular for all the masterpieces crammed into that little room. Her breath caught and caught again with each new painting and print that Manuel hoisted, so that she had to cover her eyes from time to time not to swoon from lack of air.

Awa had dyed wool, of course, but had no idea so many colors could be replicated on the canvas. Having only seen his sketches, nothing could prepare her for the holly greens, rose reds, and daisy yellows the artist used—during her adolescence atop the sparse mountain, she had hardly remembered such colors existed at all. The ladies were her favorite, the willowy and the plump, the dark-haired and the fair. That she would be allowed to sleep in the room where all these ladies dwelled pleased her immensely, and dispelled some of her nervousness. Then Awa noticed a painting unlike the rest.

"It's you!" Awa marveled at how much more handsome Manuel appeared in the painting. In the image the artist was painting in an uncluttered, lavishly adorned room, an apprentice working in the background, cherubs overhead, a large window displaying the countryside behind him. "Where are you, in the painting?"

"Er"—Manuel scratched his head—"well, it's less any *specific* studio as it is the ideal studio, right, one where I'd have more room to work, and a lad to mix the color and everything."

"But it's so real!" Awa peered closer. "What is that gold circle floating behind your head?"

"I think it's about time to eat," said Manuel, reluctant to own up to artistically rendering himself in a similar fashion to what he did for the men he had struck down on the Lombardy battlefields, even if he had nominally done the painting as one of Saint Luke—it would take too long to explain, anyway.

That night, after a dinner that might have been awkward even without the revelation that the nun in filthy bandages was actually a Moor, and the arrival of a rather drunk Monique midway through, and the eventual disclosure that Manuel had not actually earned very much money at all, the artist and his wife finally escaped their guests and household, closing the door to their bedchamber with the finality of masons sealing a crypt. Then they fucked with far more passion than they had been able to raise over the last hour of entertaining, Katharina only giving her husband enough time to rinse his business before kneeling before him, kissing his stomach as she worked his member with a practiced hand. Manuel sighed, more content than he had been in ages, and then she took him in her mouth and he tousled her hair, groaning happily.

"Did you miss me?" Katharina asked, dropping him from her mouth and scooting backwards just as he reached the edge of the slope upon which there is no purchase. He teetered, clenching the muscles he did not know the names of, and the pressure relaxed. He scowled happily at his wife, who had gotten to her feet and was quickly undressing.

"Like a leper misses his limbs," said Manuel with a bow, pulling his trousers the rest of the way down. He had washed and changed upon gaining his house that morning and almost wanted to keep them on, so much had he missed the feel of genuinely clean clothing upon his flesh, but for some reason Katharina always insisted they be completely nude after dark. During the day she delighted in finding ways to accommodate him through her sometimes cumbersome dresses, in sliding his codpiece aside just enough to flick his foreskin with her tongue, to have him squeeze her breasts almost to the point of pain through her bodice, but once the sun had set she would not tolerate so much as a stocking upon him or her.

"Not more?" she pouted, the light of the full moon making her body glow like alabaster, and making Manuel once again contemplate taking up sculpture to better honor her.

"More than words can say," he said through a mouthful of shirt as he got the last garment over his head. "More than art can show, more than—ah."

Her foot had intercepted his chest as he reached the edge of the bed, intending to crawl on top of her.

"Ah," he said again, gently lifting the foot to his lips. She kicked him lightly on the chin.

"How many, Niklaus?" Katharina said firmly, her voice unwavering even as he took her big toe into his mouth. "It must have been quite a few, for you not to confess freely. The Moor?"

"No!" said Manuel, genuinely taken aback. "She wouldn't even let me sketch her, and besides, she reminds me of Lydie."

"Really?" Katharina had no idea how the stone-quiet and spruce-stocky Moor reminded her husband of their niece. "The big dyke, then?"

"Dyke? Really?" Manuel clicked his tongue at his wife, although his friend had more than once referred to herself as Schielands Hoge—the biggest dike in Rotterdam. "Mo'd break it off if I suggested it, and she won't let me sketch her, either."

"Hmmm," said Katharina, stretching her foot past her husband's ear, finally letting him lower himself. "Let me work on them, they'll have their skirts over their heads before you can mix your flesh tones."

"That's, well, that's, beautiful, really," said Manuel, but he wasn't thinking about painting his companions, he was gazing raptly at his wife's profile as he slid down beside her and kneaded her breast. "Christ Christ Christ, have I missed you, Kat."

She gasped and he squeezed harder but then she was sitting up, tearing his freshly scarred hand away and holding it up toward the window. "Niklaus, what's happened?!"

"Oh, that?" said Manuel, putting his unmarred right hand on the nape of her neck and squeezing gently. "That's a story for later, full of witches and bastards."

"But is it alright?"

"It is, it is, but there's another region that's troubling me..."

"Oh really?" Katharina began kissing the fingertips of the hand she held. "Now, I thought you just said witches."

"I did, I did," said Manuel, pulling his hand away from her mouth and replacing it with his own. "Later."

They did nothing but kiss for a very long time, and then she cried briefly but fiercely, holding on to the hand von Stein had shot, and then they fucked until Manuel came, which was far too quickly for both of their liking. Then he finally confessed to masturbating on five different whores, on nine separate occasions, as he used his hand and mouth on his wife—the taste of his own paint was a fitting penance, they agreed as she squirmed and he postponed her climax as he detailed the way he had made them hold up their skirts, the way it had run off their breasts like oil whites, but before he got to the last night with the last whore, where he had sketched a French girl no older than his niece with his charcoal in one hand and his cock in the other, splashing her chin and tongue and breaking the charcoal in his passion, before he got there Katharina had heard enough and drew his head back in with her nimble feet as he tried to break away to continue his tales, and she came harder than she had since he had left to go to war. Exhausted from the ride to Bern, and his wife, Manuel opted to wait until the next evening before asking her about the men she had enjoyed while he was gone.

"You could," Katharina said after they had both caught their breath. "I really wouldn't—"

"Hmph," Manuel snorted, cupping her breast firmer as he pressed himself against her. "Don't want to. The sketching's enough until I get back to you."

"It makes me think you're playing martyr when you say it like that," she said, more sharply than she intended. "I actually, you know, fuck other people, I fuck them, Niklaus, and you make up dirty stories. As long as the whores—"

"I don't want to jerk off on whores, let alone have sex with them," said Manuel. "I want to sketch them, and occasionally paint them, and then I want to come home and make gentle love to my wife as I invent stories about jerking off on whores. And call me old-fashioned, but I'm still perfectly happy with you sleeping with other men when I'm away so long as you love me best."

"Mmmm," said Katharina, snuggling closer to her husband. "I sometimes think it wouldn't be as... weird if you really did, instead of making it up."

"Oh? Weird, eh? A pity, then, it would be *so* much more

normal if I painted whores with my prick instead of my brush." Now Manuel pretended to sulk, but Katharina's hand had fallen to his, her fingers running over the gnarled scar tissue.

"Tell me what happened," she said, her tone now somber, and so he did, leaving out nothing. Before he had even stormed out of von Stein's tent for the first time she had gotten up and retrieved the special schnapps, and then they sat on the edge of the bed and drank little sips of the fiery enzian water as he recounted his story. She stopped him, bidding he confirm and confirm again the details of Awa raising the dead, and of her raising Manuel from the little death. She did not cry even when he did, and at last he concluded his story, wishing he could see her face in the dark—the moon had long since deserted them. He waited quite a while before she spoke. When she did, her voice was very flat, in the way it became when she was quite furious with him.

"So you risked me, and Lydie and the baby, all for a fucking witch, Manuel? A real witch? That creepy fucking Moor you brought here, into our home? With an Inquisitor searching for her?"

"The Inquisitor, he, ah, he's been excommunicated, and—"

"Niklaus Manuel!" She slapped him across the face as hard as she could, his left eyelid immediately swelling. "You're such a fucking idiot!"

"I didn't have a choice, they—"

"We always have a choice, Niklaus!"

"You're right," he said quietly. "I just kept, kept imagining it was, it was..."

"It was what?!"

"I kept imagining it was you under the sack they'd covered her with, or Lydie. And when they were going to rape her I kept thinking it, I couldn't stop, and I thought you'd want me to help her, whoever she was, and I, and I—" Manuel's voice broke, knowing his wife was right, that he had risked her, the most kind and wonderful person he had ever met, and his growing family besides, for a fucking witch, and only the hand of Providence had saved him; had the Inquisitor not been excommunicated they would all be dead, or worse, von Stein was a barbarian, and—

"Oh, Niklaus," Katharina whispered, taking her husband's head in her arms and stroking his hair. "It's alright, it is, and I'm proud of you, really I am, you just scared me—"

"I know!" he moaned. "I know I—"

"Shhh," she said, her own eyes filling not at her husband's tears, which were not so uncommon as some men's, but at the invisible sword he had hung over her head for who knew how many days until that Inquisitor had been discharged from the Church. "I love you, Niklaus; you're just too sweet for your own good. I'm proud of you, though, I am. I don't know if I would have saved her, if it meant risking you and our family."

"Katharina," he sniffled. "You're so good...you're so...so good, and I knew you'd, I knew you would be waiting for me, if I didn't, if I didn't lose my soul. It was a test, it had to be, and I passed, I did, and to prove it He cast out the traitor in His Church, He got rid of him."

"Who cast him out of the Church, Niklaus?"

"God," said Manuel, realizing how ridiculous he sounded.

"Now, that's impossible," said Katharina, and when this stunned her husband into silence she waited only one, two, three heartbeats before saying, "I'm an adulteress, you're a killer, and we don't pay nearly enough to the Church for Him to intercede on our behalf, you filthy artist."

They laughed in the dark, both scared and guilty for what they had thought, and then they finally went to sleep, the husband and wife forgetting everything but their love for one another as they fell into their dreams together.

XXI
Breakfast in Bern

While Katharina and Manuel spent their night engaged in wanton fucking and earnest conversation, Awa and Monique only did the latter. Both apologized, though each felt they really should not have to, and in the morning they were closer to friendship than they had been for days, if not quite warm. They ate fresh biscuits that Lydie had made, Katharina and Manuel coming down from the second floor midway through the meal.

"Nun sacks!" Manuel picked up one of the cocoon-shaped confections and bit into it with relish.

"Bozolati," Lydie said, glancing at Awa and blushing. "Nun's bozolati, uncle."

"Fu—fantastic, is what it is." Monique waved her biscuit at Manuel's niece. "Real choice, Lydie. Sweet, too."

Awa snorted, wondering what Manuel thought of the gunner flirting with his niece. Then she realized that several sets of eyes had settled on her, and she coughed, taking a sip of water. "Very sweet, young miss," said Awa. "Thank you very much."

"Manuel was telling me you both will be leaving for Marseilles at once," said Katharina as she got herself a plate before joining them. "A pity we did not have more time to get to know each other."

"Well, time's a fickle bitch," said Monique, biting into another biscuit.

"She is indeed," said Katharina mildly. "She is indeed."

A servant came in, only to take a step back at seeing Awa. Then he sheepishly hurried around the now-quiet table and whispered in Manuel's ear. Katharina heard what the man said and promptly dropped her biscuit, her eyes growing large.

"Pardon me," said Manuel, but Awa saw he had gone quite pale. On his way out after the servant he paused, looked at her, and then quickly exited into the hall. Even though he closed the door behind him they heard raised voices almost at once, and Katharina quickly stood up.

"If you ladies would care to join me," Katharina said, both Awa and Monique noticing that while she had discarded her biscuit she still held a small knife in her right hand. She was shaking slightly, and as Lydie opened her mouth to speak, or maybe sigh or yawn, the full attention of her aunt fell upon her. "Lydie, please take a walk outside."

"Where should—"

"Outside," Katharina repeated, and the two strangers realized that despite the levelness of her voice the woman was incensed. As soon as the girl had removed herself and the rear door swung shut Monique rose from the bench beside Awa.

"Right-o, what in hell's the rumpus?"

"Oswald," said Katharina, staring at the still seated Awa. "The abbot of the Dominican monastery."

"Oh," said Awa, recalling Manuel's story of the abbot who was not supposed to like ladies but did anyway. "Is he here to commission Manuel again?"

"The Dominicans are the ones burning witches," Katharina said softly, and Awa flinched from the sharpness of the woman's eyes. He had told her, then, and she had not been happy. Not at all, and now the chief Dominican in the area was talking to Manuel in the next room.

"Come on, then." Monique nudged Awa. "I'll get my pistols ready an' we'll scoot out, aye?"

Awa looked up at her friend. "They've caught me. Manuel's told me the sort of men they are, that those who try to help these women are accused themselves. I've endangered you all enough, so let me surrender and—"

Monique stuck out her tongue and blew, the raspberry deafening. Then she seized Awa and jerked her to her feet. "You're not that fuckin weak, an' neither am I. Let's go, little sister."

"What? Mo, I'm caught, they—"

"The window at the back of his studio." Katharina was looking at the biscuit she had dropped on the table. "Give me a moment, I'll, I'll spill something on myself and run in crying, keep them from looking out the front. Go straight out and left, there'll be more people on the road that way."

"No," said Awa, pulling her arm away from Monique, "I—"

"Don't think I won't fuckin carry ya," Monique hissed.

The door burst open and Monique's hand fell to her hip but her guns were still in their brace, hung over a chair in the studio, and Katharina gave a little yelp. Manuel beamed at them, shutting the door softly behind him and striding proudly over to the table. Looking at each woman in turn, he sat back down on the bench and picked up his half-eaten bozolati.

"Should I stab him?" Katharina asked Monique and Awa.

"Alright, alright!" Manuel put his breakfast back down. "The abbot's just called. Father Oswald?"

Katharina put the knife against her husband's cheek.

"And-he's-commissioned-me-to-paint-something-big," came out in a rush. "Very big, and very lucrative. It's finally happened, Kat, it's finally fucking happened!"

"Mary's mercy, Niklaus." Katharina's knife clanged onto her plate. "We heard shouting."

"He's just loud, and happy to see me. He's been waiting for my return." Manuel looked to Monique. "He commissioned me before, a small piece, but I was still excited, and so I had a drink or two since Kat—"

"Manuel," said Monique, sitting back down. "I've 'eard that story far too many times ta even pretend I give a fuck bout the 'orny bishop."

"Abbot," said Manuel, crossing his arms. "Oswald's an abbot."

"Don't make the story any more interestin." Monique took another biscuit. Meeting Awa's eyes, Katharina smiled. The necromancer smiled back, and they finished breakfast.

Monique claimed to need most of the afternoon to follow through on a few leads and Awa was not in a hurry to see her future employer fawning over pig-assed whores, and so as the table was cleared they parted until the evening. Later in the day, and after much soul-searching, Manuel went to his studio where Awa was preparing to leave.

"Awa?" She was admiring the dress Katharina had given her and Lydie had quickly altered, the accompanying veil draped over the stool as she held up the strange garment. The stained bandages and habit were disposed of, and Awa had been delighting in the feel of cool air on her bare skin when the knock came at the door. She pulled the dress over her head, battling the puffy sleeves onto her arms.

"Yes?" she said to the door.

"Can I... can I come in?" Manuel asked on the other side.

"Oh! Yes, yes, come in!" No one had ever asked her permission before entering a room, and the experience gave her a quiet little thrill.

"Ah," said Manuel, again asking himself how in heaven the strapping, dark-skinned woman reminded him of his little slip of a niece. The thin tunic and brown, ratty leggings she had retrieved from her bag by the river were no more flattering than the nun's habit or the clothes she had stolen from Bernardo, but they did suit her more than the soft dress she now wore. She seemed too big and too sharp for it, as though the cloth would be shredded to ribbons as soon as she took a step. "You look nice."

"Am I a woman of Bern yet?" Awa plucked up the veil and held it over her face.

"Good as, or better," said Manuel. "I'm glad Lydie was here, she's better than Katharina or I at tailoring."

"I'll be happy when I can knit my own clothes again," said Awa, dropping the veil. "I feel like this thing will rip as soon as I take a step."

"We do have a loom here, so—"

"Your wife doesn't like me, Manuel," said Awa. "You should have asked her instead of inviting me in without her knowing—"

"Katharina is, can be, ah, cautious, is all," said Manuel. "It's not that she doesn't like you, she just...doesn't like you being *here*."

"Oh," said Awa, angry with herself for letting such a valid sentiment hurt her. "We're leaving now, so she won't have to worry."

"About that..." Manuel suddenly wrung his hands. "Might you consider staying? Not in the house, but somewhere nearby where—"

"I don't need you to protect me, Niklaus Manuel Deutsch of Bern." Awa smiled.

"No, I suppose you don't," said Manuel, recalling all too well his poorly conceived and even poorer-executed escape plan back in the hazel wood with Werner and the rest. "But I do need your help, if you'd be willing to lend it."

"Niklaus Manuel Deutsch of Bern, I'll kill the Pope and every priest if it would please you," Awa said, her face doing its too-serious, vaguely sinister expression that always gave Manuel pause.

"Nothing, ah, so strong as all that," said Manuel. "Mo's talk has been rubbing off on you, I see."

"Not all she's been rubbing off on me," said Awa, and Manuel's eyes widened, the artist gaping at her. She stared back at him and shrugged. "Well, *I* thought it was funny."

And then he did laugh, far too loudly and weirdly for it to be genuine, but Awa appreciated the gesture nonetheless. "Niklaus Manuel Deutsch of Bern, I—"

"How in hell did we get back to the *of Bern*, eh? Manuel, it's Manuel, or Niklaus or—"

"Niklaus is what your wife calls you," said Awa, vigorously shaking her head. "Manuel. What is it I can do for you, Manuel?"

"Wellllllll," said Manuel. "You could stay the night, maybe in the brothel Mo's whores are at? And once the sun starts to go down you could—"

XXII
Dancing After Midnight

V

This is how it goes, thought Manuel as he crept down the street along the wall just after midnight, *this is the first step down. Don't be coy*, he thought next, *you're already seven flights down and dropping, by Alighieri's reckoning. Shall we do a recent head count of your mortal sins? Thirteen dead men before, plus the seven planks you've added to the compendium of saints from this last tour, plus Werner... did the other three count, Bernardo and the Kristobels?* They would still be alive if she had not been loosed, and he had loosed her, so—

A stone thumped his scalp, a lump quickly rising on his unadorned, and thus uninsulated, head. Looking up, he saw a shadow crouched on the top of the wall, and then she had his wrist and up he went. *This is how it goes*, he thought again as the moonlit churchyard came into sight beneath them, *break bread with a witch and before you know it you're digging up bodies and— Don't put this on her*, thought another part of him, *this idea is yours and yours alone, God forgive me.* Would the confessor wait for him to finish or drag him out of the box with his sins half recounted?

Awa dropped down on the other side of the wall and Manuel followed, the planks in his satchel clattering as he landed. Looking guiltily up at the monastery's church, Manuel wondered how many candles he and his wife had given over the years, how many bright mornings they had entered the building with the rest of the neighborhood instead of jumping the wall under cover of darkness. Then his eyes settled on the small chapel jutting out of the nave and he wondered if it would be a serviceable hiding place if the monks were to hear them in the graveyard and investigate. They slunk along the wall like burglars, which was what Manuel supposed they were, even if they just intended to borrow the property. Isn't that what thieves always said? *We were just borrowing?*

Then a figure loomed out of the darkness, a short, thin figure, a figure with holes punched through it by the moonlight, a grinning skull for a head, too-tight skin clinging to its bones like a damp shift on a sweaty whore. Manuel had seen the dead walk before but he still squeaked in surprise as it stepped back to prevent him from running into it, and as the other three corpses emerged from the shadow of the wall their smell hit him. He had smelled worse, and often, but even though they stunk of little more than wet dirt and old bones he felt himself beginning to gag and clapped a hand to his mouth.

"You were late so I got a few ready," Awa explained, and to his horror he saw she had changed back into the moldering nun's habit.

"Why are you wearing that?" he hissed, the walking dead momentarily forgotten at her heretical flourish. "That's not right!"

"So asking me to raise the dead for you is alright, but wearing this robe isn't?" Awa crossed her arms—walking around in both the habit and the dress without her leggings had chafed her thighs dreadfully, and to have him whine about what she had done for his benefit sat poorly with her indeed. "Monique found your servant throwing it away and saved it for me, and when I told her where I was going she surprised me with it. She said it would help me blend in, since we're at a church and—"

"Keep your voice down!" Manuel almost shouted, his eyes flicking to the dark building leering over the too-small cemetery. "Blend in?! In a churchyard, after dark, at a *monks'* monastery?"

"How is my wearing it here any worse than wearing it on the road or in your house or—"

"Point." Manuel clenched his hands into nervous fists. "Point. We should have gone to the hospital graveyard instead, with you dressed up like that. Or the nunnery across the Aare."

"Shall I light a—"

"No! Don't light anything!"

"Fine," Awa groused. "I was just trying to help. I didn't know your eyes were as good as mine since you walked past where I was sitting on the wall twice before I hit you with the pebble."

"The moon's all I need," said Manuel, giving the dark building a final once-over before kneeling and opening his pack. He should have been studying the corpses, taking in every detail, but he could not bring himself to look at them until he had plank and charcoal ready. "This commission is for the Dominicans, I suppose, so they can't object too strongly to our presence. It will probably go on the outside of the wall, though."

"I thought you'd drawn a lot of dead men," said Awa, sitting on a gravestone as he set up. "And what sort of church wants pictures of them?"

"Most of the men I've sketched aren't nearly so dead," said Manuel, picking out one of the corpses and focusing on him. Or her, the artist could not really tell. "And this is to be a Dance of Death."

"Oh," said Awa, not really understanding. "You should have told me. I can have them do anything you like."

Before Manuel could begin telling her about revivals of medieval tropes and the significance of Death as an artistic image, the four corpses had paired off and begun to dance. The only dance Awa knew was a rather spastic Andalusian routine the bandit chief Alvarez had taught her long ago on the mountain, on the night she first sampled wine, and to keep all four at it she had to focus so intently that she did not realize Manuel was speaking until he shook her arm, breaking her reverie. By this time the dead were in step and did not need her guidance, and as the two whispered back and forth the corpses pranced around the graveyard, kicking their feet and hopping on top of tombstones.

"Stop them!"

"Why? You said—"

"I know what I said! Fuck this, and fuck me for—"

"I'm stopping them, see? All done."

Manuel closed his eyes tightly, then opened them and looked over his shoulder. The undead corpses had gathered around him, leaning in closely as if they expected a great speech. He jumped.

"Just—no." Manuel shuddered, not even the continued darkness of the monastery a relief at this point.

"Right," said Awa, more than a little annoyed. She had vowed never to use the undead without their permission, yet she had broken her word to herself for the sake of her friend, reasoning that it was a relatively innocuous request. Had she more time, she would have asked if any of them minded, but Manuel had told her people were executed for what they would be doing and they had best be fast and silent, and so on the off chance that she brought back their spirits only to have them start screaming, or worse, she had raised them as mindless ones. Manuel was not being particularly fast or silent himself, and Awa took a drink from the bottle she had brought. "What do you want them to do, Niklaus Manuel Deutsch of Bern? Just stand there? I thought you said model, and I thought you said models did poses, and I thought—"

"I'm sorry, I'm sorry, I... is that wine?"

"Schnapps." Awa breathed a hot gust of pear vapors in his face as she handed him the liquor.

"Are you…are you drunk?" He took the bottle and found it half empty.

"No," said Awa. "But I fucking will be soon if you don't get a move on."

"So you can pose them, eh?" Manuel took another pull. "I hoped so. Here, hold on a moment…"

Leaning over his bag, he removed a lump of cloth, which he unwrapped to reveal a small drum. Then he took a similarly muffled drumstick from the satchel, then a flute, then a toy scepter or club, and finally a hat. As he shook out the bits of cloth he had wrapped the instruments in, Awa saw they were linen scraps. Grinning up at her, he said, "Props."

Getting the corpses fitted with hat and draped with cloth was easier than having them hold the instruments properly, but a cadaver that had somehow kept its mustache in the grave while losing its lower jaw seemed more adroit than its fellows, so Manuel gave him both the flute and the drum. Awa noticed a definite change come over Manuel as he instructed her and she instructed them on how to pose, the artist's nerves calmed more by the charcoal in his hand than the drink. Then he set to, and Awa peered over his shoulder, more impressed than ever with both his speed and skill. They drank the rest of the bottle as he worked, which encouraged him to draw wilder poses yet instead of packing it in.

"Perfect. Think I'll include Peter in that last one, old Falcky will get a kick out of it. Another mercenary, used to have all sorts of talks on faith and the Church and all. Wish you could've met him. Now stand a little to your left, and cross your hands. Perfect." Awa did as he asked. She had relented some time before to let him sketch her, and her initial disappointment that he was doing so here, in a graveyard surrounded by the walking dead, instead of in his studio, lasted only long enough for her to finish the schnapps. He paused, and as she watched he removed a cord from around his neck and tossed it to her. "Hold it in your, your left hand. Dangle it over your right."

Awa picked it off of the ground where it had landed and held it up. It was the necklace with the gold crucifix she had found in his bag the night they had met, along with Lydie's old doll. She let it hang from her hand, resuming the pose he had instructed her to take.

"Wait...pull the wimple higher over your head, but not so much's to cover your face. Good. Now hold the necklace tween your fingers, like it was a rosary."

"A rosary? Oh, the beaded necklaces people are buried with, yes?"

"Oh. Yes, those." Manuel supposed people *were* buried with them. "Like that. Good. I'll make it look like a rosary on the wall, no problem there. Now turn sort of toward Mustache, him with the flute and drum? Gooooood. Now look away. No, not your head, just your eyes. So face forward, eyes away? Perfect! Fuck, that's perfect, Awa...no, don't smile, look...concerned, very concerned. Death's right fucking beside you, isn't he, but you don't want to look, right?"

"I suppose not." Awa fought with her face, the battle made all the harder by the admonishment to stay serious.

"Thank you," Manuel said at last, stretching his arms and straightening up. Awa relaxed, too, the process not nearly as thrilling as she had hoped once the initial excitement waned. "Wish I'd known you were game, I'd have had you bring another set of clothes."

"Tonight is a fortuitous night for Niklaus Manuel Deutsch of Bern," Awa said with a wink, and before he could protest she had squirmed out of the nun's habit, revealing the hand-me-down dress Katharina had given her. Its yellow coloration looked jaundiced in the moonlight, and the red ribbon bow dangled lower than it ought to at her waist, and it was still so large that the ribbon-trimmed bodice and puffed sleeves hung down in a fashion that a less fatherly pair of eyes might have thought of as provocative. "What say you, Manuel? Another sketch?"

"Let's have the king pose with you," said Manuel, gesturing to the skeleton with the hat.

"Why is he a king?" asked Awa as she had the boneman stand beside her.

"His crown, for one," said Manuel, "which will look more like a crown once I'm done with it, and the scepter in his hand."

"Oh, that?" Awa took the toy from the corpse and waved it at Manuel. "His hands are busy, so let's put it somewhere more visible."

"Busy? Visible?"

"Here." They had needed to affix a chinstrap around the skull to get the hat to stay on the slick bone, and Awa jammed the haft of the scepter through this strap, so it jutted up beside his crown. This pleased her immensely, and she nodded at Manuel knowingly.

"What are his hands busy with, then?" said Manuel as he got his plank into place.

"Me, of course," said Awa, having worked toward this, or something like it, all evening. She still had not recounted her farewell speech to Manuel, but as they had drunk and laughed as quietly as they could in the churchyard a deep, breath-snatching guilt had come over her for even thinking of saying a fond farewell and leaving him with false pretenses. She realized that she needed for Manuel to know just how wicked she was, just how fucked up and crazy. She had tricked her friend into being her friend, had acted normal and kind instead of like the beast she knew she was.

Somehow the words had not come, though, all night they had secreted themselves away from her tongue. In the morning she would be gone, would probably never see him again, and she owed this fine friend the truth, so that he would not miss her or remember her fondly. Then she would return to the brothel and tell Monique the same thing, and then she would be done lying to people, to friends, done with leaving out the nasty truth of who she was, of what she had done. Then she would go back south, to Paracelsus—if there was one person who would not care if she had raped the dead it would be the mad physician, who probably would not mind if she raped him so long as she disclosed her necromantic secrets.

Manuel was staring at her, mouth wide, and then she felt the finger bones she had guided to her chest worm their way under the edge of her bodice. She smiled a crazed, too-wide smile as she looked at Manuel, and linked her right arm through that of the king of the bonemen. His skull came ever closer toward her cheek, and she batted her eyes at Manuel. Now he would cast down his plank, demand to know what was, no, what *the fuck* was wrong with her, and she would tell him, laughing or crying or both, she would tell him about Omorose, about what she had done to her corpse and he would hate her, he would tell her—

"That's perfect!" said Manuel, and then his hand was off like Omorose fleeing over the glacier, a blur on the plank, and Awa stared at him, her miserable smile losing its wild edge, and she struggled to keep in another of those damn giggling fits. She had rarely suffered them before making his acquaintance. He was some friend, she thought, as Manuel drew the seemingly lecherous king skeleton copping a feel. "Yes, keep looking at me, keep that smile. Perfect. I used to tell old Tiziano, have the girls look out of the painting, really confront the viewer, but I didn't take my own advice, except with the smut commissions I'd do for the boys, and Tiziano, the master I had in Venetia, he'd berate me, said it was scandalous, the dirty old dog, though secretly I think he rather liked it, wouldn't be surprised if he started doing—"

"I fucked a dead girl," Awa blurted out. Manuel did not say anything, but he did not stop drawing, either. She tried to keep her pursed smile but the choking wind was coming out of her lungs, catching in her throat, tearing up her eyes. "My friend, my mistress. Omorose. I dug her up and I raped her, and I didn't ask, and her spirit, when I put it back in, wants to kill me, and—"

She was crying too hard to see he had put his panel down, and then he gently unhooked her arm from the king and held her as she sobbed and blathered, holding her stiffly but firmly. Manuel wondered if it surprised him, this lonely, half-mad witch who had come from nowhere confessing to such a deed. *This is what happens*, he thought, *when you consort with witches, you find yourself in cemeteries hoping the monks don't catch you and— Fuck you, and fuck them*, he thought, and held her tighter. She pulled herself together quickly, and pushed him away, wiping her cheeks.

"It's alright," said Manuel, "we all—"

"It's not," said Awa firmly. "It. Is. Not."

"Well, I think—"

"Get a plank, Manuel, get a plank and I'll pose, and you draw what I show you, and it will be, what did you say, less *vivid*, than what I, what I really did, and then tomorrow, when you're not drunk and graverobbing and excited, then you take your little picture and you look at in the light of day, and you tell yourself then that it's alright. You show it to your wife, and ask her if it's alright, or anyone else. I'm a beast, Manuel, a filthy beast, and I raped her, I made her, I did, I—"

"Shut up," Manuel said sternly, his tone harder than she had ever heard it. "People will hear, people we don't want hearing us. I'm getting my plank, so pick your partner and we'll sort this out right now."

"What?" Awa had not been thinking, and now he was really going to make her, which was what she deserved, but—

"Quickly, Awa." Manuel had a new plank up. "We're losing the moon."

What she deserved. Awa glanced at the corpses and had the foulest, wettest mold-swaddled carcass walk to her, and knowing it incapable of deception, asked if its spirit would mind her attentions. It would not, and so, glancing at Manuel, Awa dragged it to her and kissed it full on the mouth. Her hands groped its body, grabbed the rancid penis that mashed between her fingers, vomit competing with the sob to breach her mouth, and then Manuel pulled her away from it.

"Awa," said Manuel, his face in shadow, his eyes dark as ink. "That's not what happened. That's not you. I know you better than that, and if I require one thing from my models, be they whores or ladies, children or crones, it's honesty. You can't fool me. Now show me what happened, and don't be afraid."

Walking back to his plank, the artist heard her retching behind him. The internal voices that sometimes had things to say, things to ask, were all silent now, as if frightened into silence by the strange, mechanical change that had come over him. His mind was as blank as the pine panel before him, and taking a deep breath, he looked up. Awa and the corpse were appraising one another, and then the cadaver made its move.

Awa drew back, but he recognized the coquettishness of her movements, the playfulness of her retreat. Its hands were on her, leaving dark smears on the dress, and though he sometimes thought she was glancing at him for help, for mercy, he sat and he watched and slowly he began to return to himself.

"Stop," the artist finally said to himself and Awa, and both woman and partner went as still as the dead man's heart. The corpse's right hand was drawing Awa's curl-wreathed head toward his open mouth for another kiss, and his left was pressed up between her legs, her dress hiked almost to indecency, only her right hand on his wrist arresting his assault. Her dress fluttered between his legs in the cold breeze that picked up across the cemetery, and Manuel began to sketch.

"There," Manuel said at last, the crown of the moon dipping behind the cemetery wall. "Come and have a look, Awa."

She broke the embrace with the corpse, whispering an apology to it and walking to where Manuel stood. Looking at the picture, she could not express what she felt. The image captured her crime perfectly, but the woman in it, her, seemed the victim instead of the perpetrator.

"Awa," Manuel finally said after the moon had sunk and they were enveloped in darkness. "I think with some time in the studio, this will be my finest work. I have never had a better model, and I thank you for your patience."

"You're welcome," said Awa, her voice just as stilted and dead as his. She was not sure what his drawing her had done, save strip her of the little self-respect she had managed to knit for herself from the small compliments he, Monique, and Paracelsus had paid her—and, of course, the praise of the dead, who for so long had been her only friends. The nauseating urge to kill him unexpectedly flared in her, but then he took her shoulder tightly in his hand, his breath hot on her face.

"We do evil, Awa, that is what we are born for. We sin against one another and against ourselves, whether we mean to or not. We are born into this. There are none, *none*, who escape the fact that in our very nature is a compulsion to annihilate ourselves. And each other."

"What I did—" she began, his clumsy attempt to make her feel better even more insulting than making her re-create the act for his voyeuristic pleasure.

"I know what you did," said Manuel, those tiny voices inside him howling their displeasure at his calm, at his understanding. "You showed me. The first was not what happened, you didn't lay into a dead body like a hungry beast, you, you, the second time... you resisted, it forced itself on you and—"

"No!" Awa said far too loudly, a chain of dogs linking themselves to the sound, and then Bern was rattling with barks. "No, I, I made her. I didn't know it, I didn't know she didn't want to, I thought she did, but I was still doing it. I made her force herself on me, as you say, which is worse than—"

"No," said Manuel. "I don't understand the how of your, your ways, nor do I want to, but I heard you say, right now, that you didn't know exactly what you were doing. Is that the truth, Awa?"

Awa nodded, suddenly unable to speak, but he somehow saw in the dark and nodded himself.

"Then I don't want to hear any more. I knew what I was about when I went to war, when I cut open boys younger than Lydie to buy a little paint. I could have given up the art, I could have taken up nobler work, but I took money to kill boys far more innocent than myself. I knew, yet I did it. Tell me how your crime is worse, Awa, tell me how doing evil in ignorance is worse than doing it voluntarily, than doing it for a few fucking crowns instead of out of, out of love? That's why, isn't it? You loved this girl, and she died, and so you made a mistake? How is—"

Awa's arms were around his neck, and as they held each other neither was sure whose tears were whose, and were happy for the ignorance. It was very dark in the cemetery.

"God loves you," said Manuel as they tamped down the earth over the graves of his models, the corpses returned to their beds and tucked in with the help of the spade Awa had found by the nave. "He loves us all, and will forgive you if you ask Him. We can go together, straightaway, and if the confessor betrays you then the evil will be his, not yours, and—"

"Niklaus," Awa said quietly. "Do you forgive me?"

"Of course."

"That's what matters."

"Oh."

"And going to one of your holy men seems like a terrible idea."

"It does, doesn't it?" Manuel yawned. "He'll find you, in time, or you'll find Him. For now I'm fucking exhausted."

"Me too," said Awa. "Thank you, Niklaus Manuel Deutsch of Bern."

"And thank you, Lady Awa," Manuel said with a bow to match what the four dead men had given them when Awa momentarily returned their souls to their bodies to properly apologize before reburying them.

Over the wall went the artist and the necromancer, and as the dawn began to bleed over the rooftops of Bern they said their farewells in the street beside the monastery. Awa's improvised goodbye was not the eloquent speech she had rehearsed, nor were Manuel's awkward verbal fumblings much more than that, but they meant every word. There they parted, Manuel returning to his wife and family and studio and station, and Awa to the companionship of a would-be whoremonger who made a far better friend than a lover, neither knowing if they would ever see one other again.

XXIII
The Rise of the Hammer

It was not easy, being a bastard, but Ashton Kahlert managed to pull it off. Had his father acknowledged his birth and given him the love and affection he so craved he might have turned out conceited and proud, with unrealistic expectations about the world. Worst of all, he might not have appreciated how brilliant his father truly was—most of his peers took their fathers for granted, ignoring greatness if it sprung from their patriarch as though their own abilities were in danger of being overshadowed by the very existence of the men who gave them life. Ashton had no such pride, no such conceit, and so he saw, albeit from a distance, just how important his father was.

His mother was, well, his mother, and the best that could be said for her was her candor in disclosing the identity of Ashton's father. If the boy's grandfather had not taken his fallen daughter back into his home life might have proven much harder for Ashton, but as it stood the lad grew up inside a decent enough house in Salzburg instead of on its streets. The streets were still there, of course, and rare was the day that he could avoid them and the bullyboys who beat and mocked him for having a whore of a mother, but at least he had a bed and four walls and a roof to return to, red-eyed and bloody-nosed. He was almost old enough to seek an apprenticeship when he found out the identity of his father, although his mother, being his mother, tried to make herself the martyr in the rendition she told.

"Heinrich Kramer," she had told him as they cleaned up after dinner one winter night, keeping her voice low so her father could not hear them from his chair by the hearth in the only other room. She had promised him she would not tell the boy what had happened but the fantasy father her son had invented for himself was so wrongheaded, so misplaced, that she had to set him straight, even though it would hurt him. "*The* Heinrich Kramer, Inquisitor of our fair little saltheap, and of all Tyrol besides."

Seeing her son's jaw drop, she went on before he could get carried away with his fancies. "He's a cruel man, Ash, a very cruel man. Do you think I'm a witch?"

"What?" Ashton smiled. "Of course not. If you were you'd not be so miserable all the time."

"Thank you for that," she said. "He didn't think I was, either, but that didn't stop him from making a veiled accusation or two. He'd come into the bakery I was working at, when I'd gone to Tyrol, and he took a fancy to me, and that was that. So in he comes and tells me he'll put me on trial for putting the blood of babes in my bread if I don't do as he says. I'm not kidding, Ash."

Yet Ashton could not stop smiling. His father was a great man, just like he had always insisted to the bullies who worked him over. His father was a great man and, better still, a living man. His mother was going on now, doing her little sniffling act she always did when he was "being difficult," but Ashton had heard enough to know what really happened. His mother, well-meaning and kind and thoughtful though she might have been, was a slut, and Ashton had seen her bring home enough men when his grandfather was away to know she must have seduced Inquisitor Kramer, then been put out when he denied any responsibility for the child. She was his mother and he loved her, but he could hardly blame his father for not wanting some low slattern for a wife.

"Father?" The Inquisitor looked the boy up and down, Ashton feeling his hard eyes running over the yawning seam where his shoes needed cobbling, the patches on his trousers that were only a little off-color, the sweat stains on his linen shirt, the slightly too big hat he had taken from his grandfather. "Impossible. Do you know what it is that you do, boy? You accuse me before God of being an adulterer. Me."

"I didn't...I don't..." The years Ashton had spent preparing for this moment had dragged by so slowly that he had thought the day would never come at all, yet now that it had arrived it was flying by far too quickly, and the angry expression on the man's face told him just how naïve he had been. Of course his mother had made it up to make herself sound more important, to say that for one night at least she was found desirable by a great man. This was all her fault, and as the Inquisitor reached for the small brass bell on his desk Ashton felt the tears come, and rather than be cast out with this great man thinking he had invented the story himself for his own gain he fell to his knees and quickly blurted out an apology. "This wasn't—it wasn't my idea. My mother told me you were, you were with her when she worked at a bakery. In Tyrol. She was lying to me, I see that now, she's a lying slut and I'm sorry, I'm so sorry I came, I meant no, I meant no malfeasance, I—"

"Malfeasance." Kramer smiled, his hand hovering over his bell. "A fine word, a topical word, but not the word you meant, I don't think. Are you sure you're not trying to blackmail me, to get a little something from your malfeasant papa?"

"No!" Ashton said, trying to calm his breathing, to stop his tears, to remember the words he had rehearsed. His father was supposed to have acknowledged him, to offer him a place and opportunities, and he was supposed to nobly turn them down, to say, as he was saying now, despite how inappropriate the words had become, "I just, I just wanted you to know I'm going to be better than any other son my mother would have bore, because you are a great man. I am going to be a great man, because you are—"

One of Kramer's black-gloved hands had slipped in front of his square jaw, and a long finger shot up before the man's smiling lips. Ashton trailed off as the Inquisitor slowly got to his feet and walked around the table, the coils of his hair bobbing around his ear as he peered closer at the boy. His smile grew wider, and he tousled Ashton's hair. The boy nearly wet himself.

"Innsbruck," Kramer said in a low murmur. "The little witch of Innsbruck. You're fifteen, lad?"

"I think, sir," said Ashton, not quite sure.

"Your mother seduced me," said Kramer, ever smiling at his son. "She baked some of her hair and blood into a cake, and gave it to me. By the time her witchcraft had worn off I had already put you in her belly."

Ashton tried to speak, to tell his father the lies his mother had told, but only a happy little sob came out.

"I let her live, and escape trial, because I knew I had put some good into her," said Kramer, leaning back against his desk and pointing at Ashton. "You. I made her recant her ways, of course, and swear that when you were of age she would tell you who your father was, so you could come to me and receive my blessing. I see that here she was as good as her word."

"She lied!" Ashton managed. "She said you wouldn't want, she said you wouldn't want, she..."

Heinrich Kramer went to his son then, and the boy felt the soft baized wool of his father's robe soak up his tears, gloved hands removing his oversized hat and stroking his hair as he cried and cried. Of course the Inquisitor could not publicly acknowledge the boy as his own, and of course Ashton understood. Even still, Heinrich Kramer was a gentleman and a loving father, and helped in every possible way with the boy's desire to follow in his heavy bootsteps. Within a few years Kramer was denounced by first a local bishop and then the Inquisition as a whole for his radical methods and publications, but through his eager son the good work continued.

Ashton worked his way up through the local Dominican order with the invisible glove of his father unlocking the few doors that the boy could not pry open with his natural intelligence and zeal. Low means and low birth were no longer the barriers Ashton had supposed they would be, and his father's close association with the archbishop of Salzburg meant that the boy was eventually appointed Inquisitor himself, albeit of a more remote region. He met with his father often, and together they would go over the finer points of Kramer's witch-hunting manual that the Inquisition had claimed was out of line with doctrine.

Despite the Church's betrayal of him, their most faithful son, Kramer knew that only through the flames of the Inquisition could the Empire and all her little princedoms, bishoprics, and prince-bishoprics be cleansed of the taint that had taken root, and if his son were to be his instrument, then so be it. Indeed, Ashton's illegitimacy proved most beneficial for the two of them, the myriad enemies they made within both the Church and the universities unable to connect father and bastard son in any sort of discrediting manner. Kramer died a very happy and old man, and his son, Ashton Kahlert, proudly set to ensuring that his own father's legacy would be as immortal as that of God the Father. That he had never mustered the will to properly question his mother before her eventual murder at the hands of one of the men she brought home Ashton considered his chief personal failure, but he tried not to dwell on it.

Kahlert's effectiveness at ferreting out witches was not lost on the archbishop of Salzburg and his associates, but after the enemies of the Inquisition had successfully removed Kramer from power all true believers knew a more cautious route was in order. Kahlert's official role as Inquisitor was thus obfuscated from as many records as was feasible, and his jurisdiction was expanded to wherever he set his feet.

As the most powerful living necromancer prepared to escape the prison of his body atop the Sierra Nevadas, Inquisitor Kahlert journeyed to Granada to assist the Spanish Dominicans with the ongoing expulsion of Jews and Moors from the lands united by the deceased Isabella and the demented Ferdinand—the kabbalists were up to their old tricks, adding blood to the matzos, and stranger sorceries still were credited to the Moslems. Reluctant to abandon the purging of his homeland though he was, Kahlert had learned from his father that the cleansing could not be limited to one area, lest honest men forever be taxed with the guarding of their borders from marauding witches.

Granada was a fair city, and so purged of Jew and Moslem that Kahlert could scarce believe a Moor had ruled it only twenty years before and allowed every sort of degeneracy to flourish. The Spaniards—some of them, anyway—understood the effectiveness of his father's interrogation methods far better than the Imperial Inquisitors had, and Kahlert established himself in a quiet little house up in the Andalusian foothills overlooking the city. When he was not assisting in the more problematic interviews with the accused, he rediscovered his youthful love of the romance, and in only a few years had assembled a fine collection of melodramas and adventures by the greatest German, English, and Italian authors; the French he found entirely too French, and the Spanish were, well, everyone knew what Spaniards were, and it went double for their romances.

One evening, after a day sweating in a dungeon with a pair of pliers and a pair of Jewesses, Kahlert took a constitutional among the chestnut trees above his house, and there he met the most beautiful woman he had ever seen. There were no other houses for some distance, and the servants he kept were all men, and yet here was a woman sitting on a boulder, dark enough of complexion to arouse suspicion, but comely despite it. She wore an exotic, flowing garment of multicolored silk and, even as he knew she must be brought in for questioning, Kahlert found himself looking for an excuse to delay such an engagement.

"Good evening," Kahlert said in Spanish with a bow. "You are lost?"

The woman looked up, and he saw from the tears still shining on her cheeks that she had been crying, though her kohl-darkened eyes were not the slightest bit puffy or red. She seemed to hesitate for a moment, and then replied in a husky voice. "I am indeed lost, good sir. Indeed, I doubt any in all this world are more lost than I."

"Perhaps I may be of service, then," said Kahlert, the encounter seeming more and more like one of his romances. "My house is not far from here, and from the patio we may overlook all of Granada. I have found a delicate pigeon sofrito after a leisurely stroll helps orient oneself marvelously."

"That is a most generous offer," said the woman. "If it would not be an imposition I would be pleased to join you."

She was not jabbering at him in a foreign tongue; on the contrary, she spoke with obvious care and intelligence. Having seen a few Spanish ladies with only slightly lighter skin, Kahlert let himself hope she might actually be a lost Christian of unfortunate pallor and nothing worse. Then he realized she was clearly waiting for him to help her from her seat, and he quickly extended his hand. Through his glove her fingers felt even thinner than they looked, the delicate bones hard in his palm.

"What is your name, my lady, and from where did you hail prior to being lost?" Kahlert asked her as she released his hand and stood beside him.

She began to tremble anew, the pools of her greenish-brown eyes filling, and as if speaking the words caused her physical pain, she groaned, and he barely made out her words: "Um... a...Rose. Call me Rose. I'm from...there." She pointed south, her face contorting with emotion.

Kahlert realized how insensitive he was. His work had not allowed for much polite contact with decent women, and he cursed himself for a low-mannered clod. "Forgive me. Of course you are exhausted and in need of rest and nourishment, not an interrogation. Please accept my apologies, Lady Rose. My name is Ashton Kahlert, and I confess that I am a terrible host."

She nodded, too well-bred to sniffle despite the obvious appropriateness of the occasion for it. Kahlert's mother would have sniffled. If, during his lengthy tenure as a witch-hunting Inquisitor, he had encountered even one actual witch Kahlert might have paid more attention as he led her back to his house. He might have noticed little things, like the way the hem of her dress never became dusty, or how, despite wearing little brown sandals, she left bare footprints upon the dirt track. But he had never captured anyone more sinister than a mundane midwife and so these telltale signs were lost to him.

The servants were surprised to see their master returning with anyone along the trail that wound into the hills behind the stucco-framed house, let alone a beautiful, immaculately dressed woman. Not having any women in the house meant he had not needed female servants, but the woman insisted she was perfectly capable of bathing herself once the bath was heated. Kahlert retired to change for dinner, not something he was accustomed to doing.

Omorose settled into the bathwater with a sigh, and while her illusory appearance remained unblemished, scraps of the young corpse began floating loose in the water. She frowned at that. She would need to acquire bandages to wrap her flesh in, lest an ear fall off mid-conversation with her host—at the very least, the strange particulars of necromancy meant she would keep her tongue and her bones, which would be sufficient so long as she kept the ring on her finger at all times. She had stopped daring to hope she would ever enjoy another bath around the time she had died, and while the sensation of warm water running over exposed tendons and bone was less fulfilling than it was on her few remaining patches of skin, a bath was a bath was a bath, and she was happy to have it.

Omorose had not allowed herself to relax since fleeing the mountaintop days before, convinced her former slave was right behind her the whole time. The fleeing corpse had avoided the few houses and towns she had glimpsed, terrified she might be caught and banished back to the grave by Awa if she were discovered eating in a farmhouse or dozing in a barn. Yet when the pasty man had discovered Omorose in the woods and offered her succor the idea of further flight lost all appeal. Let the beast find her, so long as it meant a hot bath and a meal of something other than chestnuts and longpig. Being dead, Omorose needed neither food nor drink, but wanted them desperately, and the longer she went without them the less real and the more deranged she felt.

Her mind turned to Ashton Kahlert. He would have to be informed of Awa, at least in some fashion, so that if the black beast arrived, he could…

What was left of Omorose's lips curled back in delight. Ashton Kahlert was not dead. Ashton Kahlert was a man of some means, clearly. Ashton Kahlert was not prevented by Awa's curse from harming the little beast, from killing her. Why scour the ends of the earth for a book when all she needed was to find one of the living to exact her vengeance for her? She could watch, of course, she would have to watch, it would be too wonderful to miss, and if he took it slow…

Then again, Kahlert seemed a little old and soft, hardly the sort of man to indulge Omorose's need to watch Awa being taken apart by degrees. She would have to be very careful and very convincing, for he was alive and she was dead, and therefore she could not tell him a single lie. Worse still, if the beast had not been following her, if she had fled in the other direction, then she might already be a week or more away, and who was to say this Kahlert would employ his resources to capture her?

The man had hungry eyes, to be sure, but that might not be enough. Clearly no women lived in the house, which was curious for a man of means, and might denote a difficulty rather than an advantage in securing his favor if he were unaccustomed to indulging a lady. Omorose sighed and sank lower in the tub, not having had many opportunities to relax as an independent, undead being.

There was a knock at the door.

"Yes?" she called, louder and more confident than she intended.

"Just checking in," Kahlert's voice came through the door. "Are you hungry?"

"Famished," she said in a much more satisfyingly quavering voice. "I shall be out soon."

"No hurry, please," said Kahlert, padding away from the door. He returned to his library and his pacing, hands clammy. Being alone had restored some of the wits she had taken, and Kahlert was not at all convinced she was not a dangerous witch. This was how his mother had ensorcelled his father, after all, through her looks and manner, a seemingly simple girl in need of the attention of her betters. He would flush her out, though, or be convinced of her purity, and to this end he hurried to the kitchen to make preparations—holy water in the carafe and blessed salt in the table bowl to burn her lips, a mug of sheep's milk that she might spoil with her presence.

Lifting herself out of the now-black water, Omorose inspected the small room and immediately noticed a book on a stool beside the chamber pot. Constipation and bathroom reading have long been confederates, so its mere presence did not interest her—it was the title. Her tutor had prepared stews for his pupils using dried tongues, and one of the tongues had belonged to a very lost Franciscan who had blundered within reach of the necromancer's bonemen. The monk had known Latin, and as a result so did Omorose and Awa.

Malleus Maleficarum. Malleus was "hammer," so the title was *The Hammer of Malefactresses.* Thumbing through the dog-eared volume, Omorose very quickly deduced that in this instance "malefactress" meant "witch." Flipping back through it, she saw an inscription on the very first page, and as she read the cramped Latin a dry, rattling chuckle rolled out of her throat.

My dear Ashton, Inquisitor Before Man and God,

What father but He Above may know my grief at being unable to intervene beyond bestowing my own humble wisdom upon so loyal a son? Hearken to the Clarion Call, heed this text, add to it with thy observations, and with brands aloft we shall rid this world of every witch that pollutes it with her licentious evil. Fear not, for I shall be thy hammer, just as thou shall be mine.

With Respect,
Heinrich Institoris Kramer, Inquisitor Before God

The woman stepped out into the warm evening, bringing the odor of honey and lavender to Kahlert's flaring nostrils. Her saya dress appeared even more lovely than it had before, and not so exotic in style, and by the light of the many candles he had lit she did not look nearly so dark as she had first seemed. The dust of the road, no doubt, now washed free. At that moment the servant cleaning the bath chamber was nearly overcome by the fumes of the water and the foul gray, green, and black residue on the towels. As the help uniformly hated Kahlert, no mention was made to him regarding this unpleasant discovery—if she was a bruja then it would serve him right.

"You appear radiant," said Kahlert, striking a clumsy bow. Most of what he knew about etiquette came from his romances, and were thus out of date and from the wrong regions besides.

"Thank you, Inquisitor Kahlert," said Omorose, bowing herself. "Why did you not mention that you were a witch hunter?"

She smiled to herself at his stupefied expression, his reddening cheeks, his nervous babbling of excuses, and with a wave of her delicate hand she quieted him. Then she poured wine from a silver decanter on the table into his glass, refusing to let herself lick her lips at the sight and smells of the dinner. Then she poured herself a glass and leaned back in her chair, the lights of Granada shining beneath them as though they were dining above the stars.

"Inquisitor," said Omorose, cutting off whatever nonsense he was saying, "I was chased here by a witch who is trying to destroy me. I was a pious girl in my youth, but not so very long ago found myself at the mercy of a sorceress, and only narrowly did I escape her clutches. As long as she exists I am in mortal danger."

Kahlert dropped his glass and it broke at his feet. Whatever he had expected, this was not it, although it certainly explained a few things. He had *known* witchcraft was involved, and he was overjoyed that his guest was innocent. Then he realized she had taken his shaking hands, and looking at her pale cheeks, her eyes blue as his own, he could not imagine how he had thought her a Moor.

"Ashton," said Omorose, choosing her words as carefully as he chose his tools when interrogating supposed malefactresses.

"I wish that I could tell you tales of this witch and her actions, but due to my condition, the condition she has afflicted me with, I cannot without risking myself. I must furthermore beg—beg with all my heart—that no matter what, you never ask me any questions about myself, about my past and what has befallen me. If you do, the witch will surely triumph. I will tell you what little I can without risking myself, but if ever you ask even a single question of me I may fail, and the witch, the necromancer, will be victorious."

Kahlert clung to her words like a romantic hero clinging to a precipice, knowing at long last his true test was at hand.

"Ashton," Omorose breathed, the fear in her voice genuine—if he asked but one question... "Ashton, will you help me find and destroy this malefactress, though I will not tell you all the details of her witchery? I cannot stop her by myself."

Well she might have asked the rain to dampen her hair, or the sun to dry it. She was a simple creature, he realized quickly, of limited understanding but a true heart, and if the trial of his faith was not questioning her further then he would obey. Preventing a victim from testifying under penalty of some curse was exactly the sort of trick a witch would employ. Once Kahlert recovered from the shock of it all they ate together, and then talked long into the night of how to find the witch. He would be her hammer.

XXIV
The Whores, the Boors, and the Moor

The road to Paris had not proved smooth, direct, or happy, but at last they were unpacked and settled in a miserable dump in the worst ghetto in the entire stinking city. Laws were changing, and every city and hamlet they passed through had already reached their quota of sanctioned brothels, which was rarely more than one or two in even the larger towns. With each failure Monique would curse and grin and the small caravan would move on, only occasionally losing whores to desertion. The gunner was adamant her business be legitimate and licensed, and that was how they found themselves in Paris with more mouths than they had loaves, and there at last Dario, a scrawny, ginger-tufted little man, returned to the wagons with all the paperwork signed, the license acquired, and the last of Monique's funds exhausted.

Awa was a little surprised to find that Monique had a husband, but soon enough realized what her friend meant by *beard*—the man had no more interest in women than Monique had in men, and so their marriage was far less tumultuous than most. He did have a rather virulent case of the pox when they had finally tracked him down in Marseilles, but Awa got him cleaned up and before long he was boasting and swaggering and drinking just as much as his wife. They had served together in Lombardy long before Manuel had enlisted, though Monique confided to Awa that Dario was no better with an arquebus or pistol than she was with a penis.

"Kin work a soup spoon or a saber like I kin work a nub, mind," said Monique. "Could turn a turd inta a currant tart, that one could, an' when we got in it he'd keep straight ahead an' I'd be ta the rear reloadin, which would've got von Wine's goat if we didn't get the results we did. Fucker was always tryin ta get us ta act like archers when these bronzies of mine are shit from more'n a few paces."

Dario had not served in the last campaign under von Stein, meaning he had a better idea than Monique of where her favorite prostitutes had gotten to. Most were still working for Paula, the madam who had previously followed von Stein's camp, and while Monique had no interest in an alliance she did hope to screw the woman out of some of her better whores. The harlots they picked up were in no better condition than the wagons they found themselves needing before very long, women worn down and scarred by life but nevertheless capable of rolling on a few more leagues.

Despite the drafty, flea-ridden room in the dilapidated brothel Awa had briefly shared with Monique before leaving Bern, the necromancer had imagined that, once they were all settled in, Monique's operation would closely resemble the harem where Omorose had lived and Awa had served. The reality was remarkably less comfortable, the half-timbered three-story building listing as though it might topple onto the village of tents and ramshackle huts beside it if a mark were to go at one of the girls with more vigor than a rheumatic geriatric climbing a steep staircase.

As promised, Awa did have a private room, even if it was the low-ceilinged attic in the gable. The garret would have been dustier than an indulgence-seller's piety if the leak in the thatch roof had not turned the dust into mud the color of gunpowder. Dipping into her small fortune of antique coins—the graveyard loot that she had decidedly not volunteered to help Monique get her business off the ground—Awa bought a pallet, blankets, a spindle, some wool to spin, an iron pot, and a large pan to burn wood in, though over the years she had become quite adept at using only the salamander eggs to cook her dinner. After she had scraped the layers of mud away, enlisted the spirits of the next storm to show her where to patch the ceiling, killed every flea that landed on her with a flick of her will, and hung the small nude portrait from a beam, Awa had a home for the first time since leaving the mountain.

They turned the ground floor into a tavern, with Dario cooking delicious food with the poorest of ingredients, and pouring wine that was a week from being vinegar and spirits that were years from being smooth. The second story was where Monique and Dario had their private rooms, as well as the common sleeping chamber the whores shared. Monique would have preferred to have her offices at the top with the servicing area on the second story, but the second floor already had separate chambers, whereas the third was a single open room, and so the third story was where the fucking took place. With the thin, colorful linens separating one bed from the next and the near-constant screams and grunts the place reminded Awa of Paracelsus's clinic. She took to drawing the ladder to the attic up after her, and fitted a lock to the trapdoor when she went out.

Awa went out often, preferring to pull a cloak down over her face and roam the streets rather than stay in the dark attic with the constant riot of Venus taking place just below her. Each expedition revealed a new marvel to her, from the recently completed urban canyon of the Pont Notre-Dame to the flamboyant, castle-like façades of the aristocrats' hôtels rising up behind their curtain walls; moldering, unique Gothic flourishes and newly built, symmetrical arcades were of equal interest to the curious young woman. Especially alluring to Awa were the gorgeous cathedrals and abbeys, and the small, charming cemeteries that abutted them, but she had not set foot in a churchyard since parting ways with Manuel and took only an aesthetic pleasure from admiring the tombstones and crypts. No matter what hour she left the majesty of the ever-growing city behind her and returned through the tightly constricting avenues that choked out the sky, she would find the brothel lit up like a beacon, and the third story every bit as noisy as she had left it.

Even had she been inclined Awa could not join in the sport on the third floor—the punishment for a woman lying with a Moor was death, in Paris and elsewhere, and the punishment for two women lying together supposedly the same, so Monique insisted Awa and any girls who shared her or her predilections did so far removed from any witnesses, lest the letter of the law by some rare chance find itself enforced. Monique, good as her word, had found whores willing to take a tumble with a blackamoor; in fact, several seemed eager to try her out, but Awa only rarely got so bored and lonely that she took one up to her attic.

Awa had once awoken to find the woman she had brought up rifling through her bags, and she gave the whore a different kind of little death than she had earlier in the evening, only reviving the terrified, confused woman after she had dragged her down and delivered her to Monique. The gunner waited until Awa returned the whore to life before administering a beating that rang in Awa's ears even after she had run back to her attic. From then on when she did fuck the whores she did not go to sleep until they had gone back downstairs and she had stowed her ladder.

All that changed a year and a half after they had settled in

Paris, when Awa met Chloé. Awa had seen the girl before—indeed, she saw her every morning when she woke up. She was the whore Manuel had painted on commission for Bernardo, the girl whose portrait had saved the artist's life back in that wet cave two years before, the portrait hanging on Awa's wall. Chloé was curvaceous yet fit, black-haired, green-eyed, and foulmouthed, and Awa fell in love as she had only once before in her life. Or rather, fell deeper in love, for she had loved the girl in the portrait with that feverish intensity hearts reserve for imaginary paramours. Unlike Omorose, Chloé was far from proud; despite being one of the youngest women in the brothel she was willing to take on the crustiest, rankest beggar who had robbed or murdered his way into enough coin for a fuck or a suck.

Chloé was in the early stage of the pox when she arrived, but upon inspection Awa saw that half a dozen other wayward spirits also infected the young woman's nether regions. Breaking them all, as well as running her hands over the girl to kill the inevitable ticks, fleas, and lice, took quite a bit of energy, and by the end Awa was barely remembering to apply the mundane paste she mixed to cover her necromancy. Chloé did not even wait until Awa had finished before making a move, rubbing against the necromancer's fingers as she shakily smeared the ointment.

"Your boss asked if I'd fuck a blackamoor, and I told her nay," said Chloé as Awa looked up from her work in surprise. "But I thought she meant blokes. You're not a bloke, though, so if you got the francs to match that interest I'll make myself obliging."

"What makes you think I'd have an interest?" said Awa, unable to meet the woman's eyes.

"Everyone's got an interest in something," said Chloé, "and you're interested in putting your tongue up there or I'm a blackamoor myself. What say you wash me off and get first taste of the new pottage, eh? Didn't even let the monger have a go, said I wanted to get clean first."

A year or two before Awa might have turned away or at least blushed, but instead she met the young woman's olive eyes and nodded. Upstairs they went, Awa leading her out of the whores' sleeping chamber and quickly past Monique's closed door. When they reached the attic Awa lit a candle and pulled up the ladder.

Then they sat facing each other on the pallet, the younger woman suddenly demure, and Awa found herself pinning Chloé down, kissing her hard, more excited than she had been in ages, the dark-haired whore letting out little gasps. It was strange, taking the initiative, and even when Chloé traded places with Awa the younger woman maintained her beguiling modesty, repeatedly leaving Awa shuddering on the edge to adorably ask for guidance that they both knew she did not require. It was unlike any fuck Awa had enjoyed since arriving in Paris, and when they were both exhausted she tightly held the warm little creature. Feeling Chloé's willowy arms intertwined with hers, Awa drifted off remembering two junipers she had once seen that had somehow merged their trunks and become a single beautiful, twisted tree.

"Who's Omorose?" Awa started awake, the warmth and darkness suddenly cloying instead of comforting. She rolled away from Chloé, scolding herself for falling asleep.

"Nobody," said Awa, her eyes not so quick to adjust as they once had been, the girl beside her in the bed still just a pale lump. "How long have I slept?"

"I don't know. I was asleep, too," said Chloé. "Do you have anything to smoke?"

"Smoke?"

"Poppy oil? I suppose not." The girl sighed. "A Moor I knew shared it with me. He said it was not so rare in your land."

"And where is it you think I come from?" asked Awa, retrieving a bottle.

"I suppose I was being foolish," said Chloé as Awa took a drink. "You don't all come from the same place, of course."

"Of course," said Awa. "Would you like a drink?"

"Of course." The girl sat up and took the bottle. "Say, this is a sight better than what they keep down there. What's your name?"

Awa told her; she had long since given up on keeping it a secret.

"Well, Awa, can I ask you something?"

"Certainly."

"Can I sleep here? It's late, I think, and I... I like sleeping against you. You smell nice." Awa's eyes had adjusted enough to see that the girl had dropped her head, and Awa felt her throat tighten, her stomach hot and nervous.

"You can stay as long as you like, Chloé," said Awa, and then the girl looked up, tears shining on her cheeks in the dark for some reason, and Awa held her tightly. Then they kissed, softly, much more softly than before, and lay back down together. Much later, after she was sure the girl was asleep, Awa sat up on her elbow and stared at the ivory creature beside her, wondering how long she could feel this happy. Longer than she expected, as it turned out, but, of course, not forever.

The only nights Chloé did not sleep pressed against Awa were when a mark paid the extra franc to have her stay until morning with him on a lumpy pallet surrounded by cheaply perfumed curtains. Those nights were harder than Awa expected, though she was not so foolish as to think loving a whore would be easy. She managed it, though, and took a quiet little thrill in keeping her own secrets as Chloé let one after another slip out with the errant tear; she told Awa about her absent mother, her abusive father, and her molesting uncle, about running away from home to work in the city only to find herself on her back, about her dreams and nightmares.

"I'm going to be famous, a poetess," said Chloé as they sat on the edge of their pallet early one morning. She stunk like the man she had just left and Awa drank more to kill the scent. "That Moor I told you about, he had a book by one of them, courtier, no, courtesans. Italian bird, sang poetry into her books, and now everyone from the Grand Duke of Muscovy to the caliph of wherever are singing her praises. I'll write like her, sad poems and sweet, and be the queen of the courtesans."

"Can you read and write?" asked Awa.

"Not yet," said Chloé, taking the bottle. "But I learned to suck cock when I was ten, so learning letters at eighteen ought'ent be worse."

"I can teach you," said Awa. "If you like, I'll buy, I don't know, a book or something and teach you to read."

Chloé was silent for a time, then burst out laughing. "Yeah, why not?! Teach me!"

"It'll be fun," said Awa, taking the bottle as Chloé rolled onto the floor and squatted in front of her, putting her hands on Awa's knees. "Fun."

"My first fucking sonnet will be an ode to the soft wings of the raven, eh?" said Chloé, moving in as Awa lowered herself down with a sigh, the portrait of the girl watching them from just over the jet-haired head now nodding between Awa's legs.

Complications and jealousy were as inevitable as pox in that house, though not so easily remedied. The occasions when Awa passed through the third floor and saw Chloé at work, or worse, chatting up some slob in the tavern below, gnawed at Awa more than she would admit to herself or her lover. An especially loud and obnoxious Englishman named Merritt took a shine to Chloé, and he more than all the anonymous marks put together rubbed Awa wrong.

Merritt delighted in talking immense amounts of shit about the other patrons and whores, flexing and strutting like an especially immodest peacock, and picking fights at the slightest provocation—provided his opponent was smaller or drunker than him. Awa noticed that he had become a regular, and that he favored Chloé, but did not pay him much notice until one night when her last bottle went unexpectedly empty and she was forced to march down to the tavern for some of the local swill. It was quite late and she was already a little drunk so she had not bothered donning her cloak, which was still drying anyway, and so she went downstairs with her head held high only to hear Merritt crowing in the worst French she had ever heard.

"Blackmoor! Fuck, blackmoor!" Chloé was sitting on his lap and glanced up at his outburst. Awa looked to her instead of him, and when Chloé quickly turned away, whispering in Merritt's ear, Awa set her face and made straight for the bar. Then it came again. "Fuck blackmoor! See! Why you telling me not they are had blackmoor, chit? Me buying her!"

Awa's face must have given away far more than she intended, for Dario already had two bottles off the shelf and held out to her, his smile more grimace than grin. Through his frozen expression Dario murmured, "Fucking English're the worst, eh, Awa? We fleece that mutton closest, believe me, so just go—"

"Blackmoor! How much for you eating the shit of me, blackmoor?" Dario winced, as if the shouting drunkard were addressing him instead of Awa. "Not, not *story*. You eating the shit of me, me paying, me watching, girl watching. How much?"

"No fucking charge for what I'll give you," Awa heard herself say, and she was already halfway across the tavern when a great Dutch shadow fell over her. Awa felt her hand extend to kill Monique, and then Merritt and Dario and everyone else in the tavern, and then she would burn the building down, and if Chloé didn't like it she would kill her, too. Then she caught herself and yanked her hand back, her fingers almost brushing Monique's arm.

"Upstairs, Awa. My room," Monique said softly, then, raising her voice and turning to Merritt, "Oi, Saxon! Don't know bout on your gloomy native rock but 'ere bouts we got laws gainst doin nastiness with blackamoors."

"Me wanting not fucking it!" Merritt protested loudly, addressing the other patrons as much as the brothel's nominal bouncer. "No, not fucking blackmoor!"

Awa heard him spit as she went up the rickety stairs, and had a single other voice joined in or even laughed she would have wheeled around, murdered them all, then brought them back so that she might murder them a second time, but no one else spoke or chuckled, and she went down the second-story hallway to Monique's room. It was locked. Fuck this, and fuck them, and Awa was storming back down the hall when Monique appeared, and she looked so miserable and tired that Awa's rage began to steam off her, and she let herself be led back into Monique's room.

"That fucking asshole! Who the fuck does he think he is?!" Awa drained the drink Monique offered and slapped the clay mug back into her friend's palm. "I don't have to take that shit!"

"No," agreed Monique, refilling the mug and drinking it herself. "Ya don't *'ave* to take that shit—only if ya wanna stay under this roof, aye?"

"So that's how it is?" Awa took the bottle from Monique's hand when the cup was not refilled and stalked around the room. The bed was nice and soft, by the look of it, and there was a table against one wall with scales and canisters on it, a trunk underneath it and a chair beside that, but otherwise the room was empty save for the clothes strewn about the place, frilly things far too small and delicate for Monique to ever fit into. "Some fucking loudmouth idiot over me."

"Ya got a real tidy thing goin on here," said Monique, sitting down on her bed. "*We* got a real tidy thing goin on here. We don't 'ave ta take the shit, but we will if we like it as it is, if we wanna keep it as it is. Understand?"

"Easy for you to say, without some squinty piece of shit taking that tone with you!" Awa took another long pull on the bottle.

"Right, right, I forgot, it weren't me gettin zero fuckin credit for this affair while that ginger-lout I pay ta embezzle my fuckin bar inta his belly gets the praise an' Christ knows 'ow many tips an' perks for bein born with a prick. Weren't *me* gettin the short end, was some other Low Country cunt." Monique sighed. "Ya gonna bring that bottle back here or am I gonna 'ave ta chase ya down?"

"So I just take it? When some shit-eyed bastard talks that fucking way to me, I just bend over and take it?" Awa returned the bottle, the fiery gutrot matching her acidic mood.

"Smallest, softest cock you'll ever take is the ones what come out they mouths," said Monique. "For any of us it'd be hard, but for those sisters of our circumstances this's good as it'll ever get, believe you me. Not many places in this wide, wonderful world the Lord made for us'll tolerate a fuckin blackamoor witch, an' dyke besides, sittin up most nights gettin her business tended by the fairest fanny in fuckin Paris. No?"

Awa looked at Monique, and smiled the slightest bit. "No, I suppose they wouldn't."

"So maybe turnin the other cheek when some greasy Saxon runs 'is gob ain't too steep a price for the ass I found ya, especially when said ass is chargin triple what she oughta from that particular greasy Saxon?"

"Just burns me up, seeing her on his lap, knowing what she'll be doing before the night's out." Awa shook her head, teeth clenched so hard that her jaw began to ache. "That *asshole*!"

"Call'em Roast Beef, ya ever want ta take some of what he's been robbin."

"Roast Beef?"

"What the locals call them Saxons what come down all pale an' pink up in the sun."

"Pet insults don't take the sting out of her kissing on him and everything else."

"Well, she's an earner, a true earner, an' that's what it takes." Monique put her arm around Awa and gave her a tight squeeze. "Most 'ores can't juggle private with business, but that minky pink of yours seems more'n capable. Be careful, though—a mink got teeth, don't it?"

"What the fuck's that supposed to mean?" said Awa, removing Monique's arm from her shoulder and standing up. "You wouldn't be jealous, would you, Mo?"

"Of her or you?" Monique shook her head. "That bitch is too bony for my likin, an' too damn clever by 'alf. On occasion I'll take a bony 'ore, or a smart one, but never the two in one. Recipe for trouble."

Awa stared at Monique for a moment, then burst out laughing. "That's the stupidest thing you've ever said. That...that makes absolutely no sense!"

"It don't, does it?" Monique smiled. "Philosophy's a pretty personal affair, don't always translate. Oi, let's get us a new bottle. I tell ya I got the shithouse fair ta sussed?"

The shithouse was Monique's saltpeter farm, a small brick building she had built behind the brothel. She filled it with dung from the nearby stable and the contents of every chamber pot, and woe to the ear of the whore who dumped her pot in the street instead of the special gutter draining into the shithouse. The gunner had endeavored to get Awa to assist in managing the balance of excrement, urine, and other elements to ensure the proper conditions were maintained, but the necromancer would have none of it, insisting that such esoteric matters were more the forte of Paracelsus than she. Eventually Monique got it sorted well enough on her own, and after she had separated—and sold off—the table salt from the mineral deposits that grew in the shithouse, she mixed the resulting saltpeter with willow charcoal and sulfur in her room, and had started bringing in almost more money from the blackpowder she sold than from the whores. Never in her life had Monique been happier.

They sat up most of the night drinking and talking, both realizing it had been far too long since they had simply relaxed together and shared a drink, and both realizing how much they missed it. Neither woman let the whores—regular visitors to their beds or not—in on their secrets or their pasts, and being with another individual who knew more about both than either were necessarily comfortable with felt liberating, and they had a proper night of it. When a soft knock came around the end of the second bottle Awa wasn't sure she entirely wanted to leave the company of the Dutch gunner, but Monique shooed her off after making a lewd innuendo or two, and Chloé helped her drunk lover up to the attic. Awa tried to go straight to sleep but Chloé made her drink some water, and as she did the whore apologized.

"He's harmless, just an idiot, really—I've never met anyone so conceited and stupid."

"Gotta do what you gotta," said Awa, no longer as annoyed as she would have liked.

"He's just a mark," said Chloé. "Nothing more'n a piss-taker."

"Eh?" Awa heaved herself back out of bed, reminded to relieve herself before passing out. "Who said he was more than that?"

"He's not...he's really not so bad," said Chloé, so quietly Awa could barely hear her over the sound of piss hitting the chamber pot.

"What are you sayin?" Awa clambered back into bed. "I don't want to hear about his fucking style."

"What? How much did you drink?"

"A lot."

"Oh. No, like...like as far as they go, he thinks he's funny, sure, but he's harmless. I talked to him, told'em I'd cut him off, he talked that way to you again."

"Don't go missing out on wages on account of my fucking sensitivity to loudmouthed assholes," said Awa, though she appreciated Chloé threatening the bastard. "Heard you get triple from him."

"Trip's what I tell the boss," said Chloé, snuggling against Awa. "It's more like four times the usual minge money."

"So long as you're happy," Awa muttered sleepily, and they both dozed off as dawn crept under the eaves.

XXV
The Judgment of Paris

Awa's time was running out. The days were passing far too quickly, the nights even faster, and not even Chloé could distract Awa from the truth of the matter. All the signs were there—the brothel's boost in business as harvest arrived, the few trees Awa passed on her walks losing their leaves like skeletons shedding desiccated skin, the pinch in the air, her own memory that would not be quiet, no matter how much alcohol she poured down her throat. She had reached her final year before the necromancer would claim her.

It had been easier than Awa had anticipated to forget, especially with the help of Chloé and Monique, and Manuel, who had come to visit a year before, no, two years before, bringing Katharina with him. Not to the brothel, of course, but to the city, and Awa and Monique and the artist's wife had all posed for him. It had been fun, much more fun than the only other time she had posed for Manuel, though she had to argue vehemently with him before he agreed to tweak her features and lighten her skin, lest she be identified by the completed painting. Little details like this told her she had not yet given up entirely, that she would not roll over and let death take her, but she pretended it was modesty instead of self-preservation, and so she convinced herself she would not rage against her fate as she once had.

The sketch for his painting, though—Manuel had wanted Monique to be nude, which had led to blushing instead of blows but nevertheless Monique's staunch refusal. They had talked it over, the three models and the artist, and if he was annoyed when they hijacked his vision he did not dare voice it. Monique would be the mother instead of Awa, and keep her modesty even if it meant wearing a fashionable dress for a change. Dario was dragged along, but by this point they had a few more hands employed at the brothel and so the five were able to nip off to an uncleared acre of trees and shrubbery in the outskirts without being missed.

The barkeep and official whoremonger sat on a rock facing Katharina, the artist's wife nude save for a transparent shift that concealed her charms no more than a light breeze might. She held an apple in her hand, the very image of Venus to Manuel's eye. They had been right, of course, and as he worked he could scarcely believe he had gotten Awa's and Monique's roles reversed. The gunner made as perfect a Juno as Katharina made a Venus, but there could be no denying that of the three Awa most embodied her goddess—though Manuel was perhaps a touch mixed up over the historical roles and identities of the goddesses in the first place.

Manuel felt guilty adding the long curls of hair on Awa's shoulder that she had insisted upon, at softening her at all, at lightening her flesh and masking her features, but still she shone through the disguise he gave her, Minerva as she had first appeared to him in the cave, his sword in her hand, a borrowed shield on her shoulder, his hat upon her head. Catching himself comparing his models, Manuel smiled to himself—he was more in Paris's position than the seated model, and made sure to replace the barkeep's face with his own in the finished painting. For now he sketched them as carefully as he could, and upon returning to Bern would have the apprentice he could finally afford make a cartoon of his sketch, which in turn the boy would copy onto a panel for Manuel to paint.

"You look like shit," Manuel had told her earlier in the day, Awa's eyes sunken and purple-rimmed, her breath hellish, but now she looked perfect.

"So do you," she had said, and she was right, a few years away from mercenary work enabling him to acquire a bit of a paunch.

"Come visit sometime," said Manuel. "I want to show you some things I've been working on."

"I'll come..." Awa paused. "Soon."

She had not, and now time was running short. Awa was beginning to lose sleep, to grow distracted even when Chloé was tending to her, and she went from drinking every night to drinking every morning as well. Monique commented on it, as did Dario, but Awa did not pay much mind until Chloé brought it up.

"What the hell's wrong with you?" the younger woman demanded.

"Huh?" Awa blinked, unsure if it was morning or dusk. Not enough light was coming in for it to be midday, but too much for night. "What?"

"You've been calling me that name again," said Chloé. "You can call me Rose or anything you want, but you need to pay extra."

The girl had grown quite lippy since Awa had run out of her stock of coins and had to start collecting a stipend from Monique to keep Chloé in clothes—going to a churchyard to refill her coffers no longer appealed to her in the slightest. Reaching around for a bottle, she found them all empty, which did little to improve her mood. Chloé watched her, shaking her head. "Pathetic."

"Get fucked," said Awa, finding one with a little slosh to it.

"Maybe I will. Merritt's offered me means if I want out of this game."

"Yeah, marry Roast Beefy and have his calves," said Awa,

tilting the bottle back and disappointed to find wine instead of stronger stuff. The Englishman no longer bothered her, much as he tried whenever they crossed paths in the tavern. Awa and Chloé had been fighting more than usual, however, about this and that and the other, and though Awa could read all the signs she paddled harder into the brewing storm. "I don't care what you fucking do, you dizzy slut."

"All right then," said Chloé, and up snapped the trap, and down went the ladder, and out went Chloé. Awa lay back on the bed, her heart pounding, the wind whistling outside, and tried to stop herself from shivering. He was coming to get her, right now he was out there, bobbing on the breeze, smacking his spectral lips, getting his affairs in order. Fuck that, and fuck...

Awa sat up with a start, and now it was dark in the room, very dark. The dream was running, weaving away from her, but she clung to the edge of it, and drew her legs up to her chest. She had not so much as thought about her mother in years, certainly could not remember her face, or the sound of her voice, or all the specifics that had been so vivid moments before, and she set to work before she found herself downstairs opening a bottle.

It had never occurred to Awa before, not once, and even as she splashed water in her face, trying to think straight, the absurdity of it gave her a chuckle. Blood was not enough; she needed a skull to call them back, and of course her blood was not the same even if it had been sufficient... but what was the harm? She casually cut into her forearm, not too deep, just enough, and then daubed the blood in a circle on the floor, then drew a second circle beside it. She let a bit more blood run off her elbow into a pool inside this second ring, and then she sat cross-legged in the first circle. Without bothering to stanch the wound, Awa focused intently on her dream, on the sound of the voice, on the appearance, on the smell.

She had never before tried to call back a spirit without a body, had not tried to call back any kind of spirit in years, but almost at once she felt its arrival. The circles of blood were bubbling, burning, the stink like scorched hair only sweeter, sharper, and a column of smoke rose from the puddle of blood in the second, empty circle. The shape was indistinct, swirling, and the voice was a strange warble, closer to an insect's than a person's, yet Awa was sure she had succeeded, and the pleasure at this victory was only surpassed by the pleasure of seeing her mother again, no matter how dimly.

"I...I'm sorry for what I've done," said Awa, but the spirit could not answer in any tongue that Awa knew. So they simply stared at one another for as long as the blood smoked, and then the woman began to fade, and then she was gone and Awa was alone.

"I will see you again," Awa told the air, and the certainty of that decision rocked her to her bones, the folly of what she had been doing, of the time she had squandered, no longer important. There was time, there had to be; she would not hide in a garret, drunk and slobbering, until he arrived and ended her, until he swallowed her into oblivion. Fuck that, and fuck him.

She must have been laughing or crying, for each bed she passed on the third floor went quiet, and then she had gained the stair, banging on Monique's door until it swung open. Awa pushed the pistol away as she barged in, Monique cursing as she stepped back and removed the sizzling matchcord she had almost used to fire the gun into her friend's face. A newer whore was sitting up in Monique's bed, her open mouth growing wider as Awa approached her.

"—fuck?!"

"Out, please." Awa ignored Monique, addressing the harlot. "I need to discuss some life-and-death business with the lady."

"Mo?" The whore looked over Awa's shoulder, and whatever

she saw encouraged her to hop quickly out of bed, the sheet wrapped around her ample form.

"Wait in the hall, I don't wanna go an' find ya," Monique was telling the girl as Awa went to the table and picked up a half-full mug of wine. Then the door shut and they were alone. "Life-an'-death it better fuckin be, Awa, I was—"

"I'm leaving," said Awa, emptying the cup. "Now. Apologies for not giving you more notice, but time's a fickle bitch, yeah?"

"That she is." Monique's wide shoulders slumped and she pulled her robe tighter around her. "An' she ain't the only one, apparently. If you've been fightin with that mink of yours again—"

"You know you mean *minx*, right?"

"Mink's soft an' pretty an' bites if ya ain't careful, an' I can't say what the fuck a minx is, so no, I mean fuckin *mink*. Rhymes with pink. But point is, ya been yellin again?"

"Monique." Awa smiled, knowing she never would have made so happy a home without the madam's help. "You've been a grand friend, grand, but I'm away, and that's it."

"That's it?"

"That's it." Awa poured another cup from the bottle, handed it to Monique, and hefted the bottle to her own lips. "Away."

"Why? Where're ya goin? What's so fuckin urgent?"

"Better not to know." Awa winked, tugging her ear. "Witch business."

"Ah." Monique set her gun on the table and swished the mug in her hand. "This witch business might allow ya ta pop in from time ta time, let us know you're well?"

"I don't know," said Awa. "I very much hope so."

"Me too," said Monique, putting the wine down beside her gun. "Me too, little sister."

They stood facing each other for a time, and then Monique

turned and went to her trunk. She unlocked it with a key she kept on a necklace around her bull neck and removed a purse. She started to untie it but then thought better of it and tossed it to Awa. The necromancer caught the pouch, the weight of the coins stinging her palm.

"Takin that prime mink with ya?" Monique was perfectly lousy at faking a smile. "If she stayed behind I'd 'old a brighter 'ope of ya comin back."

"I don't know," said Awa, the thought she had kept at bay now barking in her face. "I hope so, but she's a free woman."

"Aren't we fuckin all," said Monique, her smile becoming more genuine.

"Oh! Oh, Monique, I have something for you—but you have to make me a promise, alright?" Awa had set down the satchel she had hastily packed with the portrait of Chloé and all her other treasures. She took out the hawthorn box as Monique lit a second candle from the nub burning on the table. "Now, your word, Monique!"

"My word, right enough," said Monique. "I'll do as ya wish... but what're those, rocks?"

"Salamander eggs," said Awa. "I'm going to keep one in case I need it, but the other five are yours, so long as you promise to let them go when you're done with them."

"Eggs?" Monique looked suspiciously at them, perhaps worried they were about to hatch. "What do I do with'em?"

"Whatever you wish. You're smarter than you let on."

"That's a little outta order!"

"Listen, when you're done with them, or if you don't find them useful, just go out to the woods, and build up a big pile of logs, and put them all in the middle. Then let them go."

"Riiiiiight." Monique was giving Awa a strange look, so Awa hurriedly went on.

"They start fires. Their mother whispers the word for fire to them, and they immolate themselves, but if there's no tinder atop them they just go out again before they hatch. They need a mother to build a nest for them to burn up as they hatch, to help them leave their eggs. I don't know how many years they've been waiting for someone to help them hatch, and I was going to, but I owe you so much, and—"

"What in fuck, Awa? Really? I think you've maybe been drinkin a bit—"

"Watch," said Awa firmly, dropping one of the eggs onto the metal plate the candles were burning on. "Lean in, lean in… *fire*."

The round stone flashed white-hot, the brilliance making their eyes water, and almost at once the two candles on the plate toppled over, their bases melted to liquid in an instant. Already the little stone was extinguished, a thread of black smoke rising up from it, and Monique stumbled backwards away from the table, the room going dark as the fallen candles went out. By the time Monique relit the candles Awa had repacked her things, including the one salamander egg she was keeping for herself.

"Just focus on the one you want to light, focus and address it like you were telling someone something instead of addressing a room, and it'll light right up. But when you're done build them a nest, and let them go. Right?"

"Right, Awa, right," said Monique, staring at the box. "Just say… *fire*?" Monique whispered the last word, and Awa smiled.

"Perfect. Take care of them, Mo, and take care of yourself." Awa shouldered her bag, eager to be off.

"Aye, an' you. Fill your bag from the larder, an' all the sternwater you want, an', an', fuck, I dunno, be careful?"

"Of course!"

"Will you, er, are you seein Manuel anytime soon?"

"I…" Everything had been happening so quickly that she had not thought about it. "I'd like to, very much, but I don't know. If I don't, don't get to see him, you'll tell him that I love him, won't you?"

"What?!"

"Tell him that I love him." Awa nodded sadly, realizing she might well never see Monique again, either. "And I love you, Monique. Be happy."

"I—" Awa threw her arms around the giantess, who quieted at her embrace, and they held each other tightly for a time, neither speaking. Then Awa sighed and released Monique, each wiping their cheeks as they straightened up.

"She's asleep." Awa winked at Monique as she opened the door and saw the woman she had kicked out dozing on the floor.

"Fuck me." Monique frowned. "Forgot about'er."

"Goodbye, Monique," said Awa, giving her a peck on the cheek, and then the necromancer disappeared down the dark hallway.

The only ones awake in the tavern were Dario, Merritt, and Chloé, who sat drinking at a table. Awa strode directly up to the trio, who had quieted at her arrival on the stair, and informed Dario she would be taking food and drink. She set to packing rations while he scuttled upstairs to clear it with Monique, and then she turned to Chloé.

"I'm off to find something I should have gone after a long time ago," Awa told Chloé.

"Your Omorose?" The girl crossed her arms.

"What? *No*! She, she hates me, and I can't say that I'm terribly fond of her, now that I've had ample time to consider things."

"Oh." Chloé looked at Awa's bulging satchel. "What are you after, then?"

"The most important thing there is. If I succeed it'll mean I can really take care of you, forever, and not be a drunk layabout hiding in a rabbithole. I'll, I'll really be able to take care of you."

"Can I come?" There was no hesitation in Chloé's voice.

"I..." Awa had not seriously considered the girl accepting an invitation, let alone inviting herself along. "I hadn't—"

"She was going, me was going," said Merritt, sitting straighter in his chair and blinking at Awa. "We three was going."

"No," said Awa, looking at Chloé. "No fucking way."

"Awa," said Chloé, sliding out of her chair and going to Awa. "I know he's been bad, but really, he's got a sword, and is good with it, and—"

"How the fuck would you know that?" said Awa, her enthusiasm rapidly dwindling. "I'd rather eat shit, breakfast and dinner, than—"

"What saying she?" said Merritt, standing up. "We three was going."

"He'll get tired of it and come back here a day out," pleaded Chloé.

"Why? Why the fuck should I put up with that?" said Awa, crossing her arms.

"Because you love me," hissed Chloé, "and if you love me you'll say yes, and we can leave now. Otherwise—"

"Fuck it," decided Awa. "I'll kill the beef if he gets mouthy. You hear me, you goddamn son of a bitch? You keep that mouth of yours shut or I'll fucking gut you."

"Eh?" Merritt's eyes grew big indeed, the man ill accustomed to anyone taking such a tone with him, especially a Moor. "What?"

"Let's get on with it, then," said Awa, her smile nowhere near as strong as it had been in Monique's chambers. For fuck's sake.

XXVI
Necromancers and Other Scavengers

Ɛ

Awa tried to maintain the optimism that had powered her out of the brothel, and had Chloé been her only companion she might have kept the chill of hopelessness at bay, but within a week of keeping close quarters with Merritt despair and frustration returned. It might have helped if she could have talked to Chloé about the true nature of her quest, but Awa had never told her partner anything about her past and the present seemed like an especially poor time to start, as every time she tried Merritt returned from checking the snares Awa set or otherwise mucking around in the wood. She was all too aware that as far as Chloé knew she was a simple Moor, albeit a strange one. That was what Awa had wanted her to think, but now that circumstances had changed she found herself without anyone to confide in as her unhappy, seemingly undeterrable demise loomed.

One chill evening Merritt and Chloé chatted about saints after dinner in the lean-to Awa had put together, a dusting of snow already sparkling atop it in the firelight, and, of all things, that was the conversation that drew Awa deeply into bitter memories she had tried to blot out, memories of the first time she had searched for her tutor's book. Merritt said something about Saint

John and Awa excused herself, unable to feign indifference. When Chloé tapped her on the shoulder, asking again if she was determined to take first watch, Awa started back to the present, apologizing.

"Are you...Awa?" Chloé squatted down and extended her fingers, brushing her lover's wet face. "What is it?"

"Nothing." Awa took Chloé's hand and kissed it, tasting her own tears. The snow continued to drift down on them and the necromancer was again reminded that this would be her last winter if she did not find the book. "It's nothing, girl, just the snow melting in the fire."

"It's almost out. You'll freeze. Come and lay down, we don't need a sentry every—"

The fire flared up at Awa's silent request and Chloé drew back in alarm, staring at the blaze. Awa tossed another windfall branch onto the flames and forced a smile. "The pitch deposits in these—you mustn't get too close. I'll wake you when it's your turn."

"Right." Chloé shivered, then went to Awa and kissed her sweetly, her hands sliding under Awa's hood to press her damp cheeks. Then she went back to the lean-to without another word and vanished into its shadow. Awa turned back to the fire and her reminiscences, gingerly fitting the pieces of her memory together like the scattered bones of an old skeleton.

Awa had come down from the mountain, torn between hunting Omorose and hunting the book, and for the next four years she had wandered from churchyard to ruin to ill-marked barrow, skulking through the snow and rain until every pair of leggings had lost its stripes, until each tunic was thinner than cheesecloth, until she was little more than a shadow herself, no markers remaining to signify where dusty rags stopped and ashy skin started. She starved almost constantly, and on the few occasions she found herself rich in food she ate to overindulgence, to sickness, and everywhere she was alone save for the little bone-bird she had created to keep herself company. Almost alone.

"You'll never find it," he had said one misty spring morning, the necromancer's shade having taken up residence in her skull. "Never, ever, ever."

"If you thought that you wouldn't be here, watching me," said Awa, though his voice had worn her purpose down from the peak it had been atop the mountain to a rough little pebble. "You wouldn't have come back."

"It was simple business that I had, and as I went directly it took the week and no more, and back I flew. I like to watch you being stupid," he said. "Stupid black beast."

At first she had thought he was imitating Omorose to needle her, but as the voice prattled on while she covered herself with deadfall branches in the dawn gloom, an even more terrible possibility occurred to her. She let the thought steep in the back of her mind like wormwood in a kettle, in the blurry region where she had hidden her intention to murder him on the night she had—for all the good it had done her. Yet when she rose that evening and he started in again she was ready for him.

"—fruitless as a winter orchard, you stupid—"

"What's your name?" asked Awa as she shouldered her bag.

He did not say anything at first, and then said, "I won't tell you."

"You will if you're really him. He said the dead have to answer the living, and have to answer them honestly."

"The dead cannot *lie*. I never said they had to answer."

"Shit," said Awa, unable to remember if that was true or not, and knowing how foolish it had been to try and catch him with such a trick. As soon as a thought occurred to her she knew she had thought it, of course, and if she knew she had thought something then he knew she had thought it and—the only thing to do was blunder ahead and hope for the best. "Why will you not answer me?"

"Because knowing would give you power over me," said the necromancer's shade, but he spoke slowly, carefully. She had put him on guard and—

"Why are you answering me at all if you don't have to?"

"Because I like to see you squirm. Truth burns hotter than ignorance, little Awa."

"Why didn't you try to stop me from doing what I did to Gisela? If you had something then—"

"I never cared about that bag of bones! I rather liked watching you interrogate her, you reminded me of myself at—"

Then he went silent and Awa sat down, though she had just started the night's march. Only the day before he had said he was gone the first week, which would have been when she dug up Gisela, but now he claimed to have seen that, too. That was it, then. No scream of defeat, no justifications or clarifications or backpedaling, just silence. She was too practical, as usual, she thought, and too stupid—she was so stupid she had fooled herself for a very long time, and now had just fooled herself again. Stupid.

Of course he was off running his errands; he would no more follow her about than one would forgo a summer holiday to stay at home and stare at their mittens. She had been talking to herself with his voice for quite some time now, and even when the voice had sounded more like Omorose's she had explained it away as another trick of his. She looked down at her trembling hands and wondered how a crazy, stupid little beast could ever hope to find a book that might be hidden anywhere in the entire world. The concubine had implied the air spirits would not have the strength to move it far but Awa had very quickly lost any sense of where she was and how far she had gone—as a child she had been sold from one master to another, journeying farther in a few years than most travel in a lifetime, nearly a thousand leagues, and then came of age on a spit of rock less than a league across.

Graveyards seemed the logical place to search, for he would be able to command the dead to hide the book, and some of them had weatherproof mausoleums and ossuaries that would keep it safe from life's unavoidables. Awa recognized at once the aversion the living had toward cemeteries, but she also noted their keenness to keep them tended and guarded behind walls, and so she established a routine for investigating churchyards instead of marching blindly in with a spade. She would observe them for a day or two, from hiding if possible, or by wandering near them several times a day in the more urban areas. She had taken to pulling her cowl down as far over her face as possible to avoid being recognized as a Moor or a woman, and even still there had been a few uncomfortably close calls that had resulted in her killing men, or beating them near enough. Only once had a party pursued her through the wood, hounds baying and torches shining, and while she had escaped with only a little dog blood on her hands the experience had instilled her with a strong aversion to drawing the attention of men.

Awa suspected his voice would return, or rather, she would summon him back like a spirit to its bones, and she would resume talking to herself in his voice with some perfect explanation for the contradiction she had tricked him—tricked herself, the contradiction she had tricked herself into saying. She argued with herself, told herself she would not be fooled again, that now that she knew she was safe, and what sense had it ever made, really? The worst part of it was when she came to miss the voice when it did not return, and she tried to mimic it to relieve the monotony but now it always rang false to her ear.

Awa was in the mountains again, which suited her, though whether she was still in Spain or had blundered into Castile, Navarre, or France would have caused some conjecture amongst the cartographers of those fair kingdoms. These mountains were far lusher with grass and pine, little emerald leaves covering the ground like an endless phalanx of shields, white flowers spearing out of the carpet on purple and green stalks.

Soon enough the snows were coming and she stayed to the low mountains, dipping into the deep valleys and canyons to exchange the wealth she gathered in graveyards for food and wine from what outlying farmers would sell to a filthy vagabond. The men and women who worked the granite-flecked valleys of the Pyrenees were no more happy to see a Moorish wench than were the Basque shepherds of the high country she encountered the following spring, but all were willing to take a fortune for a little food, and those who followed the ragwoman into the wood to relieve her of any other burdensome wealth she might carry were found stone dead the next morning, or not at all.

The Black Lady was soon frightening children all across the mountain range, a woman in mourning who would offer you riches in exchange for a loaf of bread, but woe to the man who tried to rob her, the woman who tried to cheat her, the child who cursed her. Awa pushed on, the mortal remains she resurrected in the cemeteries no more helpful than those she had raised in the previous churchyard, or those she had raised a year before, or three. At least the churchyards seemed to have emissaries, with one spirit usually quicker than the rest to return to its bones and speak on behalf of the cemetery.

"Has a book been hidden in this place?" was the question she would ask, and then she would release the spirit. It would return to where the spirits of the dead go, and then promptly come back to shake its skull.

"No grave in this churchyard has been disturbed to hide a book," would come the reply, and, because Awa would not simply raise the bones but always insisted on giving the spirit back as well, sometimes a request would be given, such as, "Donna Stefanie asks that you, who can speak with both we and they, inform her husband that she knows he was having it with that Vittoria, and she forgives him, and wishes that he cease mourning and marry the girl."

Just as often it was, "Donna Patricia asks that you tell her husband that his dead wife knew he was cheating with that haughty blond bitch, and she was pissing in his porridge every morning until she died," but Awa did as she was asked all the same, and would have even if she were not told where to find this hidden treasure or that buried purse in exchange for her trouble. It was the least she could do for the dead, and she had yet to have a recipient of one of their messages do worse than make the cross at her and back away gasping in horror. The legend of the Black Lady took on stranger and more diabolical permutations with each incident.

Awa was simply relieved that through some esoteric system of their own each churchyard never made more than one request of her. She wondered how they determined whose wish was most important, or how the returned spirit remembered what it had been told in whatever place the dead go, from which she thought no memories were supposed to be taken away. She imagined she would find out herself when she died, but then remembered that unless she found the necromancer's book her soul would be devoured, and then she would know nothing for all time.

It was on such cheery thoughts that Awa was musing when she heard the child singing. A harvest moon shone over the sharp canyon walls as she walked the path to the cemetery she had staked out, but at this elevation snow had already been sown over field and forest, the actual harvest having come a month before. Awa stopped, the ill-fitting new shoes she had traded a priceless necklace for crunching gravel and ice, the wind that brought her the song slicing through her threadbare cloak and leggings. It was a little girl, Awa realized, singing an Ave in the moonlit cemetery, and the young necromancer left the trail lest she startle the child in the night. When the song ended and then began again, she resumed her pace, intending to circumnavigate the low wall of the cemetery and wait in the rear of the grounds until the singer returned home.

Awa kept to the treeline, eyeing the window of the church in front of the cemetery even though she knew from her reconnaissance that the building was empty, the ancient priest sleeping with his brother's family in a warm adobe house at the edge of town. The graveyard was perched on top of a little hill behind the church, and with the low wall ringing the grounds Awa could not see the child but her voice grew clearer and warmer as Awa reached the back of the rise. Squatting at the base of a shrouded tree, Awa rubbed her hands and hoped the child would finish soon.

She did not, her Ave concluding but then beginning anew after only a brief pause. She might even be singing louder, her joyous little voice lacking the solemnity the words implied, and Awa stood up with a sigh. She began creeping ever so slowly up the hill, having heard the song enough times now to recognize when the girl's voice would rise sufficiently to crunch another footfall of snow without the risk of being heard. Once she gained the wall she could see if the girl was alone, and if so, kill her quickly.

Only a little, of course, and just long enough to inquire of the corpses about a certain book, and then she would bring the girl back to life. No, then she would take the dead girl back to town, jump the wall, deliver her to the house where the priest slept, *then* she would restore her to life, bang on the door, and be away. Then she would have a fire in the cave she had found, a hot, blazing fire, and she would stop being so unbelievably cold. She reached the wall of the cemetery, and the girl's song abruptly ended just before Awa's hoof crunched loudly down into the snow.

Awa ducked even lower, one shoulder against the rough wall,

and before her lips could even form a silent curse she heard the child call out, but quietly, as if she were just as afraid of being heard as she was of being missed. "Papa?"

No father answered, and Awa exhaled. Spooked, the girl would run home and—

"Papa, what is it?" The girl spoke in German, her voice loud and sharp despite the wall and the wind and her obvious attempt to restrain herself, a chirping, birdlike voice. "Papa, what is it? I see it. I see it."

Awa frowned, straining her neck to look at herself, and saw that her shoulder was definitely below the top of the wall. What—

"It's looking at me," the girl said, her voice cracking and warbling, "looking at me it's looking at me looking at me go away go away…"

The girl gave a squeal, and Awa chanced looking over the wall. Nothing but the snow swirling between the gravestones, and then the squeal came again, from just behind the single large crypt in the center of the churchyard. There was no one else in the cemetery, and Awa realized the girl must have heard her outside the wall and scared herself silly. Still, Awa found herself possessed by a sudden impulse to duck back under the wall and dart to the treeline, to run through the forest and not look back, to—she shook her head, her smiling teeth shining in the dark. Childish—

"Bad." The girl was crying now, the dying wind bringing her tiny sobs to Awa. "Ba-ba-bad, ba-ba-bad doggie. Gooooooo a-a-a-a-way. Ba-ba-bad doggie."

Awa's smile faded with the chill breeze, and she jumped the wall. The ibex-handle knife reassured her palm, which reassured the rest of her, and she strode quickly toward the mausoleum and the crying child. She sent her bonebird winging from her shoulder to wait in the trees, lest it frighten the girl. Whatever fit the child was having could— Awa stopped, her breath snatched away by the gust of wind that snapped between the gravestones, her mouth dangling open, her eyes huge.

"Ba-ba-bad, ba-ba-bad doggie." It walked slowly around the side of the crypt, its yellow eyes shining in the moonlight, its tongue twisting around the child's voice wafting out of its long muzzle. "Gooooooo a-a-a-a-way. Ba-ba-bad doggie."

It was much, much larger than a dog, its shaggy coat spotted along its flanks, scrawny legs jutting down under its thick body. No creature could have a head and neck so disproportionately large, thought Awa as it approached, it must be the angle, the perspective. Difficult as thinking had become, moving proved impossible, its eyes locked with hers, eyes that despite the distance smiled in a way its canine maw never could, the sharp teeth and dripping tongue somehow perfectly replicating the sounds of a little girl.

"It's looking at me," the creature whined, "looking at me it's looking at me looking—"

Awa ran, the worst thing for it but there it was, Awa ran and even as her eyes watered from the wind scratching them and the nightmare reflecting in them she saw it run, too. No, it trotted, those legs swinging straight beneath it, legs capable of moving much, much faster if it wished, the monster ambling parallel with her along the uneven rows of the churchyard. *No no no*, Awa thought, almost turning her back on it completely to jump the wall, but then she caught herself, tightening her hand on her dagger, and she skidded to a stop in the snow, wheeling to face it. It was closer than she had thought, one row over, and it stopped as well.

"I am more dangerous than I look," she told the creature, and it laughed, not like a child but like the grotesque horror that it was, the cacophony leaving its slavering mouth like a thousand ravens cawing in broken unison. Dogs had to be shown you were not afraid, something her tutor had told her when lecturing on the outside world with its mobs of men and their hounds. This was no natural dog, no dog at all, but the risk of giving it a little more leverage over her was worth it if it showed the monster she was not afraid, and so she addressed it: "I am Awa, a necromancer. I have come here to raise the dead, not be barked at by dogs. Go away."

The creature cocked its head at her and sat back on its haunches. Awa took this to be a great improvement, until it spoke with her voice. *"I am Awa. Awa. Awa."*

"Ohhhh." Awa could see its spirit now, in the moonlight, but it was buried deep in the creature, bunched up in its rear, and she wondered if she had erred in telling it her profession. The spirit coiled even tighter, as far from her as possible—killing the beast with a touch would be almost impossible; in most things the spirit flowed evenly throughout, and so severing it was as easy as brushing an arm, touching a tail. It was listening, though, and so she added, "I mean you no harm."

It again echoed her but altered the meaning by roughly inserting new words in a gruff, masculine accent, the jumble of her voice and another even worse than the simple imitation had been: "*I am* also *more dangerous than I look*, nor am I to *be barked at*, bitch."

"Bitch?" said Awa, licking her lips. "Is that a dog joke? Funny."

It rose back up on all fours, a low growl giving way to her voice again, and a single word with a much deeper inflection. "*I have come here to* eat *the dead, not to be barked at by Awa. I mean you harm. I have come here to* eat *Awa*."

"Well shit," said Awa, and it lunged forward.

Her dagger punched through its cheek and glanced off its jawbone, the creature emitting the scream of a young girl as it wrenched itself away and dashed past her, skittering around the gravestones and disappearing in the thicket of stone markers.

Her knife hand was dripping with its blood, and Awa almost laughed, the battle won before it had started, when she noticed her fingernails were digging into her slick palm. She did not have to look down to realize her knife was gone, that the monster had bit down on the blade and yanked it out of her hand and run off with it, and Awa was dashing toward the crypt even as it called out from the shadow of the wall behind her with the child's voice, "Looking at *Awa*, looking at *Awa*!"

It had been years since Awa was genuinely terrified, but she fell back into it easily enough. She was not breathing, which was a good start, and her vision was blurring, and she could not make herself turn and fight even though she knew it could outrun her, knew it was right behind her, knew she was doomed. Her bone-bird was dipping through the air in front of her and she followed the course it charted through the cemetery, the avian construct leading her toward the high crypt. Like a hounded stag bounding over a stream, she saw a stone slab jutting out of the snow and leaped for it. Instead of propelling her up to the safety of the crypt's roof, her right foot slid on top of the snowy gravestone and she fell forward into the side of the mausoleum.

Unlike her childhood escape attempt from the necromancer's hut, when she had jumped across a chasm only to have a dead tree knock the wind from her, Awa had not taken a breath in nearly a minute and so had no breath to lose, and the sensation of three ribs cracking like kindling no longer brought the debilitating pain it once had—almost, but not quite. Her callused fingers closed on the edge of the mausoleum's roof, ignoring the agony her elbows shot into them as they too struck the crypt, and Awa hauled herself up over the top of the structure. Her palms slapped the icy stone, dragging her stomach over the sharp lip of the crypt roof, her legs curling up behind her instead of trying to find purchase on the side of the mausoleum as her bird frantically fluttered above her.

Then it rose like a fish breaking the surface of a pond, the furry ridge of its back tickling her thigh, and iron-hard teeth bit into her hoof. She had no breath to scream with and so she gasped, her fingers stretching out toward the opposite end of the roof, to cling to the edge so it could not pull her off, and then she was falling. Awa tried to scream, so that the villagers in the town would hear and help, so that anyone would hear, even Omorose or her tutor, anyone, but then that precious scream was knocked out of her lungs on the frozen ground as it brought her to earth, the pain in her chest every bit as monstrous and powerful as her attacker.

Awa lay contorted on the ground, the beast towering over her. It had her hoof in its mouth, the ensorcelled string that normally disguised it having come loose or been bitten clean through, and those shining pink gums strained as it bit down harder, its delighted yellow eyes squinting from the strain. Then her hoof cracked, blood running off its hot tongue and dribbling down her leg. It dropped her, its purple tongue running over its wide teeth, and Awa saw that in addition to her mangled hoof, the leg was twisted, broken, and blackening.

The bloody muzzle jutted forward, Awa's life lost, but then her little bonebird dived out of the air, pecking at the creature's face. Awa willed it to fly away, to stay high above the monster, but it did not listen and then the beast snapped the bird between its jaws. The mouse bones crunched as it chewed, and it looked back down at Awa.

Awa could not even cry but the creature cried for her—not with its ever-happy eyes, but with its bloody, foam-flecked mouth, the sound of the little girl blubbering as it mocked her: "Ba-ba-bad, ba-ba-bad *Awa*. Ba-ba-bad, ba-ba-bad *Awa*."

Those teeth were growing larger and larger, its breath blowing the pungent stink of blood and gravedirt and old marrow in her face. She tried to reach out, to snatch its spirit and break it, to do something, but as its eyes met hers she found herself frozen, and she wondered if she had already died. She had not, she realized as it put a leaden paw on her stomach and pressed down, her fractured ribs screaming, and to deny it what little pleasure she could she closed her eyes.

With her eyes closed, Awa could not see if they all burst from the hard earth at once or if they had emerged one at a time and converged in the darkness, gathering like rumor, until their numbers were large enough to move. All she knew was that the crushing weight on her stomach and the fetid wind in her face were suddenly snatched away, and the only sounds she heard above her own wheezing whine and the monster's surprised yelp were the clattering of bone on bone, of rot-greased limbs sliding around hollow sockets. She could not believe it but her ears were always the most honest of her senses, and so she opened her eyes.

Awa could not tell how many there were, the canine creature thrashing on the ground as the skeletons clawed and clubbed and kicked and beat it, and as it threw half a dozen off and gained its feet three bonemen pounced onto its back and rode it through the cemetery, their fingers wrenching out clods of meat and fur that they threw into the snowy air like wet confetti. The beast was screaming with that little girl's scream, but to Awa's dismay it reached the wall of the churchyard and bounded over it, disappearing into the night with its undead riders still in tow. Awa heard it scream for a long time, its voice echoing down the canyon as she looked around for the necromancer who had saved her. She was still alone, save for the thirty or forty animate corpses staring at her, but she could not get to her feet to see if her savior was on the other side of the mausoleum.

Five of the walking dead quickly came to her and hoisted her up, as careful as she would have been herself to keep the splintered hoof from brushing the ground, and as they slowly turned her around she saw nothing but the empty cemetery. Instead of an unbroken white churchyard Awa saw black pits yawning all around her, several tombstones tipped over, and the gory trail the monster had left as it fled, bloody clumps of its hide littering even the far edges of the grounds. Glancing toward the previously dark town she saw it was blazing with light, but no brave souls had yet dared investigate the noisy disturbance in the cemetery. Through her shock Awa took note of the dead men holding her aloft, and realized who had saved her.

Awa had not thought herself so powerful—she had always dug up the bodies herself before trying to raise them, even if she did employ their help in refilling their own graves. Now the militia of the undead that she had conjured all stared at her, some from oozing sockets and others from dry skulls, and Awa smiled weakly at them. She had vowed not to raise the mindless ones, not to use the dead without the permission of their spirits, but this seemed like a reasonable exception. She did not know how much time she had before the villagers found their courage and came with lanterns and cudgels, and so she bade her animate palanquin lower her onto a stone cross marker to supervise the reinterment.

"Someone find my knife," she tried to say, but only a little blood came out. The monster had nearly killed her, she realized, and she would need a volunteer or two to help get her through. As she mused how to go about it, one of the bonier fellows—no, a woman, Awa saw by the pelvis—returned with her dagger and, she saw, the disguising string that had come loose from her ankle when the creature bit her. Awa shook her head in bemusement. Just to make sure she was correct she had the woman do a little jig, and Awa smiled through her hurt. She did not even need to speak aloud for them to hear—how useful was that?

There were always a few whose spirits had not quit their bones for what other worlds await the dead, perhaps those with unfinished business in the mortal realm, and Awa singled out the three corpses present whose spirits clung to their flesh like a drowning sailor to driftwood. They were still mindless, of course, as the spirits could not actually reenter their old homes without her help, and so help them she did after ordering the rest of the mindless ones to bury each other.

There was a recently deceased man, his skin barely blackened by the grave, and a man and a woman with less skin between them than Awa had on her two thumbs. Once the restored spirits had stopped marveling at the event, all three faced Awa. She would have returned their polite bows had her injuries not crippled her.

"I am in your debt," said the freshest of the dead. "That monster had dug me up and would have eaten my body as surely as he ate the dozen before me if you had not interrupted him. He would eat one of us, sing his song, and eat another, and I would have been next."

"Why care?" Awa managed. "You're dead."

"He ate them, bones and all, and if he had devoured me I would not have been able to meet you, and ask the boon I shall now beg."

Awa was accustomed to the dead making little sense to the living, and so she simply nodded.

"My request is a simple one—I promised my heart to the sea, and had no intention of dying, and being buried, anywhere but within her. I was born on the coast, but not long ago life pushed me far from her, and fate has made a liar of me. I beg that you take this heart of mine with you on your travels, and before it rots away to nothing cast it into my beloved."

"The rest?" Awa said with a wince. "Ribs, say? Legs, say?"

"The rest?" The corpse took a step back. "Well, the rest could just..."

"You can hear as well as I what she thinks, what she needs," said the woman's skeleton, both she and the other old corpse having salvaged operative tongues from their mindless neighbors before they had fully reburied themselves.

"Yes," said the male skeleton, clapping his finger bones on the fresh corpse's shoulder. "The hyena would've eaten you anyway. If it's only your heart you care about, where's the harm in helping our mistress?"

"No harm, I suppose." The dead man smiled nervously at Awa. "Use of me what you will, mistress, though I beg you remove me first so I do not feel it."

"Come," said Awa. "Come and rest."

The dead man knelt as if in prayer before Awa, who still half sat, half leaned on the tombstone. Awa gently pushed his spirit out of his bones, then went to work with her knife. His heart was already well on its way to putrescence, but Awa wagered that with the help of the sun spirits that drifted down even in cruelest winter she could dry it enough to last the duration of a trip to the ocean. She was surprised to see that the man's spirit had not drifted away to wherever they went, nor had it stayed in his skull, but had somehow come loose and settled in the wet lump of muscle Awa held in her hand.

"Mistress?" the male skeleton said quietly but firmly, shifting from one foot to the other as though he were a child in bad need of a piss. "Ah, mistress? Mistresssss?"

"Yes?" Awa was intent on her task, wrapping the dead man's heart in the wet rags rotting to his skin.

"Ah, lights? Lights."

"What?" Awa looked up.

"The village is coming," the female skeleton said. "Let us away."

"But I haven't heard your requests yet," said Awa. "How will I know—"

"Let us away," the dead woman repeated. "Hurry."

"Right," said Awa, trying to get up and falling from her seat into the snow. She felt bones closing around her, low voices murmuring to one another how best to handle her. Then she felt them raise her off the ground and she cried out despite herself—she hurt so much she knew she must be dying. They moved very quickly, the two skeletons carrying her while the mindless body of the man whose heart she held in her hand staggered after them. Once they cleared the wall of the cemetery and the harvest moon cleared the wall of the canyon the night became very dark indeed.

XXVII
The High Cost of Living

"You called it a hyena," Awa asked Johan, the male skeleton. "How do you know that's what the monster was?"

Awa had not heard of hyenas from her tutor, though well he might have warned his pupil against that bane of grave and graverobber alike. Her parents had cautioned her of them when she was a child, though she had forgotten that particular boogeyman until the skeleton had used the term. The hyena had come as close to killing her as even her tutor had managed, and she was horrified to recall that in her panic she had so freely given it her name. Even after consuming all the requisite pieces of the heartless dead man Awa found herself unable to move from the cave she had found without the assistance of her two skeletal companions—they had only that night carried off a goat from a nearby village, the hoof now boiling down for Awa to consume.

"My line o work meant being appraised've mythical whatsits," said Johan, putting his finger bones in the bubbling pot and giving the hoof a squeeze to see how it was softening. The rest of the creature smoked on spits strategically balanced around the stewpot, and the skeleton removed his hand and blew on the steaming bones. "Not so mythical, I suppose, but there it is. Hyena. Got magic rocks in his head, too, shame you didn't catch'em."

"Magic rocks?" Ysabel, the female skeleton, glanced at Awa.

"Well, it's not so credible like magic string that hides a hoof, or, you know, resurrecting the dead like our names is Lazarus, I'll give you fair," said Johan. "But Philosopher's Stone in the ol' eyeball mightn't be so far-fetched."

"And what was your line of work?" asked Ysabel. "I'm sure our mistress is curious."

"Awa," said she, "please, I'm not your mistress. Just call me—"

"Mistress wants to know, she'll ask," said Johan. "Think your hoof's about ready, if—"

"Does graverobbing sound like a business to you, mistress?" Ysabel asked Awa, who was having a time of it adjusting to voices outside her own addressing her on a regular basis.

"That," said Johan, "is pure shit. *Pure shit.* I look like I got a beard to you?"

Without any skin or musculature it was difficult to tell if he was genuinely upset or only joking, and he and the woman bickered on as Awa closed her eyes and listened. They had stayed with her for days now and neither had volunteered why they wanted to return to life, and if they kept this noise up much longer Awa would demand a damn good reason or banish them back to death. The thought, harsh though it surely was, curled her lips into a smile that caught the attention of her companions.

"Course, she don't mind you being a graverobber," said Ysabel, and, opening her eyes, Awa saw they were both staring at her.

"Heard've resurrection men afore," said Johan. "But didn't think they meant nothing like her."

"Look," said Awa, the pain in her leg faded to the point that holding a thought long enough to voice it was easy, if not exactly pleasurable. "I gather you both have your reasons for wanting to come back..."

"Her first," said Johan, pointing at Ysabel.

"Now, how's that fair?" protested Ysabel. "He should have to go first for trying to do me like that!"

"Out with it, Johan," said Awa. "What do you want?"

"I want to be a relic," said he, clapping his hand over his jawbone as soon as the words left it.

"You what?" asked Awa as Ysabel laughed and laughed, her teeth chattering.

"I want," Johan repeated slowly, "to be a relic. I don't expect it's in your powers to make me one official-like, but I thought you might be able to, you know, pull a switcheroo?"

"What?" Awa squinted at the skeleton, as though she might see what he was about if only it were not so smoky beside the fire.

"It's like this," Johan explained, making an obscene gesture at the still chortling Ysabel. "I was something like an entrepreneur, made my coin selling relics and all."

"Relics?" Awa had not wanted a drink so badly in a very long time. "What kind of relics?"

"The regular kind?" Johan rubbed his palms together.

"The *regular kind* are made've saints, not random old bits of beasts, you cheat!" said Ysabel.

"Says you!" shouted Johan. "I was in the business long enough to set you straight there, and anyone else! When they weren't stealing'em from one another they were making their own."

"Who were stealing what?" asked Awa.

"Priests and all, and men what worked for'em," said Johan, clearly pleased that she had taken an interest. "Like me. I'll allow I went freelance after a time, but I started off legit as the rest. I was one o the boys what got the saints out've Stantinople when we crusaded it."

"He was slinging chicken bones, trying to pass them off as old Popes!" said Ysabel. "I took pity on him getting run off by the priest, and the thankless fraud got me killed for my trouble."

"Harsh, Ysabel, very harsh." Johan crossed his arms. "So much for personal responsibility, eh? And the few times I didn't have real bones with me they was pigs', not chickens', so that's slander atop o slander."

"Listen," said Awa, rubbing her temples. "You can't lie, so let's go from the beginning. Starting with you, Johan. You were helping people leave Constantinople?"

"Yessss?" Johan fidgeted. "Well, alright, yes and no. See, people what do real right by God get turned into saints, and the bones them saints leave behind is powerful holy. So over the years Stantinople buys up a load o these saint bones, relics is what they is, and the people pilgrimaged there to pray. And when Constanty was being sacked on direct orders o the Pope, well, my brothers and some others who was there decided to help out this abbot was reclaiming the relics. So we nicked some bones and took'em back to France and all, to where the bones, relics, right, where the relics belonged."

"Why did they belong in France instead of Constantinople?" asked Awa.

"Cause the priests what paid us for the bones told us so," said Johan with a shrug. "Not being a priest myself, I couldn't say. But belong they did—saints wouldn't let no one move their bones otherwise. Furitive sacrum, they call it."

"And what happened after that?" said Awa.

"I seen the coin I made off one set o bones, so I thought why not make a little more? I, ah..." The words started falling out, to Johan's obvious dismay and Ysabel's delight. "A man died on the way home with the relics so I cut off his hand. After, right, after, but I cut it off and cleaned the meat and little white ropes and all and got the bones out, and ah, rubbed'em with sand and filth and all, and got'em cracked a bit, and traded ol' Saint James a left for a left. So after we got the coin in France I took the show to the road, selling his finger bones."

"Oh," said Awa. "Selling them to other priests?"

"Exactly! And the random noble what'd stay at the sort o inns I did. Got myself a monk robe, made a box for the bones, and that was that. Thing is, not everyone believed I was the last brother o this order or that trying to find a proper reliquary for beloved James's hand in exchange for some funds to save the abbey. Some uncharitable souls, and I'm talking clergy's well as gentry here, didn't believe the hand was even his."

"Imagine that!" said Ysabel. "I wish you'd seen him with his skin on, mistress, the old villain looked like Reynard himself, red as the devil and twice as shifty."

"I was handsome, is what she's getting at," said Johan.

"Is that so?" Now Ysabel crossed her arms.

"Sooo." Johan turned back to Awa. "You see where my mind started going next?"

"I do?"

"You don't." Johan sighed.

"Sinning don't come natural as breathing to some folk," said Ysabel. "He starts thinking if those who buy his relics take it on faith they're real, maybe like-minded honest souls'll take it on faith any old bones a priest tells them is holy is just as holy as the real relics, even if they come from any old barrow. That's what you were thinking, wasn't it? Exploit them who believe a priest?"

"Less eloquent than I would've put it," said Johan. "But true for the coarseness."

"Coarse, am I? Well, that's a touch coarser yourself than last you commented on my texture, you—"

"Ysabel," said Awa. "I think I understand what Johan was up to. Now, what happened when you met him?"

"I was passing by when the old priest run this fox off, and I took pity on him, being far from in that particular rooster's good graces myself. I come down from a Waldensian upbringing and my husband of course tells the priest, who's none too fond to hear it, especially with me tending to women up at my place without his holy ears hearing the specifics. So I invited this cheat back to my house, which was a ways out of town, so I thought none would be the wiser of me taking in a scrawny ne'er-do-well out of the goodness of my heart."

"Goodness of your heart," said Johan, "or a lusty thought to poach my eel and eggs? We'll get the truth out you yet!"

Ysabel made a low groan, then said, "...I thought him fair for being a rascal, and my husband had moved back in with his mother the next town over, and he and I, my husband, I mean, we were about done with each other, or at least I was done with him and...I thought I might get something from the ginger goat."

"And get it she did!" said Johan, then ducked as Ysabel threw a stone at him.

"So he lays his dirty bag of bones out on my table, and starts laying in his lies as we eat, and the whole time he's coming off fishier and fishier, cause I'm country but I'm not stupid, and finally I tell him if he's sport we might have a game to play, if only to shut him up. So in we get to it, his bone the shakiest of the lot—"

"Hey! No call—"

"And my husband decides this is the time to get the priest's help in patching things up twixt me and him, so up they come as I'm doing the same, and that's that," said Ysabel.

"That it was." Johan nodded. "Got myself done in for doing an old woman a favor."

"Favor? Old?" Ysabel was feeling on the ground for another rock.

"What do you mean, that was that?" asked Awa. "The priest and your husband discovered you? Then what?"

"Well, then they killed us," said Ysabel, glancing at Johan and shrugging.

"What!" Awa shook her head. "How could they?! Why would they?! For what?"

"For fucking," said Ysabel, "though if my husband or the priest had a decent bone in their bodies they wouldn't have. They said we were both witches, and that was that."

"Witches?" Awa could not believe it. "But why would they think you were witches for, for—"

"Well, he had just blown into town dressed like a monk, and right after pissing up the priest's leg he went over to the resident witch's, me, I mean, and was caught with his wick in the wax, still dressed like a monk and with bones hither and yon," explained Ysabel.

"Ahem," said Johan. "A-hem."

"Resident... you're a witch?" Awa had never met another of her kind since leaving the mountain, but her excitement was short-lived.

"Well, not as such," said Ysabel. "I knew what herbs to help get rid of a babe, or help keep it, and I might've had one or two nights when me and some friends got into the belladonna and, you know, ridden a broom or two"—she made her hand into a fist and pumped it in front of her pelvis—"but not like, real witchery. Nothing like you, to be sure."

"Oh," said Awa. "And they killed you for that?"

"A pretext on the part of my shitty husband and that shitty priest." Ysabel sighed. "Or maybe they thought they were doing the Lord's business. End result's the same."

"Once my foot's better we'll go down there." Awa nodded slowly. "We'll see to this priest, and we'll see to your husband, and... what?"

The skeletons were both looking curiously at her. Johan made a sound like he was clearing the throat that had rotted away ages ago. Ysabel had knit her finger bones and was clicking her thumbs together.

"What?" Awa repeated. "Don't you want revenge? I do and it wasn't even me!"

"Revenge is overrated," said Johan. "It's a drain, if nothing else, and—"

"Don't act pious now," said Ysabel. "If mistress had brought us back a few centuries gone you'd be singing a different song, says I."

"And whose tongue did I find you but a descendant o that husband o yours, by whatever woman he took after you burned? More than like the reason we got what we did was to clear the way for him to poke some other girl."

"Ah," said Awa. "I'm... I'm late, aren't I?"

"Better than never," said Ysabel. "And you've put me at rights on that, at least."

"I have? On what?"

"On witches," said Ysabel. "I wanted to know if they were real, and if so, if they were the devil-sucking, baby-eating things that priest talked about at my trial, cause if they were I'd maybe see where he and my husband was coming from a bit keener. That's why I wanted to come back, to see the cut of your cloth. And witch you definitely are, but don't seem too bad for it."

"And a Moor besides," said Johan, shaking his skull.

"Thank you?" said Awa. "So... do you want to go back to the graveyard now that you know I'm not a, a baby-eating devil-sucker?"

"Hmmm," said Ysabel. "Maybe not here? Maybe we could find a nicer place for me to bed down, like that sailor whose heart you've got."

"That's my aim, too, though it's more specific, I'll allow," said Johan. "Switcheroo of this skull o mine with a saint's in some churchhouse, right?"

"I hope she trades you out for some phony head you sold them," said Ysabel.

They were bickering again, and Awa leaned back against the wall of the cave. So very odd to have other people around to talk to, even if they were dead. At least her hoof would be healed soon.

They went north, and at Johan's suggestion disguised themselves as lepers to keep anyone who might stumble upon them in the wilds at a safe enough distance to avoid revealing their cadaverous nature. Rags were obtained easily enough from fresh graves at the next few churchyards, and the wise-fingered Johan built noise-makers out of rough paddles of wood and rope. Swaddled in layers of moldering cloth they looked appropriately terrible, and clacking their paddles at the first sign of civilization worked marvelously at keeping people away. Obtaining food, fresh clothing, and other alms was actually easier now than it had been when the villagers and travelers got close enough to see that Awa was a Moor, although once an especially good-hearted priest had approached them, the old boy fainting dead away when he noticed Ysabel's finger bones holding the edge of her cowl.

The heart of the unnamed sailor was cast from the cliffs of Gascony into the Atlantic before the trio changed direction. Awa had unburdened herself to the two skeletons, who strongly approved of her quest to find the book and thwart the necromancer. The skeletons offered to help her as best they could until finding their idyllic resting place, and as each monastery and church with a reliquary that they passed was not quite what Johan had in mind, and each scenic glade they camped in was not quite right for Ysabel, the three eventually wandered farther into France and then down to the blood-soaked hills of Lombardy.

Fulfilling the requests of the random unquiet dead that they heard in the churchyards along the way stopped seeming like a chore to Awa, and with Ysabel and Johan to stand guard over her she slept better than she had in years. She missed her little bonebird but did not make another—it seemed disrespectful to even consider it. No trace was seen of the hyena, thankfully, but no sign of the hunted tome was found, either.

"I'm telling you, Awa," Johan insisted as they passed along a wooded ridge overlooking a small town a year after they had met, "go down in there and find a parish, bring in this pinky finger o mine, and tell the priest they come from Johnny Baptist by way o Armenia. Stake my bottom rib that's us into a bottle or two o wine."

"And what would you do with wine?" asked Ysabel. It took a skilled eye to notice when a lipless skull intended a grin, but Awa caught Ysabel's smile and winked back at her friend.

In their travels, the two skeletons talked a great deal about what they had seen of the world so long ago. They explained customs and beliefs and jokes, until Awa wished she could wash the color right off her skin, stride into a town, and have a hot meal and a good talk with the guests at an inn, or hear a mass, or see any one of the marvelous cities Johan described. Her two friends talked more and more of her finding decent folk who might overlook a Moor in their midst, if she did not behave in too witchy a fashion, but Awa would hear none of it and the skeletons held their own counsel when she slept. Finally they had an intervention, and when that did not take they staged another one, their joviality fading and their demeanor hardening as again and again Awa refused to listen.

"If I don't find the book, he will destroy me," she said, exasperated with them, but even more exasperated at herself for knowing they were right but refusing to give up. "Not kill me, but, I don't even know, end me, take away everything! How can I stop!?"

"All the more reason to pack it in," said Johan. "If I thought there was the slightest chance, I'd say, *Alright, Awa, let's find it*, and help you look til Judgment. But you got what, five years? And no way of knowing if it's even in a graveyard, which is where you've been looking exclusive-like, yeah?"

"He's right, Awa," said Ysabel. "We've been over this enough times you know it by heart, but let's have you hear it again—spending your last bit of time on God's grand earth prowling about in churchyards, dealing with the dead—it's not right. You should enjoy life, not hide from it."

"Thank you for that," said Awa, knowing what was coming next. "And I should take up prayer to your god, too, yes?"

"He forgave me, He'll forgive you," said Johan.

"How do you know?" demanded Awa. "You don't! You don't know where your soul goes when it's not tied to your bones out of some, some sick obsession with a, with a switcheroo! Or some need to justify your husband murdering you, waiting around in hopes a witch will come along and dig you up!"

"But dig us up you did," Ysabel pointed out. "You're right, we don't *know*, but we believe, and what greater proof can there be than your ability?"

"No more proselytizing," said Awa. "Please. I'm tired of all this! You don't think I'm tired of going to one graveyard after another, always wondering if some dog's about to bite my ass, if someone's going to see and try to string me up! I'm tired! Tired!"

"Then pack it in," said Johan. "Ysabel and me, we talked it over, and we think maybe it'd help encourage you to, I dunno, do something else with your life if we weren't, if we weren't..."

"What?" said Awa, looking away from them. Through the trees she could see the river they had been following faintly glowing in the sunlight. She knew what they were going to say, and she knew they were right, and still the tears came.

"This looks like a good spot for me," said Ysabel firmly.

"Me." Johan made a swallowing noise. "Me too."

"So that's it," Awa said, knowing she was being petulant but unable to stop herself. "After all this it's just, *Goodbye, Awa? Good luck? Hope the immortal evil doesn't get you?*"

"You need to stop chasing clouds," said Ysabel. "Enjoy yourself. Make friends that aren't dead. *Live*, Awa."

"Live." The word felt mealy on her tongue, but through her disappointment and loss a little spark of excitement was building in Awa, of an end to the monotony of graveyard on top of graveyard. "Live."

"There's places Moors don't have it so bad as Spain and all, probably," said Johan.

"And what about the skull swap, eh?" said Awa, and both skeletons' sets of shoulder blades relaxed at the smile on her tear-streaked face. "Given up on sainthood?"

"This is a prettier spot than them churches," said Johan, though he was looking at Ysabel instead of the sun-dappled, sandy clearing. "My bones'll rest easier here, knowing no entrepreneurs never going to steal'em away to a rival city."

"It's not that we don't want to help, or we don't think you deserve—" Ysabel began, but then she picked up on Awa's thoughts and went respectfully silent as her mistress approached her and Johan. She hugged them until their ribs groaned and Johan's clavicles popped out of their sockets, and then released them.

"Let's get you both tucked in, then." Awa smiled, and the three friends dug two graves by the river.

"Wait!" said Johan just before Awa released their spirits, and, clawing at the side of his grave, he soon dug his way through to Ysabel's. He stuck his arm through and they joined hands. "Right. If you need some relics you know where to dig."

"Goodbye, Awa," Ysabel said. "Live."

Then they were gone, so much bone in a shallow grave. Awa let herself sob then as she filled in the holes, terrible, painful sobs, for the two of them and Alvarez the bandit chief and Halim the eunuch and Omorose and her little bonebird and the heartless sailor and especially herself, who was again alone, alive but alone. The very notion of her finding living people who could understand her, or even want to, was ludicrous, but she nevertheless made ready to free the last creatures she carried with her.

She built a huge pile of brush, and after dumping the salamander eggs in the center tossed down the box and cracked her knuckles. Her tutor had told her there were almost none left, that if they hatched finding more would be impossible, and that made her smile. He would find her, and he would destroy her, but he would not have these six innocents to warm his kettle with. First, though, she stripped off all of her clothes, so that as soon as the inferno was ignited and her skin warmed she could leap into the shallow river and wash away the fear and frustration of the last few years.

Awa opened her mouth to address them all, to be their mother and ignite them and set them loose into the world, but then a branch snapped behind her. Before she could spin around someone tackled her into the brushpile, the sharp branches slashing and stabbing her as she flailed. A hairy arm was around her waist and she grabbed it, his spirit fat and stupid and right there to sever, but while it recoiled from her touch like a large rat struck by a small viper it did not fade immediately, and she heard metal sliding on metal as the man latched the iron chain in place around her waist.

She struggled and his meaty fist was punching her in the back of the head. Then his hand was over her mouth, his fingers pinching her nose, and as she began to swoon Awa wondered if the necromancer would not have a living body to take after all. As she went limp the mercenary Wim clumsily slid the sack over her head and down her body, wrenching it underneath the chain around her waist and fitting a second chain around her neck.

The man had not believed in witches until she had touched him but now he felt feverish and queasy, a black lump rising on his arm. He dared not disturb the witch's belongings, lest they be cursed.

Wim spit on the half-conscious Moor. "Von Swine didn't pay extra for you kickin I'd gutcher wicked belly, bitch. I don't doubt killin you'd make the angels sing."

XXVIII
A Happy Reunion

"She needs our 'elp, ya fuckin lump!" said Monique, and Manuel reddened to hear her preferred term for true degenerates fired at him.

"We've given her more help than Moses gave the Hebrews," said Manuel. "She's more than capable of looking after herself."

"Maybe fore she fell in with us," said Monique. "You ain't seen her since ya painted'er naked in the park with us, an' that's years past—lose interest once you've seen some ass, Manuel? Friends stop meanin more'n coin once you gander their bush, lump?"

"I've been busy, as have you and she, else you might have called on me instead, yes?" said Manuel, only mildly more angry at her than at himself. "As you point out, I was the last to visit, meaning custom would dictate that you and she come here."

"Fuck your custom, Manuel, I've a business ta run!"

"And I don't?" said Manuel, keenly aware that the sketch he was in the middle of copying was no longer receiving as much of his attention as it really ought to command—one of the corners he had secured with a nail had torn slightly and now the whole damn thing might be off-center. Worse still, his apprentice was gone for the day so he could not simply pass it over to the boy. "And I very much doubt a few years of brothel life has wholly removed her, her witchcraft, which proved more than a match for me or four stout mercenaries back in—"

"Don't be callin her a witch, Niklaus," said Monique. "Don't want your precious studio havin an accident, do ya? Lots a powder in my purse, an'—"

"Don't you fucking threaten me!" Manuel finally set his stylus down. "Our friend, Awa, is a witch. I've seen what she can do, I've *felt* what she can do, so don't you act like you didn't know! Did I say she was wicked, Mo? Did I? The fuck I did. But she's a witch, a real fucking witch, and—"

"What the fuck is that?" Monique shoved past him, and he gave a little yelp as she knocked his arm into an easel. Steadying it and turning, he saw what she had pulled the rest of the way out from under a stack of planks and his stomach rolled. For a moment he considered calling for a servant but then he saw that her face was hurt, not angry. She looked up from the paper, and said in a voice far quieter than he had ever heard her use, "You knew."

"That was ages ago," said Manuel, glancing at the closed door over her shoulder. "Katharina told them she'd gone to Muscovy."

"You fuckin knew an' let me go on bout this." The stupid confusion on her face was maddening, as if it were difficult to understand. How the illiterate had even recognized the bill for what it was he could not fathom, though he supposed the men who had come to her brothel must have delivered a similar poster. The sketch of Awa on it was pure amateur work, a black head with distinctly European features, and—

The clicking of his teeth as she punched him in the chin was somehow louder than the easels toppling, the planks clattering, the pots and glasses shattering, and then he landed on his back. She did not strike him again but went back to staring at the poster, perhaps puzzling over the different squiggles underneath the image. Hers would have been in the French vernacular if the author had any sense, and he must have a little if his men had found both artist and gunner, whereas the bill Monique now held was in German. Manuel winced as he flexed his jaw, then he saw the paint spreading across his floor, the scattered planks and tipped canvases, and he winced again. Monique crumpled the bill in her hand and looked down at Manuel with the expression of one who has just realized that the meal they were in the midst of enjoying was seasoned with rat droppings.

"I thought you was different, Manuel, an' so did she. You're just like'em, though, aye? Von Wine, them Lombardy mayors, all of'em. How much ya sell me one of your kids for, Manuel? How much ya sell me your wife for? How much'll it cost me ta watch ya fuck a pig, you little shit?"

"Look," said Manuel, his voice cracking as he looked up at her, "they came here when I was out with Margaretha and Lydie, two men came here. To my fucking house. Tomas, the servant, Tomas wasn't going to let them in but they forced the door, and one held him and the other found Katharina with, with Hieronymus, with my little boy. He was on her tit and they just barged in. They didn't talk long, just enough. Katharina was terrified—"

"An' ya didn't fuckin tell me." Monique was shaking her head. "Ya didn't tell me first thing when I come in the door. Ages ago, aye? An' ya didn't even send fuckin word?!" She slapped another canvas over, and that brought Manuel to his feet.

"Kat knew who they were fucking after, Mo, and she stalled and cried until she thought she sounded convincing, and then she told them Awa had stayed a night and then gone to Muscovy. Muscovy, Mo, how much farther from Paris can you fucking get?! And you ask why I didn't send someone from my fucking house directly to where she was, you ignorant pimp?! Did it ever cross your mind that my house might've been watched?!"

"It ever cross yours it might not've?" Monique kicked the base of an easel, bringing a painting he had been tweaking for half a year facedown into a spreading pool of paint.

"Stop!" Manuel went for her, the smirk breaking her face like a rock through a window telling him this was just what she had in mind. His fingers went numb as his punch struck her cheek, and then he was down again, unable to breathe or even see straight as first a jab to the stomach and then a boot to the armpit sent him rolling across his floor, the forest of stands toppling around him.

"—'eard the way she talked bout ya," Monique was saying as the artist moaned, wiping the smear of blood from his face. Paint, he realized, which was somehow worse. "Only 'eard lads on the line talk bout their da's like that, or preachers preachin bout the All-Father. You're a saint ta her, Saint Manuel the fuckin Brave. She'd tell 'ow you saved'er from Werner an' them more times'n you talk bout the 'orny fuckin bishop, talk bout your little pictures like they was treasures of Heaven. Have you even fuckin thought bout her since them men came lookin?!"

Manuel had thought of hardly anything else, but had almost convinced himself she would do better without his blundering about, leading her hunters to her hiding place. Things were better than they had ever been in Bern, he wasn't some fucking peasant anymore, he was coming up fast. Von Stein, asshole though he certainly was, had found his little cowherd even more useful on these obscure political battlefields, and so vanishing from society for who knew how long to ride to Paris to maybe get his friend killed, and himself and his growing family besides, had not seemed exactly judicious. Tell that to the raging lummox in his studio, though.

"I should've written," he admitted, still not moving lest she deliver another kick. "I should have fucking found a way to get word to you, alright? They said if she were lying, they'd, they'd take measures. Measures with Kat, and our fucking kids! She sent them to Muscovy and—"

"How in fuck ya know she said that, Manuel?" Monique sat down on his stool, one of the few untipped items in the room. "How you know that wife of yours didn't point ta Paris an' say—"

"She's not a liar," said Manuel, the fear one he had harbored ever since that day, to his shame and frustration. "We've never lied to each other."

"And 'ow you know that? You her confessor, too?"

"We don't go anymore," said Manuel. "We're, we've broken. You should, too—God doesn't need you to pay some—"

"Manuel!" She was using her battlefield voice, and he knew a servant would arrive soon, praise God. "I don't fuckin care how ya do your prayin, I want ta know how ya fuckin know your wife ain't a fuckin snitch!"

"She fucks other men!" Manuel shouted back now, furious at her for voicing that needling doubt, for opening that box he had locked up and weighed down with volumes of Katharina's proven honesty. "She tells me about that! And she tells me when she's been selfish or nasty, which she is sometimes, being fucking human and all. We're not all fucking saints, Monique! We're not all fucking heroes who only pause their prayers long enough to enslave other women, to foster lust, to, to, to fuck girls who'd puke at the thought if they weren't drunk, broke, and starving! So ask me how I know my wife isn't a fucking liar and I'll tell you how I know—because she doesn't even lie to herself, so why—"

"I told them where she was." Katharina was in the doorway. She looked tired. "I didn't lie to Niklaus, though. They came, and I told them she had gone to Moscow. They didn't believe me. They showed me something they had in a little case, a sort of bracelet with metal spines on the inside, and pointed at my baby son, and so I told them to look in France. I told Niklaus they had come in and asked, and I had told them Muscovy. So I didn't lie to him, and he didn't lie to—"

"You're an evil fuckin cunt," snarled Monique.

"I'm a mother and a wife," said Katharina evenly. "And I lack much motivation to protect a witch. Did Manuel tell you what they did together, in the graveyard before you two left? Did she tell you? Has he shown you the *art* he's crafted based on what she showed him? Call me evil if you like, but I sleep very well at night knowing I've done all I can to protect the people I know to be good."

"You wanna tell me again she ain't a fuckin liar?"

"I knew," said Manuel, and laughed a stupid, weird little giggle. "I knew. Or I should have. The look on your face when I got home, Kat, the panic in your eyes when you said Moscow to me, and I said *do you swear*, and you just nodded, as frightened as I've ever seen you. I knew right then you'd told them more but I didn't ask, did I? I just said you, you'd done a good deed. Ah!" Another part of the conversation came to him, and he giggled again. "You said I should write! You said I should write to warn Awa, and I said no, we were, we were probably being watched and she could take care of herself, and and and—"

"Stop crying," said Katharina, and he tried. Turning to the other woman, Manuel's wife said, "I don't expect you to understand."

"I understand," Monique said. "I seen enough in my day ta know what direction the piss flows. Devil always shits on the biggest pile."

"But pray tell," said Katharina, "how is it that you come here looking for her? We thought she was with you."

"She left, didn't she," said Monique. "Dunno where she went. Cut out not a week fore them prats showed up talkin bout gettin me locked up, closin down the shop an' all. So don't act like I wasn't threatened, too."

"And what did you tell them?" asked Katharina. "What clever ruse did you employ to send them on their way?"

"I didn't," said Monique, "an' they didn't go no place but face-down in the shithouse. Come in *my* fuckin place usin words like *dyke*? That term's reserved for we what hold back the sea, and a select few who're in our good graces, not some stoat-lookin ass-holes come tryin to bring the scares with fuckin toothpicks at they waists an' a matchlock what requires more'n earnest prayer to get primed an' lit."

"So now you're a murderer, and threw away what they threatened to take?" Katharina shook her head as though she were talking to a child.

"Been one longer'n I 'aven't." Monique shrugged. "An' I sold the whole kit to Dario, who's well aware of what's ripenin in the shithouse an' was more'n happy to pay a mite lighter than he might've otherwise due ta the inconvenience. There's a time I could've done better by forgettin to mention a detail but didn't, so maybe the both of you assholes could do with followin the example of Saint Cuntlick 'ere."

"I think you had best leave," said Katharina.

"I think that's fuckin sound," said Monique, glaring at Manuel. He had not gotten to his feet again but lay on his back in the wreckage of his studio, propped up on his elbows. She walked over to him, leaned down, and extended her hand. He moved to take it but she reached past him and fished a small canvas off the floor beside him. It was a portrait of Awa, one of the few where he had not disguised her by blanching her skin or substituting his wife's nose, his niece's lips. Monique held it up and brushed it off, and without looking at the prone artist said, "Should I give'er your apologies or ya gonna come deliver'em yerself?"

"She'll understand," said Manuel, and that was the worst, sharper than Monique's boot or fists, the knowledge that Awa would understand, indeed, she would insist he had no choice at all, and neither had Katharina. People always have a choice, Manuel knew, and looking from Monique to his wife he made his. "Let me give you some crowns before you go. I can spare—"

If she had spit on him it would have been better, but her phlegm struck one of the few paintings not cast about in her rage. He did not watch her leave, instead scrambling up and hurrying to clean the canvas. She had narrowly missed herself, the clod of lung-butter dripping down between Paris and Venus, between Manuel and Katharina. Carefully peeling the slick matter off with his apron and daubing the spittle up, he tried so hard not to remember working on the painting in that Parisian park that when his wife put her hand on his shoulder he jumped.

"It's gnawed at me," Katharina said quietly. "But I didn't have a choice. You would have gone to her."

"Probably." Manuel smiled weakly. "Probably led them right to her, gotten everyone killed. I'm not very good in tight spots."

"What is it about her?" Katharina looked down at the scattered sketches and prints and paintings. "You've been obsessed ever since you met her. Witches everywhere. Why didn't you just fuck her instead?"

"I never wanted that," said Manuel heavily. "I'd make more sense to myself if that was it. I love you, Katharina, and I love our family, and I won't jeopardize you again, not for her, not for anyone. I gave you my word the first time I went to war—when children arrive I'm finished, the sword goes on the mantel, and there it stays. I'm a man of my word."

"Except when you took that sword to Novara not so long ago?"

"That was different," Manuel said, knowing it wasn't. "Von Swine just needed a clerk, not exactly frontline action, or at least it wasn't supposed to be—and it was the worst I've ever seen, Kat, the things they did, the things we did, and I told him I was finished, didn't I, and came home early, and—"

"We're talking about the Moor, remember? I thought you said you were an instrument of God? He wanted something of you, wanted you to help her. Isn't that why you've had me stop going to the confessor, why you've made me talk to myself like a madwoman? Because you think God's more interested in talking to we sinners than the Pope?"

"Pope's a dick," said Manuel.

"Nice."

"Well, you know." Manuel smiled.

"Why don't you get your gear and go after her?" said Katharina. "Monique's right, you love her and—"

"I don't! Not like, like that," protested Manuel. "And she doesn't need my help. She's a fucking witch, remember? If anything, being around us made her soft, and if she left so close to those bounty hunters arriving she must have known, and got out first. They'll never find her, and neither will Monique."

"If I had known that's what they were, hired men and not real Inquisitors—"

"Hired men are worse, Kat," said Manuel. "I know from experience, don't I? You did the right thing in telling them. And not telling me. I can be... excitable."

"Foolish."

"That too."

"Go after her," said Katharina, staring at the Judgment of Paris, at the dark spot where spit had dampened the contour of her naked breasts, the apple Manuel had made her hold out to the seated man. One of his so-called Classical pieces, but the apple, and her nudity, had invoked a different garden to Katharina's mind then, as it did now. "Be safe."

"I'm a painter," said Manuel, as he set to cleaning up his studio. "And I'm a father, and a husband. She'll be fine. She doesn't need a Saint Niklaus any more than you or the children."

"If you change your mind I'll understand."

"I won't."

"I'll try to understand."

"Better. We'll make an honest woman of you yet," said Manuel, his smile almost genuine.

"I'll send Tomas to tell the abbot that you're ill and—"

Manuel cursed, having completely forgotten about his meeting with Oswald to discuss a referral to Rome, of all places. "This is too big, Kat, for all I know he's already shown my work to some cardinal or bishop. Fuck! Can you get this or—"

"Go on." She shooed him off, and he raced around the house, washing the paint off his face, pulling clods of it out of his hair, and would have carried on like this for some time if his wife had not cornered him in the bedroom. "You're an artist, Niklaus, he'll be disappointed if you're not a little scruffy."

"There's this public office I might be, well, I was waiting to tell you, but I think between Oswald and von Stein I might get the appointment and—"

"Out, Niklaus!"

Pecking her on the cheek, out he went. Watching him gain the street from the bedroom window, Katharina went down to the kitchen and poured herself a drink. Tomas came in, and after surreptitiously drawing the curtains, the servant stepped beside his mistress and put his hands firmly on her shoulders. When she did not relax at his touch he sighed and walked around the table, getting one of the glasses Manuel had blown for himself.

"I lied to him," Katharina said. "I don't know if I ever have, not really, but I lied to his face."

"I heard the row." Tomas nodded. "Is everything alright?"

"I don't know." She drained her glass. "I don't even know why, why I did it, it just came out, they were like dogs at each other's throats, and out it popped. Apparently Niklaus isn't the only fucking martyr in this house."

"What did you say?"

"I told them that those men who came about the Moor, I, well, I told them I had disclosed the girl's location to those men."

"She really did go to Russia?" Tomas loved a good bit of gossip as much as the next servant but was not quite following his mistress.

"Of course not," said Katharina. "I was really scared, of course, the thought of lying terrifies me, which somehow makes me rather adept at it, apparently. I kept pretending I didn't know who they were talking about, and then I cracked, I was going to crow *Paris!* at the top of my lungs, but then I heard myself say Petersburg, and that was that, they were gone before I could even ask myself what the hell I'd done. I was so proud of myself! And he was so proud of me! Sinful, really, all the pride-taking that went with that little lie. I saved her, me, the meek little housewife, I saved her! Or at least risked my life and family to try and save her." She sighed, her shoulders relaxing, and raised the glass Tomas had refilled.

"So why tell Master Deutsch and his friend that you had given up the secret?" The servant set his own emptied glass down and laid his hand on top of hers.

"Because we really should have sent word to her, at the very least," said Katharina after pondering the question for a moment. "That must be it. It's not enough to do a little good, is it? We've got to do everything we can, especially if God's not honoring indulgences and deathbed confessions anymore."

This latest development in the Manuel household was even more surprising to Tomas than the couple's creative definition of fidelity, though it certainly went a way toward explaining it. The young man very much loved his mistress, however, and knew that just because she took her pleasure from him when he was lucky he did not have the right to address his reservations about their abandoning the Church. At least his master was still meeting with the abbot, which implied they had not quit it altogether.

"I quit it altogether, you puffed-up pigeon!" Manuel said, interrupting the abbot. Oswald blinked, no doubt intending to spout more anti-Luther rot, and Manuel quickly clarified, "I mean your church, I mean this house of lies, this, this midden, with Old Leo king cock! How dare Luther speak? How dare Leo excommunicate a man with more piety in his ballsack than you lot have combined! And now that Leo's dead you've elected a Dutchman?! Really, man, the Frog Pope? It's like a bad joke!"

Oswald had begun to turn the same bright fuchsia color he had in Manuel's studio upon first seeing the nudes, and Manuel paused. Certainly he was being harsh, and it was not as though he had actually met Luther or anything; he just agreed with some, but certainly not all, of his ideas. Manuel had been thinking about Awa, and then Oswald had said something exceptionally, offensively foolish, and then—

"Sacrilege!" Oswald finally managed. "You blaspheming—"

"Horseshit," sneered Manuel, a few of his voices cheering him on, others mortified into silence, and a few content to watch his mouth work its magic. "You fucking clergy blaspheme more in a day than I do in a year, and I've been known to hide in the closet and watch my wife stick rosary beads up the ass of the help, so I know from sacrilege. Come, come, if they weren't meant to go there why'd the Good Lord make them such a perfect shape? I wouldn't be surprised if that Borgia Alexander had you jam a few up there yourself before God struck his ass down!"

Oswald did not have anything to say to that, but he did stand and make for the door. Manuel leaped out of his chair and intercepted him, knowing the difference between burning a bridge and setting oneself on fire in the process. The abbot was gulping like a landed carp, and Manuel moved quickly to gut him.

"Those pictures, Oswald, all those filthy pictures I sold you," said Manuel in a low voice, and then chanced a bluff. "We both know I'm not the only one who knows you have them, eh? Quite a scandal, if a confidant of yours and the artist himself both outed you for collecting such lewd, lustful images."

Oswald drew back as if struck, and Manuel felt the slightest tinge of guilt. This was a collector he was shaming, a patron, an aficionado. There could be no hesitation now, however, and when Oswald began parroting Manuel's excuses back at him the artist was ready to twist the knife.

"They're art, art! Beauty is—"

"Art? They're pictures of whores fingering themselves, Abbot, pictures of women fucking women and men and who knows what else I put in there. Tell me quick, Oswald, and tell me honest that you've never jerked off looking at them and I'll trouble you no more!"

"Trouble me no more," groaned the man, choosing neither to confirm nor deny the allegation.

"Gladly," said Manuel, "eagerly, and with relish. You don't even have to make good on your referral to Rome."

Oswald groaned louder. "Who was the Judas, Niklaus, whose sweet kiss betrayed me? Tell me that, I beg!"

"What?" Manuel blinked.

"Which of my friends told you I showed them?" Oswald spat. "Who must I settle accounts with after you've exacted your blood money?"

"I'll take care of it for you, if you get me what I want," Manuel lied effortlessly, overjoyed that his wild stab had struck home. Now there was only Katharina to deal with. She was waiting when he arrived, and with an exaggerated sigh he sat down across from her at the kitchen table.

"Well," she said blandly as he poured himself a drink into the glass already waiting on the table. "When do you leave for Rome?"

"The damndest thing happened," said Manuel. "I lost the commission."

"Oh my."

"I know. Terrible. We'll be destitute."

"Oh my."

"The thing is, I think I've also turned Oswald off putting in a word for me about that civic position."

"Oh my."

"So there's nothing for it, really, but going back to the mercenary work." Manuel examined his wife, trying to determine the rules and stakes of the game they were playing.

"This is the last time, Manuel," she said, and he winced to see the sadness in her eyes. "And you need to know I lied to you and her earlier—I never told them where Awa went. I've thought it over and don't want to be the clever, clever wife who knows the best way to help her husband is through clever, clever lies—if you go, it's your choice, yours alone. Your things are in the studio."

"Ah," said Manuel, wondering for an instant if this confession changed matters in the slightest but knowing it did not. It had always been his choice. "After dinner then I'll—"

"If you want to catch her you'll have to leave immediately. I packed you a few meals."

"But Lydie just took Hieronymus and Margaretha and won't be back until later."

"Yes." Katharina was still looking him in the eyes, and he had to break her gaze.

"I'd have to leave without saying goodbye."

"Yes."

They sat in silence in the late afternoon warmth, and slowly Katharina stood and went to her husband. She held him for a time, then scratched his head and slapped him on the back. He stood, and she followed him to the studio. She had cleaned the room from top to bottom, so that no one would have known of the Dutch whirlwind that had blown through it earlier that day.

On his table was a pack laden with pine planks, charcoal, his stylus case, several pairs of clean trousers, shirts, blankets, cheese from their cousins' goats, bread from his favorite baker, four sausages, three empty waterskins, and two bottles of schnapps. Beside the pack were his ostrich-plumed hat, his dagger, and the sword she had removed from the mantel.

Manuel was genuinely impressed that Monique had not tarried at the brothel but departed immediately upon concluding her business. He decided to try south, thinking if he were to write a play or a poem, something about witches and mercenaries and such, the obvious downward symbolism of the direction could not be passed up, and he arrived at her roadside campfire just after dark. She had told herself she would not smile but could not help herself, feeling like an idiot as she stowed the pistol she had brandished at the sound of hooves.

"You're going the wrong way," said Manuel, still on his horse. "Get your gear and mount up."

"Well, I didn't want ta get too far ahead lest ya lose the trail," said Monique. "And how in fuck ya know where Awa is?"

"I don't," said Manuel. "But we're not looking for Awa."

"We're not?"

"No."

"Then who're we lookin for?" said Monique.

"Ashton fucking Kahlert," Manuel said triumphantly, but when Monique just blinked at him he sighed and pulled out the parchment he had received from Oswald after the flustered abbot had returned from checking his records. "The former Inquisitor who's paying muscle to track down our little friend, printing posters and getting himself kicked out of the Church and such."

"Ahhhh!" Monique's crooked teeth shone in the firelight as she booted sand onto the blaze. "Ya got a beautiful brain inside that ugly head of yours."

"Thank you, madam."

"So where's this cuntsmack gonna get 'is?"

"Well, the good news is Kahlert came from Salzburg, so the abbey at Bern had a few places to look for him. The bad news is that he hadn't been through in years, so who knows how out of date the addresses are. But it's a start."

"That it is, that it is." Monique mounted her horse. "Where're the possibilities?"

"Well, one's near Granada, which is the last place Oswald was sure Kahlert went before being excommunicated, but that's almost ten years old. The other address is outside some shitty backwater in the Schwarzwald, a property he inherited from a dead superior of his."

"Holy Roman, then," said Monique. "Helluva lot closer, an' bad as Imperials are, Spain's full of evil cunts."

Manuel wondered at this, for everyone he had ever met from Spain had been nothing short of lovely. They turned their horses and doubled back past Bern, the pretty red millwheel Manuel adored nothing but a black blur in the night, and together they began their hunt for an excommunicated witch hunter with the funds to send mercenaries all over Europe after Awa. For fuck's sake.

XXIX
A Fast Night in the Black Forest

♂

The records Manuel had extorted from Oswald mentioned a house outside of Calw that Ashton Kahlert listed as his personal property, and with the last hard snows of winter behind them Manuel was confident they would gain the city by Lent. Not that he would be fasting this year—that was the first thing to go, although it might make getting decent food at the inns difficult. They were entering the land of Luther, though, so hope sprang eternal.

The slow, meandering river they had followed that morning now joined another just outside one of the dozy hamlets that popped up far less frequently than Manuel would have preferred. The Schwarzwald was every bit as black as its name, owls gliding just overhead in the middle of the afternoon; he had stowed his hat lest the birds mistake his bobbing toque for something edible. They crossed clearings and meadows as they wound up through the hills, but these breaks from the forest only made the artist more nervous, as if the entire surrounding wood were watching him venture out into the open, and always the road took them back under those brooding firs and the occasional elm, whose bare branches appeared almost reluctant to bud in so grim a forest.

"Wolfach," Manuel told Monique as he returned to the table she had secured despite the throng of already piss-drunk locals.

"Never 'eard of it." She took two of the four mugs he clung to as the sea of drunkards pushed and pulled around him.

"Nor I, but we're close to Calw." Manuel frowned, seeing she had the only stool.

"An' will 'is Majesty be sharin a room with the lady?" Monique wiped ale foam from her mouth. "After a night or two beddin down under them evil trees I'm inclined ta take your pallet-minded ways ta heart."

"What?" Manuel squinted, as if that might help him hear better over the hullabaloo.

"Did ya get us space in the common? I ain't springin for a room less we ain't got a choice."

"No room," said Manuel. "No rooms, and no room in the common. We'll be camping out, though the keep says on nights like this folk are allowed to set up by the rivers once the party dies down."

"Fuckin Fastnacht," she spit, Manuel noting how much cooler her tone was now that they would not have a warm building to stumble inside after the festivities. He shrugged and drained his first beer. It was quality stuff, dark and stern as the woodland, and Manuel was thrilled they had found a decent town instead of spending the festival eve hunched around a fire in the loneliest fucking forest he had ever had the misfortune to ride through.

"I'm going to head down there after this, set up and get some sketching in."

"I won't join ya," Monique belched. "Not til I get some fuckin meat in me. Unless they're outta that, too, in which case I suppose I'll eat my fuckin pony."

"You want me to take her with me then, lest you lose control?"

"Huh?" A band had struck up somewhere in the packed tavern, a hurdy-gurdy moaning and a rumble-pot roaring.

"Do you want me to take your horse with me?!" Manuel

shouted in her face, and she nodded. He guzzled his second beer, overjoyed to escape her company for a spell. She was not bad, not really, but Christ could the loudmouth tax one's patience—a sentiment shared by Monique, as far as the artist went.

Out in the streets the people of Wolfach, farmers and cowherds and miners, were already celebrating the eve of Ash Wednesday with the sun still high overhead, stalls set up and hay cast down to catch the influx of dung from all the hayseeds journeying into town for the festival. Manuel grinned, and wondered when the hell he had last taken the time to come out to one of these. Masks that might be doubles of the ones that had haunted his nightmares as a child leered all about him, witches and monsters everywhere, and he wondered if they would have a running of the Bright Ones. How had it gone... the Perchten, the Bright Ones, were lords of the beasts, and could be fair or foul. The young, pretty ones chased the old witches, and—

A shapely girl in a white robe bumped into him as he led the horses through the crowd, and as he began to apologize he noticed her mask, a bright red wooden hag face, a ram's horn and a stag's antler jutting off at wild angles. She shrieked and shook his arm, then capered away, one phantom amidst many. Manuel had stopped cold, staring after her, the horsetail pinned to her robe swishing behind her.

"Eat it," Manuel's great-aunt rasped, her voice sharp in his memory even down all the years. "You eat or she cut your belly open, stuff you fulla straw."

Perchta was not just some creature of the wilds, Manuel remembered, the memories swirling like the crowd around him, she was a pagan deity, one of the old gods that still haunted these hills. The mad old woman was the exact opposite of Manuel's overzealous Christian grandfather, and even as a child he could not tell which ancient minder was more terrifying. His great-aunt had a secret shrine to Perchta she hid from her pious siblings, and she had made Manuel set out offerings, made him eat that disgusting fish gruel, which might have been tasty if she had not been the one making it, salted fish who knew how many years overripe mixed with moldering oats, while his mother was off doing whatever it was she did.

Manuel had always imagined his father's side of the family would have treated him better, but the artist was a bastard, albeit one who knew the identity of his sire. It was not easy, being a bastard, but Manuel had managed the best he could, and the apothecary who could not formally acknowledge his son at least provided them coin enough that Manuel only had to stay with his demented relatives some of the time, instead of all of it. Manuel no longer tasted the phantom of the beer in his mouth, he tasted that wince-inducing, salty gruel of his great-aunt and smelled her almost sweet breath, and he moved faster, the dancing devils no longer quite so amusing.

From heretical altars on dirt floors to modest piety to rejecting the Church and fine city living in only a generation or two—impressive, thought Manuel as he kept along the river. He stabled the horses, then walked the length and breadth of Wolfach, plank and charcoal in hand like sword and shield.

Following a side street to the eastern wall, he paused by a gate looking up the cleared hillside bordering the town. Several late revelers were dashing down the cowtrail toward the artist, laughing and whooping, and seeing they were still some distance off he idly began sketching their approach. He would wipe the plank clean with a damp piece of bread later, but such exercises were good at keeping his speed up—rarely did even the perfect model keep the perfect pose for more than a few moments.

They were a curious bunch, the man in the lead dressed like a monk, which seemed a little strong even for an isolated town like Wolfach. At least he did not wear a mask, unlike the devils who chased him, their monstrous faces sliding about as they raced for town. Then one of the bestial men hoisted a blunt-looking flail and easily as threshing wheat knocked the running monk's legs out from under him. Manuel paused. Another man, all horns and fangs and animal skins, grabbed the monk's beard as the poor fellow tried to gain his feet, and then the others were there, a man with a giant rooster mask seeming to give them orders.

Manuel ducked down, peering through the slats in the gate. As the chicken-headed man pulled his mask off to reveal a rather mundane mustachioed face, Manuel noticed two things. First, what he had taken to be the monk's beard was clearly a crude gag made out of a pelt that was now jammed back into place, and second, the monk was none other than Doctor Paracelsus. The subdued physician was hoisted onto the shoulders of three of the five men, who trotted back up the trail into the forest as Chicken-Head put his mask into place and scanned the edge of the town. Manuel ducked lower, wondering just what the hell was going on, and when he next peeked through the slats the hillside was as empty as it had been on his arrival.

Fuck. Paracelsus? Fuck. Manuel very, very much regretted leaving the inn where Monique no doubt still drank, and he very, very much regretted leaving Bern in the first place. Whatever trouble the old quack had gotten himself into was his own damn fault, and...Manuel sighed, and set to picking his way back to the inn where he had left Monique.

She was gone, and he could not find her in the next few taverns he tried, either. The sun was setting now, bonfires lit along the river, and the festival was growing wilder. Manuel had almost given up hope of finding her at all when she clapped him by the shoulder and spun him around. To his immense relief she was not drunk; on the contrary, she looked remarkably sober.

"Where the fuck've you been?" she demanded before he could do the same of her, and without waiting for an answer she whispered, "Let's get ta some back road, an' now. We gotta talk."

Monique led him through several alleys before she would even slow down, let alone speak. They were winding east between the half-timbered houses, and when they hit the wall where Manuel had seen Paracelsus he set his heels and growled, "What's happened, Mo?"

"She's here," said Monique, and then a pack of children went howling past them along the wall, pursued by a straw-covered man with a goat mask.

"What? Who?" Manuel glanced at the darkening hillside beside them, the twilight sky blurring with the treetops.

"Who do ya fuckin think? Awa!"

"Where?! When did you see—"

"Shut it," said Monique, and suddenly grabbing him in her arms, she crushed him to her chest and brought her mouth a breath from his. Before he could protest, she hissed, "Don't you ruin this. They's comin up behind an' we'd best be lovers lookin for quiet."

And then she did kiss him, harder than he had ever been kissed, though her tongue stayed on her side of the fence. Half a dozen men passed by, and with the multiple weapons at their waists, their dour faces, and the large swatches of chain and leather armor covering their traveling clothes they did not seem to be on their way to the festival. Even after the last of them had vanished along the now-dark lane Monique continued to grind against Manuel, and when he tried to push her off she grabbed the back of his neck and held him tighter, which was when another man passed them. This fellow made no pretense of ignoring them, and once he had gone a little way up the road he laughed loudly, and then was gone.

"Ever give a thought ta eatin somethin other'n cat turds?" Monique spit as she broke away from him. "That'll be a franc, son, or two if ya had yourself a moment under that cod of yours."

"I'm guessing you know those men?" said Manuel, wiping his mouth.

"Not half's well as we will fore sun-up," said Monique. "Meant to get ahead of'em but your dirty self had ta slip off for a wank, didn't ya? Let's give'em some time fore we go after."

"Monique," Manuel said as patiently as he was able. "What's going on? I saw something, I saw Paracelsus. The doctor from Milan?"

"What?" Now it was Monique's turn to let her jaw hang. "That fuckin lump?"

"You first, then I'll tell you what I saw."

"Not so much seein on my end but I 'eard the whole fuckin thing, didn't I?" Monique said smugly. "I'm finished with them beers you brought, an' unlike a proper joint there weren't no maids bringin more so I push on up ta the bar. Jus' when I'm bout ta tell the keep three more beers, an' leave out the water this time, cunt, this slight fucker cuts in front of me, one of them what jus' passed us."

Manuel wondered which of the bulky men classified as "slight" to Monique.

"I'm bout ta straighten'em the fuck out when I 'ear'em say ta the keep, loud as fuckin day, *we come ta collect the witch.* Now, I'm thinkin he's talkin festival talk or somethin, thinkin no fuckin way's it this easy, an' the barkeep says back, in fuckin eye-tie ta top it all, *keep it down, they got the witch stowed outta town.* Now I'm gettin real interested in pickin through my purse, aren't I, an' the keep an' this lump jus' keep yakkin away in eye-tie like nobody knows what they're sayin, an' by the cut of those drunk fucks no one else did. But I speak eye-tie, I speak it fuckin bella, don't I?"

"So they came to pick up Awa? Did they say Awa?" Manuel looked around nervously, the alley dark in the gloaming but the bonfires by the river lighting up little patches of the cross streets a few blocks away.

"Course they didn't say fuckin Awa, 'ow the fuck they know her name?" Monique shook her head, disappointed by Manuel's obtuseness. "They said witch, but they also said they'd been followin'er trail through some graveyards up ta this'un, an' it seems like this lump barkeep was the go-tween with the muscle. Sounds like this Kahlert cunt's spread 'is net wide, but he's also been buttonin it down local so all these fuckin hick-bergs know there's a man in Calw what'll pay for witches."

"So Kahlert *is* in Calw," said Manuel. "Good fucking thing we didn't try Spain first."

"That weren't happenin," said Monique. "Told ya."

"But wait," said Manuel. "If Kahlert's men, the muscle, were tracking her from some graveyard to here, to Wolfach, how was the barkeep involved, and—"

"In time, in time," said Monique. "I was almost fuckin there. So barkeep says them locals what got the witch caught'er up an old graveyard they don't use no more, out the east side of town off a huntin trail. Barkeep says ta go out there ta pick'er up, an' after gettin the biggest fuckin tip I ever seen the keep finally gets round ta pourin my beer while the muscle goes back ta 'is crew."

"His crew? He and the rest—"

"Drinkin it up, real fuckin subtle-like, seven big assholes bunched together in one place. So I stagger o'er, not next to'em, understand, but close enough ta catch a word or two as everyone's shoutin ta be 'eard in that fuckin place."

Manuel could scarcely believe she could hear anything after a lifetime blasting guns, but her words were starting to create an unhappy image in his mind, though a play might have served the complex story better. A tragedy, with Manuel as the lead, and—he caught himself. "I'm sorry, Mo, what was that?"

"I said three of the big cunts was trackin'er this way, an' come inta town the same day four of Kahlert's boys come down from Calw. See, one of these local chumps went up ta let Kahlert know they'd caught 'is witch, but if that was true Awa couldn't be muckin bout in them other churchyards the first three was followin'er through. So the muscle, all seven of'em, get inta town today, some from the south an' some from the north, an' someone recognizes someone else, they compare stories, an' what the fuck? Somethin don't add up, what with it soundin like the witch's in two spots at once, an' these boys pissed besides that some fuckin peasants is stealin they glory *and* they bounty."

"I know what's going on, Mo, I—" Manuel began, but she cuffed him on the head.

"Shut it til I'm finished. So the south muscle says she'd be up the graveyard tonight or next, seein as they don't reckon she's got a horse an' this oughta be the next potter's field in line for'er, an' so they an' the north muscle says why not go see if the peasants got themelves the witch, an' if aye, great, kill the fuckers an' take'er back to Kahlert, an' if nay, send them peasants packin with an empty purse an' lay in ta catch the witch if she shows her snout tonight or next. So they all runnin ta the graveyard, and we will, too, once you tell me how you got it all sussed, and what the fuck Doctor P is doin mixed up in it."

"He's the first witch!" said Manuel, the pieces fitting together seamlessly. "Maybe Kahlert isn't specific about what witch he wants, or maybe the locals think, what with him being a fucking witch hunter, that he'll pay out for any old witch they catch, and who knows, maybe he will. So Paracelsus arrives in town, running his fucking mouth, and some of the locals decide he's witchy enough."

"An' you said you seen'em? Paracelsus?"

"Just down the wall!" And Manuel quickly recounted what he had seen by the fence.

"So Doctor Lump rides in a few days back an' his fuckin mouth lands'em in witch territory." Monique nodded slowly. "Barkeep sends word ta Calw tellin Kahlert they caught themelves a witch down in Wolf. Meantimes, Awa's cuttin through graveyards for reasons obscure, with three fuckin bounty riders after'er, an' is headed straight for this shitheap."

"That's how it looks from here," said Manuel. "And that's a sight better to go on than what either the locals or Kahlert's muscle is working with."

"I don't give half a drunk-fuck what 'appens ta Doctor Lump, but if our girl's blunderin inta it up the graveyard—"

"Or if we're wrong about any of the details—"

"That's enough head start for those assholes," said Monique, straightening up. "Let's get ta fuckin work, Manuel."

They jumped the rough stone wall where they stood, then hurried up the grassy hill toward the treeline. Manuel found himself excited, actually nervous and eager and hungry to stick his sword in some piece of shit that would sell a girl to a witch hunter. A shame, he thought, that he had been unable to conjure such enthusiasm when he was actually a mercenary who stood just as good a chance of living out the battle as anyone else, as opposed to an already winded has-been embarking on a blind charge into a dark forest on an increasingly dark night against unknown odds with only a single ally at his side. He might have laughed but he lacked the air, and then the screams started, shrill but distinctly male, and Monique laughed for him.

"That's our fuckin girl, like as not! Move, lump, move!" They hit the trail where it entered the forest, and then he was huffing after her, Monique jangling in front of him with all the subtlety of, well, a furious Dutch gunner smashing up a studio. Fuck had no sake here.

The screaming trailed off as lights came into view through the trees, and Monique continued to exercise the restraint that had so surprised and impressed Manuel by slowing to a stop, her hands fluttering over her body to press the bouncing metal silent. Manuel stopped as well, not for the first time admiring her array of guns and wishing he had learned the skill himself, or at least thought to pick up a crossbow. She must have invested some of her income in new pieces, for the twin pistols she silently drew from scabbards jutting out from under her armpits were unlike any the artist had seen before, the silhouetted barrels long as short swords. Even in the dark he heard her breathing steady as soon as the guns were in hand, and before he could ask how she meant to light the cords without drawing attention she left the trail and darted between the trees.

How someone so big could move so quietly was a question Awa had asked herself recently as well, the necromancer having been taken unawares and bound in iron chain for the second time in her life—no coincidence, that. Merritt was supposed to be on watch to prevent just such a circumstance, but her immediate suspicion that he had sold her out was proven false when she spied two men shoving him into an identical sack just before the hood went over her eyes. Chloé gave a short gasp that was cut off, and Awa could only hope this was the result of a gag similar to the one Awa now wore being put into place. Then she felt herself hoisted up, their captors clearly not keen on dallying beside the churchyard where they had finally captured the witch and her accomplices. She realized that not only was she caught and most likely being delivered to someone who both knew her weaknesses and meant her harm, but this time there was no Niklaus Manuel Deutsch of Bern to save her.

Manuel stumbled in the dark, ashamed of himself for making so much noise as he tripped through the underbrush, but when he glanced up to whisper an apology Monique was gone. The artist stayed very still as he peered around, close enough to the cemetery and its lights to see that he was very much alone in the stand of firs shrugging up against the low stone wall of the old graveyard. Turning his attention there, he did not see a single man, the seven bounty hunters from Wolfach and the five costumed locals who had kidnapped Paracelsus just as absent as Monique, only a few lanterns balanced on gravestones indicating anyone had been there at all.

There were several stone markers but the only other obvious grave was a hulking barrow that dominated the rear of the cemetery, and with a silent prayer Manuel closed the little ground between him and the wall. Clambering over it he knocked a stone loose, the rock clattering down with all the volume of an angelic choir announcing the presence of the Almighty. Fuck.

Landing in a crouch and drawing his sword, Manuel waited for the mob of bounty hunters and locals, now united in purpose, to charge around the side of the barrow and martyr his sorry ass. Nothing stirred but a breeze that brought the distant drumming of the Fastnacht festivities from Wolfach, where the witches and devils and beauties all danced and danced, celebrating the death of winter. The wind felt chill enough on his neck from where he knelt, and Manuel might have stayed there until Judgment if Monique had not materialized to his right.

She marched in through the gate as if she were a noble lady taking in her gardens, a winning smile on her face as she walked casually forward, only the two pistols jutting out in front of her implying she felt any anxiety at all. Manuel stood slowly, and felt a little piss dribble into his codpiece as both gun barrels suddenly yawned in his direction, Monique's smile twisting to a frown as she saw who it was, her wrists relaxing. Then she motioned him toward the barrow with a pistol, and he hesitated only long enough to retrieve one of the lanterns from atop a leaning tombstone.

Turning the light toward the barrow, Manuel's eyes bulged and he heard a low, whining moan. Realizing he was the one making the noise, he instantly quieted, though his unease was not so easily dispelled. The side of the barrow and the ground before it was coated with blood, wide splashes of it reaching even the walls of the cemetery. Looking down at himself, Manuel saw he stood in a puddle of the old Papal paint. Monique was no longer smiling.

Taking a few a steps forward and peering closer at the earth, he saw winding smears and furrows where bodies had been dragged around the side of the grassy mound, as well as several shattered lanterns and discarded swords. So there might have been a double cross after all, and enough of one side or the other had survived to drag away the bodies. A chicken mask lay cracked against a tombstone, matted hair stuck to its edge. Looking back to Monique, Manuel saw she was rounding the barrow, and the nerve that had to date saved him on the battlefield loosened his knees. Circling around the far side, he slowed almost to a crawl as he heard the unmistakable sound of muffled digging from within the hillock itself. Monique appeared around the other side of the mound, and together they advanced on a wide tunnel dug straight into the side of the barrow.

Awa felt them set her down, every part of her aching and sore. People were moving around her and whispering, and she wondered if Chloé was still nearby or if the young woman had been taken to some other location. Then the slit in the hood was being uncinched, and even with the dimness of the chamber her eyes burned and wept. She smelled old bones and gravedirt but could not tell if the reek was her own, and then, finally, a familiar voice spoke to her. She froze, shocked beyond her ability to think, and so as her eyes adjusted and the face peering down at her came into focus she could only stare and gasp.

"Paracelsus," Manuel hissed at the mouth of the barrow tunnel, and from the corner of his eye he saw Monique's cool features ignite in rage at his breaking the silence. The man heard, however, and looked up from the dark shape on the ground he was kneeling over. The doctor looked far more crazed than he had even at his most incensed and drunk back at his clinic, and he held a shaking red finger to his pale lips. Blood dripped down his hand onto the body beneath him, and the digging sound coming from deeper within the barrow stopped.

"I mean you no harm," Awa called from the darkness at the rear of the tunnel, and Manuel felt all his fear melt into delight at hearing her voice. She sounded frightened and anxious, terrified, even, but it was her, and they were all here, and everyone was safe.

"Awa!" Monique cried, shoving the pistols back into their holsters and pushing past Manuel. "It's us, Awa, Mo and Manuel!"

Manuel felt a residual shiver at her sheathing the weapons, but the tunnel was obviously too narrow for more than one person to be back there. Paracelsus gaped at Monique as she neared him, and then snatched her leg with wet, bloody hands, gibbering up at her. Manuel moved in to drag the deranged doctor off of her, which was when the light from his lantern illuminated the figure in the rear of the tunnel. Not. Fucking. Awa.

"I am Awa." The horror spoke with her voice, the yellow-eyed canine monstrosity spoke with her fucking voice, and before Monique could turn from Paracelsus and see it, it and the bloody pile of corpses it crouched atop, before Manuel could even blink the tears from his eyes, the lantern sputtered once and went out. In the sudden and unbroken blackness they heard Awa say, "Funny! Funny! Funny!"

Then the hyena let out its riotous, horrible laugh, and there in the dark of the barrow Manuel began to scream.

XXX
The Hammer Falls

Omorose. The tears leaving Awa's eyes were no longer only from the faint light searing them after a week blindfolded inside a sack as the bounty hunters took her west after catching her just outside Troyes. She had been directing their search to take them toward Bern, and if only she could have seen Manuel one last time, laughed and shared a drink and taken in his newest masterpiece...

"Well well well, beast, it's been a long time." Omorose beamed at her old slave, as unblemished and beautiful as she had been the day she left her harem, unlike the weather-burned, haggard witch who cried in her bonds, only her chestnut-dark face jutting out of the cocoon of sackcloth and chain like some miserable caterpillar interrupted mid-metamorphosis. "You look good, beast, quite good like that, all tied up and bleating."

Awa realized she had been trying to speak through the gag, and went silent. She had to think, she had to find out what had happened, where she was, what they had done with—

"We've got your friends, beast," said Omorose, and Awa felt herself lifted up. She was in some sort of dungeon. Not that she had seen one before, but she made out stone walls, long wooden tables with shackles and cranks, an utter lack of windows—a dungeon to be sure.

"Is it safe to, to move her?" An older man she had not seen before had spoken as he hoisted her off the ground with the assistance of two of the bounty hunters.

"They got her here, didn't they?" snapped Omorose. "If a week on a horse didn't rattle her loose then putting her on the table shouldn't be too risky, should it, Ash?"

The man grunted even with the bounty hunters to help him, and then Awa was laid flat on one of the tables. From up here she could see the two other swaddled shapes on the floor, and then they rolled her on her side and the man, Ash, looked across Awa at Omorose. She held up a knife, Awa's ibex knife, the necromancer realized with a shudder, and then a cold thought came to her—what if Omorose had found the book, found a way to break the curse, to hurt her despite being an undead creature? Then the knife sank into the sweaty cloth bundling Awa and Omorose began cutting around the chains, tearing away the sack in wide swaths.

One of the bounty hunters said something to Kahlert, who glanced sadly at Awa and then disappeared from view. They had used much more chain this time, the man who had initially seized her holding a loop of it around her shoulders as his fellows beat her until she went still, and then they had locked it into place, covered her with the hooded sack, and applied yet more chain. Bands of the iron links tightly encircled her ankles and knees, and a single length of it wrapped around her torso many times over, pinning her arms to her side; even with the sack cut away from her Awa had no hope of squirming loose, and she looked helplessly up at Omorose.

"—an extra ten to ride down to Wolfach and find Olaf," Kahlert was telling the man. "Obviously the lead there is useless at best and fraudulent at worst, and if they already purchased the alleged witch then the barkeep at the Wolf's Step will know who has taken my money. I know there's plenty of room for duplicity in such a convoluted matter, so I shall make it simple for you—so long as the money I gave to Olaf for the acquisition of the witch is returned to me, you shall have a reasonable cut, and I don't care if the money is currently held by Olaf, the barkeep, or the amateur witch hunters of Wolfach. Once you've acquired my funds please inform Olaf, and the barkeep, for that matter, that until further notice I'm not paying out for sorcerers and—"

"You're going to suffer in here." Omorose rolled Awa onto her back again and leaned down, her face hovering just above Awa's as she whispered to her, "He's alive, beast, think about that. He can do anything he wants to you. Annnnything I can think of. And I've thought of *a lot* since last we saw one another, since last you tried to murder me."

"Thank you, Inquisitor," said the bounty hunter. Awa heard a door open and close, and then the sound of metal sliding on wood. Omorose straightened up and Kahlert came back into view at Awa's feet, his face grim. No, Awa realized, not grim, but trying to look it—the man was trembling all over, nowhere near as calm as he was pretending.

"They're gone," Kahlert said, switching from German to Spanish. "I had him dismiss the lot, so I'll go and make sure all the servants have cleared out, and then we can..." His fingertips were extended, almost brushing Omorose's cheek, and the woman gave a little sigh. Awa's surprise was wearing off, and she began to extrapolate what was going on. She did not have to do much guessing, however; as soon as the man disappeared Omorose positively gushed.

"His name is Ashton Kahlert, and he was an Inquisitor when I found him," said Omorose, smiling down at Awa. "You chased me right into his arms, and before you know it he's doing everything I say, because of you. Because of *what you did*. I told him a bit of it, of what you did, only a bit, and even still you should have seen the look on his face! So he told everyone he knew about you, and even when it cost him his position in his church he kept at it, an *obedient* man, a *loyal* servant, the sort of slave that a woman might find herself admiring, appreciating. Loving."

Awa would not have had a great deal to say, even without the gag.

"So his men found you." Omorose sighed. "It's almost *too* perfect. Daddy's favorite caught in the only place she ever goes to meet girls, and with a pair of friends, too! One of them's a woman, I gather—is she your *girlfriend*, beast? Is she a stupid little cunt who doesn't know what you do? What you've done?"

Keeping Chloé—and Merritt, for that matter—oblivious to what she was up to as they had scoured the churchyards of France had not been easy, but Awa had managed. Both assumed she was simply a graverobber, albeit a remarkably successful one given the coins and jewelry she returned with, and as she limited her raising and questioning of the dead to the times when she was able to ditch her companions, usually on her turn at watch, neither ever suspected that they were traveling with a necromancer, and Awa had never found a suitable opportunity to tell Chloé. Awa did not see how she could have given away anything with the gag in place but perhaps her eyes or her nostrils twitched, for Omorose smiled even wider.

"She *is* your little girlfriend, isn't she? And she *doesn't* know, does she? Oh, this is too perfect, just too, too perfect." Omorose spun around in place, then caught herself, setting down the knife and planting her hands on either side of Awa's face. "Oh, how I wish I could spit on you, beast! Don't have the moisture, I'm afraid—I had to take all my skin off because of you. I started *shedding* and so I had to shave it all off, skin, muscle, everything else, lest I give myself away. Do you know how badly I miss my skin, beast? About as badly as you'll miss yours, I imagine."

Omorose glanced up at something, then leaned closer. "I was going to have him rape you, beast, like you did me. Well, not quite... we can't make you pretend to like it. But he'll rape you if I ask, you know, he's capable of more than anyone I've ever met. I thought he was so soft when I met him, I thought it would take so much work to get him to even let me at you... but you wouldn't imagine the things he does! It's, it's ingenious, is what it is. But you'll see, yes you will, you'll see what he does. But not to you, not at first."

Awa moaned then, much as she fought against it. If only Omorose would loosen the gag she could talk to her, reason with her, say something.

Would it matter, though? The realization was sobering, and chill as ice water on her back—nothing Awa could say or do would stop Omorose, nothing. The woman's mind was irrevocably broken and she had spent almost a decade plotting for this occasion, and there was nothing to be done but suffer whatever she had planned. Awa had raised Omorose, raised her more than once, and she had brought Chloé along, had suffered that asshole Merritt to be with her, all so the plucky young harlot could be tortured to death over who knew how many hours, how many days. Awa shook with sorrow and terror, and Omorose shook with laughter.

"They're gone." Kahlert closed the second door, and locked that as well. "Shall we start?"

They did. Awa was rolled onto her stomach and the chain around her ankles was removed, but before the bruised skin could enjoy the sensation of freedom for even a moment manacles were slid into the grooves the chain had left in her skin and locked into place. Then they removed the chains wrapped around her knees, and by working a crank at the side of the table heavy ropes attached to rings in her manacles tightened and then pulled her legs apart until she felt like she would be split down the middle. They repeated the process with the chain binding her arms to her sides, and then the second crank was tightened and Awa was splayed out facedown on the table, a board shoved underneath her chin to keep her looking straight ahead. All the chains had been removed, but when she gritted her teeth and focused despite the strain in every muscle and tendon she found that the iron shackles around her wrists and ankles were completely smothering her ability to work any sort of necromancy.

"Start with the slut she brought," said Omorose eagerly. "Take her on the floor so the witch can see. While you fuck her I'll use the comb to peel back her scalp."

That was without a doubt the single evilest thing Awa had ever heard. She moaned again, hoping against hope that the mild-looking man would balk at this, perhaps even remove her gag, hear her side of the story, listen to—

"I want to shoe her first," Kahlert said firmly. "If she's as powerful as we suspect, the iron on her arms and legs might not be enough. I still think we should take care of her—"

"Fine, fine." Omorose twitched, clearly displeased. "But you'll do it, won't you, Ash? You'll do it so the witch has to see?"

"Of course," said Kahlert, knowing that what a witch hates most is what most needs doing, no matter how distasteful the act might be were an actual human involved. "What choice do we have?"

Omorose shrieked with laughter, dropping down to look Awa in the eye as she did. Awa was hyperventilating, her pupils dilating, and Omorose yanked out her gag.

"I gave you another chance," Awa finally managed as Omorose shimmered before her. What Awa at first took to be a spell revealed its mundane cause when the tears tickled her chin. "Life, I gave you another life! I gave you everything I could!"

"You gave me everything, alright," Omorose whispered. "You think I wanted you to dig me up and play with my bones, you nasty bitch? You think I wanted to become some rotten monster instead of lying at rest? You're just as selfish as you were on the mountain!"

Omorose laughed again, and Awa knew they were both lost. Kahlert came over beside the still tittering Omorose and held up a small V-shaped piece of iron, several holes punched through the flat surface of the metal.

"This is your test, witch," the man said softly, almost kindly. "The lady Rose has told me you conceal a cloven hoof under the skin of your left foot, like the devil himself, and that she knows the method of removing the glamour you disguise it with. If you are innocent obviously your foot will remain your foot, and I will release you, and your friends. Conversely, you may admit to your crimes now, in which case you will be burned at once, your soul cleansed."

"The *fuck* she will," Omorose growled at Kahlert. "What's the meaning of this fucking pardon?!"

"It is not Christian to use the stronger methods when—"

"I confess!" Awa wailed. "I confess I confess I confess!"

Omorose was livid, her pretty face taut and wild, but Kahlert held up a gloved hand and said, "You confess to what?"

"I confess!" Awa hiccupped. "I confess to whatever you want, to whatever she said!"

Kahlert shook his head slowly. "You know what you have done. Confess."

"I confess to being a witch," said Awa, eyes darting between the patient Inquisitor and the fuming Omorose. "I confess to bringing Omorose back from the dead, and raping her, and trying to kill her again, and—"

"What?" Kahlert furrowed his brows. *"Back from the dead?"*

"She's dead!" said Awa. "She's dead dead dead!"

"Don't listen to her, she's trying to turn you against me," Omorose murmured, desperately hoping he would not ask her if this was true. It had been a very careful dance she had led him on down the years, and the thought of being tripped up by her irresistible compulsion to honesty now would be worse than never having crawled out of the ground. To her relief Kahlert nodded, clearly disappointed with Awa's confession.

"No!" Awa blubbered. "She's dead, and I brought her back but she'll kill me, and I never meant, I never meant—"

"All of the farriers I spoke with said it wouldn't work," Kahlert cut her off, wiggling the iron V in front of her. "They said it would ruin the goat's foot, that such things were only for horses. Even still I found one who would make an appropriately shaped shoe, and having applied it to several beasts myself I assure you that it does indeed impede movement instead of aiding it. But by the fourth or fifth goat I had gotten the knack for deeply affixing the nails without splitting the hoof wide."

Awa had not paid a great deal of attention to the hooves of the few horses she had ridden, but his meaning was clear enough and she moaned again, "I confess!"

"Well, Rose." Kahlert turned to Omorose, who was once more exuding a sunny smile now that it appeared Awa would not be proceeding directly to the stake after all. Omorose stood without a word, and Awa felt the woman's finger bones running up and down her calf. They dug under the manacle, and as Awa gave another low cry she felt the string tug and then come loose. Omorose came back into sight, dangling the fraying length of twine that had disguised Awa's foot. Kahlert took it gingerly, his breathing shallow, and looked wide-eyed down the length of Awa to where her hoof stuck out from the manacle.

"Bring the hammer and nails," Kahlert breathed, standing up and walking out of Awa's field of vision, down to her legs.

"Please!" Awa squealed, looking to Omorose. Her former mistress was twitching all over, her nose and lips and even her eyes jarring from tiny spasms. The woman smiled, and blew Awa a kiss as she walked out of sight. Awa suddenly had to urinate very badly, and then Omorose came back before her, holding up a small hammer in one hand and a tiny bouquet of iron nails in the other. Then she smiled even wider, and went to Kahlert.

It was a cloven hoof. Kahlert giggled. He suddenly, desperately wanted to stop everything, to unshackle her and put the chains back into place, to bag her and gag her and take her without delay out of his house, out of the Empire. She must go to Rome, they must go to Rome, and then unmask her before that swamp-Pope Adrian. It would slap the Church in the face with a real, live witch, it would convince them, it would make them stop punishing the loyal and rewarding the wicked. His father would posthumously be brought back into the Church, *he* would be brought back into the Church, everyone would know, and then the good work could begin in earnest. This was God's gift to him, Ashton Kahlert, Inquisitor before God, and soon, Inquisitor before Man once again.

The lady Rose stood beside him, a very curious expression on her face as she held out the hammer and nails. He took one of the nails and held it up. They would never believe him. Even if he brought this Moorish witch before them they would deny it, that was the way with the wicked, they would claim he had faked it, attached the foot himself, something. Yet here was a lamb who believed him, who believed in him, who had delivered to him this abomination, and all she wanted was justice, not a commendation by an officer of the Church, not the Pope's blessing, just real, honest justice. She had not trusted the Church, she had trusted him, and even when the Church had turned its back on him she had believed, and now, even though he had doubted both her and himself many times over the long years, he believed, too. There must be something to this Luther's ideas, he thought, God must be just as sickened by the Church's corruption as he was, and then Kahlert smiled and shook his head.

"I wish my father could be here," Kahlert told Omorose as he reached for the hammer. "I'm sure he watches us from Heaven, though. Hold the shoe for me and—"

Omorose screamed in his face, terrified in a way that Kahlert had only previously seen on the rictuses of the doomed women he interviewed, and even then only when substantial portions of their bodies had been put through his crucibles. He spun around, expecting a demon or worse to have materialized behind him, the witch's familiar, but there was nothing there.

The lady Rose was still screaming when he turned back to her, the poor girl's entire body rattling as she shrieked in horror, and he knew at once that she was bewitched. Keeping the black sorceress alive even a moment longer would be a mistake. She had a hoof so it was not as though he could be mistaken, and clearly the iron was not binding her as well as he had hoped. Best to kill her at once, rather than risk being ensorcelled himself as he exacted a full confession.

Kahlert opened his mouth to tell the lady Rose to be strong, that he would break the spell, which was when she smashed in his teeth with the hammer. He spun away onto the ground, his jaw afire, blood and broken teeth choking him, and as he tried to get up she fell on him with the hammer, wailing like a tortured witch as she struck again and again. He crawled along the length of the table with Omorose riding his back, gurgling blood as the possessed woman broke ribs and bruised muscle, and then he collapsed directly under Awa.

The noises behind her had been almost worse than the prospect of the shooing, Awa's imagination unable to process what was happening. When Kahlert dragged himself beneath her, covered in blood and making wretched moans very similar to those she herself had voiced only moments before, a thought occurred to her. Then Omorose appeared, squatting down in front of Awa and continuing her unbroken shriek as she caved in the back of Kahlert's neck, a thick black porridge welling out around his collar.

Omorose had not found the book, Awa realized, and a strange, terrible laugh burst from her mouth as she felt Omorose remove first the shackles at her wrists and then those at her ankles, and Awa rolled off the table onto the floor, meaning to put some distance between herself and her unexpected savior. Unfortunately, a week of being restrained and cramped, followed by the vicious overexertion the table-rack had inflicted, had rendered Awa's limbs nearly useless and she lay sprawled on the floor. Omorose had finally stopped screaming and stood shaking by the table. The manacle pins she had removed were still in her bloody hand, and giving a little sob, she cast them away into the corner.

"Not fair," she cried. "I had you I had you I had you."

"You didn't find the book," said Awa, the idea making more and more sense. "You didn't find it and thought you could have a living person do what you couldn't, but the curse compelled you to protect me."

"I hate you!" Omorose shrieked. "I hate you I hate you I hate you!"

Awa looked down at the bloody furrows in her wrists and ankles where the iron had cut her, knowing the dead cannot lie. It was not fair, then, but then what about life was? She sighed heavily, still nauseated from the harrowing experience. She looked up to say something, to say anything, but Omorose was gone. Then Awa heard the dull thump of a hammer striking meat, and a high-pitched whine. No.

Awa's neck snapped around and there was Omorose, straddling a squirming, sack-covered body. The hammer came down again, a beatific grin on Omorose's face as the tool struck home, the handle gripped in both hands. The shrouded body underneath her was convulsing now, and the hammer went up a third time. Awa tried to stand but still her legs thwarted her, and she screamed impotently at Omorose.

Omorose turned that smile to Awa, that mad, sadistic smile, and the hammer fell. The sound it made when it connected with the sack was wet, and the body stopped thrashing as violently. Then Awa was screaming at herself, screaming at the top of her lungs because she was a necromancer, an unbound witch, and as easy as spitting or blinking the spirit was snipped from Omorose's body, and then Omorose's body was gone, a skeleton collapsing into loose bones atop a bloody sack.

Awa crawled across the floor, little nonsense words bubbling out of her mouth as the necromancer's ring slipped off of Omorose's finger bone and rolled away. It was Merritt, it had to be, the sack was too large and the spreading pool leaking through it was too cold to belong to her hot-blooded Chloé, and, picking up Omorose's skull, Awa smashed it on the ground, shards of bone spinning across the floor. She closed her eyes, bit her lip, took a deep breath, and opened her eyes again. Then she unlaced the hood with numb, clumsy fingers, and pulled open the slit to reveal the bruised, swollen, and utterly dead face of Chloé.

XXXI
A Slow Night in the Black Forest

Chloé was not dead. Her eyelids fluttered, the girl's left eye a bright red puddle, and beneath the blood-filled eye her nostril was smashed flat and black, and as she opened her mouth Awa saw that her jaw was split and crushed. Awa killed her before Chloé could feel the bones of her face sliding apart, before she could feel her battered organs fail, before she could feel cold air on exposed marrow and muscle, and though it was a little death the necromancer knew that once she revived Chloé, which she must in a day or two at the latest, her partner would not have long at all, certainly not enough time to force-feed her enough meat and bone to heal her. Then Awa wondered if she would be able to raise her at all, if, little though the death she had administered was, it had been enough, given Chloé's condition, to kill her lover entirely, and she whimpered to herself.

Something whimpered back in the room, and Awa lifted her head. Merritt. The Englishman's sack twitched, and Awa turned back to Chloé's corpse. This was all her fault. As soon as she had escaped from the table she could have killed Omorose, could have ended her forever, but instead she had fumbled for something to say. How fucking stupid was she? She stayed with Chloé, mulling it all over, until one by one the candles began to sputter and die, and then the last went out and she was in the dark.

Awa awoke, not sure how long she had slept. She pawed around the dark room for what felt like hours until she found the bag the bounty hunters had taken from her, and in the blackness of the windowless dungeon she removed the portrait of Chloé, which brought on another crying fit. When she had pulled herself together she went back to digging in the bag until she found her last salamander egg. Setting it on the ground, she turned her back on it before giving the command so that she would not be blinded. The brightness gave her a pounding headache, but by the third time she had ignited the egg she saw an unlit torch in a sconce by a door, and retrieving it she soon had more light than she cared for.

The pool of blood that had leaked out of Chloé's sack was nothing short of ridiculous, the girl seeming to have more on the floor than inside her skin. Still, even if the little death failed and her partner truly died Awa could bring her back. It was not much, but it was better than nothing. Then she began to cry again, imagining Chloé as a rotting horror, or a thing of hard bone instead of shapely flesh. Merritt groaned again from his sack, and Awa knew she had to let him out. Just not now. She could not handle his idiocy at present, and so she left him trussed and bagged and left the dungeon by way of the smaller door.

Awa stood blinking in a pleasant, sunlit bedroom, one wall lined with books, the wide crown glass windows overlooking a creek that wound through the meadow of Kahlert's yard all the way to the edge of a forest. The blazing torch forgotten in her hand, she wandered through the house, her mouth wide, her head cocked. The contrast between the torture chamber and the rest of the simple but impressive house was as sharp as the difference between the living and the dead. Everything was intricately carved hardwood and sparkling marble or granite, with rooms to spare and a kitchen housing more sumptuous food than a prince's larder.

Awa sat on the kitchen table and opened a bottle of wine, then bit into a loaf of bread—she wanted the bread to taste like potash or sawdust, for the wine to taste like sour rainwater, for the world to deny her pleasure now that she had gotten Chloé killed, but her traitorous tongue relished the food and drink, and she nearly wept at the taste. She was alive, and could not pretend otherwise. Pleasure would be had, then, and she filled a sack with bread and early cheese and dried fruit but no meat. During her time in Paris, with the abundance of cheese and bread and produce to be had, and Dario's willingness to experiment with all things related to cooking, she had finally been able to dispense with eating flesh, save that which was absolutely necessary to heal herself—if her spiritual balance were ever to be restored she had to stop feeding on the dead like the hyena, and besides, the less iron she took into her body the more powerful were her arts. After adding bottles and bottles of wine and spirits to her already bulging sack, Awa tossed the still smoldering torch onto the stack of cordwood beside the stove. Then she heaped the table and chairs and everything else that looked flammable on the smoking woodpile, and smashed a bottle of schnapps onto it for good measure.

Watching the wall of the house catch, Awa smiled and retrieved a brand from the fire. The flaming chair leg would have gone out almost at once but she politely asked the spirit of the wood escaping through the flame to humor her by burning a little longer, and so it did. She went from room to room lighting the embroidered linen curtains, but then the smoke from the kitchen began thickening in the rest of the house and she knew her time was running out. Looking in the bedroom, and the black doorway leading to the torture chamber, Awa considered turning around and leaving, letting Chloé and Merritt burn to ash, but the thought twisted in her guts and she angrily hurled her brand against the bookshelf. Chloé deserved better than that.

Just as Awa turned to enter the dark chamber where Omorose had finally fallen, she heard a faint whine, almost a squeal, from over her shoulder. The spirits of the wood whined as they became spirits of fire and then air, but this was something else, something she had never heard before. The sound quickened her heart, made her chest ache and her eyes water, and she was suddenly more aware than ever before of the blood coursing through her veins, the essence of her life. Her hands and feet were going numb, and she felt a weight coalescing in her body, in her face, a weight pushing her head to look behind her. Awa obeyed her blood, and then her heart stopped completely.

Her blood was pushing her eyes, wrenching them the way she might wrench an arm out of socket, and there could be no doubt of where they fell. One book, a thin volume on the top shelf, and she could not have looked away had she wanted to. Flames were scrambling up the shelf, faster and faster as the books caught, and Awa was over and up in an instant, singeing her clothes and the hairs off her arm as she jumped for it, her fingers pulling it out, and then she was back on the ground, the book in hand.

Backing away from the blazing wall, Awa looked at the book in her hand. *The Romance of the Rose*, a French text. Flipping it open, she gasped and slammed it shut, then dropped it altogether as she saw the cover had changed. Instead of a flowery gold font on a red velvet background the cover was blank, untitled, and bound in old brown hide. Even if the cover had not reverted to its true state she would have known from the glimpse she had taken of the contents—even though she had only ever seen the first page, the ever-changing first page, there could be no doubt. It was the necromancer's book.

"Fucking witch?!" Merritt scrambled away from her after she had loosed his chains and his eyes had adjusted enough to the firelit room to see her. "Me understanding Spanish words!"

"That's right, I'm a witch," Awa said evenly, though behind her calm features swelled an impossibly large smile. She had found it she had found it she had found—

"Blackmoor cunt!" Merritt was clearly terrified but she needed him to help move Chloé before the entire house caught fire, and her patience with the man was limited in the best of times. "Fuck! Witch!"

"Merritt," Awa said, switching from French to his native English to ensure he understood. "You listen to me, and you listen good—pick up Chloé and carry her out. Once we're outside you can go your way and we can—"

"Fuck!" Merritt noticed the second door and broke for it.

"Merritt," said Awa, advancing on him as he fumbled with the door's lock. "If you don't do as you're told I'll kill you. Right now. Pick her up."

She was right behind him and then he got the door open, but as he swung it wide she brushed his shoulder and down he fell, his lifeless head cracking against the doorframe. Awa stood over him, and a moment later he shambled back to his feet and obediently retrieved Chloé's body. Then another thought came to Awa, and as Merritt passed by her, exiting the burning house through the stable that adjoined the torture chamber, she went and raised Kahlert's corpse. Giving Omorose's bones a kick for good measure, she spied a glint of burnished bone on the floor and retrieved the ring she had given her mistress so long ago.

The ring reminded her of the string that Omorose had removed from her hoof, and she ordered Kahlert's corpse to find it. He did, his head flopping from side to side atop its broken neck, and as the room filled with smoke she hastened outside after the walking dead. Pausing in the stable, she opened the stalls and released the panicking horses. She did not particularly care for the animals but bore them no grudge, either, and knew she had much to atone for. Balance was everything, good with evil, light with dark, life with death, greed with sacrifice.

Maybe.

At any rate, she had the fucking book.

Awa marched Merritt and Kahlert far away from the burning house before she let herself examine the tome. She held it in her hand, in her fucking hand, and did not want some bumpkin or bounty hunter coming upon her as she did some light reading beside the inferno of Ashton Kahlert's country house. There were no neighboring buildings in sight but she still took them away from the path that wound out the front gate, instead having them slosh up the creek to cover their tracks. Soon they dipped under the canopy of evergreens but Awa made herself wait until just before sundown before stopping and opening the book.

The first page was blank and crisp, but every page thereafter was covered from top to bottom in script, the text occasionally broken by diagrams and illustrations. Flipping through it, she saw that every few pages the handwriting changed, sometimes a little, sometimes a lot, but always the same brown ink. Not ink, of course, and as she thumbed through it she saw that each page contained much more than words and pictures and skin and blood—scraps of spirit clung to the book, many, many little pieces, and closing the book softly she let out a very long sigh. She would not be obliterated completely when he claimed her, then, but some small part of her at least would live on through his book. Small comfort.

"Inquisitor." She addressed Kahlert's mindless corpse, recalling from her teenage experience with the concubine on the mountain that interrogations went much quicker if one simply addressed the bones instead of the willful spirit. Not once in her dealings with the animate remains of Kahlert did she think about her oath to ask the spirit's permission before using its body, nor did she consider the feelings of Merritt's spirit as she had his corpse fetch firewood—ever since her initial encounter with Manuel in the cave, she had wondered if it would be possible to administer a little death to a person, raise them as a mindless one, and afterward restore them to life, and now at last she had her answer: no. She had not intended to really murder Merritt but raising him back at the manse had evidently made his little death a permanent one; given the man's general attitude, Awa had a hard time feeling broken up about it.

"Yes." The inquisitor's corpse left his position standing watch at the mouth of the small clearing, a deer trail having given way to a small patch of open ground hedged in by thick holly.

"This book." Awa wagged it at him, unable to stop grinning. "This was in your library."

"I did not know. I did not see it," said the corpse.

"It, it was disguised," said Awa, recalling that strange detail. "It looked like a book called *Roman de la Rose*, a French book bound in red velvet."

"I remember that volume," said the corpse. "I read part of it once, in a library. I did notice it on my shelf but could not recall where or when I had acquired it, for I disliked it as much as most French romances."

"Then why did you keep it?"

"I thought that if it were a gift I could not remember receiving then I did not wish to offend the giver by discarding it, lest he peruse my shelves and see his gift absent. That, and I thought having a wide range of texts would make me appear intelligent."

"You were vain, weren't you?" Awa smiled.

"Yes."

"How could the book know that?" Awa asked herself. "And how could it disguise itself?"

"I do not know," said the corpse, but as it answered the book twisted in Awa's hands. She clumsily juggled it, the book opening of its own accord. The pages were flipping to the front, and when the blank first page was reached a bright red dot appeared in the upper left corner, like a handkerchief pressed to a pinpricked finger. Then a jagged red line arced out of the spot, and words began appearing in wet blood on the blank hide.

We had made ourselves discreet, the bloody text read, *the spirits of the air delivered us against one side of a row where we could blend in with the wood of the shelf. Then the man mentioned the name* Roman de la Rose *when he was showing the corpse who called herself Rose his library, and mentioned his dislike for it, and so when he left Granada and had his servants pack his library we took the form of a book we knew he would not be interested in examining. Nevertheless he picked us up, sometimes, but we made our interior into an obscure dialect, and so we did not need replicate the text we claimed to be in order to maintain the ruse.*

"You..." Awa's mouth hung open as she read. Not scraps of the spirits, not tiny little pieces, but enough to respond, enough to answer. The dead cannot lie, and this book, written in blood, on skin, this book bound with spirit, must answer the same as any corpse or soul. *We*, the book wrote, the previous apprentices of the necromancer, the—

We contain the blood and skin of his tutor, the book continued, *as well as his pupils, which enables us to change our form to better disguise ourselves.*

"Why would you?" said Awa. "It helps him, doesn't it, if you stay hidden? Why would you help him when you're just like me?!"

We are no longer more than a book, and books serve whatever purpose their master ascribes to them. The text paused, and then resumed, even more quickly. *But the master of a book is she who holds it and knows its potential, and that is you until another hand lifts us, another eye reads us. We serve you now, as we served him then.*

"Do you"—Awa could scarcely believe that she had reached this strange and terrible place, that even though she had succeeded in achieving the impossible and found the book, all might be for naught if—"do you know a way to break the hold he has over me? Is there, inside you, the means of stopping him from,

from"—the book was already answering but she did not read, pressing ahead—"from claiming my body? Do you know a way?"

A single word can contain more power than a million, and the simple *no* Awa saw before her made her cast the book to the ground and scream, her cool, practical mind doing nothing to stop her outburst. That was that. *Of course*, she thought, *of course of course of course*, if the book knew a way wouldn't one of her predecessors have thwarted him already?

Once she had calmed a bit she retrieved the book from the grass and muttered an apology, but did not open it again until much later, after she had eaten and gotten a little drunk and grown tired of staring at the bloody sack that housed Chloé's mortal remains. By the same time the next night Awa knew the little death would have to be removed lest Chloé actually die from the experience. Yet restoring her as she was would kill her anyway, and Awa could not very well avoid that topic any longer.

With a sigh Awa picked up the book, and asked, "Is there a means of restoring a dying person, or a corpse, to life, with its spirit intact, in such a way that the body does not decay but instead stays as it was in life?"

Yes.

Ah, the joys of one-word answers. Awa wondered if the book would burn, but pushed the thought away, and focused on the positive—there was a way. The undead she raised certainly putrefied at a slower rate with their spirit inside them, but Awa had enjoyed enough of the love of the dead to last a lifetime.

Only a dying person, though, the book wrote after a pause, as though it were considering her query. *Once life has left the body then what you ask is impossible.*

"Not much time, then," said Awa. "How do I do it?"

You cannot. Only one of them can make another.

"Fuck!" cried Awa. "One of who, one of what!?"

Instead of scribbling an answer the pages began turning, and settled on an entry near the end. It had read "something" *of the Schwarzwald*, but the something was angrily crossed out and a new word written in, so that it read *BASTARDS of the Schwarzwald*. The old word had begun with a *W* or a *V*, but she knew she could find out the proper name by asking the book after she had read the entry. Settling in, the first thing it said was *Avoid*, followed by a catalog of attributes: *shiftless, vain, difficult, obstinate, opinionated, boorish, gluttonous.*

The cramped writing was broken up by the author, as though he were putting together a taxonomical volume.

Lifespan: Indefinite, unless one is of a mind to do some mischief with an iron stake and a stout ax.

Appearance: Hideously mundane. They eschew the charms of the grave, just as an idiot child, if allowed, would refuse to advance past a prepubescent state.

Corporeality: Mutable, but disposed toward physical materialization.

"Very nice," said Awa. "Perfect, even."

Scanning down, she noticed *Cause* near the bottom. *Only they can create more of their kind, proving what a useless variety they are. They refuse to share their recipe for generation (or any other recipes, for that matter) and cannot be controlled by any known means. Again: avoid at all cost.*

"Hmmm," said Awa. "Hardly surprising that old asshole didn't get along with things he couldn't manipulate. Even if I can't learn the trick maybe I could barter with one of them to do it for me. But how do I find one?"

The book flipped to the last page—a poorly sketched map of what Awa presumed must be the continent she had searched. A key set at the bottom confirmed this, and distracted by this new discovery, she set to orientating herself. There was a tiny island that must lie between her native land and the Spanish coast, and one of those peaks there must be where she had been indentured by her tutor, and here, this forest north of the Lombardy battlefields, must be her current position.

"Is this where I am?" Awa asked herself, and to her delight a small drop of red welled out of the page in the center of the wood. "Book, you're fabulous! Now can you show me where to find the Bastards of the Schwarzwald?"

She eagerly watched the crimson drop sink back into the map. A moment later it reemerged an encouragingly short distance away. The drop grew larger, however, and her smile shifted downward as the bright red smear thinned and spread across the entire forested section of the map.

"That's enough of that," she said, closing the book and turning to the mindless corpses of Kahlert and Merritt. "Let's go, lady-snatchers."

Awa hoped she was leading them toward the spot on the map where the drop had initially appeared before spreading, but she had never used a map before and each time she consulted the book she seemed to be in the same place. She nevertheless drew closer and closer, her Paris-dulled eyes sharp again after half a year back in the wilds, and the wood grew thicker and thicker around her as the night grew ever deeper under those boughs that suffered the trespass of neither starshine nor moonglow. The corpses blundered after her, making such a racket as they carried Chloé that Awa could not hear the wolves gathering around them or the bats that congregated overhead.

At last they reached a clearing, and in the center of the small glade stood a small brick house with a single red door. Awa checked the map and saw she stood on the very spot she had made for, with dawn still many nightmares away. When she took her first step from the trees the animals that had followed her announced themselves, the wolves fanning out from the trees to cover the clearing while the bats swirled over the building until neither the structure nor the open sky could be seen for the flurry of wings.

"Shit," breathed Awa, thousands of eyes staring at her in the dark.

"Good evening," a deep voice came from behind the curtain of bats and wolves, and then the two swarms parted and a tall man stepped out of the building, a living corridor formed between where he stood at the doorway and Awa. "Please do come in. We have been expecting you."

It took a moment before Awa could force herself to step into the lupine sea, but once she got going she found it difficult not to break into a run, hundreds of muzzles lining her path, the ceiling of hovering bats billowing down a rank breeze. Approaching the smiling man in the doorway, she saw he was pale and hairless as an ivory statue, and every bit as nude.

"I am Awa," she said nervously, unsure if volunteering her name would be a mistake or the token of goodwill she intended it as—in any event, divulging it had never been the catastrophic disaster her tutor had implied it would be. The naked man stared at her with unabashed interest and concern, as if she were the naked stranger controlling mobs of animals. "I, I have traveled far."

"Come in, come in." The man beckoned to the doorway. "Please come in. We have all the answers in here, and the questions you've forgotten as well. Bring your friends, and enter freely, Lady Awa."

Glancing behind her at the emotionless corpses and the bloody sack, Awa wondered if these were indeed her friends. They were the only friends she had with her, at any rate, and Awa wondered if Monique and Manuel were sleeping in warm beds with warm bodies beside them. Then she put them from her mind and went willingly into the darkness.

XXXII
The Convergence of Trails

Manuel dropped the dead lantern and ran, telling himself he was going for more light, that he had to go for more light, but as he skidded around the side of the mound and heard Paracelsus's scream joining his own, and then Monique's joining their merry little choir, he knew he had no fucking intention whatsoever of going back. He was outside in the light, the abandoned lanterns propped on gravestones casting a soft amber haze on the screaming artist. Then he realized he was the only one still shrieking, the other two now silent as, well, the graveyard around him, and he shut up, too. As soon as he did he heard it, the panting, the shuffling of dirt, and try as he did to stare straight ahead and run for it his traitorous neck turned and looked back over his shoulder.

At first Manuel saw nothing but the face of the barrow and the black forest behind it, but then a shadow moved along the top of the high mound and he would have screamed again, he would have prayed and wept and swore, but as soon as he saw the hyena atop the barrow it pounced. Spindly legs stabbed his back like spears, and he smelled his own death wafting out of the brown muzzle that clicked shut beside his cheek. Then Manuel was falling forward, the beast riding him to the ground, and he landed at the base of a tombstone, the weight of the monster grinding him into the earth.

"Fuck fuck fuck," Manuel chirped, a frigid wet nose snuffling his ear. Then its tongue was lapping him, the hot, sticky muscle plastering his hair up and out of the way of his neck. Manuel lay on his face with the hyena crouching on his back, several stiff lumps in its engorged belly rubbing the base of his spine as it breathed against his cheek, and his next *fuck* was washed out on a tide of vomit, the rotten-meat stench coming from the creature's maw positively evil. Before he could even stop gagging it rose from his back and circled around, jutting its nose against his, and then it lapped up his spew, one yellow eye winking at him.

Not like this, thought the artist, *not here, not now*. That was probably what everyone thought when they died, he knew, but he had been spared at least a dozen deaths before this one, deaths that would have been far better than being gobbled up by a devil or monster or whatever the fuck it was. He would really have to write a play where he died properly, one without all these witches and fiends, and Manuel giggled.

The hyena stopped slurping up his vomit and giggled back, foul cords of the artist's bile tethering its open mouth to the earth, and then tilted its head to the side and bit Manuel's face. Not off, not yet, the jaws settling on either of the artist's cheeks and pressing down, the rows of teeth reaching his ears. Manuel struggled then, struggled as he should have when it first pinned him instead of letting it take any pleasure from him, and he realized as the teeth pierced his skin and dug into the bone that it was still playing with him, that what he thought was pain was only a prelude, and then the hyena's jaws tightened against his skull and Manuel screamed into its throat as it bore down like a nutcracker straining against an obstinate walnut.

The lantern was right there above them and shone down the bright red, ribbed throat gaping in front of him, a tunnel so wide and slick Manuel wondered that it did not eat him whole, and then he felt his cheekbones begin to give, his sinuses bursting, and he heard a resounding crack. He realized his skull must have split from the pressure. It dropped him, and through the tears and drool coating his face he saw the tombstone towering above him, memento mori and all that, and wondered if he would be called up or pulled down. Then he heard the shrieks of the damned and closed his eyes, knowing himself a fallen man.

"Up, lump!" Monique kicked his leg and Manuel opened his eyes, wiping the film from his face. The wailing hyena had not fled entirely but howled from the dark side of the barrow, and Monique snatched Manuel, hauling him upright. "Get your sword out, lump, an' take this. Pop the fucker in the face when I hold'em still for ya."

"What!?" Manuel did not realize he was shouting as he took the proffered pistol. His ears were ringing but he was relieved to see that the second pistol she had set on the gravestone beside the lantern was smoking; a more likely culprit for the thunder in his head than a cracked skull.

"Sword an' pistol, lump, an' if ya ain't sure ta hit with mine then stick it with yours." Monique was striding forward, leaving Manuel trembling with a gun in one hand and his hilt in the other. Looking down, he saw that, as if in a nightmare, the trigger and firing mechanism had somehow fallen off the gun and what he now held was a very long and heavy L-shaped piece of bronze with no means of firing. Before he could alert the gunner she began shouting into the darkness with a voice that could deafen a cannon. "Out, bitchdog, out! I took a paw for a paw, so let's settle this fair an' now!"

Manuel forgot whatever he was going to say when he saw her draw a third pistol from a sheath at her waist and set it on a tombstone, and then take its mate with the same hand. She raised both arms and waved them in the air, and the artist saw that her right was mangled, the bitten hand soaking through whatever rag she had tied onto it and splashing the barrow as she dropped her arms and set her last gun down. She flexed the fingers of her left hand, peering around the edge of the light, and shouted, "Don't need tools ta take down a fuckin bitchdog! You scared, bitchdog, you scared out there in the dark?! Come an' 'ave a taste without your tricks an' skulkin in the dark, bitchdog! Come an' take a mouthful—"

It did, shooting out of the night beside the barrow and latching its jaws onto her uninjured left forearm. Instead of toppling over, Monique spun around the monster, teeth dragging along bone as she fell onto its back and wrapped her bloody right arm around its throat. Manuel heard the splintering of her arm from where he stood but Monique did not relinquish her grip, instead settling all of her weight on its spine and clumsily kicking at its hind legs. She tackled it in a strange parody of how it had pinned Manuel, with the hyena flat on its stomach and Monique half atop it, one arm broken in its mouth and the other gripping it in a headlock. She screamed as it bit harder, blood and marrow bubbling around the viselike muzzle clamped onto her forearm, and the sound finally rattled Manuel out of his shocked stupor.

Running to where she had placed the other two guns, Manuel cursed when he saw that these also lacked lock and trigger, the smooth metal pistols identical to the worthless one she had already given him. Before he could examine them more closely and see where the touchhole was located on the primitive firearms, before he could fetch the lantern to fire them once he had found the touchholes, the hyena began to thrash and roll like the crocodiles its kind would sometimes mate with. Manuel abandoned the pistols, comforting though it would have been to press a barrel to the creature's canine temple and pull the trigger instead of stabbing at it with Monique so close, but by the time he had raised the sword they were a blur on the ground, Monique screaming ever louder, and Manuel moaned impotently, unable to tell one from the other for more than an instant as they rolled away from him.

Then the hyena was up and before Manuel could close the distance between them it fled, limping. He saw that even though Monique had shot off its right forepaw while it was biting his head it was still hobbling quickly, dragging Monique after it by her mauled arm. She was screaming and screaming as Manuel chased them through the cemetery, the light failing as the monster passed through the gate, Monique bouncing after it, and as Manuel breathlessly reached the edge of the graveyard they vanished into the dark wood.

"Fuck!" Manuel howled after them. "Fuck!"

Going after them, he thought as he ran back to the lanterns, *going after them, going to find her, going to save*—she's dead, he realized, Monique's scream having trailed off, she's as dead as Awa. It had met her, it must have, to replicate her voice, and it must have gobbled her up, must have gobbled her up and now it was gobbling up Monique, and if those two had not stood against it then what hope did he have? And Monique had let it take her, had put down her guns, the fucking idiot, or maybe it had broken them all somehow, it had—

"Ahhh!" Manuel yelped as a figure lurched out of the shadows toward him. "Paracelsus!"

"The same." The man looked like his own shade, pale and terrible as a body dragged from a river. "The same."

"Fuck me."

"Where is it?" Paracelsus looked around anxiously. "Where did it go?"

"It's got her," said Manuel, handing the confused doctor one of Monique's pistols and the fullest lantern. "Figure out what's gone wrong here, and hold this."

The physician looked in bafflement at Manuel, as if the lantern and gun the artist had handed him were made of rock candy. Then Manuel tightened his grip on his hand-and-a-half and walked out the cemetery gate, Paracelsus following close at his heels. As soon as they passed the wall their visibility tightened to the paltry circle the lantern cast, but the creature had not tried to cover its trail and the wet smear Monique left guided them sure as a path deeper into the forest, Manuel praying they would be in time even though he knew she was already dead.

The hyena dropped Monique after a half of a league, the woman having gone silent after it had dragged her into and over a few fallen trees. Looking down at its pulsing, oozing stump, it licked at the wound, watching the woman who had maimed it. She lay on her back, the right hand it had initially bit in the barrow folded behind her, the left arm it had dragged her by twisted and lame. It licked her face until she woke up, which it smelled even though she kept her eyes closed and her breathing even. It stanched its bleeding stump by pressing the wound into her armpit, and mimicked her voice.

"Paw for a paw, bitch? Don't need tools ta take down a fuckin bitch?" Then it chortled, obviously struggling to restrain itself from howling with laughter. Monique began to pull her arm out from under her back but its laugh turned to a growl and she lay still. She opened her eyes the tiniest sliver and realized with horror that either all the lanterns had gone out or she was far removed from the churchyard. It giggled. *"You scared, bitch, you scared out 'ere in the dark?"*

"On my fuckin arm," Monique groaned. "Lemme get it out, brute, you're fuckin killin me."

It laughed again at that and she tugged harder, wondering if this was to be her last act, her final words. It did not kill her as she squirmed to get her arm free, the pinky, ring finger, and half a thumb she still had after its bite barely holding on to the slippery grip of the pistol she kept shoved down the back of her trousers. Her left arm, her shooting arm, was fucked beyond repair, the pain of it the only thing letting her ignore the fact that a real fucking demon was breathing its stink in her face.

"Hunted *often*." Each word borrowed from a different victim, the hyena addressed her in a dozen accents as she got her arm out from under herself. "Know *guns*. Smell *gun* dust. Took *fingers*, can't *use* guns. *You* different. *Wrong* hand, *wrong* fingers. *Ba-ba-bad doggie*. Now *better*. No *arms*, no *hands*."

It cackled in her face, the fit so bad its eyes closed, though Monique could see nothing but a shape leering over her, a fiend even darker than the black night enveloping them. Then its laugh stopped abruptly and she heard it sniffing, a low growl building as it did. She raised her arm a little higher, the burning where her middle and index fingers used to be growing hotter as the open, leaking stubs hoisted the heavy bronze.

Monique felt it relax and it chortled again in its broken staccato, "No *fire*, no *fingers*, no *gun*. *Stupid* bitch."

"No fire?" Monique breathed back in its face, and focused as intently as she could on the pistol balanced in her mangled hand. *"Fire."*

Manuel and Paracelsus heard the roar of a gunshot and quickened their pace. They were far away and moving slowly, and so by the time they reached Monique and the hyena she had extracted all the information she expected to gather from the creature. It was still alive when Paracelsus's lantern fell on it, the ragged hole in its stomach pushing ripples across the pool of blood it wallowed in as it drew wheezy, ragged breaths. Both men had started back at finding the creature alive but now drew closer in wonder, like pilgrims beholding a miracle, and Manuel looked at Monique with equal measures of respect and horror.

After rolling it off her Monique had stomped all four of the monster's legs, the hyena crying and whimpering and snapping weakly despite the agony she knew the gutshot must be causing. The interrogation had not taken very long, it telling her all she needed to know, the distinct voices lent a more uniform cadence by the miserable whines accompanying each syllable. It hurt to talk, but it hurt worse to have bones broken, to be kicked in an open wound.

Monique did not look much better. Her right hand was missing two fingers and half her thumb, and the awkward angle she had fired the gun from combined with the recoil had broken her wrist, the appendage dangling loose and dripping. Her entire left arm was black with blood, the bones cracked all along her forearm. She was smiling, though, and awake enough to berate Manuel as she slid down the tree she had leaned against.

"Stupid fuckin bastard," said Monique. "It's fuckin killed me, thanks ta you."

"No," Manuel moaned, going to her, but Paracelsus snatched his arm.

"The lady is in dire need of assistance," said Paracelsus, his eyes glancing to the hyena. "We must act quickly if we are to save her limbs. But I cannot work unfettered of anxiety with this, this beast at my back."

"Right," said Manuel, but his sword hand felt as numb as his rattled brain. For an instant he considered going back for his charcoal and planks, but then the monster begged for help with the plaintive voice of a little girl and he advanced with his weapon.

"What are you about, boy?!" said Paracelsus, though the pudgy doctor was obviously the better part of a decade younger than Manuel. "I didn't say kill it, I said watch it!"

The doctor had actually said neither of these things but Manuel did not debate this point. "You don't mean to let it live?!"

"No," Paracelsus scoffed. "Do I look like a suicidal madman? No no no, by dawn that monstrosity will be dead as iron."

"Then what are you waiting—"

"I have a patient to attend," said Paracelsus. "Afterwards I will examine the monster, thoroughly, and inspecting it after it is dead will be worthless."

"What do you mean, worthless? It—"

"If you wish to learn about life, you study the living!" Paracelsus turned his back on Manuel, clucking to himself as he saw Monique had passed out. "How else will you see how it all fits together? I've examined enough corpses to tell you that if you want to see how it all works you need a living, responsive subject."

Paracelsus kept on but Manuel stopped listening, walking around the creature's head. From here it looked like an exceptionally large dog, one with a small stumpy tail and a very large, boxy head, but just a dog. Then one of its eyes focused on him, the voice of a child crying out in fear, and he stumbled back. It could not be real, it could not, and yet it was.

"Oi!" Monique came to. "What're ya doin?"

"Saving your life, my lady," said Paracelsus as he splashed water on her ruined right hand.

"Alright then," said Monique, shock helping her relax. "Ya know where she's at?"

"No," said Paracelsus. "I was looking for her, have been ever since she left my employ. Manuel did not tell you I barely missed the both of you in Bern, what, six years past? Shortly after you, ah, quit my clinic."

"Didn't mention it," said Monique, resolving to have a little chat with her artist friend about being more forthcoming with information. "So what's this? He said you was 'ostage of some chickenheads?"

"Certainly, certainly. Our friend Sister Gloria—"

"Who? Oh."

"Our friend Sister Gloria speaks in her sleep, habitually, at least when she stayed with me, and so I gathered she spent the bulk of her time in graveyards—"

"Nah, not Awa, that don't sound like'er," said Monique.

"Indeed she does, or at least did. I have been... misled, I fear." Paracelsus scowled over his shoulder at Manuel. "I was told that you and she had gone to Petersburg, or maybe Spain or Africa, they were not sure which, and so I scoured the sunbaked southern deserts, the once-great Granada, the icy steppes of the far north, all with predictably little success, realizing as I do now that you made no such sojourn. Or did you?"

"What? Nah, Spain's full of—fuck!" Monique swooned as he gently pressed on her shattered left arm.

"So I took my time, making many, *many* advances of my own, but of course found no trace of her, and so I set to searching the countryside near the last place I knew she had been—Bern. And as I gathered from her unconscious mumblings it was her custom to speak to the stones in churchyards and ask them strange questions, I took to camping in cemeteries myself, in hope, vain though it proved, of finding a trace of the necromancer. Instead something found me..."

"The devil there?" Monique felt hot and cold and sick.

"The same. I did not know I was being followed, but followed I was. She had left a pair of old leggings at the clinic, and I kept them with me—"

"*Nasty* fuckin man." Monique shook her head.

"What? I kept them so that if I caught her trail I could secure dogs to follow her—"

"Dogs?! You was gonna hunt'er with dogs, lump?!"

"If need be," Paracelsus said defensively. "Unfortunately, something else picked up the trail. That monster. It thought I was she, from the scent in my bags, and it followed me here. I came into town a few days ago, inquired about the churchyard, and next thing I knew found myself held captive in a bandits' den, a shack not far from here. They hardly fed me at all, and kept me gagged, and after thwarting my ingenious escape attempt they took me to the churchyard to give me to another band of brigands. I inferred they were operating as agents of some Inquisitor, which is hardly surprising—as a magus they don't dare attempt to put me on trial, me, who would expose them as frauds, as corrupt, no no no, they tried to do it on the sly, knowing that as easy as it is to trick uneducated women into damning themselves the scholar will unmask them, will call attention to their—"

"It's moving!" Manuel called. "It's trying to get up!"

"Oh? Good," said Paracelsus. "Tell me if it succeeds. Where was I, my dear?"

"I ain't your dear, shitlips," said Monique, her eyes rolling as he prodded farther up her arm. "You was gettin traded from chickenheads ta bounty riders."

"Yes, of course. Well, that was that—the monster attacked from the darkness, and the one or two men that held their ground were disarmed or killed outright. One fiend against a dozen stout men, and they all fell, some running, some hiding, some praying, but they all fell. Then it gnawed through my bonds, curious why I smelled of she, I imagine, and the answers I gave it delighted the beast... I pretended to know where she was, and so it consented to let me live so long as I took it to her. I agreed, of course, and it set to making a den in the barrow. It meant to spend the night in its lair, eating all the men it had killed, and that is when you found me, tending the last dying man."

"I—I think it might be dying," said Manuel, and that decided things for the physician.

"You won't bleed to death now, and amputating that arm ought to wait on better light and equipment." Paracelsus stood, coated from brow to boot in caked blood and dirt.

"Amputate?" Monique said quietly, trying to move her broken arm and nearly passing out again. "Nah, no need, I broke bones afore an'—"

"It comes off or maggots will materialize," said Paracelsus as he picked up his bag and advanced on the hyena. "Take comfort that you have your life."

"Then maggots materialize, ya fuckin quack!" Monique screamed after him. "Fuckin piece of shit!"

"Yes yes, blame the doctor." Paracelsus smiled at Manuel, who looked greener than the dark pines overhead. The physician was in better spirits than he had been in years, and turned his attention to the dying hyena. It looked up at him with its pleading golden eyes, and he walked around it thrice, like a dog preparing to lie down, then squatted just out of its reach should it muster its strength and try to bite him. In Latin he asked, "Can you understand me?"

"*Ita,*" it whined, the voice that of a boy not yet through the trials of manhood.

"Good." Paracelsus reverted to German as he unscrewed the pommel from his sword. "Though *ita vero* is really more appropriate for conveying assent—must have eaten a novice, eh? Is that how your faculties work?"

"Help me," came the little girl's voice again, Manuel stumbling away and dry-heaving in the shadows.

"Certainly," said Paracelsus. "Now, we don't have much light left, this lantern's almost empty. But before we got started I thought you might help me coin a term for the sort of examination we'll be doing. I love language every bit as much as you evidently do, so since you'll be contributing so heavily I thought you could offer your opinion."

"Examination we'll be doing?" The doctor's voice bounced back at him, which only widened his smile as he removed his Stones of Immortality from their hidden compartment in the pommel of his sword. Technically they were not stones, being a compound of poppy oil, quintessence of gold, a few binding agents, and preservatives, and they certainly did not bestow immortality,

although they did provide a wonderful buzz, but he thought the name had quite the ring to it—a fascinating drug, one of the finest discoveries to come from his time in the Middle East.

"Stick out your tongue... that's a good doggie."

"Ba-ba-bad doggie," wept the creature, but it did as he asked, and when he had crumbled some of the laudanum onto its tongue it made a pathetic coughing sound.

"Noooo, *good* doggie. It will calm you, take away the pain," said Paracelsus, and as the mighty head began to sag even lower he scratched behind its sharp ears. "Good doggie. Now, before your tongue grows too heavy, what do you think about the word *vivisection*? The Latin *vivus* is obvious, but something about *sectio* strikes me as being apropos, don't you think?"

"Vivus?" The hyena's tongue was lolling, its eyes contracting as Paracelsus took something long and shiny from his bag and set it on the ground. Next the doctor removed a bandage and gingerly helped the creature roll onto its side. The animal was not responding as strongly to the stimulation as he plugged the gunshot wound, but it got another word out. *"Sectio?"*

"Yes, yes." Paracelsus nodded as his fingers peeled back its gums, prodded its cheeks. It clearly wanted to bite him, tried, even, but it could barely stay awake. That changed soon enough. "Vivisection. A lovely word, don't you agree?"

XXXIII
Bastards of the Schwarzwald

"Your companions must wait here," said Awa's host as he closed the red door behind them. The walls of the hut's only room were smooth, dull metal that glowed and shimmered from the single torch set in a sconce. The only other exit was a round portal in the floor.

"Why?" Awa looked up at the gaunt, pale man, wondering just what his nudity indicated—madness or simply different societal mores.

"The iron will keep them insulated," said the man as he put a foot under the handle on the portal, and with a light kick the metal door swung up to reveal a black pit. The trapdoor was as thick as Awa's wrist but the man's scrotum was barely swaying from the exertion of opening it. "Down, if you please."

"What's your name?" said Awa, warily noting that his spirit did not keep inside his body but stretched out from his skull in all directions, barely visible translucent tentacles swaying around him.

"Carandini," said the man, and bowed. "It is an honor to make your acquaintance, Lady Awa."

"Right," said Awa. "So...down?"

"Down."

"Why?" Awa glanced at her two mindless assistants and the

dripping bag they carried containing Chloé. "And you said iron would insulate my mindless ones, my new bonemen. From what?"

Carandini's left eyelid twitched, the pinkish eye it covered dilating ever so slightly. He sighed, plucked the torch from its mooring, and stepped forward, dropping straight down the black shaft. His fall stopped abruptly at shoulder height, and then he began descending a flight of stairs, his head dipping out of sight. Reasoning she had little choice, Awa lowered herself the short drop to the first stair and hurried after. She heard the iron portal somehow close behind her and knew she was sealed in with Carandini, his torchlight reflecting on the iron-lined walls of the spiral staircase. She was powerless, but she had not come to test her prowess against beings that even her tutor could not master.

Carandini was talking quietly, she realized with a smile. He was dead, undead but dead nevertheless, and so compelled to answer the questions of the living. It was a fine little loophole, Awa had to admit, answering but doing so out of hearing.

"I couldn't hear you," said Awa. "Why are we going down, and what will the iron room insulate my bonemen from? And please speak up."

"Certainly!" His voice echoed up and down the stair as he paused and smiled up at her. She saw his canines jutted out and down like pearl tusks, yet as he closed his mouth there was no bulge to his lips. Awa supposed the clip-clopping her left foot made on the stair might seem similarly odd to her host. "We are going down because you came here looking for answers, and unlike some we do not believe in punishing the curious by keeping them prisoner in drab little rooms. The iron lining above will keep your so-called bonemen insulated from our leaking wisdom."

"Leaking wisdom? What is—" Carandini broke into a trot down the stone stair, and Awa hurried after him.

"We are a collective of scholars," his voice echoed up to her.

"As such, it does not behoove us to keep our individual minds isolated from one another. We have adapted ourselves to share our intelligence with one another, but once you let something as vaporous as intellect out of its vessel it can go any old place, including into normally mindless servants."

"The wolves and birds outside," said Awa, impressed with herself for coming to the conclusion so quickly. "They're normal animals that absorbed your leaking wisdom?"

"Bats aren't birds," Carandini said aloofly.

"Oh," said Awa.

"And not my personal wisdom, thankfully. One of our servants noticed you, and so I volunteered to monitor your progress through the wood. When it was obvious you were coming here I alerted the others, some of whom went above to orchestrate my entrance, and ensure you were who we suspected. If you were not the lady Awa, but instead that insane tutor of yours wearing the flesh of yet another apprentice, then we would have been ready with beast as well as brains."

"I knew my tutor had come here before, and I inferred you didn't care for one another," said Awa. "So when you're around other creatures they become as smart as you?"

"Not at all," said Carandini, slowing to a walk upon finding Awa more than capable of keeping pace with him. "We leak, as I say, so that here, when we work in the laboratories together, we are all of equal intellect. When we go above, however, or allow others into our sanctum, our carefully cultivated intelligence seeps out of our skulls and infects anything in the vicinity. This does not make them equal to us, at first, but the longer we are near them the more we lose, and the more they gain, until the balance has shifted."

"The balance has shifted? So were there, were there just as many of you up there with the wolves and bats as there were animals?"

"Of course not. Simple beasts cannot, alone, drain more than the slightest fraction of our intelligence, which is why so many of us keep familiars. They are far more useful than your so-called bonemen, and just as loyal—their borrowed wits allow them to realize that loyalty is the soundest option for their continued self-interest."

"I see," said Awa. "So you become less clever the longer you're around other beings. At what point does it cut off? Your leak, I mean, what is the minimum intellect you can have? Say you were trapped in a room with a hundred human doctors, smart as you are that would put quite a drain on you, wouldn't it?"

"Yes," said Carandini, grinding his teeth. "To even master that number of wolves and bats my associates lost themselves, I fear, for there is no *minimum intellect*, as you put it. The volunteers who went up are no doubt loping around on all fours as we speak, no better than wolves themselves, and if they have lost so much of themselves that they no longer realize that they should seek what solitude the forest affords to recover their wits we will need to send up others to capture them and bring them back down. Otherwise they'll be pillaging farms and gnawing the udders off cows by dawn."

"I see." Awa smiled to herself, quite liking all of this—she was completing his sentences in her head before he even voiced them. Most of them, anyway. Then a concern regarding the practicality of transforming Chloé into one of these bizarre undead impressed itself upon her, and she asked, "Is there no way to arrest the leak? Surely that is part of the reason for your isolated, subterranean dwelling, but if you were to travel out in the world—"

"Many of us travel, or have traveled," said Carandini. "It is slow, the leak, unless we wish it to be faster, and stopping the leak is easy. We put bands of iron around our brows, and that is all that is required. Such bands can easily be hidden in a hat or a wig, so they do not arouse as much attention as you might think, but doing so obviously has its own share of detriments."

"You're not wearing one, and we're not sealed from one another the way my bonemen are, so that means you're voluntarily allowing me to borrow some of your intellect." Awa nodded, delighted to hear that all of Chloé's wits would not leak out as soon as they returned to Paris. Paris? That was a terrible idea, indeed, going anywhere except the most isolated regions was a terrible idea—she had been gambling with her life every time she entered a town, let alone a city. She, a Moor and a witch, should know better than to—

"Not voluntarily." Carandini scowled. The stairs terminated in another small red door, reminding Awa that they had been descending the entire time and must now be quite deep in the earth. How she would get out if he or his fellow bastards meant her harm—"I took the iron from my brow before traveling up to greet you. Not of my own volition, but... a compulsion took me. Your ward, I imagine."

"My ward? I—" Carandini swung the door inward and strode into the dark room, and Awa again trotted after to keep up with his breathless pace. The floor resembled ice and was just as smooth, the surface sparkling in the torchlight, and then Awa saw a curious, shallow wave rushing over the ground toward them. The tide drew closer, and Awa realized it was not liquid but countless brightly colored adders roiling over one another, the carpet of snakes making directly for Awa and Carandini.

"Interesting." Her host's pale brow creased as he dropped the torch and swept her up in his arms, dancing over the polished glass floor just as the wave of vipers came crashing down around his ankles. His hands were so chill they froze the sweat infusing Awa's leggings and she gasped at both the sensation and the sight beneath her. The squirming snakes were only able to scale up to his knees before the intense cold emanating from Carandini put the serpents to sleep and they fell away without getting within striking range of Awa's dangling feet. "It not only prevents me from personally hurting you but actually compels me to protect you from the traps I had set to circumvent that very ward. It is just as Breanne said, but interesting to see in action. I don't regret the time I invested one bit."

"Sorry?" Awa was growing dizzy as he swung her onto his back, putting his chest between her and the darts suddenly fired at them by some unseen device in the shadowy chamber. She saw oily black blood bubble out around the small shafts prickling his chest, and then they were through the snakes and past the darts and at yet another red door. Setting her down, he opened the door and ushered her through as she asked, "Who's Breanne?"

"An associate," said Carandini. "It was she who dealt with young master Walther."

"Walther?" The room Awa entered was dark, and as Carandini closed the door behind her the light of the abandoned torch was blotted out, leaving them in perfect blackness.

"Your predecessor. Light." And light there was, light of every imaginable color reflecting out of dozens of glass globes that spotted the enormous workroom. The globes were full of liquid that swirled and flashed, some set atop stands on the long tables, many more suspended from the scalloped ceiling by braided wires, and these as much as the bizarre apparatuses that adorned the room made Awa gape in wonder. "This is one of the laboratories. The others are in use so you cannot see them, lest you take more than your due."

"More than—oh." Awa saw him tapping his shaved scalp. "My predecessor came here? This Walther was the last apprentice of the necromancer, the one whose skin he wears? Er, wore?"

"Yes," said Carandini.

"And your associate, Breanne, dealt with him?"

"Yes."

"I must speak with her!"

"No." Carandini smiled, showing his fangs again. "You speak with me."

"Oh. Well, you tell me, then—what was he doing here?"

"What?" Carandini blinked at her. "The same thing I presume you've come for."

"And what's that?" asked Awa.

"To find a way to break the curse your tutor has afflicted you with, to postpone or prevent the loss of your body and soul." Carandini looked warily at her. "Isn't that why you sought us out?"

"Oh! That would be wonderful!" Much as she wanted to indulge her curiosity, Awa had resolved to be as forthright with the dead as they were with her, and that meant honest answers given at the time of asking. "I just came here to ask for your help with my, my lover. She was the one in the sack, upstairs? She's dying and so I killed her, but only a little, and I hoped you would turn her into one of you before she dies all the way. I don't want her to start rotting, and the book said—"

Carandini shook his head. "You sought us out to help with your *girlfriend*?"

"Well, yes. But since I'm here and you know about everything having to do with my tutor, why don't we talk about that instead and deal with Chloé later?"

"Chloé's your lover?"

"Yes. In the sack."

"Very well," said Carandini, throwing his hands in the air. "Ask away."

"Well, first of all, why are you so helpful?" Awa sat on one of the benches.

"Because I must," said Carandini. "I am compelled. And besides that, your tutor is an old enemy. He is a cheat. He came here long, long ago, volunteering an alliance. We accepted, despite our caution in aligning ourselves with a breather, and soon enough he had taken what he could and snuck off instead of putting in the years of labor he had promised. Indicative of your type, was he, more concerned with personal advancement than the common good. The hunt for knowledge oughtn't to be competitive." Carandini glared at Awa. "*Ought not be* competitive."

"I agree! Really! And I'll do what I can to help, and—what was that about being compelled to help? The ward you mentioned, the curse that keeps the dead from harming me?" Awa narrowed her eyes at Carandini. "How would you treat me if the ward did not compel you to this or that?"

"I would peel you like an onion," said Carandini, clearly overjoyed she had asked. Those eyes, pink and shiny as salmon flesh, came alive in a way the rest of him never would, and his bright red tongue flicked over his ivory teeth. "I would commandeer an entire theatre to take you apart, to find out how his wards work. Of course, if you did not have the ward I wouldn't have anything to study, which is a paradox. What was I saying? No, I would just kill you, I think, for your audacity, for one, in coming here to ask for assistance with your... relationship, but also because it's the only way to thwart him, I think, but then he, then you... another paradox." Carandini looked confused.

"Only way to thwart him?" The hope he had fostered in her quickly felt the pinch of frost. "Of course you don't know another way, otherwise my predecessor, this Walther, would not have been possessed. But obviously he was."

"Obvious now," said Carandini. "The boy stood a decent chance, to hear Breanne tell it."

"But you won't let me hear Breanne tell it."

"No."

"What did she do for him? How did she deal with him, as you said?"

"The issue," Carandini sniffed, "is that if you die it would probably thwart him, indeed, it is likely the only way *to* thwart him, but that pesky ward prevents us from counseling such a course, or allowing you to consider it. Breanne was forced to perform surgery on Walther when it became evident he intended to kill himself upon leaving our company."

"Surgery?" Awa glanced nervously at the array of too-bright metal tools covering the tables. "What kind of surgery would prevent him from, ah, doing that?"

Carandini tapped his head again. "Cut him off from thinking about most things, other than eating and keeping warm. Unfortunately that route didn't work, otherwise I'd already be up to my wrists in your skull. Again, these abominable compulsions—it must have gotten the boy killed, or whatever you want to call what your tutor does when he steals your body, and so that avenue is denied me."

"How would, would hurting his brain keep him safe?!" Awa demanded. "What kind of solution is that?"

"A pretty good one." Carandini crossed his arms. "It kept him from doing himself harm, which was the point in the first place, and no doubt caused some difficulties for your tutor upon taking over the body—we had hoped that if he did manage to possess Walther he would be in the same bestial position as the boy, but apparently the old breather managed to overcome the deficit of reasoning long enough to trap some traveler or another and eat their brain. That's how you lot repair your physical injuries, isn't it?"

"Yes." Awa sighed. Why had she even allowed Chloé to come along in the first place—so she could watch Awa become possessed, or maybe help her kill herself? So she would be close to Awa when her body was stolen by an utter bastard with a predilection for dead flesh? What the hell was wrong with her?

"The surgery wasn't the only precaution." Carandini had

taken up a pair of pliers and was wresting the darts out of his breast. He dropped the bloody quarrels on a metal plate to punctuate his sentences. "Breanne found a mountain peak riddled with thick, unbroken veins of iron. Those natural deposits, when combined with a great deal of time and energy and our own arcane wards, would allow an ethereal spirit to pass through but prevent the necromancer from leaving once he bonded with the flesh of his pupil. He would have been imprisoned there upon possessing Walther, yet somehow you fell within his grasp and he manipulated you into doing exactly what all your predecessors had done—studying his arts to prepare your body, then freeing his spirit from the aged mortal shell after he cursed you. And all without ever escaping the mountaintop! A little impressive, I must admit."

"So you took the apprentice to the mountaintop and left him there? How was that different from killing him, and how could you if the ward—"

"It was the only way, and obviously Walther had a chance or we wouldn't have been able to leave him there. Initially Breanne wanted to dump him on some empty island or in the middle of a desert, where the boy could live just long enough to become possessed and then perish, but she couldn't, the ward wouldn't let her. Compulsions compulsions compulsions. I didn't want to let you in, I didn't, I wanted to lock the door and leave you to fend for yourself, but next thing I know I'm ushering you downstairs, giving you the grand tour, so why don't you tell me what it is I can do for you and be off." Carandini stood and walked along the benches toward a metal door set at the end of the hall.

"I need the wits that are leaking into me, your wits, to find a way to stay alive," said Awa, brightening. "Why don't I stay here, and you and your collective can study me without killing me, and then when he comes we'll all have figured out something together!"

"Out of the question," said Carandini, opening the iron door. "We would succeed, I presume, in removing your ward if we were to examine you, which would allow us to kill you, which is why I can't allow you to stay."

"Well don't, then!" Awa followed him. "Why be so nasty to me? Why not make a friend, form an alliance, and defeat the necromancer together! You don't have to kill me once the ward is removed!"

"I didn't say we could remove it, just that we might. Dark." All the globes in the laboratory winked out. "Light."

The rear wall of the new room lit up, thousands of luminescent insects squirming across it, pale green light spilling out over a spacious, comfortable stone chamber. The chairs and bed looked as soft as the floor and walls were hard, and Carandini ushered her to sit as he went to a tasteful wooden cabinet and fetched a bottle. Awa settled into the chair, and though she told herself she would not display anything of the sort, a happy sigh involuntarily left her lips. Her host set a beautiful yellow glass bottle on a small table beside her chair then sat opposite her in the seat's twin.

"If you stay here you will die," said Carandini wearily, rubbing his temples. "That's obvious. I don't particularly wish to help you but it seems I must do something or you will die, which I am compelled to prevent. So what next?"

"I don't know," said Awa, picking up the bottle. "Is this wine?"

"Yes," said Carandini, and, waving his hand, two glasses appeared on the table beside her, sparkling quartz goblets that blazed with the light of the wall. "Pour me one, too, if you please, might as well enjoy being foolish for a night."

"I drank with a skeleton before," said Awa. "But he really couldn't keep it in, of course, and it couldn't affect him. I suppose you are different?"

"I am." Carandini winced.

"Tell me about your type, about your differences from the undead I am familiar with," said Awa as she filled his glass. As soon as she finished it floated off the table and drifted over to his languid fingers.

"We require blood to stay alive," said Carandini. "As you will eat a finger to replace a missing digit, we must drink fresh blood to preserve ourselves. We do not have a heartbeat unless we wish it, however, and as our bodies maintain a very cool climate the blood inside our veins will last a very long time and we do not need to refresh it very often. If we choose to use it, it goes bad much quicker and we must ingest fresh human blood."

"Choose to use it?" Awa sipped her wine and found it delicious, but much as she wanted to throw back the glass and pour another she knew that getting sloppy with this monster would not further her cause. "How do you use your blood if you do not have a heartbeat?"

"We do not have a heartbeat unless we choose to. I've turned mine on now, for example, in order to digest and savor the giddiness this beverage affords. If we're of a mind to enjoy a nice meal, or other physical pleasures, then we activate the dormant organs required for the task and set to. The blood goes bad much quicker when we do this, though, so we usually avoid it."

"Where do you get human blood down here, so far from everything?" The question made her a little uncomfortable, as she doubted the answer would be pleasant. It was not.

"We have a farm further down," said Carandini, draining his glass. "We raise them, humans, and keep them in pens downstairs. They're never in the best of health but we're rather good at tending to their maladies, and so we always have something on hand. They don't taste as good as those that live above—not enough exercise, probably, or maybe the sunlight has something to do with it. At any rate—"

"That's terrible!" Awa set down her glass. "What gives you the right to do that!?"

"The same thing that gives them the right to eat cows and sheep and everything else—there's no one to stop us. Of course at this point we've developed artificial tonics that serve just as well, but it really doesn't taste as good so we just keep it on hand for an emergency, like a plague outbreak or—"

"Doesn't *taste* as good?! You mean you don't really *need* the blood, you just prefer it?!"

"That's it." Carandini burped and the bottle floated from the table to his hand. He refilled his glass. "But shouldn't we be worrying about you, Lady Awa? Why the curiosity about us?"

"Chloé," said Awa, more than a little disturbed and doubtful he would help her if he did not have to. "She—"

"She's one of us now," said Carandini. "You were heard when you told me in the lab what you'd really come here for, and Breanne's taken care of it."

"What?!" Awa stood up. "When, and how—"

"They've been listening in, of course, and the little death you gave the girl was easily undone. You did arrive just in time, it sounds like she was almost gone. Why you would prefer her to be one of us instead of simply restored to health is a question I wouldn't mind answered, in light of how ignorant you seem to be of us."

"Wait... what?" Awa looked around the dimly lit room, wondering just how many ears were listening in. "I didn't want her to die, and since she was hurt beyond repair—"

"Beyond whose repair?" Carandini was on glass number three. "I could have restored it, your Chloé, to full wellness in the time it took us to walk downstairs. Hemorrhaged brain, broken bones, ruptured organs? Child's play."

"I... I didn't know," Awa murmured, wondering for the first time how well Chloé would take the news that she was now a supernatural creature that must occasionally consume human blood. Not very well, she expected. "I thought it was the only way."

"It wasn't." Carandini chuckled. "She's one of us now."

"You said that," snapped Awa. "Are you going to keep her hostage or will you let her go?"

"She can do whatever she wishes," said Carandini. "We don't bestow our boon lightly, but I gather Breanne took a shine to her. Still, Breanne can't very well hurt you, so she was probably just setting things in place for the girl to have somewhere to go after the inevitable transpires."

"You mean after I die? Some place for Chloé to go after my tutor finds and destroys me?"

"Yes." Carandini nodded. "Exactly. You're getting smarter, see?"

"I want to go." Awa stood, no longer sure she appreciated the increased intellect that made it so difficult to draw absolute differences between herself and her ghoulish host. "I've had enough of this, this nastiness. Living underground, eating people you don't have to, plotting to steal my girlfriend—what's wrong with you things?!"

"We're just practical is all." Carandini shrugged. "Anyway, you can't go yet."

"Why not!?"

"Dunno. Compulsions. Can't let you out until you've come up with something feasible, I gather. So think, Awa, think!" Carandini had stopped using the glass and drank directly from the bottle.

Awa sulked. She could not stop worrying about Chloé—was she awake? How much had they told her about Awa? She had been waiting for the right time to tell Chloé everything, but somehow it was never the right time to tell your lover that you are actually a necromancer afflicted with a terrible curse.

The longer Awa stewed, however, the easier it became to think past her immediate concerns, her emotional concerns, and slowly a smile started to spread across her face. It was so simple, so obvious, that she could not believe it had not occurred to her before. She knew how to find a way to defeat the necromancer.

XXXIV
Sharp Truths

B≠B+

Carandini had crawled into bed and lay moaning, clutching his scalp. Awa let herself out and closed the iron door behind her, bedding down in the empty laboratory so that her host could gather his wits. Then she fell immediately asleep, exhaustion keeping her pinned to the floor until nearly a full day and night had passed.

Her host was sitting on a bench watching her as Awa awoke and groggily made her way to the bowl she had found on a table and used as a chamber pot. She noticed he now wore a crown of iron but otherwise remained nude. She turned away from him and pissed, wishing he would stop staring at her.

"Time to go, then," Carandini said after she finished, and he escorted her back to the surface. In the little iron room the mindless corpses of Merritt and Kahlert waited, the bloody sack that had housed Chloé draped limply over Merritt's arm. "I gather your, ah, girlfriend is waiting outside."

"Wait," said Awa. "Please."

"You are quite welcome," said Carandini.

"No, not that," said Awa. "I want to show this one. He deserves it. Will you wait? Please?"

"You *are* a strange one," said Carandini, but he obliged her.

Awa called Kahlert's spirit back to his body, the suddenly sentient corpse backing into a corner and crying, "Stay away!"

"Ash," said Awa patiently. "We are a day's march from your home, and here we find a nest of undead sorcerers with more power than even I can conceive."

"Sorcerers?" Carandini snorted. "We're scholars, philosophers, alchemists."

"Can you control animals with your mind?" said Awa, annoyed with the bastard. "Can you bring the dead back to life?"

"Of course."

"Ahhhh"—Kahlert's head snapped back and forth between the two on its fractured neck, his mind now remembering everything his body had experienced since his death—"aahhh!"

"A day from your house, Inquisitor, a single day out. They've been down here for who knows how long and you didn't suspect a thing!" Awa smiled and shook her head. "And when you took a witch-hunting holiday in Spain you were just down the road from a necromancer, did you know that? So close he hid his mystical treasures in your library—last place a witch would look, but the last place a witch hunter would look as well, apparently. So your house is on top of a warren of bloodthirsty monsters, your summer home is next door to a warlock, and to top it all off you've been letting your undead witch girlfriend call the shots. You're a credit to your profession."

"Help!" Kahlert closed his eyes. "Please, God—"

"Just thought you should know," said Awa, and dispelled his spirit.

"That was perfectly charming," said Carandini. "If you are quite finished I will ask you to leave. Don't come back."

The iron portal rang out as Carandini disappeared back down his hole, and Awa sighed, staring at the little red door. What would Chloé have to say? Would they have told her that apparently Awa could have simply asked for them to heal her instead of transforming her into whatever she now was, another Bastard of the Schwarzwald? Nothing for it but to find out, and Awa swung open the door.

Chloé was waiting in a pool of moonlight on the edge of the forest, more beautiful and alive than Awa had ever seen her. Her skin shone, as did the iron circlet crowning her pale brow, dark hair falling over her shoulders and breasts like night falling over snowy hillocks, and Awa nervously went toward her, keenly aware she had not so much as washed her face since spending a week shoved in a witch hunter's sack, her clothes soiled, her hair a lumpy mass jutting out from her skull. She paused in front of Chloé, rubbing her hands together, nearly crying at her lover's unbroken jaw, her unbruised skin, her sharp teeth.

"Were you ever going to tell me you were a witch?" asked Chloé, her tone less severe than Awa had feared but nowhere near so warm as she might have hoped.

"Would you have come with me if you had known?" Awa smiled, weak but hopeful.

"No," said Chloé, and flinched. "I mean, I don't think so. Maybe? I was superstitious."

"Oh," said Awa, confused. Remembering Chloé could not lie, she focused on something that had been bothering her for a long time. "Why did you insist Merritt come with us? You had a new excuse every time I asked, and you knew how much I hated him."

"I...I liked him," said Chloé uneasily. "I know he wasn't as funny as he thought he was, but he was alright enough. I know what you did to him, incidentally."

"Oh," said Awa, no more comfortable with the conversation than Chloé. "Liked him like you liked me?"

"Not quite," said Chloé, "but close? He was just as lost as the rest of us, run out of his birth home after some business with their Henry getting a whim and putting the spurs to honest men. So down he came to Paris, and he was a good enough sort. Kind of an asshole about foreigners, but I was working on him about that. Nobody ever had their mind changed about blackamoors, or witches, for that matter, by being killed by one."

"Why come with me at all, then, if you liked him *close* to how you liked me?" said Awa bitterly. Why the fuck were they talking about that asshole anyway? "Thought there was more fortune to be made tagging along with me, is that it? After all the clothes I bought you, the books you never had time to study, thought you'd make money and keep your boyfriend in the bargain and—"

"That's not fair, and you know it," Chloé said, crossing her arms, and even if the girl had not been dead Awa would have known she was telling the truth. "Taking to the road's the most dangerous thing in the world. You really think I'd abandon a comfortable position in the best brothel I've come across because I thought there was more to be made risking my neck on the open road with you? And so what if I was confused, if I liked the fellow who drank too much and was a cunt to people he didn't understand almost as much as I liked my girl who drank too much and was a cunt to people she didn't understand? I should've been more honest with you, about my feelings for him, but I never loved you any less for it, and you weren't exactly upfront with me, either."

"I only ever loved you," said Awa. "I was scared I would lose you if, if you knew about me, about what I am. No one understands—"

"No one understands if you don't give them the chance," said Chloé.

The two women were quiet for a long time, the silent corpse of Merritt looming behind Awa. Finally Awa could bear it no longer and blurted out, "So what about us? I saved you, and I made some mistakes, sure, but—"

"You killed him!" Chloé's voice cracked. "You killed him, Awa, and for what? Because he was scared of you? Because he tried to run away instead of doing what you said? God's fucking wounds, Awa, you murdered him like I'd swat a flea, and even hearing what he meant to me you've got no more remorse!"

"He was an asshole, he was always—"

"No," said Chloé firmly. "I can't. It's over."

"What?" Awa could hardly believe it. "Because I killed that piece of shit you're leaving me?"

"Yes!" Chloé cried. "Yes! I love you, I do, and we both know I mean it. But I can't be with someone who could do that to another person, just, just end them like that, and not even say you're sorry! You're not, are you?! You're not sorry at all!"

"No." Awa felt cold and sick. "He was—"

"He was alive, and you killed him because he pissed you off. How can I know you won't do the same thing to me?"

"I wouldn't!" Awa cried. "Never! I brought you back, I had them bring you back!"

"And that's something I'll have to work out on my own," said Chloé. "I didn't bring it up, I, I knew you'd be hurt enough, but really, Awa, what the fuck? I'm a monster! They, they say I need to drink blood, to hide underground, to hide from the sun! What the fuck, Awa? You didn't give him a choice, and you didn't give me one, either."

"If you don't like it dying's easy enough for all of us," said Awa, and instantly wished she had not.

"I forgot, didn't I? Life and death's like hooding a lantern to you." Chloé was crying. "I don't want to see you anymore, Awa. I want you to leave me alone."

"You're fucking welcome!" Awa almost screamed at her. "For everything! Sorry I took a fucking interest!"

"I'm not," Chloé sniffled. "Even now, I'm not. I love you, Awa, and I always will. But not like before. Never like that. Before, if I were still... alive, I might be able to convince myself, you might be able to convince me... but no. I'm wiser now, much wiser from what they did to me, somehow, and I'm smart enough to see now that I would never be able to trust you again, to really forgive you. I can't lie to myself any more than I can lie to you—we're over."

Awa was trembling and took a step toward Chloé. The girl took a step back. Then it finally sank in—Chloé was genuinely afraid of her. Awa crumbled, and then Chloé did go to her, and held her, and they talked in quiet voices until just before dawn. Then Chloé kissed Awa's cheek and, with the wisdom of the dead, left her to sort through her pain alone.

Alone, as if she had been anything but. No words could capture the sorrow Awa felt, and why would they wish to? The two corpses approached their mistress, picking up on her unspoken desires, and she lay limp in their arms as they began carrying her back to the ruins of the Inquisitor's manse. Better for her to have died there in that house along with Chloé than to live and suffer so.

As dawn made what headway it could in the shadowy forest, Awa tried to focus on the necromancer and her curse, on the epiphany that had struck her in Carandini's chambers, but her mind kept masochistically returning to Chloé. Light was skulking through the trees as the two corpses stopped at the edge of the clearing beside the ruins of Kahlert's manse. Awa clambered down from their arms, muttered an apology to their spirits as she returned their bodies to true death, then walked out of the forest toward the stream crossing the glen.

She pulled her clothes off as she walked, no longer crying, her mind as cold as the creek water she lowered herself into. In one hand she held the last salamander egg and in the other the ibex knife, and as the frigid water shocked her into taking a sharp breath she floundered back to the edge of the shallow creek. She placed the egg in a pile of grass on the bank, then hacked off her greasy, matted hair with the knife, clipping pieces of her scalp as she heaped the hair and grass ever higher over the egg.

Finally she breathed the word onto the stone egg, and as it caught fire the stink of burning hair cut into Awa's nose. She piled more grass onto the small fire, which burned ever hotter, and then added a small fir branch that had floated down from the forest and become hung up on the bank. The wet wood caught and burned as though it had been seasoning in a shed for years. Then the fire died down, the smoke thickened, and Awa saw a small shape moving inside the miniature pyre.

It looked like a newt. Not a flaming newt, or a mysterious newt that glowed like coals in a furnace, but a simple newt. When she tried to pluck it out of the ashes it scalded her fingers, however, and she popped them in her mouth as it crawled away from the creek, its tiny legs moving ever so slowly and carefully as it wound through the grass.

Awa sighed a happy sigh as she had upon first sitting in Carandini's marvelous padded chair, and then she lay back down in the creek, the spirits of the water doing what they could for her seared fingertips and bleeding scalp. Fuck her, and fuck her tutor, and fuck all of them, and Awa put the knife to her own throat. The blade pressed against the skin and Awa looked straight up at the cloudless sky, a river stone her pillow, the water her shroud, the banks rising sharply on either side the walls of her coffin.

XXXV
A Tale for a Colder Night

There is always a choice, and Awa made hers. Fuck that, and fuck him—she had to try, no matter if she was as terrible a person as Chloé seemed to think, no matter what. The creek suddenly felt as hot as it was cold, and with a gasp she tossed her knife over the side of the bank and scrambled up after it. Surely somewhere along the line one or two of his apprentices had done themselves in or perished of external forces; for all she knew that might be exactly what he wanted. Besides, giving up was the same as letting him win, and she would fight until she lost.

It was so simple that Awa grinned as she dried herself with her discarded clothes and put on her least filthy leggings and tunic. She found a large flat boulder where the creek met the forest and, clambering onto it, took out the book. Her book. She asked her question and the pages dutifully began to turn.

The book settled on a page that began *Pity Boabdil*, and Awa took the time to read his version of her life. That he had seen so much from his prison atop the mountain brought all of her anxiety back to her tight throat, her pounding heart. How could she hope to compete with such power? It was the nature of the book that as she read the writing pulsed and changed, so that while she read for quite some time she only turned the page once, and she saw clearly how he had folded the rectangle of skin and stitched it into place, creating two full pages—only the front and back of the first was written upon, the second blank as one of Manuel's fresh canvases. Taking the knife, she sliced into the first page.

The book hurt; Awa felt it quivering as the iron knife dug through the page. The words were dripping off it, and by the time she had the leaf free her hands were covered in blood and the page was a wet clod of old skin. She wiped it in a small circle on the stone then put the crumpled page in the center, and put the knife to her arm. She only went in with the tip a little, and as the blood welled out she daubed a wet ring around herself on the boulder.

She tried to recall a face she had struggled to forget, a voice she had replicated perfectly until she realized what she was doing, the smell of his breath, everything. She could do this. Then the bloody page began to smoke and smolder, the red ring surrounding it crackling, and then he was there.

Rather, the thing he had become. A pit opened in what must be his head, the serpentine shadow as black and lustrous as when she had last seen it, immediately after he had tricked her into killing his physical body. The hole of a mouth twisted into a crescent, and then he began to speak through it.

"Little Awa." The necromancer sounded happy to see her. "What have we here, eh? I don't suppose you've killed all those babies, hmmmm?"

"No," said Awa, remembering all too well the concubine's claim that were she to kill a hundred children with the necromancer's dagger she would be spared. The notion had never appealed to her. Strange, she thought, that despite the nonchalance toward death she had possessed in her youth she had never even considered the one obvious escape he had offered.

"No," he said, piling on top of himself until his increasingly skull-like face floated just in front of hers. "But you found my tome! I couldn't believe my luck, having a book-collecting witch hunter move in so close. Mind, he never caught a witch, not one."

"Yes he did," said Awa, smiling crookedly at her tutor.

"Ho-ho! What a clever young woman you are!"

"Clever but stupid."

"Did I say that? Cruel, cruel and unnecessary, you—"

"Shut up," Awa said, still smiling. She was actually starting to enjoy herself. "What's your name?"

He told her, his jovial smile narrowing to a tiny hole that voiced the syllables. She smiled wider, which made him thrash against the invisible walls of the circle, greasy black smears hanging in the air. Then he drew himself up short, facing her again.

"Doesn't matter," the necromancer hissed. "Think it makes a difference, knowing that? Think there's anything in the book to save you? Think I don't know you've got a few more months left on your sentence, a few more precious summer days until I can claim you? Your time is running short, little Awa, your time is running up, and I'm going back to where I was before you so rudely invoked me."

"Why does the curse, the ward, whatever you put on me that keeps me safe from the dead, why does it last ten years?" said Awa.

"That's as long as I can persist without a true form," he said, the question restoring some of his good humor—he might be a monstrous necromancer with pretensions at some sort of immortality, but he was still a pedant at heart. "Any longer and I start to lose my abilities, degenerating in quality, and we can't have that. Being freed from flesh is the most marvelous experience possible, although I expect you lack the imagination to see why. I fly like a tireless bird, across mountains and oceans, from pole to pole and back again, learning all the secrets our physical senses keep hidden. But after a decade or so I begin to slide, and if I'm not careful I'll wind up as some mundane poltergeist, able to interact with this world on only the faintest level. So I give myself ten years at a time, which is proven to be safe, and fairly easy to keep track of, especially as I time it to expire on memorable dates... such as Christmas, or the Autumn Solstice. *This* Autumn Solstice."

"What would you do if I died before you could return for my body?" Awa recalled all too well the feel of a blade against her throat an hour before.

"I would take another body." The black smile spread even wider, a chasm in the smoke. "I would lose much time, for the body would not be trained as you have been, prepared, seasoned. I would have to take a child to make sure my arts would find a home, to ensure the vessel would be capable of overcoming its innate iron as you are, and I might well make a bad choice and not be so powerful as I once was."

Not even that bitter remedy would stop him, then.

"But in time the body would grow, *my* body would grow, and I would retrieve my book and train a new pupil, and try again. It has happened before, indeed, it has happened more often than not. Our world is perilous, after all, and living ten years without the protection of my wing is a trial not all are capable of. But I have always regained what was lost, and I have always punished those who sought to hide in death. There is no escaping me, little Awa, and we both know I cannot lie."

"If escape is impossible..." Awa felt her stomach fall through her bottom, knowing she was down to her last hope, but also certain that this final possibility that had come to her in Carandini's chamber was the key to everything, and as close to a sure thing as she would ever come.

"This page is almost used up," he said, languidly swimming around his circle, "so unless you've got another piece of my skin, a piece of bone, something to prolong my visit, I'm afraid I'll be going back to the so-called New World for a little while longer. New! I've been there a dozen times, but even old things are interesting with new eyes. I think we'll go there in the flesh, you and I, once I've returned. I'll be seeing you soon, little Awa, I'll be seeing you very, very soon."

Awa did not want to use the other page of his skin lest the means of thwarting him somehow require it, and besides that she suspected that if she broke the circle to place another artifact inside the ring he might be able to escape. There were still a few tiny scraps of the skin burning in the circle, meaning he could not flee just yet, and Awa mustered the courage to ask. She had him.

"How do I defeat you?" Awa said. "Tell me how to destroy you, to banish you from this world, to stop you from stealing my body."

The oily shadow stopped swirling around its circle, the eye holes growing larger, the mouth hole shrinking. It shuddered violently. The features were more distinct than ever, the face in the smoke almost that of her tutor. It shook harder, and Awa realized he was afraid.

No. She heard it then, the noises he was making, and they were not fearful whimpers, desperate cries. He was laughing.

"Tell me!" Awa screamed. "You have to tell me!"

"You think I know that?!" Her tutor made a sound like a clicking tongue or a clicking bone. "Think I kept reading any grimoires that seemed to be going in that direction? Think I went out of my way to ruminate about such conundrums? Think you're the first to ask? No no no, little Awa, why would I try to learn the answer?"

"How..." Awa's fists were clenched. Not fair. "Where might I find an answer? Where might I look to find a way?"

"I haven't the foggiest," beamed the eel-like apparition. "No idea whatsoever. But you're a clever, *clever* girl, so I'm sure you'll—"

"Get fucked!" Awa shrieked. "You fucking piece of shit, I'm going to fucking end you!"

"Language!" The necromancer's spirit recoiled. "No soap around for leagues, by the looks of you, or I'd advise you wash your mouth, young lady! But in all seriousness, we might find another way, together, you and I—"

"You're fucking dead! Think I'm some beast for you to beat, some dog to come lick your hand after all you've done?! You fucking bastard! I'm going to fucking ruin you!"

"Look, this page is burned out, so I don't have to stay any longer than I wish and if you won't be civil—"

"Be gone! Fucker!" Awa shoved him back the way he had come, and then she was alone on the comfortable boulder by the pleasant creek winding through the scenic glade beside the burned-out house of the dead Inquisitor. "Fuck!"

Awa did not shed a single tear, nor did she waste another breath. She had perhaps half a year, and she would use it well—that she had even considered giving up made her sick. If she died, regardless of the cause, it would inconvenience him but by no means thwart him, and thwart him she fucking would.

"What in fuck witchery's this?" Awa looked up to see Monique standing on the opposite side of the creek. "With that cunt-smack's house a hot mess of ash an' coal jus' down the crick, you think profanin at the top of your lungs is best?"

"Mo?" Awa wondered if this were some resurgence of the old madness that had made her think her tutor's ghost was haunting her skull and speaking with her. That had just been her talking to herself, not a bona fide hallucination, but even if she were but a phantasm brought on by an overtaxed mind Awa was overjoyed to see her. "Mo!"

"Mind the arms, love," said Monique as Awa leaped over the creek to embrace her friend. The gunner's voice was level despite the rivulets pouring down from her squinting blue eyes, and Awa saw that both of the woman's arms were bound in stained bandages, her left in a sling at her chest and her limp-wristed right held clumsily out in front of her, as though she did not know what to do with it. "Kin I jus' say that you're a welcome sight, shit-lookin though ya surely are?"

"Monique." Awa touched the giantess's shoulder. "You're really here!"

"In the flesh, or what's left of it." Mo leaned closer. "Oi, wipe these eyes for me fore the others come along an' see me actin the feeble, eh?"

"Others?"

"Awa!" Manuel came trotting out of the woods. "For fuck's sake, what are you doing out here?!"

"Manuel!" Awa laughed with delight. "Niklaus Manuel Deutsch of Bern! Who else do you have out there, Johan and Ysabel?"

"Who?" Monique shook her head. "We got the fuckin quack with us."

"Not Paracelsus?!" Awa cried, and then he emerged wheezing after Manuel, and there on the bank of the creek Awa laughed and wept to see her friends appearing one after another when she needed them most. She gathered her gear and followed them deeper into the wood where they had camped for lunch upon finding the manse burned to the ground. After she had eaten and achieved a tidy little drunk from Paracelsus's schnapps, they all began talking at once, all four faces struggling to contain their grins.

Before the telling of tales could begin in earnest, Awa insisted on examining Monique's arms against the woman's protests. Paracelsus tried to explain that the obstinate gunner had not allowed him to amputate but Awa would hear none of it, one look at the spirits infecting the wounds confirming that she was already in mortal danger. Manuel's bitten face would require a bit of tending as well, but Monique had no right to even be alive. Awa set out immediately with stewpot in hand to retrieve the necessary parts from the discarded bodies of Merritt and Kahlert after securing the promises of her friends not to follow her.

No sooner had she left than Paracelsus had dire need of a shit, and after quitting the campfire the physician crept after Awa, watching with interest as she cut flesh and bones from two fresh corpses that lay close to where they had found her. She knew the noisy doctor was watching her grind up the meat and bone with the aid of her knife's pommel, and on the return trip she made sure to catch up with him and have a little word on the propriety of the occasional judicious silence.

Otherwise she was as honest as the dead with her companions as she prepared the stew that only Monique was allowed to sample, much as the smell of fresh pork excited Manuel. She made a much smaller batch for the artist soon after, which he found stringy for his taste—thankfully the sinuses and cheek meat of the dead men did their work well enough without his palate's approval. As they ate Awa told them everything, about her servitude to the necromancer and her onanistic romance with Omorose and her curse and her years of searching graveyards and the friends she had made amongst the dead, and her enemies as well. They only occasionally interrupted her with their questions, and when she was finished they took their turns, Awa immensely relieved to hear they had dispatched the hyena.

"And when we got to Calw we heard that Ashton Kahlert's estate had burned down, so of course we came over to have a look ourselves," concluded Manuel. "Camped out here so as not to arouse the local ire by picnicking in the ashes, though we gathered that the barkeep at least was no friend of Kahlert."

"An' I'm walkin down ta see if all's still quiet so's we kin get out the way we come in," said Monique, "an' I hear ya shoutin them fuckwords Manuel an' me taught ya, an' I wager they 'eard, too, so we all come a'runnin."

"But why come all this way?" said Awa. "I understand Paracelsus wishes to study my methods, but you two have lives away from all this. Manuel's family, and your brothel, and—"

"Well, the cleanest 'ores in Christendom didn't stay quite so clean without your attentions," Monique said sheepishly. "Sides, Manuel here needed your help in fulfillin a certain fantasy of 'is what relates ta those of the skeletal persuasion."

"It's not like that!" Manuel protested but he was smiling, too. "I'm an artist, damn it!"

"Yes, yes, of course you are," said Paracelsus. "And of course Paracelsus will risk his life a dozen times over to study someone else's *methods*, of course it's all business for *him*, of course *he* has no fondness for anyone or anything but esoteric knowledge. It's all just research for the magus, the only nourishment he requires."

"Eat up," said Awa, lifting another spoonful to Monique's thick lips. "It'll only help if you eat."

Monique and Awa took the first watch together, catching one another up having taken some time and Paracelsus's addition of laudanum to his schnapps making the day float by all the faster for the reunited friends. Monique waited until she was confident Paracelsus and Manuel were asleep before putting the problem to Awa directly: "So what now? If the ol' wizardly cunt don't know a way, an' you don't neither..."

"I don't know," said Awa. "I've got his book, but if it doesn't know and my tutor doesn't know and the Bastards of the Schwarzwald don't know, then I certainly don't, either."

"What bout what he did, then? Couldn't you do the same, nick out an' take some other body fore he gets yours?"

"Even if I knew how, I wouldn't. I couldn't do that to somebody. I'm not like him." Awa knew she was trying to assure herself as much as Monique.

"What if they was willin, like?"

"Willing? I don't think most—" Awa saw the look on Monique's face and shook her head vigorously, her heart twisting in a bittersweet contortion that is only possible on the rarest of occasions. "No. I…no. I can't ask that of you, or anybody. The spirit…the spirit is destroyed, obliterated, or else trapped in his book, I think, oh hell, I really don't know. But no."

"Maybe we could share?" said Monique. "Like, if you wasn't keen on, on pushin my soul about, maybe we could both set up shop. Room enough for two in 'ere. Rest of my family's right dwarfs, maybe that's the reason I come up so big?"

"I—I've never heard anything so generous." Awa took her friend's hand. "But like I said, even if I wanted to I don't know how. I can talk to spirits, and make bargains with them, but I'm not so wise about controlling my own spirit, or who knows what else goes into what he does."

"Whatta the, uh, the dead say on it, then?" said Monique.

"Which dead?"

"I ain't the expert," protested Monique. "Jus' askin, right? You told of helpin out all them dead people fore meetin up with Manuel an' me, thought you might've asked one of them dead or spirits or what bout how ta deal with dead wizards tryin to do stuff an' all. What?"

"No." Awa had sat up straighter, a sudden thought setting her teeth on edge. "I just…maybe…Monique, is there a war happening?"

"A war?"

"Yes, like the ones you were fighting when Manuel and I met?"

"Hell, there's always a war goin down Lombardy-ways," said Monique. "Emperor Charles ain't just a fuckin Spaniard cunt but the king of the fuckin Spaniards from afore he got the 'oly Roman crown, so ya know he'll be mixin it up with the cheese-eaters an' the eye-ties even more than the old Emp. What's war gotta do with it?"

"I...I..." Awa was getting excited, her thoughts swirling around something but unable to stick to it. She was on the edge of salvation, she felt it. "We need to go there, Mo, we need to go to war."

"Might's well ask Manuel if he'd like ta paint a pretty 'ore." Monique grinned. "Them sally eggs ya gave me's changed the whole fuckin game, Awa. Traded a smith some mink for time in 'is shop, an' made me some commissions. An' I'm talkin *dread* fuckin cannons, no locks ta jam, no cords ta die in the rain, no trays ta spill—I jus' keep'em in the bottom of the barrels, add a charge and round, an' pop goes the fuckin hyena, Barbara bless us. Go on down the front an' get some honest blood on'em sounds fun, 'specially if my arms get as good as you say. But mark me, this is my last go—I'd rather crawl back on bended tit ta Dario than keep workin the von Wine shaft."

"One go is all I have," Awa said nervously, wondering if the plan she was forming had any chance of success. "I'm out of time."

XXXVI
The Requiem of Bicocca

🜍

In the predawn gloom the corpse of Niklaus Manuel Deutsch, artist, soldier, and pretentious know-it-all, was somberly carried through the camp by the Dutch gunner Mo and a Milanese man who had not campaigned under von Stein in years. Those who had not seen their old ally in over half a decade were warned away by his dour face and cold eyes that nodded down at the body he helped carry whenever one of his former friends tried to ask him just where the hell he had gotten to after cutting out with Manuel and disappearing all those years ago. At von Stein's tent the guards did not give them much trouble, for von Stein overheard before Monique's voice could become too loud and hurried out to see if it was true. He had no idea Manuel had come down to find sport at the little park just north of Milan, indeed, if he had he would have gotten the boy a cushier location than the front, and he gnashed his teeth to see his useful pawn as cold and dead as the trout he had left half eaten on his plate to investigate the ruckus.

"What's this, what's this?" said von Stein. "I thought you died of the pox ages ago, my maid, and yet it's poor little Manny I see at his reward? Baffling!"

"He wanted ya ta be left lone with 'is corpse," said Monique sadly. "Said it often, he did, fore he went—said you'd 'ave a pray o'er him in private, that you'd understand."

"Did he?" Von Stein blinked down at the body. "Well I don't, not at all. Morbid, morbid as hell, such a thing."

The pallbearers held their breath, then von Stein sighed and held open the flap of his tent. They carried Manuel in and set him down on the ground, and von Stein stood over the body shaking his head. Then he looked again at the man who had helped Monique carry in Manuel's body and the captain blinked, now more interested in the soldier than the corpse.

"Ber... Bernardo?" asked von Stein.

The man nodded.

"I sent you with Manuel all those years ago, didn't I?"

The man nodded again.

"I recall you, I do." Von Stein waggled his finger at the mercenary, pleased with himself for remembering the man's name. "Manuel absolutely hated you. I thought you died."

"I did," said the man, and slapped von Stein's extended hand. The captain took a step back, then toppled over, his eyes rolling back in his head as he died with all the glory of a glutton choking on a chicken bone. Awa quickly knelt and restored Manuel from the little death she had given him outside the camp while Monique pointed her guns at the tent flaps lest the guards enter upon hearing von Stein's body fall. They did not, and Manuel, having had some experience in bouncing back from a little death, helped Awa drag von Stein under the captain's massive table. Manuel glanced nervously at Monique and when he looked back at Awa he saw she no longer appeared to be Bernardo but now looked exactly like von Stein. It was bizarre and terrible to see the man hunched over his own corpse, and then she looked up at her old friend, grinning with teeth the color of the trimmed beard that wreathed them.

"Do I look the part?" asked Awa.

"Need to start writing plays," muttered Manuel. "Or poems. Something with tragedy."

"No tit in plays, an' poems're for ponces," said Monique, creeping to the mouth of the tent to peek out. "Can't fuckin believe that worked."

"You're dealing with a witch of the first water." Von Stein's doppelganger puffed out her chest. "I think it's time to, how did you put it, inspect the lines?"

"The lines." Manuel gulped. "Yes, I, that's where the worst will be. But what about his, his body?"

"Oh, that's an even better idea! I'll just raise his corpse, make myself look like Bernardo again, and we can all—"

"Oh fuck it all," Monique hissed, and tiptoed quickly to where Manuel and Monique stood. "It's Lautrec, it's fucking Lautrec! He's coming in!"

"Who?" Awa asked.

"*The* Lautrec?" said Manuel. "Oh fuck."

"The big boss," Monique began, "Frenchman who—"

"Allll-brecht!" The dark-haired, squinty man stepped into the tent, the flaps held back by von Stein's guards. "Just what is the meaning of this?!"

"Ah." Awa looked desperately at her two friends. "I, ah—"

"A fish breakfast?" The Vicomte de Lautrec walked around the stunned trio and poked von Stein's trout. Manuel held his breath, wondering if the man could see the commander's corpse shoved under the desk from his vantage. Spinning around, Lautrec said, "Might we speak in private, Albrecht?"

"What?" Awa squawked. "They, they need to be here."

"Tosh." Lautrec shooed them away with his fingers. "I just want to have a quick little word, Albrecht, then you can have your advisors back."

Manuel and Monique dejectedly marched outside and stood at the mouth of the tent, wondering if everything was about to turn to shit. One of the guards glanced at them, did a double take at seeing Manuel up and about, and swooned. Then the duo set to explaining to the other guards how Manuel had needed to fake his own death lest there be spies in the camp, obviously, and—

The tent flaps swished and Lautrec stepped out, a curious smile on his thin lips. He looked mischievously at Manuel and Monique. The other guards were standing rigidly in salute and Lautrec looked around, then stepped closer to the artist and the gunner.

"Awa?" Manuel whispered.

"A what?" Lautrec whispered back in French. "Normally I'd take offense to you scum addressing me in your incomprehensible accents, and your uppity refusal to even salute, but thanks to your captain all of you are going to die. Die. Give the Infinite my regards, cowherds."

"Right!" von Stein boomed, exiting his tent. "To the lines with us, then!"

All heads turned and cocked in his direction, just as the embedded Imperial arquebusiers would soon turn and cock their guns on the advancing Swiss that von Stein would lead. The morning moved very, very quickly after von Stein's announcement that he would personally lead the contingent of mercenaries from Bern, and as the lines were formed at the front Manuel prayed more and more vigorously. Incomprehensible though it seemed, their orders were to march straight across a field toward a fortified road the Imperials held with pikemen and gunners. As for the boisterous Swiss, their own pikes swayed like wheat, exactly like wheat, and Manuel knew what happened when the wheat grew tall enough to properly sway. Fuck fuck fuck.

"So," Awa explained after ducking back to von Stein's tent, altering her appearance to resemble Bernardo again, and returning with the reanimated body of von Stein in tow, "just before we got here von Swine told his master, that Lautrec, that all the Swiss would abandon the fight unless they were allowed to attack immediately. Lautrec was coming to try and change his mind, I think, or maybe just yell at him. But anyway, we're at the front!"

"Yes." Manuel panicked at the realization that he had left the satchel with all his planks back in the tent. "We've got to go back, I've got—"

"That's the fuckin signal," Monique observed as a horn lamely tooted somewhere behind them. "Get walkin, lump. Jus' like von Wine, sendin us straight inta a fuckin killin field. They'll 'ave all they gunners at the front, mark me, an' just mow us fuckin down. Only way to use fuckin guns, not that von Wine ever understood that. Never thought I'd say it but wish Doctor Lump had stuck it out with us stead of pissin off ta find those bastards of the Blackwood you was on bout."

"So what do we do, Awa, what do we do?" Manuel tried to get himself under control. In the past he had not become so flustered before a battle, so goddamn scared, but all he could think about was his wife and his children and his studio. *Focus, Saint Niklaus,* he thought, *focus on what needs must.* "I sent a letter. A few days ago. Inquiring about a civic position, begging for it, really. I'm done, this is it, I'm done, after this, I'm done, it's charity and tithing and—"

"You tellin us or God?" Monique winked at Awa, who always stood close enough to von Stein to control the walking corpse and have it parrot a word or two if needed. "But lump's got a point, don't he, Bernie? What's the scheme?"

"When the killing starts we secure a small area we can keep people out of, and you, if you're sure—" Awa began.

"We're sure, we're sure," said Monique as the column began to move. "What we gotta do?"

"Protect me," said Awa. "That's all. Make sure no one disturbs the circles I draw."

On an open plain without cover such a seemingly simple request might prove impossible, but her two friends nodded. *Saint Niklaus enters the scene,* he thought with a smile, and they were off, moving with agonizing slowness across the field. The stiffly marching corpse of von Stein did not respond to the coded orders one of Lautrec's pages gave him to wait for the French artillery to bombard the fortified position of the Imperials, instead pushing ahead across the field of Bicocca. The second column, led by a provincial Swiss captain jealous of von Stein's bravado, did not wish to be left behind and likewise ignored the order to hold.

Then light appeared in the east and the Imperials, embedded atop the earthworks they had built immediately behind the sunken road that cut across the field, opened fire, a second dawn blooming in the south as a hundred muzzles flashed. The noise was deafening, not of the guns but of the pikemen screaming as they fell by the score. A mist of blood enveloped the columns as they rushed forward, scrambling over their fallen comrades, and every few breaths another volley would cut down the first few rows of charging Swiss. Awa had never experienced anything like it, but neither had Manuel or Monique or any of the men present, and only the sight of their brave captain von Stein trudging ahead with half his arm blown off kept the troops from routing.

"Cowards!" Manuel screamed, his voice cracking to see the Imperials hiding atop their wall. "You fucking cowards! Cowards!"

Awa kept a wall of marching dead men in front of her and her friends, and if any of the Swiss mercenaries noticed that their companions rose despite mortal wounds they themselves were killed before they could spread the word. Then the columns reached the high wall of mud the Imperials had built and the massacre worsened. Looking beside him, Manuel was horrified to see that two of the dead men carried Awa between them, the witch no longer disguised as Bernardo, her eyes twisted back in her head and foam running from her lips, a piece of damp parchment clutched in her hand.

"Fuck!" Manuel screamed, pressing himself flat against the wall as gunners leaned over the edge to fire down into them. "What do we what do we what do we—"

"Lump!" Monique slapped him in the mouth. "Shut it! She's been 'avin that fit since 'alfway cross the plain, so jus' fuckin shut it! The, the dead ones are still walkin, aye? So she knows what she's bout, aye?"

"I don't know," Manuel whined, his face covered in blood. "I don't fucking know!"

"Well I do." Monique grabbed Manuel's arm and impatiently began dragging him along the wall, as if it were a country hedge they were strolling beside and not a deadly fortification. The corpses carrying Awa followed them, which encouraged Monique even if she was not sure what it portended. "There, that cart stickin out the fuckin wall. Let's get under there an'—"

Another volley from just overhead brought bells to their ears, and as the cloud of black smoke rolled down the wall to envelop them Manuel saw von Stein's corpse methodically climbing straight up the mud embankment, pikemen rallying behind him. Couldn't they see that the morning light was spilling through dozens of wet holes piercing his fat frame? Maybe they were already dead, Manuel suddenly realized, maybe he and Monique and all the rest had fallen and Awa was just marching them forward, and—

"Down!" Monique dragged Manuel underneath the abandoned cart she had found just as the mud around them spit up clods of earth, another volley dodged, another ignoble, anonymous death avoided. Then Monique turned and saw the dead men holding Awa swaying beside the shelter and with a curse she left the cover and snatched the girl from their arms. Back under the filthy tipped cart Monique looked anxiously from Awa to Manuel, then gently slapped Awa's cheek. "Oi, up, blackamoor, there's work ta be done."

The world came back to Awa, the real, living world, but all the light was gone from it, and everything was the color of old blood and ash. Monique and Manuel were hunched over her and Awa could not tell if they were alive or dead, or which she was, for that matter. She decided they were all still alive, but that meant they were all about to die, and Awa was afraid.

Death was not to be feared. Awa thought she had believed that, thought that what her tutor intended by stealing her body was obviously different and that true death was natural, benign, sometimes welcome, even, but on the field of Bicocca that conceit was broken.

The magnitude was what changed everything for her, the sheer volume of spirits ripped from their beloved shells by hard iron plentiful as raindrops in a storm. Those that were blasted out at once were lucky compared to those who lay drowning in their own blood, and as if they were stones to be picked up and thrown she had hoisted one corpse after another and marched them forward, her eyes flitting around the field, her concentration so intense that some did not even hit the dirt before their dead bodies were reanimated, the young Swiss staggering as his throat was shot, his stomach, his heart, his groin, staggering but not falling and continuing to march on the low earthwork wall where row after row of arquebusiers discharged their weapons into the disintegrating columns.

When Awa was confident she had resurrected a sufficiently deep wall of mindless corpses to march in front of them she had ordered two of them to swoop her up. As they carried her Awa shifted her focus from the physical remains to the almost invisible spirits being ejected from their bodies, from life, and she called out to them. Not all of them listened, many shimmering and fading, not to be recalled unless forced by necromancy, but a dozen heard her call and paused, spirits hovering between worlds, and then another dozen paused, and another, and soon all of Awa's world was a cloud of spirits, a great thunderhead of death building higher and higher over the field as a hundred men died, then another hundred, and another, and Awa addressed them with her own meager spirit, a spirit protected from the deceased but one of such insignificance when weighed against that dire contingent of dead souls as to flatten her with fear. Awa pleaded, she begged, lost in a miasma of gunsmoke, mist, and death, and then Monique slapped her once, and she was still alive, but the sheer weight of the dead almost crippled her, and she lay shivering like a dying child, eyes staring in horror at the ever larger mass of spirits hanging over the world.

"Awa, please," Manuel begged. "Awa, do something! Awa!"

"Get on up, girl." Even Monique seemed concerned, a pistol in her scarred but whole right hand. The gunner had not wasted a shot marching in, but the shouting atop the earthwork was growing closer and the tipped cart on the sunken road was not likely to withstand even a single volley were they to be targeted. "Do whatcha come for!"

Awa closed her eyes and tried to find her breath, then opened them again, careful to focus only on the mud in which she lay. Not letting her vision rise to look at her friends or what loomed beyond them, she rolled over, got onto her hands and knees, then sat back on her haunches. The single torn page she had held as they marched lay crumpled in the dirt beneath her. She faced the wall of mud and smiled to herself, daring to think her mad scheme might actually come to something. Even if the plan failed she was still safe from the dead, and—

Not safe, Awa caught herself as she wiped the muddy earth beneath her as smooth as she could, nothing about this was safe. The report of another volley shook the cart to punctuate this thought, and she swung her slingbag around, jamming the loose page back into her satchel beside the leather tube Manuel had given her and removing the book. Manuel and Monique were behind her in the cramped hollow, their voices low, but she knew time was running out and addressed the tome.

"Show me the last page he took from his last body," said Awa. "I already used one but there were two."

A thick scab ran from the top of the book to the bottom where she had removed the first page taken from Walther's skin, and this second leaf did not come any easier, even when she ordered the book. When the binding finally gave up the page a trickle of blood began running down the spine, as if the folio were a deeply embedded hangnail. She had it, and placing the page in the mud, she dug deeper in the book's binding until the flow quickened and she was able to surround the loose page with a ring of black blood.

Then Awa cut her forearm with the ibex knife. In her haste she went deeper than she intended, and leaning forward she quickly splashed a red ring around herself. She would have continued despite her sudden lightheadedness but Monique had torn her own tunic and grabbed Awa's bleeding arm. In the shadow of the cart three pairs of eyes focused on Monique's ten fingers tying the rag around the wound, particularly the disproportionately thin thumb and forefingers on her right hand.

"Wish we 'ad Doctor Lump or some of your famous stew," said Monique.

"That's good." Awa dragged her arm away, the phantasmal shapes lurking just behind Monique almost capturing the necromancer's attention before she turned back to her work. "Now go away, both of you."

"Fuck that!" Manuel was shaking his head vigorously. "And fuck you both if you think I'll go out there! No!"

"Niklaus Manuel Deutsch of Bern, if you don't leave you'll distract me, maybe get us all killed," said Awa. "Maybe worse."

"Fine! Fine! Fuck fuck fuck—"

"Niklaus!" Awa shouted in his face. "What happened to you? You were brave, gallant, fearless, you saved me and—"

"Fearless, she says." Manuel looked between Awa and Monique. "Never fearless, Awa, and brave? More like stupid. Reckless. I—"

"You saved me," Awa said quietly. "I'm asking you, Niklaus, to try and save me a second time. To save us all. I won't be able to do it if you're here, I'm too scared he... If I, if I don't have complete concentration I'll fail and he'll kill me, Niklaus. Not even that, not death, but worse, he'll—"

"Damn you. You told us." Manuel sighed, the old Manuel, the Manuel who, in that instant, regretted not his decision to leave his comfortable home and loving family, nor his choice to march into the mouth of Hell with his countrymen and these two friends, but only his forgetting of pine planks and charcoal. We always have a choice, and Manuel made his. "Well, Mo, ready to say good morning to the Imperials?"

"'Eard they give'em prime matchlocks of different make than we's used ta down 'ere," said Monique. "Let's get a closer look, then."

"Let no one disturb me," Awa told them. "But stay close, if, if this even works, we'll still be, well, right here, with all those—"

A volley cut her off, and before it quieted Monique had given her a kiss on the cheek and dragged Manuel out after her, the artist flashing Awa a crazed smile as the descending cloud of black smoke covered them. No goodbyes, no speeches or tears, just the tide of gunsmoke swallowing them up and leaving Awa in her cart-cave at the edge of the earthwork.

The rays of sunlight punching through the smoke cloud would have formed the shapes of skulls to the artist if the vapors had not blinded his eyes, and the mud squeezing up between his fingers as he climbed the earthen wall would have looked like worms. Instead everything looked like a blur, which was in and of itself a sort of symbol, but he could not be fucked to sort out what it might mean. Mo had gone straight up the wall and he went after her before his mind could betray him with its logic. Besides, logic was subjective, and as suicidal as scaling the wall might be, they would do Awa no good at all milling around beside her cover—the two corpses that had been guarding the cart had been decapitated by a volley and were as dead as was natural, and atop the wall he and Monique could at least distract the arquebusiers from the obvious cover Awa hid beneath.

Mo stopped climbing. A pikeman or gunner or, if they were really fucked, one of those plate-covered Imperial assholes, must have tickled her brain, and Manuel almost let himself slide back down the wall, but then she crawled a little higher and he clumsily squirmed to her left, and with much sliding and slipping he was able to scramble up beside her. The cloud had dissipated, and with the edge of the earthwork just above them he assumed she was waiting for the next volley to blanket the wall before making their charge. He tried to pray, then, but could not fully concentrate, the best he could manage a muttered promise never to paint again if God would only let him live out the day.

Manuel began to panic but caught himself—this was the bravest thing he had ever done, this was his noblest act. Saint Niklaus, the muddy martyr, the man who gave his life so that a witch who denied Christ might live. At least he was not a fucking coward Imperial hiding behind a wall instead of fighting like honest men. His mind began to slide back down the wall, across the field, past the little red millwheel, and up the walk to where his wife and niece and daughter and little boy and even that terrible cat all awaited his safe return, then his eyes fell on the overturned cart beneath him. Smoke was trailing up from the slats like the mud squishing between his fingers, but before he could go back or tell Mo the next volley shook the wall, and with the wave of smoke washing down over them Manuel realized the arquebusiers must be just over their heads, firing at the Swiss who huddled a short distance east along the wall. Fuck them, fuck them and fuck him, and over he went.

The wind was carrying the smoke down the wall and over the Swiss, which was grand for the pikemen clustering at the base of the earthwork but rather fucked for Manuel, who rolled over the top of the wall to find himself utterly exposed in the early morning light. Thankfully Mo had captured the attention of the dozens of arquebusiers they had emerged on top of, the giantess leaping into their rows with a pistol in each hand. Manuel saw the lines instantly become a disorganized mob as she fell amongst them, both guns discharging as she kicked men down and stomped them into the earth.

"Ay dios mio!" one of the gunners cried, which only incensed Monique further.

"Spaniards!" she howled as she dropped the pistols in her hands and drew the pair from her waist-scabbards. "Evil fuckin Spaniard cunnnnts! Fire! Fire!"

Two heads split, fountains of blood and brains erupting as her second volley struck home, and then the pack of arquebusiers broke, the devil amongst them, and as they ran Manuel went to work with his hand-and-a-half. He had only hacked a few legs out from under the fleeing gunners before his stomach dropped and he took a step back—a dozen landsknechte, the Imperial equivalent of the Swiss pikemen who had proved so effective against the Empire in the past, were pushing through the fleeing arquebusiers. *Must have crossed myself with the wrong hand this morning*, the artist thought glumly. Then he noticed the plated man at their forefront, and the eager voices of the old Manuel shouted down the less brave ones of Niklaus Manuel Deutsch, would-be civil servant and fusspot. A real fucking knight had come to play, and Manuel would have charged at once if Mo had not dropped to her knees over her discarded guns.

"Are you—what the fuck are you doing?!" His concern that

she had been shot or stabbed by the routed gunners turned into incredulity at her foolishness—she was reloading her pistols from pouches at her belt, as if such a thing were at all acceptable in the midst of battle. "Get up, you fucking cow!"

"You want me doin what I do best." Mo winked at him, then raised a pistol in each hand and aimed past him. "Fire. Fire."

Her pistols blazed and two of the charging pikemen fell, tangling up the legs of their fellows. Manuel had no more time to reprimand her, the others almost upon him. The heads of the pikes were bobbing at him, and he pictured himself as Sebastian, pincushioned with shafts. Then he cleared his throat and hoisted his sword—this time his last words would amount to more than a string of fucks and a squeal.

"I challenge you to single combat!" Manuel shouted at the knight, hoping he was an Imperial, or at least bilingual—the soldier didn't have time to repeat his challenge in Spanish. "Let God hear that I challenge you, in the name of honor!"

They were almost upon Manuel, the knight's conical visor reflecting the dawn sun as the pikes jutted out from behind him like the fan of a charging peacock.

"Let God hear that I am ready to die, and fear not death!" Manuel's voice broke. "God forgive those who martyr me!"

"Halt," the knight said, to Manuel's tremendous surprise and relief. He came to a stop, as did the pikemen. Manuel heard Mo reloading behind him but over the shoulders of the looming landsknechte he saw the arquebusiers were all engaged in the same act. "Thinking highly of yourself, cow-toucher? Martyr you? Honor you? I'm going to cut you in half, you piece of shit."

The knight came forward, a noble out to earn his name or some such asshole, and Manuel smiled a wry, ugly smile. "Hiding behind that shell, hiding behind those gunners, hiding behind this wall?! You fucking bastard! I'd rather be a cowherd than a coward!"

The knight was only a few paces away and then, like dogs who have growled enough, they went at each other. The knight seemed almost to fall forward on top of Manuel, the sword he held in both hands coming around fast, and Manuel deftly hopped forward and jabbed his own sword into the slit of the man's visor. He put both shoulders into the stab and the point of his hand-and-a-half ground through the knight's left eye socket and killed him instantly. There was an awkward pause as the knight toppled over, and then the ten standing landsknechte all brought their pikes to bear on Manuel.

"Fuck," said the artist.

"Fire. Fire." The reports deafened Manuel, and so he did not hear Monique repeat the word twice more. The pikemen fell back, nearly half their number gunned down in an instant, but now it was the arquebusiers' turn to push forward, their rows restored, their weapons reloaded, their vengeance at hand.

"Saint fuckin Crybaby an' his ol' pal Saint Cuntlick," said Monique. "Did our fuckin all, eh?"

"What!?" said Manuel, swaying from his ruined equilibrium. "What?!"

"Never mind," Monique said sadly, putting her arm around Manuel as the arquebusiers raised their weapons. "Never mind."

XXXVII
Death and the Maiden

Awa focused on the circle before her, and then the ring of blood started to bubble and the edges of the page in the center began to brown and blacken. The circle she had drawn around herself was bubbling as well, and soon the page caught and the muddy alcove under the tipped cart filled with acrid, yellow smoke. He was coming.

His shade swirled inside the ring of burning blood, its shape as nebulous as those of the dead spirits congregating over the battlefield, but there could be no doubt that it was him. Awa was trembling, suspecting just how much worse what he threatened was compared to the mundane deaths going on all around her. He could not leave the circle so long as it was unbroken, and she focused on that to calm herself.

"Decided to trade in that last page?" The black specter looped over and under itself, its eye holes sliding around its head to stay ever fixed on Awa. "Changed your mind about offering up a hundred sacrifices? Hit on a bright idea to *fucking end me*, as you said? Come to grovel?"

"I'm done talking to you," said Awa, the air muggy and cloying. "And I'm damn sure done listening to you."

Awa left her circle, crawling over to the edge of his with the book in her hand. Then she set it down just outside the ring of hissing, evaporating blood and opened it at random. Winking at her tutor, she hoisted the pistol Monique had given her, the short-barreled Last Resort that the gunner normally kept in a hidden holster at the base of her spine. He was saying something but she refused to hear him. Dumping the shot and powder out of the gun, Awa let the salamander egg roll into her palm, placed it on the ground, then put the open book facedown over the egg.

"I might not be able to beat you," said Awa. "But I wanted you to watch me fuck you over as best I can."

"Awa?" The necromancer's voice had grown plaintive. "Awa, I can't lie, you know this, and when you summoned me before I mentioned that we might find another way together, remember? Before you lost control and banished me? If—"

"Fire," said Awa, and the necromancer screamed inside his prison. The egg ignited, the book shrieking like an owl-nabbed field mouse as the flames engulfed it, and Awa rocked with laughter. The powder she had dumped out of the gun caught as well, the ground sizzling and popping around the burning book, and then a deposit of the powder popped at the edge of the circle containing the necromancer. A smoking piece of blood-soaked earth spit up into the air from the tiny blast, and before it had landed or Awa's laugh could turn to a scream the necromancer came billowing out of the sliver cut from the circle, bringing his vaporous body down atop the book. It went out instantly, and he reared up before Awa, his old face forming on the head of the cloud.

"Spiteful, nasty little thing! Think I have to obliterate your spirit when I claim you!? Think I can't keep it around for a few centuries, in constant agony!? Think I have limits!?"

"Yes," Awa said from where she lay sprawled on the ground beside the broken circle, and then she pointed at him and said his name.

The dead came howling from the sky, hundreds of spirits falling through the cart onto the necromancer before he could flee back into his circle. The dozens of black claws he sprouted to fend them off were not enough, nor were the few arcane tricks his ethereal body was capable of, and they drove him to earth. They knew his name, she had told them his name, and with it they found him and held him. A dozen or two would have been little trouble, a few score a touch difficult, but the hundreds of spirits adhering themselves to his spectral form were too much, and his voice cut through the roaring gale of the dead, a single desperate word.

"Please!" he howled, and Awa smiled, and then they were gone.

Awa was alone, the morning light spilling under the edge of the cart blinding, her ears ringing from the necromancer's final scream. It would take her a very long time to fulfill all the requests the dead had made, every single fallen mercenary demanding a unique boon in exchange for his service, and each request was recorded in blood on the first page of the necromancer's book that Awa had judiciously removed before summoning her tutor. Some of the spirits had ignored her plea, going to wherever the dead go without a backwards glance, but the legion who had postponed their journey to the realm of the dead, from which none can return without the aid of the living, had proved strong enough to drag the necromancer with them. The old cheat.

The charred book settled, a puff of ash rising, and then it wiggled a little. Awa pulled the ruined tome off the hatched salamander, the creature waddling away out from under the cart. She gathered her bag and Monique's gun and followed it into the light.

The dead were everywhere, but packs of the living still clumped at the base of the wall, planning their next doomed attempt to take the earthworks. Awa went to the corpses closest to her, the light warm on her skin, and brought their bodies back. She would have preferred to ask their spirits permission but there was no time, there had not been time in quite a while, and once she had six draftees she pointed to the wall.

"Find Niklaus Manuel Deutsch of Bern and Monique," she said, and unrolled the canvas Manuel had given her outside the ruins of Kahlert's manse on the day of their reunion. Monique's spit had dried and Awa had kept it in its leather tube so the image was nearly intact, and she pointed first to the figure of Paris, then to Juno. "Niklaus and Mo. They're over the wall. Bring them back. Fast!"

The arquebusiers leveled their guns at the pair of mad Swiss who had single-handedly killed eight of their number, as well as six pikemen and Sir Isengrin, which is when another half-dozen Swiss gained the wall behind them. Twenty triggers were pulled in broken unison but the dead travel fast and Monique and Manuel were both tackled by undead pikemen just as the muzzles flashed before them. The hail of shot blasted the skulls of all but one of the reanimated mercenaries, who drooled blood as he informed the prone artist,

"Mistress wants you."

Monique and Manuel scrambled to their feet and fled, the crack-crack-crack of arquebusiers echoing their footsteps as order again broke down and the gunners desperately tried to shoot the two Swiss butchers. Then the pair reached the wall and jumped over the side, falling down the embankment and dislocating this ankle and that shoulder. Then Awa was there and they were limping across the field, von Stein again immaculate and unharmed at the lead of the tactical retreat, his two advisors at his shoulders, a dozen corpses shambling behind them as a meat-shield. Those who claimed to have seen von Stein back in camp were rebuked when his ruined corpse was brought in from the field much later in the day, and his advisors could not be found for questioning by a disappointed, but not entirely surprised, Vicomte de Lautrec.

The three friends parted ways outside Bern, in front of the red millwheel they had all passed many times before. After all the possible words were said Awa and Monique rode back down the road to begin honoring the requests of the dead souls who had spirited the necromancer off to where he should have gone so many centuries before, and Manuel looked at the wheel grinding through the water, round and around. The artist smiled. It did not look like a symbol for life, nor war, nor anything else—it looked like a fucking millwheel, albeit a pretty one. It was time to try his hand at some plays instead.

XXXVIII
Eternity in the Tomb

Paracelsus rapped again on the little red door, his palms damp despite the chill in the air. Wolves were moving through the underbrush, bats were winging overhead, and the doctor took a deep breath and tried the handle. It was unlocked. He went inside, leaving the door open so that the moon could provide some measure of light. Creeping into the room, he saw that a metal portal stood open over a pit, and then the door slammed shut behind him. In the blackness Paracelsus held his breath, and when he heard no other creature breathing he relaxed.

"What is your business?" a man's voice said just behind him, and the physician jumped.

"I'm an associate of Awa?" Paracelsus took a step away from the voice, then remembered the open hole in the floor and tried to orient himself in the dark.

"She is no friend of ours." A woman's voice came from the other side of Paracelsus. "If she sent you here it was not for your benefit, friend of Awa."

"I said associate, not friend," said Paracelsus, his right hand dropping to the hilt of his sword. His palm fell past where the pommel should have been, and he tried to maintain his composure as he pawed the empty scabbard in disbelief. "She strongly advised me against coming, in fact."

"Oh," said the male voice. "Then perhaps she was a friend."

"More than an associate, at least," said the woman. "We should listen to our associates. Very foolish to ignore the counsel of the learned."

"I came here because I wish to learn from the best," said the doctor, his pride trumping his fear. "Theophrastus Philippus Aureolus Bombastus von Hohenheim is my name, and I have come because my *associate* Awa informed me there were no greater minds in the entire world than those assembled here. If such a thing were true then I should not be made to feel bullied, but instead welcomed, by the intellectual elite. Instead you wish to twist my words against me, just like those turds at the universities, instead of hearing them for what they are."

"Theophrastus inherited Aristotle's school, did he not?" said the woman, her voice just behind him.

"If you seek meaning in my name, I prefer Paracelsus," said the doctor, the schnapps he had steadied himself with outside the door abandoning him to a sudden and dreadful sobriety.

"Celsus, the philosopher? *Para?* Greater than he, are you?" The man's voice was right in his ear but Paracelsus felt no breath stirring his long, manky hair.

"*Para*celsus, as in *beside* Celsus, not greater than," said he. "My detractors might have you believe otherwise, though."

"Well then, Herr Beside Celsus," said the woman. "What do you bring us?"

"What?" Paracelsus swallowed. "Why, a mind eager to unravel the cosmos and the alchemical, and a most impressive body of knowledge already accumulated."

"Not enough," said the man.

"Not nearly," said the woman. "Too bad. I was beginning to like him."

"What else could I bring?" asked Paracelsus, keenly aware his voice was rising.

"Something," said the woman.

"Anything," said the man. "Save for a physical form and spongy brain. We have recently had a new addition to our society, thanks to someone's predilections for appearances and potential."

"Only one of which you possess," said the woman. "With nothing else to contribute—"

"Wait!" Paracelsus had hoped to forestall the revealing of his prize until he was a full member of their little club, but circumstances were just that. "I do have something else."

"What?" said the woman.

"Something good, I hope," said the man.

"Nothing less"—Paracelsus cleared his throat—"than the Philosopher's Stone!"

"Really?" said the woman, and a brilliant light flared up, blinding Paracelsus just as thoroughly as the darkness had. "Let us see."

"Now," said the man.

"Hold on," said Paracelsus, fumbling in his pockets. He felt the pouch but kept rooting until his eyes adjusted enough to see what was happening. The man and the woman were both watching him intently, and he saw they were both completely naked and hairless. The woman held Paracelsus's missing sword casually in her thin hand. Licking his dry lips, the doctor pulled out the pouch and held it to them. The man took it reverently and opened the drawstring, then dumped the contents into his associate's cupped hand. A rough stone fell out, a jagged piece of gray rock.

"Where did you come by this?" asked the man as the woman lifted the stone up to a glowing beaker that floated between them, its yellow light filling the chamber.

"A hyena, it is called," said Paracelsus. "I remembered my Pliny, and did a little digging in the creature's eyes. The stone—"

"Is a calcium deposit and nothing more," said the woman, and the light went out. "What shall we do with you, Theophrastus Bombastus?"

"Take him below," said the man, and before the doctor could say another word his tale was cut off, leaving him in the clutches of those diabolical Bastards of the Schwarzwald.

XXXIX
Et in Arcadia Ego

O

Pity Boabdil. That is how the necromancer began Awa's tale, and when she was alone with the moon Awa wondered what simple language might end it. She knew that whatever words were used, *pity* should not be one of them, but beyond that she had no earthly idea. That is the problem with telling tales about real people, she supposed, no summary can convey every truth, every facet, and what is good for the hare is not good for the fox. Do not pity Awa, she would think, and shiver to imagine the raspy voice of her tutor voicing the sentiment. Maybe when all her tales were completed a succinct conclusion would come to her, a revelation, but she rather doubted it; the real world is no romance, where all questions are answered, all conflicts resolved, all wrongs righted, all scales balanced. Nevertheless—do not pity Awa.

One of the many tales not told here is how Awa managed to fulfill the requests of the hundreds of spirits who had saved her, or how Monique martyred herself to save her friend and lover. Nor will ink be spilled to tell of Awa's final bargain with Carandini and the rest of the undead alchemists, or of her unexpected reunions with Doctor Paracelsus and Chloé, or of the founding of the commune on the hill where she and Monique finally settled. The only story that really needs telling is of the last trip the famed poet, playwright, painter, printmaker, and politician Niklaus Manuel Deutsch of Bern made to a certain leper colony high in the foothills of the Alps.

Awa was in her kitchen as the artist trudged up the steep trail below the isolated hospice, his lantern bobbing like a firefly. When the air spirit who watched the path fluttered in and informed its mistress she kept mixing her dough—he would arrive soon enough, and would no doubt appreciate the smell of baking bozolati. Wiping her hands, Awa sat down on the bench and watched Monique weeding by starlight through the window. They had never made a great deal of sense to one another, the giantess and the necromancer, but on warm spring nights like this when the fields and forests danced with countless spirits Awa was so happy to be alive and with her partner that she could almost forgive her tutor, who had set everything in motion. She had, on most nights, forgiven herself.

"Mo!" Manuel called, spotting her in the garden. After they had embraced she led him into the small house she shared with her partner, chiding him for shouting after dark when their patients were mostly asleep. Awa could not believe how old he looked, but when she again offered him what she had secured for Monique he shook his head, just as he always did.

"I'd just as soon not wait any longer than I have to before finding out if Luther was right," said Manuel, taking the wine Awa offered. "And if we're wrong, well, I'll be waiting down in Hell whenever you two toddle in. Besides, I've never cared for crowns."

"Those Schwarzwalders won't be doing me any more favors, so it would have to be a slow rot for you anyway," said Awa. "A ring instead of a bastard's headband, but that would mean a simple disguise for your condition rather than topping off from the occasional dying leper."

"No and no," said Manuel. "True death, please, though not

for many years, God willing. Dürer's died, did you know? Never got a chance to meet him."

"I don't imagine he gave up on 'is art to pump out propaganda," said Monique, scratching under her iron circlet.

"My work is not propaganda," spluttered Manuel. "They're stories, about men and women, and so they're morality pieces, yes, but what of it? I've heard no complaints from players or audiences."

"Morality, eh?" said Monique. "The shakiest fuckin word I ever 'eard. This morality got somethin ta do with what I 'ear bout you outlawin 'ores in Bern?"

"Gossip travels fast, doesn't it," said Manuel. "What did whores ever give you but a broken heart and the pox, eh? I'll say it, and proud—I'm cleaning up the city, and not just the brothels—no more gambling, no more mercenary attire to start fights and show off their blood money, no more—"

"You're a terrible fuckin hypocrite," said Monique sadly. "Glad I didn't live ta see the day Manuel finally got himself sainted, ya fuckin boor."

"What good did it do, all that bravado, that swagger? I wrote a little something about it..." Manuel cleared his throat and shamelessly quoted himself, "*If you pay us well we'll move against your enemy, til the very women and children cry* murder! *That is what we long for and rejoice in. It's no good for us when peace and calm rule.* Or something like that, it makes more sense, is more *lyrical*, in context. Didn't Bicocca show us what mercenary work really is, what good it brings? So many dead..."

The table went quiet, but then Awa cleared her throat and poured more wine.

"Oswald, the old abbot?" Seeing Manuel blankly stare at her, Awa continued. "He comes here sometimes, to check in on the lepers and make sure we're not holding our own mass or anything, and he told me you're going after the Church, too. I mentioned that I knew you and he spit."

"Saint Manuel, the pious playwright what makes the priest spit," guffawed Monique.

"Oswald!" Manuel cried, remembering the name at last. "That crooked old bird was a Borgia apologist, the wanker!"

"Aye, cause wankin's such a terrible crime." Monique rolled her eyes. The reformed Manuel was a bit of a twat, by her estimation.

"I'm going after them, yes," said Manuel. "But it's a cover to get rid of all the pictures I did. Of you, Awa, remember those sketches I did in the cemetery? I transferred them, painted them, and did quite a few more, for the churches and monasteries and such, but we can't have all that idolatrous nonsense anymore, can we? So I clean it up, and in the process scrub away any trace of a certain young Moor cavorting with the dead. It's for your benefit, Awa!"

"I never asked you to," said Awa. "How could you destroy your work, Manuel, how could you? It was gorgeous!"

"I don't need to defend myself to you," said Manuel, crossing his arms. "I get enough at home, thank you very much. And I keep the less obvious stuff, though I tell people it was done earlier or later than it actually was, keep them off the trail. You don't know what it's like down there. The Inquisition's stronger than ever, and even with some of the papists getting run out Bern's still catching witch fever. Suppressing the Church means suppressing the Inquisition, the witch trials!"

"And 'ow long after ya start turnin a profit til you lot start burnin witches, too?" asked Monique, but before the red-faced politician could respond Awa had retrieved another bottle and winked at her partner over the top of Manuel's head.

"Fuck it," said Monique and, winking back at Awa, added, "How's Katharina and the family, then?"

"Everyone's good, I suppose," said Manuel, and on they talked into the night, the tenants of Awa and Monique's community sleeping peacefully. The disease that had wasted their flesh was arrested by Sister Gloria's ministrations, though they did not realize the true cause, and so even if she was a Moor, and even if Sister Monique did only come out at night, the lepers were happy enough to live away from the world that so despised and feared them. Awa felt the same, and she and Monique and Manuel went back to the garden just before dawn with a bundle of wood and four little stones.

"You're sure?" said Awa. "We've got a while yet, you and I, and if you think you might need them—"

"Nah," said Monique. "They saved me enough down the days I owe'em this, an' doin it while Manuel's 'ere to watch seems fine an' all. The three of us together, jus' like the ol' days."

"But your pistols—"

"I'll pick up some matchlocks ifin I get the hanker ta blow some shit up," Monique said with a shrug, and they built up a small woodpile beside the midden heap. When the eggs were all in place they stepped a few feet back, smiling at one another like children about to resume a game left uncompleted the summer past.

"*Fire*," said Awa, and the first egg burst into flames.

"*Fire*," said Monique, and the second caught.

"*Fire*," said Manuel, the firelight reflecting his grin. He, Niklaus Manuel Deutsch, practicing witchcraft—ludicrous!

"*Fire*," said Awa, and the last egg ignited.

Dawn kept its distance, and as the birth-pyre collapsed on itself and the four salamanders wriggled out of the ash they could see the tiny creatures glowing faintly in the darkness. The salamanders cooled quickly and soon the night took them, and Awa, Monique, and Manuel went back inside to finally take their rest.

The next few days they spent together were the happiest the

trio had enjoyed in years—Manuel and Awa took long walks through the hills, and even after all this time he smiled to see her left foot leave cloven tracks. One night when the artist drunkenly snored by the fire Monique dug out Awa's old nun's habit and the novice-no-more led her partner on a shorter hike into a pine grove that smelled almost of oranges, and they did not return to the house until the east had turned as pink as a blushing virgin.

On the last night Manuel even brought out his charcoal for a sketch or two, and though he protested greatly, Awa insisted on trading him the Judgment of Paris he had given her so long ago in exchange for the new drawings. They showed her as she was, she said, not for how he had hidden her under pale skin and European features. He knew she was right, and was secretly pleased to have his favorite painting returned to him. The ladies hung the new sketches beside the drawing of Awa that Monique had taken from Manuel's studio years before and the portrait of Chloé that had started Awa's collection, and after giving only a slight pause to their merrymaking for somber nostalgia, they resumed drinking and laughing.

After Monique had passed out, which she was still more than capable of when she activated her undead organs for the purpose of enjoying herself, and Manuel had drifted off on the floor beside her, Awa poured herself a final drink and watched her friends sleep. It might seem a little creepy, she knew, but then few things about her life were not to an outside observer. She sipped the schnapps and let her mind drift all the way back to those friends who would not be visiting, those faces she would never see again barring some unlikely twist of fate or postmortem reunion, to Chloé and Paracelsus and Manuel's family and the bandit chief Alvarez and Ysabel and Johan and Halim and even Omorose, and then she finished her drink and blew out the candle.

The spirits of the hearth still crackled softly as Awa squirmed between Manuel and Monique. They were both warm despite one being very much alive and the other rather dead, and Awa sighed happily—there was no place she would rather be, and she fought off sleep as long as she could to extend the night just a little bit more. When the three friends parted late the next morning they did so with only the slightest tinge of the sorrow that always accompanies the departure of dear comrades, and promised to see one another again soon.

Niklaus Manuel Deutsch died before the spring was out. His remains were interred quietly into Bern's new parish churchyard on the east bank of the Aare, but he lived on in the memories of those who had known him, and was remembered fondly by even a few of his enemies. Each year, on the Autumn Solstice, Awa and Monique made the pilgrimage to the churchyard to lay edelweiss at the head of the artist, and then the two women would walk hand in hand between the moonlit tombstones, back to their home.

Bibliography

In addition to the following texts, I had a few stand-up individuals assist me in my research. First and foremost is Armand Baeriswyl of the Archeological Service of the Canton of Bern, who provided monumental aid in rendering sixteenth-century grave-robbing, among other details, while being entirely too humble about it. I also need to thank Kameelah Martin Samuel at GSU for introducing me to some of the concepts I've explored here, Claire Joan Farago at CU-Boulder for suggesting several marvelous books that are included below, Erika Johnson-Lewis for providing me with the basics of Renaissance art when I was at FSU, and my friend Molly for sharing her own expertise with me. Finally, my high school art teacher Linda Hall deserves a shout-out, if only because she happens to be very cool.

Albala, Ken. *Cooking in Europe, 1250–1650.* Westport, CT: Greenwood Press, 2006.

Allen, S. J., and Emilie Amt. *The Crusades: A Reader.* Peterborough, ON: Broadview Press, 2003.

Amman, Jost. *Kunstbüchlin: 293 Renaissance Woodcuts for Artists and Illustrators.* New York: Dover, 1968.

Argyle, W. J. *The Fon of Dahomey: A History and Ethnography of the Old Kingdom.* Oxford: Clarendon Press, 1966.

Ball, Philip. *The Devil's Doctor: Paracelsus and the World of Renaissance Magic and Science.* New York: Farrar, Straus and Giroux, 2006.

Bambach, Carmen C. *Drawing and Painting in the Italian Renaissance Workshop: Theory and Practice, 1300–1600.* New York: Cambridge University Press, 1999.

Bay, Edna G. *Asen, Ancestors, and Vodun: Tracing Change in African Art.* Chicago: University of Illinois Press, 2008.

Burckhardt, Jacob. *The Civilization of the Renaissance in Italy.* 2 vols. New York: Harper and Row, 1958.

Cassidy-Welch, Megan, and Peter Sherlock, eds. *Practices of Gender in Late Medieval and Early Modern Europe.* Turnhout, Belgium: Brepols, 2008.

Classen, Albrecht, ed. *Sexuality in the Middle Ages and Early Modern Times: New Approaches to a Fundamental Cultural-Historical and Literary-Anthropological Theme.* Berlin: Walter de Gruyter, 2008.

Clifton, Chas S. *Encyclopedia of Heresies and Heretics.* New York: Barnes and Noble, 1992.

Curl, James Stevens. *A Celebration of Death: An Introduction to Some of the Buildings, Monuments, and Settings of Funerary Architecture in the Western European Tradition.* New York: Charles Scribner's Sons, 1980.

Duni, Matteo. *Under the Devil's Spell: Witches, Sorcerers, and the Inquisition in Renaissance Italy.* Florence, Italy: Syracuse University Press, 2007.

Ehrstine, Glenn. *Theater, Culture, and Community in Reformation Bern, 1523–1555.* Leiden, Netherlands: Koninklijke Brill, 2002.

Faderman, Lillian. *Surpassing the Love of Men: Romantic Friendship and Love Between Women from the Renaissance to the Present.* New York: William Morrow, 1981.

Farmer, David Hugh. *The Oxford Dictionary of Saints.* Oxford: Oxford University Press, 1997.

Gallonio, Antonio. *Tortures and Torments of the Christian Martyrs: The Classic Martyrology.* Los Angeles: Feral House, 2004.

Geary, Patrick J. *Furta Sacra: Theft of Relics in the Central Middle Ages.* Princeton, NJ: Princeton University Press, 1978.

Gordon, Bruce. "Toleration in the Early Swiss Reformation: The Art and Politics of Niklaus Manuel of Berne." In *Tolerance and Intolerance in the European Reformation*, edited by Ole Peter Grell and Bob Scribner, 126–144. Cambridge, UK: Cambridge University Press, 1996.

Hagen, Rainer, and Rose-Marie Hagen. *What Great Paintings Say: From the Bayeux Tapestry to Diego Rivera — Volume 1.* Cologne: Taschen, 2005.

Hale, J. R. *War and Society in Renaissance Europe, 1450–1620.* Leicester, UK: Leicester University Press, 1985.

Hall, Bert S. *Weapons and Warfare in Renaissance Europe: Gunpowder, Technology, and Tactics.* Baltimore: Johns Hopkins University Press, 1997.

Harari, Yuval Noah. *Renaissance Military Memoirs: War, History and Identity, 1450–1600.* Woodbridge, Suffolk, UK: Boydell Press, 2004.

Herskovits, Melville J. *Dahomey: An Ancient West African Kingdom.* New York: J. J. Augustin, 1938.

Jones, Timothy S., and David A. Sprunger, eds. *Marvels, Monsters, and Miracles: Studies in the Medieval and Early Modern Imaginations.* Kalamazoo: Western Michigan University Press, 2002.

King, Margaret L. *Women of the Renaissance.* Chicago: University of Chicago Press, 1991.

Koegler, Hans, and C. von Mandach. *Niklaus Manuel Deutsch.* Basel: Urs Graf Verlag, 1940.

Kors, Alan Charles, and Edward Peters, eds. *Witchcraft in Europe, 400–1700: A Documentary History.* Philadelphia: University of Pennsylvania Press, 2001.

Lawless, Catherine, and Christine Meek, eds. *Studies on Medieval and Early Modern Women 4: Victims or Viragos?* Portland, OR: Four Courts Press, 2005.

Levack, Brian P. *The Witch-Hunt in Early Modern Europe.* London: Longman, 1987.

Long, Carolyn M. *Spiritual Merchants: Religions, Magic, and Commerce.* Knoxville, TN: University of Tennessee Press, 2001.

Luard, Elisabeth. *The Flavours of Andalucia.* London: Collins and Brown, 1991.

Lukehart, Peter M., ed. *The Artist's Workshop.* Washington, DC: National Gallery of Art, 1993.

Maclean, Ian. *The Renaissance Notion of Women: A Study in the Fortunes of Scholasticism and Medical Science in European Intellectual Life.* Cambridge, UK: Cambridge University Press, 1980.

Manchester, William. *A World Lit Only by Fire: The Medieval Mind and the Renaissance.* New York: Back Bay, 1992.

Plunket, Ierne L. *Isabel of Castile and the Making of the Spanish Nation, 1451–1504.* New York: G. P. Putnam's Sons, 1915.

Reston, James Jr. *Dogs of God: Columbus, the Inquisition, and the Defeat of the Moors.* New York: Anchor, 2006.

Ronen, Dov. *Dahomey: Between Tradition and Modernity.* London: Cornell University Press, 1975.

Roob, Alexander. *The Hermetic Museum: Alchemy and Mysticism.* Italy: Taschen, 1997.

Shaw, Christine, ed. *Italy and the European Powers: The Impact of War, 1500–1530.* Leiden, Netherlands: Koninklijke Brill, 2006.

Singh, Ranjit. "Boabdil: The Unfortunate: El Zogoybi." *Free Thoughts by Ranjit Singh.* http://idyllic.wordpress.com/2009/02/26/boabdil-the-unfortunate-el-zogoybi/.

Summers, Montague, ed. *The Malleus Maleficarum of Heinrich Kramer and James Sprenger.* New York: Dover, 1971.

Sutcliffe, Anthony. *Paris: An Architectural History.* New Haven and London: Yale University Press, 1993.

Thomson, David. *Renaissance Paris: Architecture and Growth, 1475–1600.* London: A. Zwemmer Ltd, 1984.

Van Abbé, D. "Change and Tradition in the Work of Niklaus Manuel of Berne (1484–1531)." *Modern Language Review* 47, no. 2: 181–198.

Wiesner, Merry E. *Working Women in Renaissance Germany.* New Brunswick, NJ: Rutgers University Press, 1986.

Wills, Chuck. *Weaponry: An Illustrated History.* New York: Hylas Publishing, 2008.

Zambelli, Paola. *White Magic, Black Magic in the European Renaissance: From Ficino, Pico, Della Porta to Trithemius, Agrippa, Bruno.* Leiden, Netherlands: Koninklijke Brill, 2007.

Acknowledgments

Everyone from last time, plus all the people I either didn't know then or blanked on when the pressure of trying to thank everyone kicked in. Some names to add to the old list: Jason, Angie, Stephen, Marc, Mark, Tess, Robert, Josh, Amanda, Philip, Paul, Kathy, Allyson, Mike, Isaiah, Chris, Ashley, Evan, Francesca, Scott, Neil, Sandi, Kevin, Ned, Nigel, Tasha, Melissa, David, Lisa, Kelly, Alicia, Kay, Katie, the Tanzers, the Ferrells, and all the fans who took the time to write after reading *The Sad Tale of the Brothers Grossbart.* I also need to thank the owners and baristas at Folsom Street Coffee, especially J.C., Chris, Rick, Krista, John, Lily, Jessie, Staci, Teak, Shawn, and Serena, for fostering such an excellent working environment; the Widow's Bane for providing fine music to revise a novel full of the undead to; the Oskar Blues, Rogue, Stone, Ska, Odell, Left Hand, and Great Divide brewing companies for providing such delicious elixirs to soothe my overtaxed brain when I was finished; and the Fermentation Lounge for introducing me to so many of the aforementioned breweries in the first place.

Rather than the hand metaphor (and cheesy, prolonged yuck-yucking) of last time, I think simply thanking my beta readers more directly is in order. My profuse thanks therefore go to J. T. Glover, S. J. Chambers, my wife Raechel Dumas, and especially

Molly Tanzer, all of whom helped me time and again in the struggle to land this project. I should also expressly thank John Gove for dedicating his Saturdays to being a grand hiking partner—without such opportunities for decompression I might have collapsed along the way. My parents Bruce and Lisa, my brother Aaron and sister Tessa, my in-laws, and all the rest of my family should no doubt be thanked again as well, so there we are.

I also can't praise Orbit enough for being such a great publisher, especially Tim, Jack, Alex, Lauren, Jennifer, Mari, Devi, and DongWon in the U.S., and Bella, Rose, Anna, Emily, Darren, and Joanna in the U.K.

I must also thank my agent Sally and her assistant Mary for being such great friends and associates, and finally, my copy editor Roland Ottewell, without whose attentions this book would not be nearly so coherent. So again, a heartfelt thanks to all involved in bringing this book to you, the reader, who is deserving of more than a little thanks for taking a chance on my work. This wouldn't be possible without you, and I thank you for it.

Finally, I need to offer my appreciation for those individuals whom I so shamelessly conscripted into this novel: Niklaus Manuel Deutsch, his wife Katharina, Doctor Paracelsus, Albrecht von Stein, and especially old Boabdil were no doubt very different from how I have written them here, and I hope their shades accept my sincere thanks, and apologies for rendering them in such a fictitious—and often unflattering—manner. This novel would not be the work it is without the real lives of real people to inspire me, and as much fun as it was to play with their histories I would never wish anyone to mistake my versions of these individuals for the actual historical figures. Paracelsus, at least, would presumably appreciate the exaggerations.

extras

meet the author

Photo: Molly Tanzer

JESSE BULLINGTON's formative years were spent primarily in rural Pennsylvania, the Netherlands, and Tallahassee, Florida. He is a folklore enthusiast who holds a bachelor's degree in history and English from Florida State University. He currently resides in Colorado, and can be found online at www.jessebullington.com.

introducing

If you enjoyed
THE ENTERPRISE OF DEATH,
look out for

THE SAD TALE OF THE BROTHERS GROSSBART

by Jesse Bullington

The year is 1364. Hungry creatures stalk the dark woods of medieval Europe, and both sea and sky teem with unspeakable horrors. There is no foulness, however, no witch nor demon, to rival the graverobbing twins Hegel and Manfried Grossbart. This is their tale, sad but true.

To claim that the Brothers Grossbart were cruel and selfish brigands is to slander even the nastiest highwayman, and to say they were murderous swine is an insult to even the filthiest boar. They were Grossbarts through and true, and in many lands such a title still carries serious weight. While not as repugnant as their father nor as cunning as his, horrible though both men were, the Brothers proved worse. Blood can go bad in a single generation or it can be distilled down through the ages into something truly wicked, which was the case with those abominable twins, Hegel and Manfried.

Both were average of height but scrawny of trunk. Manfried possessed disproportionately large ears, while Hegel's nose dwarfed many a turnip in size and knobbiness. Hegel's copper hair and bushy eyebrows contrasted the matted silver of his brother's crown, and both were pockmarked and gaunt of cheek. They had each seen only twenty-five years but possessed beards of such noteworthy length that from even a short distance they were often mistaken for old men. Whose was longest proved a constant bone of contention between the two.

Before being caught and hanged in some dismal village far to the north, their father passed on the family trade; assuming the burglarizing of graveyards can be considered a gainful occupation. Long before their granddad's time the name Grossbart was synonymous with skulduggery of the shadiest sort, but only as cemeteries grew into something more than potter's fields did the family truly find its calling. Their father abandoned them to their mother when they were barely old enough to raise a prybar and went in search of his fortune, just as his father had disappeared when he was but a fledgling sneak-thief.

The elder Grossbart is rumored to have died wealthier than a king in the desert country to the south, where the tombs surpass the grandest castle of the Holy Roman Empire in both size and affluence. That is what the younger told his sons, but it is doubtful there was even the most shriveled kernel of truth in his ramblings. The Brothers firmly believed their dad had joined their grandfather in Gyptland, leaving them to rot with their alcoholic and abusive mother. Had they known he actually wound up as crow-bait without a coin in his coffer it is doubtful they would have altered the track of their lives, although they may have cursed his name less—or more, it is difficult to say.

An uncle of dubious legitimacy and motivation rescued them from their demented mother and took them under his wing during their formative man-boy years. Whatever his relation to the lads, his beard was undeniably long, and he was as fervent as any Grossbart before him to crack open crypts and pilfer what sullen rewards they offered. After a number of too-close shaves with local authorities he absconded in the night with all their possessions, leaving the destitute Brothers to wander back to their mother, intent on stealing whatever the wizened old drunk had not lost or spent over the intervening years.

The shack where they were born had aged worse than they, the mossy roof having joined the floor while they were ransacking churchyards along the Danube with their uncle. The moldy structure housed only a badger, which the Grossbarts dined on after suffering only mild injures from the sleepy beast's claws. Inquiring at the manor house's stable, they learned their mother had expired over the winter and lay with all the rest in the barrow at the end of town. Spitting on the mound in the torrential rain, the Brothers Grossbart vowed they would rest in the grand tombs of the Infidel or not at all.

Possessing only their wide-brimmed hats, rank clothes, and tools, but cheered by the pauper's grave in which their miserable matriarch rotted, they made ready to journey south. Such an expedition required more supplies than a pair of prybars and a small piece of metal that might have once been a coin, so they set off to settle an old score. The mud pulled at their shoes in a vain attempt to slow their malicious course.

The yeoman Heinrich had grown turnips a short distance outside the town's wall his entire life, the hard lot of his station compounded by the difficult crop and the substandard hedge around his field. When they were boys the Brothers often purloined the unripe vegetation until the night Heinrich lay in wait for them. Not content to use a switch or his hands, the rightly furious farmer thrashed them both with his shovel. Manfried's smashed-in nose never returned to its normal shape and Hegel's indented left buttock forever bore the shame of the spade.

Ever since the boys had disappeared Heinrich had enjoyed fertility both in his soil and the bed he shared with his wife and children. Two young daughters joined their elder sister and brother, the aging farmer looking forward to having more hands to put to use. Heinrich even saved enough to purchase a healthy horse to replace their nag, and had almost reimbursed his friend Egon for the cart he had built them.

The Brothers Grossbart tramped across the field toward the dark house, the rain blotting out whatever moonlight hid above the clouds. Their eyes had long grown accustomed to the night, however, and they could see that the farmer now had a small barn beside his home. They spit simultaneously on his door, and exchanging grins, set to beating the wood.

"Fire!" yelled Manfried.

"Fire!" repeated Hegel.

"Town's aflame, Heinrich!"

"Heinrich, bring able hands!"

In his haste to lend aid to his neighbors Heinrich stumbled out of bed without appreciating the drumming of rain upon his roof and flung open the door. The sputtering rushlight in his hand illuminated not concerned citizens but the scar-cratered visages of the Brothers Grossbart. Heinrich recognized them at once, and with a yelp dropped his light and made to slam the door.

The Grossbarts were too quick and dragged him into the rain. The farmer struck at Hegel but Manfried kicked the back of Heinrich's knee before Heinrich landed a blow. Heinrich twisted as he fell and attempted to snatch Manfried when Hegel delivered a sound punch to the yeoman's neck. Heinrich thrashed in the mud while the two worked him over, but just as he despaired, bleeding from mouth and nose, his wife Gertie emerged from the house with their woodax.

If Manfried's nose had not been so flat the blade would have cleaved it open as she slipped in the mire. Hegel tackled her, the two rolling in the mud while her husband groaned and Manfried retrieved the ax. Gertie bit Hegel's face and clawed his ear but then Hegel saw his brother raise the ax and he rolled free as the blade plummeted into her back. Through the muddy film coating his face Heinrich watched his wife kick and piss herself, the rain slowing to a drizzle as she bled out in the muck.

Neither brother had ever killed a person before, but neither felt the slightest remorse for the heinous crime. Heinrich crawled to Gertie, Hegel went to the barn, and Manfried entered the house of children's tears. Hegel latched up the horse, threw Heinrich's shovel and a convenient sack of turnips into the bed of the cart, and led it around front.

Inside the darkened house Heinrich's eldest daughter lunged at Manfried with a knife but he intercepted her charge with the ax. Despite his charitable decision to knock her with the blunt end of the ax head, the metal crumpled in her skull and she collapsed. The two babes cried in the bed, the only son cowering by his fallen sister. Spying a hog-fat tallow beside the small stack of rushlights, Manfried tucked the rare candle into his pocket and lit one of the lard-coated reeds on the hearth coals, inspecting the interior.

Stripping the blankets off the bed and babes, he tossed the rushlights, the few knives he found, and the tubers roasting on the hearth into the pilfered cloth and tied the bundle with cord. He blew out the rushlight, pocketed it, and stepped over the weeping lad. The horse and cart waited, but his brother and Heinrich were nowhere to be seen.

Manfried tossed the blankets into the cart and peered about, his eyes rapidly readjusting to the drizzly night. He saw Heinrich fifty paces off, slipping as he ran from the silently pursuing Hegel. Hegel dived at his quarry's legs and missed, falling on his face in the mud as Heinrich broke away toward town.

Cupping his hands, Manfried bellowed, "Got the young ones here, Heinrich! Come on back! You run and they's dead!"

Heinrich continued a few paces before slowing to a walk on the periphery of Manfried's vision. Hegel righted himself and scowled at the farmer but knew better than to risk spooking him with further pursuit. Hurrying back to his brother, Hegel muttered in Manfried's cavernous ear as Heinrich trudged back toward the farm.

"Gotta be consequences," Hegel murmured. "Gotta be."

"He'd have the whole town on us," his brother agreed. "Just not right, after his wife tried to murder us." Manfried touched his long-healed nose.

"We was just settlin accounts, no call for her bringin axes into it." Hegel rubbed his scarred posterior.

Heinrich approached the Brothers, only registering their words on an instinctual level. Every good farmer loves his son even more than his wife, and he knew the Grossbarts would slaughter young Brennen without hesitation. Heinrich broke into a maniacal grin, thinking of how on the morrow the town would rally around his loss, track these dogs down, and hang them from the gibbet.

The yeoman gave Hegel the hard-eye but Hegel gave it right back, then the Grossbart punched Heinrich in the nose. The farmer's head swam as he felt himself trussed up like a rebellious sow, the rope biting his ankles and wrists. Heinrich dimly saw Manfried go back into the house, then snapped fully awake when the doorway lit up. Manfried had shifted some of the coals onto the straw bed, the cries of the little girls amplifying as the whole cot ignited. Manfried reappeared with the near-catatonic Brennen in one hand and a turnip in the other.

"Didn't have to be this way," said Manfried. "You's forced our hands."

"Did us wrong twice over," Hegel concurred.

"Please." Heinrich's bloodshot eyes shifted wildly between the doorway and his son. "I'm sorry, lads, honest. Let him free, and spare the little ones." The babes screeched all the louder. "In God's name, have mercy!"

"Mercy's a proper virtue," said Hegel, rubbing the wooden image of the Virgin he had retrieved from a cord around Gertie's neck. "Show'em mercy, brother."

"Sound words indeed," Manfried conceded, setting the boy gently on his heels facing his father.

"Yes," Heinrich gasped, tears eroding the mud on the proud farmer's cheeks, "the girls, please, let them go!"

"They's already on their way," said Manfried, watching smoke curl out of the roof as he slit the boy's throat. If Hegel found this judgment harsh he did not say. Night robbed the blood of its sacramental coloring, black liquid spurting onto Heinrich's face. Brennen pitched forward, confused eyes breaking his father's heart, lips moving soundlessly in the mud.

"Bless Mary," Hegel intoned, kissing the pinched necklace.

"And bless us, too," Manfried finished, taking a bite from the warm tuber.

The babes in the burning house had gone silent when the Grossbarts pulled out of the yard, Hegel atop the horse and Manfried settling into the cart. They had shoved a turnip into Heinrich's mouth, depriving him of even his prayers. Turning onto the path leading south into the mountains, the rain had stopped as the Brothers casually made their escape.